P9-DFY-007

Madame Bovary's

A Novel

Linda Urbach

Bantam Books Trade Paperbacks • New York

Madame Bovary's Daughter is a work of fiction. All incidents and dialogue, and all characters, with the exception of some well-known historical and public figures, are products of the author's imagination and are not to be construed as real. Where real-life historical or public figures appear, the situations, incidents, and dialogue concerning those persons are entirely fictional and are not intended to depict actual events or to change the entirely fictional nature of the work. In all other respects, any resemblance to persons living or dead is entirely coincidental.

A Bantam Books Trade Paperback Original

Published in the United States by Bantam Books,
an imprint of The Random House Publishing Group,
a division of Random House, Inc., New York.

BANTAM BOOKS and the rooster colophon
are registered trademarks of Random House, Inc.

RANDOM HOUSE READER'S CIRCLE & Design is a trademark of
Random House, Inc.

Library of Congress Cataloging-in-Publication Data

Urbach, Linda.
Madame Bovary's daughter : a novel / Linda Urbach.
p. cm.
ISBN 978-0-385-34387-9
eBook ISBN 978-0-440-42341-6
1. Young women—France—Fiction. 2. Fashion—France—History—
Fiction. 3. Paris (France)—Fiction. I. Flaubert, Gustave, 1821–1880.
Madame Bovary. II. Title.
PS3621.R33M33 2011
813'.6—dc22   2010053286

www.randomhousereaderscircle.com

246897531

Book design by Elizabeth A. D. Eno

For *my* daughter, Charlotte

She hoped for a son; he would be strong and dark; she would call him George; and this idea of having a male child was like an expected revenge for all her impotence in the past. . . . She gave birth on a Sunday at about six o'clock, as the sun was rising.

"It is a girl!" said Charles.

She turned her head away and fainted.

—GUSTAVE FLAUBERT, *Madame Bovary*

PART 1

The Country Life

Chapter 1

Home Sweet Homais

Yonville, 1852

Was any daughter ever cursed with a mother such as hers? A self-centered, social-climbing, materialistic, coldhearted, calculating adulteress. Oh, yes, and she disliked children, too.

Everyone in the village of Yonville and the city of Rouen and all the towns in between knew the story of her mother's disastrous affairs; her wastrel ways; her total disregard for her husband, his reputation, and his finances. And her complete disinterest in Berthe, her only child. It was her mother's friend, Madame Homais, who put it into words for Berthe on the day of her father's funeral. Yes, even at her father's funeral they were still gossiping about her mother, who had poisoned herself almost a year before.

"Your poor, dear mother. She always wanted what she couldn't have," Madame Homais said as she pulled a comb through Berthe's long snarled hair. Berthe hadn't brushed her hair in weeks or possibly even months, ever since her father had fallen ill. "And what she had, she didn't want. As for your papa, all he wanted was just a little of her love. *Mon Dieu*, what a rat's nest." She untangled the comb from the girl's hair, then gave Berthe a gentle push. "Now go and put on your best dress." Did she know that Berthe only had two dresses to her name? Neither could be described as "best." All the pretty dresses that she had once owned had been sold months before. There was nothing left but the house, and that was going to be auctioned off in an effort to make a small dent in her father's enormous debt.

It was a beautiful spring day. Much too beautiful a day on which to be buried. The bright sun shone down on the small market town. Surrounded by pastureland on one side and the Rieule river on the other, Yonville boasted one main street. Lining the street and the large square were a chemist's shop, a blacksmith's shop, a simple vegetable market, the town hall—designed by a Parisian architect who favored the Greek Revival style—and the almost famous Lion d'Or Inn. On cramped side streets were the residential houses. It was a snug, self-contained little village only twenty-four miles from Rouen.

The entire village attended Charles Bovary's funeral. He had been, after all, the town physician. And beyond that, the villagers had great sympathy for him. He had died quite simply of a broken heart and everyone knew it. Berthe kept her head down so she wouldn't see all the people staring at her with their sad eyes. *They just want to see me cry,* she thought. But she wouldn't cry. She couldn't cry. On what was supposed to be the saddest day of her life she felt only a paralyzing, numbing fear. She looked down at her hands. Her nails were bitten to the quick and she had never been a nail-biter.

She knew that being orphaned was not an unusual situation. How many times had her father told her about the many orphans who littered the land as a result of sickness, war, or the normal hardships of a poverty-stricken life? But Berthe wasn't an ordinary twelve-year-old orphan, as people of the village kept reminding her. She was the progeny of the most scandalous woman who ever lived.

"How will the poor thing make her way in the world?" she heard someone whisper behind her.

"Perhaps, like mother like daughter," said her companion.

"Don't forget her father. He was a decent man, after all."

"Much good that did."

"She has the beginnings of her mother's beauty. That in itself does not bode well."

"She is a strange child. But is it any wonder? With a mother like that?"

Berthe shot a look at the woman. She wanted to scream *I'm not a strange child,* and tear the hypocritical mourning veil off the woman's head. Where were the reassuring words? Weren't they supposed to tell her everything was going to be fine? She looked around. All she saw was a row of black-clad women—a line of crows shaking their heads in disapproval. Her terror grew. She felt as if she were taking the last steps to her own funeral.

Suddenly she was visited by the image of both her parents' deaths: her mother from self-administered poison and her father from a self-acknowledged broken heart. She saw her mother in those last moments, her pale waxen features, her eyes covered with a kind of second skin, her mouth, that black poisoned hole sucking in air, and her curled hands picking aimlessly at the sheets. Her father sitting under the oak tree, his head bent, his eyes half open, his jaw unhinged. Dead to the world—and to his only daughter, who had come out to the garden to wake him for a dinner he would never eat.

So strong, so vivid was this image of her dead parents that she felt herself gag. She thought she was going to be sick in front of everybody. Sweat broke out on her forehead and she wiped it away with the back of her hand.

"Stand strong, dear child, it will all be over soon," said Madame Homais, taking her wet hand and squeezing it tight.

After Emma Bovary died her husband spent a fortune on designing and building an elaborate granite mausoleum complete with cherubs and crucifixes. He had even begged money off his good friend Monsieur Homais with the promise that he would repay the loan in a timely fashion. How he was going to do that was a mystery, considering the fact that he had already pawned his instruments and medical books. Monsieur Homais was ignorant of this and assumed that Charles would be back on his feet as soon as his mourning period was over. It was never over.

As they drew nearer to the mausoleum, Monsieur Homais looked up at his friend's final resting place. He shook his head sadly. "This could have been Madame Homais's much-wished-for third bedroom," he muttered to Berthe. It was a good thing his wife had no knowledge of her husband's loan.

The crows continued to rustle their black capes and whisper in all-too-audible tones as Berthe passed by, following her father's coffin.

"She spent all his money on herself," one said.

"And someone else," said another. "Don't forget the Some-one Else."

"No one is about to forget that little piece of scandal."

"You know there were two."

"No!"

"Oh, yes. Do you remember young Monsieur Léon?"

"But he left town."

"He may have left town, but he didn't leave her."

"Really!"

Several women gasped and covered their mouths with their black-gloved hands. Their eyes gleamed in anticipation of hearing more.

Because of the size of the mausoleum, Charles Bovary's coffin could not be placed directly next to his wife's but had to be wedged in at a perpendicular angle at the end of her triple-enclosed casket. The four men who had carried the coffin from the village struggled to fit it in. Thus, Madame Bovary's husband was laid to rest literally at her feet. And given the state of his estate, or the lack thereof, an expensive coffin for him was out of the question. He had been put in the plainest of pine boxes. It made a curious sight: the rough-hewn pine coffin lying at the foot of the lustrous rosewood casket like a humble servant at the feet of his beloved queen. The four pallbearers stepped out, rubbing their sore hands together. Then the Homaises and Berthe squeezed in what little space was left while the rest of the villagers had to make do with paying their respects from outside.

So, Berthe thought, her mother would be housed for eternity in the luxury she had always yearned for. How many years and how much money had she spent stuffing their humble home with the trappings of a much grander establishment? Silk damask armchairs, Chinese screens, crystal candelabras, brass andirons, heavy brocade curtains, a hand-carved prayer kneeler, a graceful four-poster bed. And when her husband occasionally protested, she explained: "We will need these things when we move to the new house."

She held out this vision of a grand dwelling as though it were a reality. Her dream house was based on her one visit as a young bride to the château at Vaubyessard. She described her visit often and in great detail to Berthe. It was her idea of a bedtime story.

"I walked up three flights of marble steps and into the great hall. As I looked up I saw a chandelier hanging from a glass dome. It was made of a million crystals that caught the light and glittered so brightly it hurt my eyes. There was a pink marbled staircase that circled around and up to a gallery. The walls were covered in silk. The air smelled of roses and lilacs."

But in Emma Bovary's mind, it was the effect this splendid château had on its inhabitants that was so magical. The château seemed to transform every person in it.

"They were ordinary men and women but they looked like they were another species altogether. Their hair was more lustrous, their skin had a polish and glow, their smiles were more brilliant. Their happiness was unlike anything I had ever seen before or since. It was being in that house that made them so happy and so beautiful."

Thus, Berthe had grown up with two homes, the slightly shabby lodging they lived in and the luxurious château of her mother's memory. The bills mounted and her mother began to sell off small decorative items before her husband discovered her secret debt. As little by little the house in Yonville grew shabbier, Berthe still had that other more enduring abode of her mother's fantasy. Where there would be no gossip, no suffering the opinion of others, no creditors, no shortage of love, no shortage of beautiful things to buy. And where her mother continued to live in this happy, happy home where no one and nothing could ever hurt her.

Berthe recognized a fairy tale for what it was. She knew her mother had lived much of the time in another world and that her fantasies had created an impenetrable wall around her. On the one hand, Berthe deeply resented the stories that separated her mother from their real life. On the other hand, the fairy tales held a magic that was difficult for a little girl to resist.

Her mother's favorite stories came from her beloved books. She spent hours and hours reading, happily lost in the pages of her novels. Every once in a while, she would read aloud. Emma Bovary seemed to require an audience for these recitations. Their maid, Félicité, was of course too busy, and that left Berthe as the most likely candidate.

All of the books had to do with true love, tragic love, unrequited love, doomed lovers, beautiful maidens in distress, gallant heroes coming to their rescue, fainting ladies in perfumed gardens, magnificent mansions, glorious châteaux, bloody battles, hearts won and lost and won again, dastardly villains, and untimely deaths, always in lush surroundings with exquisitely dressed women showing much ivory skin and tall, handsome men on their equally tall and handsome horses. Much later, Emma Bovary acquired a taste for modern novels by the English author Jane Austen. She also adored the stories of Mary, Queen of Scots, and Joan of Arc. Sir Walter Scott was another of her preferred authors. When she read "The Lady of the Lake" aloud to Berthe, the rhyming sometimes put her young daughter to sleep.

"Berthe, wake up. I'm coming to the best part."

"But, Maman, it is so long it makes me tired."

"How anyone can sleep through such beauty is beyond me." Her voice took on a faraway tone as she recited:

> *"A chieftain's daughter seemed the maid;*
> *Her satin snood, her silken plaid,*
> *Her golden brooch, such birth betrayed.*
> *And seldom was a snood amid*
> *Such wild luxuriant ringlets hid,*

Whose glossy black to shame might bring
The plumage of the raven's wing...

"Berthe, I'm not going to waste my breath if you're not going to pay attention. Go away and play with your dolls," she said angrily.

Berthe's sleepy head filled with visions of golden brooches and satin snoods, and she too became entranced with the stories, the romance and the richness, the drama and damsels. But most of all she loved the words. Words read aloud. Words on paper like so many stitches of embroidery. She listened to the words, long and luxurious, perfect as silk thread. She marveled at how a collection of words could create a fantastic story out of nothing.

When her mother left her to play alone (more frequently than not) Berthe created her own fairy tales using herself as the fabled princess. One day she pulled down a lace curtain that was drying on the clothesline behind the cottage and wrapped herself in it. She began humming softly as she paraded up and down the small yard. The sun shone down on her lace-covered head as if bestowing a special blessing. *I am the queen of the world. The beautiful queen of the world.*

"What in heaven's name are you doing, you wicked girl?" Her mother snatched the curtain from her. "Now Félicité has to wash this all over again!"

It was cold and dark in the mausoleum. Berthe could barely make out the faces of Madame and Monsieur Homais. She could feel the chill of the cement floor through her thin boots. She stared at the two dramatically different caskets. Suddenly she could bear it no longer. She pulled the green velvet covering from her mother's casket and placed it on her father's. Monsieur Homais patted her shoulder.

"Poor fellow. He is the one who should have had the finer coffin. Perhaps we should switch the coffins as well," he said, half in jest.

"Hush, you idiot!" Madame Homais said, hitting him on the arm. Berthe couldn't help but notice the amusement on her face. She was such a strong, warm, comforting woman. Berthe wondered what it would be like to be her daughter. In her mind, she wailed at her mother. *How could you do this to Papa? Didn't you know he would die without you? Didn't you care? You have killed everything.*

Before she could stop herself, Berthe kicked at the corner of her mother's casket so hard she felt a sharp flash of pain from her foot all the way up to her head. And then the tears came. Hot, angry tears.

"Berthe, shame!" exclaimed Madame Homais.

Her head began to pound and she gasped for breath. For a moment everything went dark and she thought, *I must be dying, too. I'm only twelve years old and I'm dying.* But she wasn't. She was alive and alone. She missed her parents terribly, for despite themselves they had been the center of her universe.

"Why are you staring at me?" her mother would say as Berthe watched her brush her long black hair. "Go out and play."

"I have no one to play with, Maman." It was true. Even though the Homais children allowed Berthe to tag along with them they never really included her in their secret games.

"Please, find something to amuse yourself. You're big enough to do that."

The days were all the same. Her mother would read in the morning, visit the town square, the shops, and the market in the afternoon, and continue reading until dinner. Most days when her mother went out Berthe would stay home and study her reading and writing with Félicité, or sit in front of the fire and sew. She would spend hours looking out the window, waiting for her father to return from his long days of visiting patients. But when he finally came home he was too tired to even speak to her.

Berthe stumbled forward and caught herself against the wall of the mausoleum. The cold marble was slick with dampness.

"Are you all right?" Monsieur Homais asked, grabbing her arm.

"Of course she's not all right. She's an orphan. She's lost everything," said Madame Homais.

"Shhh," he said to his wife.

"*Mon Dieu,* it's not as if she doesn't know."

Berthe wished she had died first, a painless but pitiful death. She pictured her own funeral. *So young, so sad.* She imagined her parents sobbing, clinging to each other in their grief. *Our only daughter. Gone. If only we could have a second chance to show her how much we adored her. This is God's punishment for a life of self-ishness. Oh, Berthe, our beloved baby girl.* And in this, her funeral fantasy, she would rise up from her coffin (exquisite but practical mahogany with solid gold fittings) and her parents would cry with joy and gratitude and vow never again to take their precious daughter for granted. And Berthe would forgive them everything.

Leaving the cemetery with the Homaises, Berthe looked up at the evening sky. Here she was the mourner, not the mourned. And because there was no one to cry for her, the tears she shed were for herself.

Monsieur Homais was a small, squat man who was many inches shorter than his wife. He had a trim little mustache, which he continually twirled into two fine points. He was forever imparting information that no one but he was interested in, on every imaginable topic. On and on he would lecture about the effect of spinach on one's bowels, or the correct temperature at which to soak one's feet in order to reduce the pain of gout. Madame Homais listened to him without listening. Monsieur Homais was the master of the house, but it was Madame Homais who ruled the roost. An enormous woman with a bosom so vast it seemed as if she might tip forward from the weight of it, she smothered her family with kisses and hugs and cuffed them about whenever they even thought of disobeying her. She was the mother Berthe always wanted and theirs was the family she longed to be part of. But it was not to be. Apparently, it had all been decided. She was to live with her grand-mère Bovary.

"But why? Why can't I live with you?" She wrapped her arms around Madame Homais's ample hips as if she were about to be swept away by some unseen force. Her eyes flooded with tears and her nose began to run in sympathy.

"Dear child, she's your grand-mère," said Madame Homais, wiping Berthe's face with her vast white apron. "You must go to her."

"She has a farm. Just think of all the fruits and vegetables, the fresh milk and cheese. How healthy you will be," said Homais, rubbing his stomach as if to demonstrate the good meals she would receive, which to him was equivalent to a perfect life.

"I hate fruits and I hate vegetables. And I hate cheese," she said, more tears spilling onto her hot cheeks.

"She has no one to keep her company in her old age. You are her one and only granddaughter. She loves you with all her heart," chimed in Madame Homais.

Who were they talking about? Berthe wondered. Her grand-mère was a woman who did not gladly suffer people, most especially granddaughters. In the few visits she had made to her son's house she had said precious little to Berthe except to ask the same pointed questions:

"Are you doing well at your studies?"

"Do you say your catechism faithfully every day?"

"Do you remember to push back your cuticles?"

It seemed to Berthe that in her grand-mère's view of the world, catechism and cuticles carried the same import. The pain of a torn cuticle seemed equivalent to burning in hell.

"Your mother truly detests the idea of being a grand-mère," Berthe once heard Emma Bovary say to her husband. "She likes to think of herself only as your mother."

It was true. Berthe's grand-mère treated her son as if he were still a young boy.

"Charles, comb your hair. You look like a derelict," she would say.

"Yes, Maman," he answered, as if he were ten years old.

"Don't make such noises with your soup," she would scold him at the table.

"Sorry, Maman," he would reply.

The idea of living with this cold, critical woman filled Berthe with dread.

"Oh, please," she begged Madame Homais, "let me stay with you. I won't be any trouble."

"Dear child." She laughed. "Where would I put you?" She gestured helplessly around the cluttered family room where indeed there were already two narrow beds set up for the youngest Homaises. The two bedrooms upstairs had long ago overflowed into the downstairs living quarters.

"Perhaps we could make her a bed on the roof," joked Monsieur, dunking a piece of bread into his morning bowl of *café au lait*. "Sleeping outdoors can be very good for one's health. The fresh air is particularly beneficial for young developing lungs."

"Don't tease the poor child. Can't you see she is serious?"

"Please,"Berthe renewed her entreaties. "Please, I'll work for my keep. I'll help Madame Homais in the kitchen. I'll mix medicine for Monsieur's customers. I'll watch the babies."

"It's just not possible, *chérie*," Madame Homais said.

Berthe grew quiet. She vowed never to beg for anything again. Not if she could help it. It hurt too much to be refused.

"The house is going to be sold," said Madame Homais. "You had better take one last look and make sure there's nothing that's been missed." Berthe had no desire to revisit the home she'd grown up in, but she did as Madame Homais instructed. It was empty of everything. Every chair, every cushion, every painting, even the curtains had all been taken away by her father's creditors. The only things that were left were the pallets she and her father had slept on. How sad the small house looked. How sad and how poor. Only the outlines of furniture in the dust on the floor gave evidence to the fact that anyone had ever lived here. And yet this house had been her whole life. It was through these small paned windows that she first made sense of the world. It was on the worn wooden steps that led upstairs where she learned to walk, holding on to the railing, taking one step at a time. Her tiny room had been a haven from her mother's moods and her father's distance.

And how she had loved the kitchen where Félicité had created the most delicious aromas out of nothing more than a dollop of butter, mushrooms, and onions. Berthe inhaled deeply. The only smell now was that of dust and something else: mouse droppings. The mice had taken over the house.

Well, let the mice have it. Let the creditors fight over the crumbs. One day she would have her own home, a beautiful house with sparkling windows, a huge kitchen hearth that never went cold, and a marble staircase that led to a ballroom big enough for fifty waltzing couples. She would fill the mansion with brocade couches and satin cushions, and paintings in real gold frames. She would have armoires . . . no, entire rooms filled with gowns made of the costliest fabrics. Satins and silks, velvets and chiffons. And she would have a long sloping lawn and flowered gardens. And acres of meadows with many, many horses so that she could choose a different one to ride each day of the month. She would build a high wall around the house with a big iron gate fitted with a lock so that no one would be able to get in unless she wanted them to. And no one could ever take her house away from her. Ever.

She suddenly stopped and yanked hard at her single braid as if to chastise herself. She had been infected with the same delusional thinking as her mother. It was all those books, and that poetry; her mother's often repeated story of the grand ball at Vaubyessard. *I won't fall into the same trap. I won't.* She would monitor herself very carefully. Whatever she gained in life, horses or houses or beautiful gowns, they would all be real. Most important of all, she would have what her mother never had: the love of someone she loved in return.

She slowly pushed open the door to her mother's bedroom. She always thought of it as belonging only to her mother even though her father certainly shared it. The small space had been crowded with all her mother's favorite things. A four-poster bed made of silken rosewood, a heavy damask bedspread, a matching rosewood dressing table, a blue and red Oriental rug, a velvet-covered chaise longue, and a freestanding gilt-framed mirror. With everything gone, the room seemed even smaller. She opened the wall cupboard not expecting to find anything. There, on the very top shelf, was a page torn from one of her mother's fashion books. It was an illustration of a woman in a ball gown. Berthe read the description at the bottom.

> *An evening dress of white tulle, trimmed with twelve narrow tulle flounces edged with rows of tiny crimson roses and garnished with crystals to replicate dewdrops. A tunic of spotted tulle is trimmed with a broader velvet, a long wreath of velvet roses, verdant leaves, and crystals. The sleeves are trimmed to correspond with the skirt. The hair is in Grecian braids. Note the wreath is of velvet leaves with festoons of crystals to match the skirt.*

Berthe's chest felt tight as she gazed at the gown in the picture. It was the most beautiful dress she had ever seen: one that would diminish an entire ballroom full of gowns. Why had this one piece of paper been the only thing left behind? Was it just to serve as a reminder of her mother's lavish, foolish tastes? Had Madame Bovary actually been planning on ordering this dress to be made? And if so, where was she going to wear it? In front of the long mirror in her bedroom? Walking the narrow streets of Yonville, infuriating the residents even more? Perhaps this was the dress in which she wanted to be buried. Berthe choked down a sob. This gown represented all the beauty her mother had ever yearned for. Taking the picture, she carefully folded it in half and placed it in her apron pocket.

It took only two weeks for the house to sell. After all her father's debts were paid, including the one to Monsieur Homais, who seemed both relieved and surprised, Berthe received a total of twelve francs and seventy-five centimes. Not enough to live on, but more than enough to send her off to what she thought of as a fate worse than death: life with grand-mère Bovary.

She waited with Madame Homais for the morning coach. She had no idea what lay in store for her. She had lived her entire life in one house, in one small town, with the same two people. And now she was moving to a whole new place. She felt as if she were falling off the edge of the earth and there was no one and nothing to catch her. She wanted to cry, but crying seemed a feeble reaction to falling into an abyss. Screaming would have been more appropriate. But Berthe was not one to make a scene. That was more her mother's domain.

CHAPTER 2

Her Grand-mère's House

As the coach took Berthe farther and farther away from Yonville, the fields became bigger and the houses fewer and farther apart. The road grew quite rough. She had to sit forward on the leather seat so that her head didn't bump against the wall of the coach.

There was only one other passenger in the coach that day: an elderly gentleman who was so fat he took up the entire seat across from her. His vest was unbuttoned and his dusty black coat barely fit around him. He began eating his lunch as soon as the horses started up. He chewed on thick slices of garlic sausage and cheese, washing them down with long swigs from a bottle of wine. Madame Homais had packed a lunch for Berthe but she had no appetite.

"You are very young to be traveling alone." Each word he uttered carried with it the strong smell of garlic. "And very pretty," he added.

He belched loudly, closed his eyes, and fell into a deep, rumbling sleep. After a few minutes, Berthe felt his knee press against hers. She moved away. He continued to sleep but his out-stretched leg kept moving closer and closer until she was squeezed as far into the corner of the coach as she could get. Fi-nally, she lifted the heel of her shoe and stomped it down hard on his foot. He snorted awake, looked around as if trying to re-member where he was, closed his eyes, and promptly fell asleep again. She gazed out the coach window in order to avoid looking at him.

Just because I'm alone doesn't mean I'm afraid. If you try to touch me I'll bite through your big fat hand. But she was afraid. She was trapped in a small carriage with a big greasy sausage of a man, and if he made another move toward her she wasn't quite sure what she would do.

It was early June and the sun was high in the sky. She saw peasants walking along the side of the road carrying farm tools on their way to or from work in the fields. Herds of brown and white Normandy cows grazed on the sweet spring grass. Small birds darted between the cows' legs, feeding on stray seeds. Everything seemed so simple and serene. She began to relax and forget her fears. She felt cheered by the beautiful countryside. She was, by nature, an optimistic child, who was greatly influ-enced by the physical world around her. As a little girl she would sit on the edge of the bottom stone step in front of her house and study the clouds. Closing her eyes and lifting her face to the sun's warmth, she savored every small shift in the breezes that blew in from the nearby Rieule.

Peering out at the pink-edged clouds now she felt, if not happy, at least hopeful. And that small bit of hope lifted her spir-its and gave her a new energy.

She thought about her grand-mère. She must be very sad los-ing her only son. *But at least she has me.* She began to imagine a new relationship with the old woman. The cold, critical woman disappeared and in her place appeared a loving grand-mère thankful for a second chance to show her granddaughter that she was capable of affection. They would start fresh and learn to love each other. After all, it was just the two of them left in the world. Madame Homais was right. All they had was each other. Her grand-mère would make up for all the love and attention Berthe had never received from her own parents. Theirs would be a close and cherished relationship. She couldn't wait for the old woman to throw her arms around her, perhaps even cry the tears that had been stored up for years. It was with these positive thoughts that she rode the rest of the way to her grand-mère's house.

Berthe half expected to see a run-down shack. On her infrequent visits to Yonville the elder Madame Bovary had pleaded desperate poverty. To hear her tell it she barely had enough to keep body and soul together. She always made a point of scolding her daughter-in-law for her wasteful ways.

"Emma, my dear," she said to Berthe's mother one afternoon at tea, "do you really need to use so much sugar? These berries are sweet enough."

"Perhaps to your taste, Mother-in-law, but I find them quite sour," Emma said with a tight smile.

"How can that be? The berries I am eating come from the same patch as the ones you are eating." The older woman popped another into her mouth as if to demonstrate its sweetness. "Mmm, like candy. Here, Berthe, have a berry and tell your mother how wrong she is. She's using expensive sugar when it's not needed." Berthe was always being put in the middle whenever her grand-mère tried to make a point. Of course, she knew where her loyalty lay. She ate the strawberry, made a face, and offered her humble opinion.

"Oh, Grand-mère, it's quite sour," she said.

"You and your mother will drive your father into the poor-house," the old woman retorted. "By the way, Emma, is that a new dress?" she asked sharply.

"No, Mother-in-law," the younger Madame Bovary lied, "I've had this for years. I just put new lace on the bodice."

Berthe thought if her grand-mère only knew how much time and money her mother spent shopping she wouldn't quibble over a little sugar.

"I myself have not had a new frock in over fifteen years." Grand-mère Bovary sniffed. "I must make do with what I have. I am, after all, a poor widow."

So Berthe was quite surprised upon arriving at the poor widow's house to discover a large, neat structure, built half in stone and half in timber like many of the houses in the region. The front was covered with crossbeams painted a pretty pale blue. A small barn sat some yards from the house. The barn and the house occupied a spacious courtyard, in the center of which was an old stone well. Everything looked clean and in excellent repair. Her grand-mère was waiting on the doorstep, her arms crossed as if Berthe was late. Her black hair was pulled into a tight bun at the nape of her neck. Her skin was very white and quite smooth for a woman her age. She studied her granddaughter with deep-set black eyes that never seemed to blink. The contrast between this, her real grand-mère, and the warm figure Berthe had begun to create in her mind was like a bad joke.

"Where is your baggage?" her grand-mère demanded, forgoing any greeting as the coach pulled away.

"Baggage?" Berthe's whole body stiffened as if she had forgotten something.

"Your things."

"These are all my belongings, Grand-mère." The old woman took Berthe's valise, opened it, and glanced at the contents, making a face as she did.

"You truly are a penniless orphan," she said. "Well, bring it along, and wipe your feet before you ruin my floor. I just swept and scrubbed it."

This turned out to be one of the last household chores Berthe's grand-mère performed.

The old woman led Berthe up the stairs to the second floor. She showed her the three bedrooms; the largest, overlooking the courtyard, was beautifully furnished: a majestic oak bed and matching wardrobe with ornately carved cornices of doves, flowers, and fruit.

"My bedroom," she announced. "Not to be entered without my permission." The other two rooms were more modestly furnished. "And this is my sewing room," she said at the door of the second room. "I don't suppose anyone ever bothered to teach you to sew."

"My mother did. I can embroider as well," Berthe said proudly.

One of her earliest memories was her mother teaching her how to embroider. Félicité had started her out practicing a simple slanting overcast stitch to be used in outlining the letters of the alphabet. Berthe couldn't follow the lines that Félicité had so carefully drawn on the muslin. Her fingers felt fat and clumsy. She was constantly pricking herself. Soon the material was covered with rust-red blood spots.

"What is this?" her mother asked, pulling the cloth out of Berthe's hands. "What are you teaching her, Félicité? How to make useless, ugly things? Come with me. If you are going to sew, at least sew something that I can bear to look at."

Her mother showed her how to do French knots, candlewicking, *point de plume,* and *point de minute*—a stitch used to make the pattern appear raised. Then she gave Berthe a large piece of soft cotton and said, "Now stop pestering me and go make something beautiful."

"But, Maman, there are no lines to follow."

"Use your imagination, that's what it's for," she said on her way to the shops.

And Berthe did. While her mother was out shopping, or at home lost in a novel or the latest fashion periodical, Berthe practiced the stitches. As she sewed she found that her fingers seemed to suddenly grow longer and cleverer. When she was all done she presented the work to her mother.

"Now what?" her mother sighed, putting down her book.

"Look, Maman," she said, laying the embroidery down on her mother's lap for her to inspect. Madame Bovary picked up the fabric and examined it briefly. Berthe had embroidered an entire garden of multicolored flowers.

"Better. Just remember, there's no point in creating something unless it makes the world a prettier place."

Berthe continued to create her own designs. She created flowers and leaves in colors and shapes not found in nature. She spent hours tracing her original patterns first onto paper and then onto cloth. She imagined embroidering entire dresses for herself and her mother, and she lay in bed at night designing these in her head. For her mother, a beautiful summer dress of white piqué with a particular design of tiny intertwined flowers and a hat festooned with pale pink peonies. For herself, a shorter dress of the same material and a small bonnet with a pink peony stitched to the crown. *No, no, that will look silly there.* She made an instant alteration, removing the flower from the bonnet and placing it . . . where? *Ah, yes, there at the center of the sash. Perfect.* In her fantasy, her mother would take her hand and, dressed

alike, they would stroll down Yonville's main street under the en-
vious gaze of the entire town. Her mother would look down on
her well-dressed daughter and smiling with pride she would say:

"Aren't we just the most elegant pair?"

Berthe's grand-mère was still talking, and she forced herself to
pay attention. "We have no use for fancy needlework here. There
is no need to go into my sewing room except to dust," Grand-
mère said. Berthe assumed that the third room on the floor was
hers. But that was not to be. Her grand-mère showed her a ladder leading up to the attic.

"You will be up there," she said. "You can have the whole
floor to yourself and you won't be in my way. Put your things
away neatly. I don't want a mess up there. I'm not too old to
climb the ladder, so be forewarned." Berthe felt an urge to
scream at her grand-mère: *I won't get in your way. In fact, I won't
live here at all. I'll go somewhere else and you never have to see me
or bother about me again.* And then she realized, of course, that
she had nowhere else to go. She took in a long deep breath and
squared her shoulders before climbing the ladder. Being hidden
away in the attic reminded Berthe of one of her favorite fairy
tales, *Rumpelstiltskin.* She just hoped that her grand-mère
wouldn't expect her to spin straw into gold.

The attic had one small dusty window. In the corner under
the slanted roof was a narrow rope bed; next to it stood a table
with an oil lamp, and under the window was another table with
a cracked pitcher and bowl. She sat down on the hard bed.
When she stood up she immediately bumped her head on the
slanted ceiling. She went over to the window and, using the inside of her skirt, she wiped it clean. It looked out over the vast
fields behind the house. To the left she saw a small orchard of
apple trees, and beyond that a narrow river sparkling in the sun

and winding its way into a wooded area beyond. She unlatched
the window, pushed it open, and inhaled the clean country air.
As close and shabby as the room was, she was happy to have a
place to call her own. And she was particularly grateful for the
lovely view. All she had to do was keep looking out, beyond the
small stuffy room. The serene fields, the whole outdoors would
be her new home.

"Berthe, stop dawdling and come down for supper," her
grand-mère called. Berthe splashed a little water on her. face,
combed her hair, and hurried down.

She felt she should say something about her father since her
grand-mère had not attended the funeral nor said a word about
his death. She must be terribly sad having lost her only son, she
reasoned.

"I'm sorry you weren't able to attend Father's funeral." She
stood at the table, her hands clasped in front of her.

"I had no desire to witness the end of a wasted life," her
grand-mère said sharply, smoothing the back of her already
smooth hair.

"Well, it was a very nice funeral." Berthe looked down at her
fingernails to make sure they were clean.

"What?" said her grand-mère, bending to pull a roasted
chicken out of the oven.

"Father's funeral. It was very nice. The whole town came."

"I should hope so," the old woman sniffed, "after he ruined
his health attending those people all times of the day or night.
Getting nothing in return. They helped drive him to an early
grave. But that was nothing compared to the damage your
mother inflicted on the poor man. She should by all rights be
hanged for murder."

Berthe glared at her grand-mère's hunched, ugly back. Was

this the woman she had imagined would love and cherish her? Had she really thought she could squeeze any affection out of this dry old woman?

"It would be difficult to hang her since she's already dead," Berthe said through gritted teeth.

"That tone will not be welcome here, miss," her grand-mère said, giving her a look filled with such venom it put to rest any thoughts of mutual mourning. "Sit down."

Her grand-mère pushed a plate in front of her.

"I wager you never ate this well at home." She was right. As angry as Berthe was at her grand-mère's indictment of her parents, she was desperately hungry. Her hunger took precedence over her feelings. She had to admit that everything was delicious. Roasted chicken with tarragon, tiny onions sautéed in butter and then smothered in a white cream sauce, roasted carrots and turnips, and finally a large slice of apple tart. "I don't suppose you know how to cook?" Grand-mère Bovary asked when they had finished the meal.

"No, Grand-mère. Before my mother died Félicité did all the cooking for us."

"You will learn how to cook, how to clean, and how to milk a cow," the old woman said, neatly rolling her napkin and placing it in the napkin ring. "You will receive an invaluable education from me. One that will prepare you for life. I did not ask God for another child, but now that I have one I will do my duty by you." She stood, smoothed her apron, and pushed her chair under the table. "Now, wash the dishes."

Water had to be brought in from the well in the courtyard. Berthe carried it in two heavy buckets, which made her arms feel as though they were being stretched out of their sockets. The water was then boiled in a big pot on the woodstove. By the time she finished washing and drying the dishes she was exhausted and ready for bed. Her grand-mère stopped her as she was about to drag herself up the stairs.

"Where do you think you are going?"

"To bed, Grand-mère."

"And the kitchen floor? Is it going to scrub itself?"

"That would be truly wonderful," sighed Berthe.

After Berthe emptied the soapy water she stood at the edge of the kitchen and admired her work. It was a big kitchen, clean, neat, and meticulously well cared for. This was her grand-mère's house in every way. It was cold, hard, and full of pride. Berthe knew she would live here, but it could never be her home. Not any more than this icy old woman could be her loving guardian.

She noticed the hearth was black with soot. She filled the bucket again, got down on her hands and knees, and scrubbed it clean. By the time she fell into bed she felt as if she had indeed earned her keep that day. She vowed that if she couldn't gain her grand-mère's love, she could at least be worthy of her respect and perhaps even her appreciation. She was determined to make the woman glad that she had come to live with her.

She took the illustration from her mother's fashion magazine out from underneath her pillow, brought it up close to her face, and imagined the gown in the faint moonlight. Tears welled up. *Could a piece of silk replace the warmth of a mother's love? Hardly.* She laid the picture back under her pillow, and before long, she was fast asleep.

CHAPTER 3

Chores

THE NEXT MORNING BERTHE AWOKE TO THE SOUND OF A knocking from below. Her grand-mère was pounding on the ceiling with the handle of a broom. It was still dark. The rooster had not yet crowed. Berthe dragged herself down the ladder and down to the kitchen half asleep.

"You are not going to lead a life of luxury here, young lady." Her grand-mère slid a bowl of coffee and a piece of bread and butter in front of Berthe. The coffee sloshed out onto the table.

She had said nothing about the clean hearth or the gleaming kitchen floor. Gaining her grand-mère's respect was going to require more work than Berthe had imagined.

"Hurry up and finish, and then we have to do something about your clothes."

Berthe sipped her coffee as she imagined a new wardrobe filled with soft cotton dresses in pastel shades. But the outfit her grand-mère provided her with was nothing she had encountered before: a scratchy homespun dress with a coarse muslin under-skirt and chemise, both of which chafed her skin. Over that she wore a vest made out of old cowhide, and over that a long apron with endless strings that had to be wrapped several times around her waist. Worst of all were the shoes.

"Fancy leather boots have no place on a farm. They'll fetch a good price at the market," her grand-mère said, examining Berthe's boots. She provided Berthe with a pair of wooden clogs that were so big and heavy it was difficult to keep them on.

"Ah, that's much better," said her grand-mère, standing back and scrutinizing her granddaughter. "Now you're dressed properly for work."

"This is so ugly." Berthe looked down at herself and felt like crying. She thought of her mother and how ashamed she would be to see Berthe dressed like this.

"Ugly is as ugly does." Her grand-mère secured the ivory comb in her dark hair.

The first day, Berthe's grand-mère showed her what was expected of her around the house: sweeping, scrubbing the stone steps, blacking the stove, clearing out the old ashes, laying a fresh fire, airing her bedclothes, and emptying the slops. She pointed to a beautiful oak kitchen dresser that had four open shelves of silver serving dishes and fine pottery.

"These are my best things. Make sure dust doesn't have the opportunity to gather." She caressed the edge of a blue and white serving platter as if it were a favored child. "And the silver must be polished at least once a week," she said grandly. Berthe wondered why she hadn't sold these things if she was so very poor. "Will you just look at this," she said, running a finger along the top shelf. "That girl wasn't worth a handful of dirt."

"What girl?" Berthe asked, wiping a dustcloth along the sides of the dresser.

"Marie, my maid."

"You had a maid?"

"Until the day before yesterday, yes. But I always had to do everything over. Lazy girl. It wasn't as if I didn't pay her a decent salary." She took Berthe's chin in her hand and looked her in the eye. "But you, *chère* Berthe, are a Bovary. And Bovarys are not afraid of hard work, are they?"

"No, Grand-mère."

"Then let's not let the day go to waste."

"I will get her pay then," Berthe said, smiling at her grand-mère.

"Whose pay?"

"The maid's."

"Don't be silly. You're not a maid. You're my granddaughter. You have a roof over your head and plenty to eat. What do you need money for?"

"I need it for my future," Berthe said, staring hard at her grand-mère.

"Just do your work. The future will take care of itself," her grand-mère said, moving the serving platter a quarter of an inch to the right.

"But I will need to take care of myself," said Berthe. "What will happen to me after you die?"

"Die!" her grand-mère bellowed. "She's barely been here a day and she's already killing off her poor grand-mère. You wicked, wicked girl!" She grabbed Berthe's braid and yanked it hard.

"Ouch." Berthe pulled away. She pressed her lips together. She was fighting back tears but determined not to let her grand-mère see her cry.

I would be better off and far better paid if I was her maid.

Anger seeped through her. She took out her frustration on her grand-mère's house. She attacked the stone floor with broom and scrub brush. She beat the rugs mercilessly. She scoured the stone sink so hard that had it been made out of flesh it would have bled.

The hardest job was the laundry. It seemed as if Grand-mère Bovary had been saving up the wash for her arrival. She loaded Berthe down with a huge pile of soiled linens.

"The laundry pot is down by the river," the old woman said, pointing the way.

Carrying two buckets of water at a time, Berthe needed to make several trips to fill the huge pot. Then she had to build a fire underneath. The sun beat down through the trees and before long she was drenched in her own sweat. She added soda crystals to the pot and stood over it, stirring everything with a big stick. Using the same stick, she pulled out the steaming items, put them in a basket, and dragged the basket down to the water's edge. Then with a square wooden paddle she beat each piece against a rock, rinsed it in the river, beat it again, and rinsed it one final time. The bed linens were hard to lift because they were heavy with water, so she devised a way to squeeze the excess water out of the sheets by standing on one end and twisting the other end until most of the water ran out. Once she finished with the washing, everything had to be dragged back up the hill to her grand-mère's where it was hung up on a line to dry. Berthe felt a great sense of accomplishment. She had never known how to do the wash, or anything else for that matter. Up until now, her greatest skill in life had been staying quiet and keeping out of the way.

Remembering that her grand-mère had paid someone to do these chores Berthe reasoned she, too, could make her living this way. She would perfect her skills and then perhaps one day she could hire herself out.

She would be in great demand; she would raise her prices,

and soon she would make lots of money. Then she could buy herself a beautiful house and hire her own maid to do this hideous work. But she would pay the maid handsomely and be sure to praise her. The harder Berthe toiled the more determined she became. Soon, she no longer even needed her grand-mère's acknowledgment or appreciation. The work was reward in itself.

Berthe was only twelve years old but she was tall for her age. Her mother had always suffered from poor health and a delicate constitution. When she wasn't actually sick in bed she was continually nursing a headache or recovering from a fainting spell. By contrast, Berthe prided herself on her physical strength. And since coming to her grand-mère's she seemed to be growing bigger every day.

One evening Grand-mère measured her against the wall.

"Unfortunately, it appears that you will take after your father when it comes to height. A pity. Big girls are not in great demand. Men want their wives to be petite," she said, looking Berthe up and down as if she were a weed that needed to be pulled. "No one wants a giantess hanging on his arm. Let's just hope you stop growing at some point before you tower over your husband."

"What husband?" Berthe asked, her heart quickening. Was her grand-mère already planning on marrying her off?

"Never you mind," her grand-mère said, pursing her lips.

The next morning, she announced, "It's time for you to take on a few of the small farm chores. Renard, a boy from a neighboring farm, does most of the heavy work. He chops the wood, cuts the hay in the summer. He doesn't have time to do the milking and feed the chickens and pigs. We have to do that."

As she followed her grand-mère into the barn, Berthe realized "we" meant her.

"This is my angel, Céleste," her grand-mère said, indicating a small sturdy cow with a white head and brown patches around her eyes like spectacles. "She won't bite. She may kick, but she'll never bite."

"I'm much relieved," murmured Berthe, taking several steps back.

"You must milk her every day, twice a day, until she dries up." Grand-mère emptied a small pail of grain into Céleste's bucket. Then the old woman set a small three-legged stool at a right angle to Céleste and sat down, resting her head against the cow's flank.

"Take the teat like this," Grand-mère said, grasping one of Céleste's pale teats in the palm of her hand. "You squeeze it like this," she added, curling her fingers around the teat, the milk coming out in a strong stream. "When one goes dry you do the same with the other three. She should give milk ten out of twelve months. Otherwise, she will be shipped off to the butcher." She gave Céleste a smack on the rear. Berthe immediately identified with the cow.

"*C'est tout,*" her grand-mère said, groaning as she lifted herself off the stool. "When you are done, pour the milk into this." She held up a beautiful copper jug which had a long leather strap attached to it. Berthe had seen women on the road carrying these jugs on their shoulders. The leather strap was used to keep it steady as they walked along.

"Hurry up with the milking," the old woman said as she left. "There's still much to do today."

Berthe had never been so close to a cow, or asked to be on such intimate terms with one. She sat down and reached for the first teat with nervous fingers. She squeezed hard. Nothing happened. Céleste turned her head as much as the rope would allow and gave Berthe a look that seemed to say, "And what in heaven's name do you think you are doing?"

"Come on," Berthe said, squeezing the teat even harder. She dropped one teat and quickly grabbed another as if she were ringing bells. Perspiration ran down her face. Her skin began to itch from the coarse muslin chemise. She squeezed and squeezed. Nothing happened. She did not want to report failure to her grand-mère. "Come on," she said, gritting her teeth. Her shoulders were stiff with tension.

"Berthe," her grand-mère called from the courtyard, "aren't you done yet? Milking doesn't take all morning, for goodness' sake." Berthe bumped her head against Céleste's side in annoyance.

"Please, Céleste, please, let go of the milk." She was ready to cry from frustration. The cow looked around at Berthe again. That sweet face that so enchanted her when she first saw it now enraged her. "You stupid, stupid cow," she growled.

"That's no way to talk to her." Berthe turned. A boy carrying a huge bundle of hay on his shoulder stood in the doorway. He had shaggy sandy-colored hair and almost painfully bright blue eyes. He was the most beautiful boy she had ever seen.

"She won't give me any of her cursed milk," Berthe said. "I must be doing something wrong. Please, can you show me?"

The boy took her place on the stool. Stroking Céleste's flank, he began to talk to her in soft, soothing tones. "Shoosh, shoosh, shoosh, *ma jolie fille*. Do you have any milk for Renard?" After he had caressed and scratched her for a few minutes, he slowly, ever so slowly reached for her teat and the milk began to stream into the bucket.

"Now you try," he said. "Just be gentle. She is like all women. You must treat her with kindness."

"And what do you know of 'all women'?" Berthe asked. He was just a boy. He couldn't have been more than fourteen or fifteen years old.

36 Linda Urbach

"I have sisters," he said, as if that explained everything. "Come. Even my littlest sister can do this." Berthe took a deep breath and sat down. She gave Céleste a look. *Don't you dare hold out on me again.* Then she followed Renard's example. The milk flowed out smoothly until the bucket was almost half full.

Forking hay into the hayloft, the boy looked down at Berthe and smiled. He had good teeth. Straight and white. She smiled back.

"My name is Renard Garnier. And yours?" he asked.

"Berthe Bovary," she said. He rested his chin on the handle of his pitchfork. The way he looked at her made her feel shy.

"How old are you?"

"Thirteen," she lied. "And you?"

"I will be sixteen on the last day of August," he said, as if he expected her to mark it in her almanac.

"Good for you." She turned her back to him.

"You're a sassy one." He threw a handful of hay in her direction. "My sister Marie used to do the housework and make the cheese and butter, but Madame Bovary let her go. You are to take her place. Has she said how much she will pay you?" Berthe shook her head. "Of course not. You will do work out of love because you are her devoted granddaughter." He laughed.

"And how much does she pay you to throw her hay around?" she retorted, pouring the milk into the copper jug.

"Don't let your grand-mère hear that you have a tongue on you," he said. "Or you will be one sorry milkmaid."

"I'm not a milkmaid." She lifted the copper jug onto her shoulder and held it secure with the leather strap. Then holding both her head and the copper jug high, she turned and walked out of the barn, knowing that she must look every bit the milkmaid that Renard had declared her to be. The sound of his laughter trailed after her. She made up her mind never to speak to him again.

Early one morning, hours before her grand-mère woke, Berthe stood in the doorway of the kitchen and watched as the sun came up. A mist lifted off the green fields. The geese emerged from the barn with an air of ownership. The chickens followed humbly behind, pecking at the ground in the unlikely event they would find leftover grain from the day before. From inside the barn she could hear Céleste mooing to be relieved of her burden of milk.

In many ways the country life suited her. The food was good and plentiful. The air was clean and sweet. And even though she labored to exhaustion from morning to evening, she did not shirk the work. She'd settled in to living here, and was determined to make her life as beautiful as possible. While her grand-mère slept she took the homespun dress and dipped it in beet juice; the result was a pleasing pale rose color. Then she took out a small case of embroidery silks that she'd saved from the house in Yonville and embroidered a design of blue and red fleurs-de-lis on the bib of her apron. She was very pleased with the result. The dress and apron were now almost pretty. It gave her a great feeling of satisfaction to be able to transform something ugly into something almost wearable.

When her grand-mère saw her she was indignant.

"What have you done to your good clothes? Well, you'll have to live with them. I have no money to waste on buying you new ones."

Several months later Berthe awoke to find her nightgown and bedsheets stained with blood. *Am I dying? So young?* Then she realized what it was. Her mother had called it the Curse without ever explaining it. Why had she called it that? Did it, as Berthe suspected at the time, have something to do with falling in love with the wrong man and having your heart broken? Whenever her mother was struck with the Curse she took to her bed for a week.

"What's wrong, Maman?" Berthe asked during one of these weeklong convalescences.

"Ask your father. He's the doctor," her mother said, turning her back and pulling the duvet over her head.

When Berthe was finally able to get a few moments with her father he explained everything in his clinical way: "The Curse is another name for a woman's menses. It is the circulatory connection between a woman's body and mind. Thus, a woman must bleed freely once a month; failing to do so will create a form of mental disorder. Similarly, she must remain quiet and calm during this time. It's been scientifically proven that any strong emotion can cause menstrual obstruction, which can lead to insanity and death."

"Every single month, Papa?"

"Every single month, child. That, you see, is the curse of being a woman."

"Oh" was all she could think of to say. She had more questions, like what was the curse of being a man? But her father was busy and shooed her away.

Now, in her grand-mère's attic without a father to ask or a mother to guide her, she lay in her bed afraid to move. She tried to keep her mind calm and her anxiety at bay just in case what her father said was true. She didn't want to get her first Curse and go insane all on the same day.

Her grand-mère's head suddenly appeared in the open hatch of the attic floor.

"Perhaps you would like breakfast in bed. Or would you prefer to sleep until noon? Just let me know and I'll tell Cook to stop boiling your egg."

"I'm sorry, Grand-mère." Berthe sat up. She tried to conceal her nightgown and stained sheets. But it was too late.

"Oh, for heaven's sake," her grand-mère snapped. "Go and soak everything in cold water." Berthe slipped out of bed, keeping her back to the old woman.

"Of course I have no rags. Why would I ever think to keep rags? You'll have to tear up one of my nice old sheets. A perfectly good sheet, torn up…" She continued grumbling as she descended the ladder to the floor below.

Berthe took off her nightgown, wrapped it in the soiled sheet, and brought everything downstairs. Her grand-mère was at the stove boiling the morning coffee. She scowled at the bundle in Berthe's arms and Berthe ducked her head in embarrassment.

Her stomach hurt. It was a deep-down tender ache. For some reason it made her long for her mother. And that was the truly painful part. Because what would her mother have done if she were alive? She thought of Félicité, the maid, whom she ran to whenever she was hurt or upset. She realized now that Félicité had been paid to watch over her, to act as if she cared. She remembered once as a small child encountering Félicité in the small park in Yonville on the maid's day off. She was walking with a new beau. Berthe ran up to her and Félicité acted as if she didn't know her. Or didn't want to know her. Remembering this now, Berthe was filled with sadness. Had she really been so hard to love?

Outside, she plunged the sheet and gown into the water trough and then suddenly brought her hand down hard on the edge of the iron container. The pain caused her to cry out.

Damn. Damn. Damn. She studied her palm. It was already bruised and bleeding. She brought the injured hand to her mouth as if kissing it would make the pain go away.

"Careful, mademoiselle, farmwork can be a dangerous thing." She glanced up. Renard had seemingly come out of nowhere. He leaned over the trough studying the contents. She felt her face turn red as she plunged the wet laundry farther down into the water.

"Go away," she said. "Can't you see I'm busy? You must have better things to do than hang over my shoulder all day."

"Actually, no. I can't think of anything better." He gave her a broad grin before turning and walking toward the fields. He must have known she was watching him because just as he got to the edge of the field where the hay had already been mowed, he turned and gave her a smart salute. She quickly bent her head so that he wouldn't see her smile.

The next evening after the milking she was washing herself outside by the pump. She had taken off her heavy muslin shirt and was wearing only a thin cotton camisole underneath. She looked down at herself. Water had soaked through the thin material and she could see pink nubs poking through. It was as if her breasts had begun to form almost overnight. Just at that moment Renard came around the corner of the barn. He smiled broadly as she quickly picked up her shirt to cover herself.

She had the beginnings of a woman's body and now the strange feelings that went along with it. Her grand-mère seemed to be all too aware of the change.

When she went inside for supper, the old woman grabbed her by her braid and pulled her around to face her.

"Don't think I'm not watching you, young lady. And I am warning you right now, stay away from that boy. He's up to no

good—and if you're anything like your mother, neither, I believe, are you."

Renard seemed to linger in the mornings so that Berthe always
saw him on her way out to milk Céleste. They never spoke, only
exchanged glances. But for her part she looked forward to that
glimpse of him. His smile was the single bright spot of her day.

One morning while she was rinsing the milk jug at the pump
he came up behind her and pulled at the string of her straw hat.

"And how goes it with you and your cow?" he asked, his blue
eyes bright in the early sun.

"It's fine. She gives her milk without an argument."

"I told you. All you have to do is be gentle." He pulled the
string of her hat again and this time it came tumbling off.

"Stop that," she said, snatching the hat from the ground and
smashing it down on her head. He laughed and made another
lunge for her hat but she jumped out of the way. She wanted to
keep the conversation going—to keep his blue eyes on her. At
the same time, she felt shy. "Is your house far from here?"

"Over there," he said with a slight nod of his head. She
looked in the direction he indicated and saw nothing but fields
of hay stacked in towering hills. "My house is beyond that grove
of trees. But it's nothing to see even if you could see it. My sister
Marie says we should burn the place down and start over from
scratch. My mother says it would only take our family a week to
ruin a new place."

"Do you have many brothers and sisters?"

"I am the oldest of seven. Four boys, three girls," he said,
kicking dirt at one of the geese who had ventured a little too
close.

"How lucky you are," she said, remembering the Homaises

and the comfort and laughter of a large family. She thought back to how, as a little girl, she'd hovered around them as though they were a good fire that provided her only source of warmth.

"Lucky to sleep three to a bed? Lucky that my father is so poor I have to work on four different farms in order to earn my keep? Lucky if I get a decent supper by the time I return home at night because they have eaten what little there is?"

"I'm sorry," she murmured. She reached out and touched his arm and then withdrew her hand quickly.

He kicked at the dirt once again, his face red.

"Why should you be sorry? It's not your fault." He hitched up his pants, grabbed his pitchfork, and walked toward the fields. This time, he didn't look back.

She thought of Renard going hungry at the end of a hard day's work, and that night when she had finished scrubbing the kitchen she took some food from her grand-mère's pantry to give to him. The old woman frequently traded her cheeses for delicacies from other farms. Her pantry was filled with all manner of good things: smoked hams hanging from hooks, jars of strawberry preserves, tiny cornichons, and boiled sweets lining the shelves. Food was something they had more than enough of. Berthe reasoned her grand-mère would never miss what she took.

Berthe had stolen only one thing as a child. She had coveted many things that had belonged to her mother: a single silver hair comb, an embroidered handkerchief, a velvet ribbon, a cut-glass rouge jar. From time to time, she would "borrow" these small treasures, play with them, and return them before her mother was any the wiser. Until the paisley shawl.

Monsieur Lheureux, the draper, seemed to become more and more of an enticing presence to her mother. One day, when

Berthe was around six years old, he brought a dozen of his finest silk shawls for Madame Bovary to choose from.

"They come from around the world," he said, laying them out on her mother's bed. "Some all the way from China. Look at the patterns: Are they not exquisite? Choose one. Choose two."

"I have no use for such a thing," Emma Bovary said, pretending disinterest as she fingered the one nearest her.

"It is not a question of use," said Monsieur Lheureux, "it's a matter of obligation. You owe it to yourself to have one of these. They are too beautiful to sit hidden away in a dark drawer in my shop."

Her mother spent the whole week narrowing down her selection. One afternoon she spread the shawls over the settee and turned to Berthe, who was sitting on the floor practicing her needlework. "Pick one. The prettiest," she said. Her mother had never asked her opinion before.

Berthe chose a shawl of the palest peach, with an intricate design of delicate blue and green leaves. Seeing which one her daughter preferred, Emma Bovary chose another, a deep red and purple paisley that she wore for a day over her cashmere dressing gown.

Some months later Berthe found the shawl on the bottom of her mother's wardrobe and took it for herself. She hid the shawl underneath her mattress. Félicité found it later while turning the bed.

"And what is this, pray tell?" Félicité asked, holding it in front of Berthe's face.

"It's mine," Berthe said, reaching up to pull it away from her.

"Oh, we shall see."

Moments later, her mother swept into the room.

"I've been looking everywhere for this," she said. "What

wonderful news. My daughter is turning into a thief. As if I don't have enough to deal with." She thrust the shawl in Berthe's face. "Here, if you want it so badly, you may have it."

Berthe took the shawl and laid it on top of her pillow. She loved having something of her mother's to sleep with every night. But one day the shawl disappeared. And as her mother sold off her belongings one by one, Berthe never saw it again.

The following afternoon when Renard was about to leave, Berthe motioned him into the barn.

"I have something for you," she said, handing him a jar of strawberry preserves and a cheese wrapped in muslin that she had hidden away in her apron.

"You don't have to feed me," he said, shoving his hands in his pockets. "I'm not starving."

"It's just a gift. From my grand-mère," she added.

He raised an eyebrow.

"Your grand-mère would kill you if she knew," he said seriously.

"Not if I kill her first," she declared. He laughed.

"You talk like a hooligan."

"You would know how a hooligan talks," she said. He pulled at her hat strings and she hit him lightly on the arm. Suddenly all her shyness was gone. He took the preserves and cheese and gave her a smile so wide it caused his blue eyes to sparkle with pleasure.

She continued to take small items from the pantry, one or two at a time. Renard accepted them willingly. She felt certain he enjoyed the idea that they were putting one over on her grand-mère even more than the treats. But one day Grand-mère Bovary grabbed Berthe as she was going out to the barn to do her morning milking. She reached into Berthe's apron pocket and pulled out a piece of pâté wrapped in cloth.

"Where are you taking this?" she demanded.

"It's for my lunch, Grand-mère."

"Pâté for your lunch? Who do you think you are, Marie Antoinette? Stealing food right under my nose. I should have known. A thief! Like mother like daughter. If your mother could have taken the food from your poor father's mouth, I have no doubt she would have. Oh, there was no end to that woman's avarice. She stole everything from him. His pride, his ambition, his reputation. Yes, even his life. Thank heavens, he had no gold teeth, she would have yanked them out of his head." She dragged Berthe by the arm into the pantry. "Everything that you see here I have saved and scrimped and worked for." She slammed the wrapped pâté down on the shelf. "You think pâté and cornichons and fresh eggs grow on trees? You think you are entitled to more, more, more?"

Berthe shook her head, clutching her apron tightly.

"Are you your mother's daughter? Are you?" Berthe didn't know how to answer the question. She nodded. "No, you are not. Not anymore. From now on you are your grand-mère's charge and you will act accordingly."

"Yes, Grand-mère." Berthe felt tears well up in her eyes.

"Your mother's father spoiled her terribly. I have no doubt that was where she learned her wastrel ways. I only pray to God that it's not too late for you.

"My son Charles just wanted to be a good doctor and lead a simple life. He spent so much money on your mother that first year. Moving from one town to another because she was bored. Buying new curtains and furniture when there was perfectly good furniture in the house already. And the hats and dresses.

And the gloves. How many pairs of gloves does one woman need? Oh, it makes me want to cry when I think of the waste," she said.

Berthe realized her grand-mère was right. She remembered all the expensive things her mother had purchased from Monsieur Lheureux when they could barely pay the mortgage. And her poor father. How hard he had tried to provide for his beautiful wife. The long hours he worked, the many miles he traveled, and for what? The few francs he managed to scrape together were nothing compared to the enormous debt his wife had incurred.

And then the awful day when the men came to collect the furniture. Berthe had been awakened by the sound of a crowd in the square. She looked out the window. A group of people had gathered around a large yellow notice nailed on to one of the posts. She saw Félicité rip the notice off the post, stuff it in her bodice, and run back toward the house. Berthe hurried down into the kitchen, where she found Félicité in tears. Her mother sat in a chair, staring at the notice. Berthe had learned to read at a young age, looking over her mother's shoulder as she read aloud from her books, and so she, too, could read the damning words:

> "... Within twenty-four hours, at the latest, to pay
> the sum of eight thousand francs. Or, she will be con-
> strained thereto by every form of law, and notably by
> a writ of distrait on her furniture and effects."

"Oh, madame, it's an outrage!" Félicité cried.

Berthe could see her mother struggling for composure. Emma Bovary put on her best black dress, donned the cape with the glittering jet beads, and tied a bonnet around her head. She looked as if she were dressed for a funeral. Her own funeral.

She glanced at Berthe as if seeing her for the first time.

"What are you waiting for?" she said. "Go on and get ready. Put on your good pinafore." Berthe had no idea where her mother was taking her. "Don't dawdle. We have a very important errand to attend to."

It was a cloudy spring morning. The air was heavy with moisture and Berthe knew it would soon rain. She worried that they didn't have an umbrella, especially since her mother was wearing her good cape. The rain would spot the silk. Her mother pulled her along the street and through the village, until they came to a large house on the outskirts of town. It belonged to Monsieur Guillaumin, the notary and the second-richest man in Yonville. He could, if he chose, save her from complete ruin.

"You will be my trump card," she said to Berthe. "Can you look the waif?" She lifted her daughter's chin and stared at her. Berthe made a sad face. "That will do." She bade Berthe to sit on a garden bench by the side of the house.

"Wait here until I call you," she said. As soon as she left, Berthe got up and peered into the nearest window. She looked in on a huge dining room. The walls of the room were paneled in mahogany. The table was set for breakfast with two silver chafing dishes, silver candelabras, and a snowy white tablecloth. In the corner a large porcelain stove crackled with a fire.

Monsieur Guillaumin entered the room, followed by Emma Bovary. He was an enormously fat man with full red cheeks and wispy blond hair escaping from his velvet skullcap. He pulled his embroidered dressing gown around his large belly, then indicated a parlor chair next to the stove; Berthe's mother took a seat. Berthe watched as he helped himself to eggs and sausages from the covered dishes. Her mouth watered. All she had had for breakfast that morning was a piece of yesterday's bread with no butter and tea without sugar. She could practically taste the food as he filled his plate.

When he had finished eating he wiped his mouth with a large white linen napkin. Then he leaned over and placed his hand on her mother's shoulder. Berthe watched as he ran his fat ringed fingers up and down her arm. Emma Bovary pulled back. And then Berthe saw him suddenly fall to his knees. She thought for a moment he had been taken ill. He pulled at her mother's skirt with his big hands. Her mother jumped up, her face red and angry, and rushed out of the room. Berthe quickly returned to the bench. Before she knew it her mother was at her side. She grabbed Berthe's hand, crushing it in her grasp, and pulled her along the street.

"Scoundrel. Beast. Wretch," Madame Bovary muttered. "I should never have gone there. What was I thinking?"

"Maman, stop, you're going too fast," Berthe said. But her mother paid no heed. She rushed down the street with her young daughter in tow, Berthe's feet barely touching the cobblestones.

When they got home Félicité was waiting for them at the door.

"Well?" Félicité asked, her brow rippled with lines of worry.

"No!" said her mother. "But I have one last hope. I am going to beg at the door of Monsieur Boulanger."

"Oh, madame, please no, don't!" Félicité cried.

"Quiet," said her mother.

Berthe could see the fear in both of their faces and it terrified her. She ran to hide in her room. She was afraid her mother would want her to go with her to beg Monsieur Boulanger for money. He had been so kind to her mother before, giving her a horse to ride, sending her a beautiful basket of apricots. Perhaps he would help her. Perhaps Monsieur Lheureux wouldn't take their furniture after all. And then there was her father. Was it possible he could find a way to get them out of this terrible mess?

Berthe watched from the window as her mother returned from Monsieur Boulanger's house an hour later. She could tell by the way her normally straight back was bent that she had failed. Rodolphe Boulanger, with all his great wealth, his mansion and many horses, had denied her request.

The elder Madame Bovary's best and, in fact, only friend was Madame Leaumont, a widow who lived in a small house a few miles away. She was as cheery as Berthe's grand-mère was dour. Her face had been ravaged by the pox, but she had beautiful brown eyes and a smile so easy and warm that one soon forgot her terrible scars. Berthe liked her very much and was always glad when she dropped by for a visit.

"Will she be going to school, your granddaughter?" Madame Leaumont asked one morning in August.

"She already knows how to read and write," Berthe's grand-mère answered.

Berthe was churning butter. She felt her grand-mère's eyes on her.

"Not that she's going to need reading and writing for anything," the old woman added. "Berthe, fetch more cake for Madame Leaumont."

"Oh, no, I couldn't," Madame Leaumont demurred, holding out her plate to Berthe and smiling. "She is already growing into quite a pretty thing," she commented, as if Berthe were not there.

"Pretty is as pretty does," Grand-mère Bovary shot back.

"You are very hard on her, *chère amie,*" said Madame Leaumont.

"I am only getting her ready for the life she has in store: no money, no family, no property. This farm, thanks to her father and spendthrift mother, is mortgaged beyond what I can ever hope to repay. When I go, it goes, too. And I won't live forever," she said with the confidence of someone who actually thinks she might.

Berthe felt a sudden, cold panic. This was the first she had heard of the farm going when her grand-mère was gone. Was she going to lose her home yet again?

"What about marriage?" said Madame Leaumont. *At least Madame Leaumont seems to care about my future,* Berthe thought. *You'll see. I'll make something of myself. I'll be rich and have the most beautiful château in all of France. And you, you wicked old woman, will be begging at the gate. And I'll let you in and I'll serve you tea from a silver pot in a gold-rimmed cup and when you ask for cream, I'll say, Cream? Oh, no, we have no cream. Do you think cream grows on trees?*

"People around here know all about her mother," her grand-mère said. "What guarantee is there that the apple does not fall far from the tree?"

Berthe couldn't keep still any longer.

"At least my mother didn't hide me up in a dusty attic and make me wear painful, ugly shoes all day."

"Berthe!" The old woman stood up. "How dare you criticize me in front of Madame Leaumont!"

Madame Leaumont put her hand on Madame Bovary's arm in an effort to calm her, but Berthe's grand-mère shook her off. "Do you see what I have to put up with? She is a devil, that girl. I give her a home and she treats me with such disrespect. What have I done to deserve this?" She turned to Berthe. "Where is my broom? Where have you hidden it?"

Berthe picked up the broom that was leaning by the door and calmly handed it to her. Her grand-mère pulled her outside and began thumping her on the legs and backside with the wooden handle. Berthe kept her head turned and stared out at

MADAME BOVARY'S DAUGHTER 51

the fields as if this wasn't happening to her. She wanted to cry but refused to let the tears come. She wanted to push her grand-mère away, but kept her arms frozen at her sides. When the old woman had finally exhausted her rage Berthe stumbled toward the barn. As soon as she was inside the barn, she laid her head against Céleste's warm flank and let the tears fall. She didn't no-tice Renard standing under the hayloft.

"What's the matter?" he asked, setting his pitchfork against the siding.

She shook her head, embarrassed by her tears. "Nothing. Just my grand-mère trying to beat manners into me."

Renard took her hand and made her sit beside him on the big pile of hay. He put his arm around her shoulders.

"I'm all right," she said, angrily wiping her face with her apron. "She didn't really hurt me. She's not that strong."

"Do you want me to teach your grand-mère a lesson? I will." He pointed to the pile of manure in the corner of the barn. "I'll take all of that manure over there and dump it on her kitchen floor. And I'll tell her the next time she decides to beat you she will have me to deal with."

Berthe laughed. "She would just make me clean it up, you fool."

"You're right. I know. I'll just go in and explain to her that she should never hit you because you are far too pretty to beat." He picked up her braid and held it between his fingers as if it were some rare and wondrous thing. "Mademoiselle of the Cop-per Hair." He leaned over and kissed her on the cheek. She laughed again, brushed her face with her hand, and slowly stood. He looked up at her and grinned.

"What are you afraid of? I won't bite."

"I'm not afraid," she said, feeling a hot blush spread to the roots of her hair. "Besides, I would just bite you back." She turned away from him, lowered her sore bottom to the stool, and began milking Céleste. She was glad of the cow's haunch so she could hide her red face. After a few moments Renard left the barn.

When Berthe finished the milking she wandered out to the small orchard in the field behind the barn. A dozen apple trees were laden with fruit. She picked up one of the golden apples that lay on the ground and took a bite. It was so bitter she immediately spit it out. She heard someone laugh. It was Renard. He was sitting on one of the lower branches of a nearby tree. He swung himself down to the ground.

"Those apples are not for eating," he said. "They are for drinking." He took a small jug out of his lunch basket and handed it to her. "My mother gives me this to ward off the cold."

"But it's summertime," she said, taking the jug.

"I know." He laughed again. "Go on, take a drink."

Berthe tilted the jug and drank a small amount of the liquid. It was terrible. It made her eyes water and her throat burn. It tasted far worse than the apple she had bitten into. She began coughing and quickly handed the jug back to him.

"Take another sip. You'll get used to it."

"It tastes like poison." As soon as she uttered the word she immediately thought of her mother and the deadly arsenic she had taken to end her life.

Renard held the jug out to her. "It won't kill you, I promise," he said, as if reading Berthe's mind. After the second sip it didn't taste as bad, and she understood why Renard's mother said it would keep him warm. She felt as if the sun were shining inside of her as well as outside. For the first time in months, she felt almost happy.

"Did you know my mother took poison and it killed her?" she asked.

"I heard the story," he said. Berthe was not surprised. Word traveled quickly from town to town. Especially tales about the disreputable woman married to the only doctor in the region.

"It's not a story. It's true," she said, drinking again from the jug. "She was very unhappy."

"It's a sin. She's probably in hell," he said matter-of-factly.

"Don't say that," she replied angrily. She tipped the jug and took another long drink.

"They say your mother was in love with love."

"Who said that?" She was beginning to feel dizzy.

"Everybody. Your mother was much talked about in these parts. Are you like your mother?"

"No, I'm not. Not even a little."

"Give me a kiss. Let's see if you have a taste for love." He reached for her but she pulled out of his grasp.

"Go kiss a cow." She twirled away, but he reached around and yanked the jug out of her hands.

"That's enough. Pretty soon you'll be reeling all over the farmyard and your grand-mère will sack me for getting you drunk."

"I'm not drunk," she protested. "What is this called?" she asked, pointing to the jug.

"It's called drinking too early in the day." He grinned, taking a big swig for himself. Swallowing, he said, "Calvados. It's the only thing those sour apples are good for. It is drunk during the meal to help with digestion."

"I thought your mother gave it to you to ward off the chill."

"I lied," he said. "I stole it from the pantry before my father could finish it off."

Berthe laughed. Renard was a kindred spirit. He lay down on the ground, folded his arms behind his head, and stared up at her through half-closed eyes. She had a tremendous urge to crawl into his arms. He was older and stronger and seemed ever so much wiser. She felt a wave of gratitude for the fact she had found him in the middle of the lonely countryside. It suddenly didn't matter that her grand-mère hated her. She had Renard and he would be her friend. And that made her feel warm all over.

CHAPTER 4

The Artist's Model

IT WAS A STEAMY HOT DAY WHEN BERTHE TOOK CÉLESTE FOR A
cool drink by the small river behind her grand-mère's house. As
Céleste drank her fill, Berthe dipped her feet into the stream.
The cold water felt wonderful on her hot, blistered feet. She
hitched up her skirt and tied it with her apron strings so that she
could get her legs completely wet.

"*Bonjour,* mademoiselle," a voice said. She looked up, startled. A huge man with a thick beard and long, dark curling hair
leaned against an oak tree several feet from where she sat. He was
about thirty-five or forty years of age and his beard and mustache
were so thick she could not see his mouth. He had strong, stern
brows and intense gray eyes above a prominent nose. He wore a
blue tunic and a floppy straw hat, and carried a canvas bag over
one shoulder. Suddenly, he smiled and his whole face changed.
His mustache turned upward, his beard quivered, and his eyes
gleamed warmly.

"*Bonjour,* monsieur," she said.

"The water feels fine?" he asked, staring at her bare feet and legs. She suddenly felt very self-conscious but struggled to conceal it.

"*Oui,* monsieur, it is very refreshing."

"Do you live nearby, mademoiselle?"

She hesitated. "Yes, I live with my grand-mère over there." She pointed to the house through the trees.

"Perhaps you will take me to see her." He put down his bag and, drawing a handkerchief from his pocket, he removed his straw hat and wiped his brow. He must have seen the question in her eyes. "I would like to ask her permission to draw you," he explained.

"To draw me?" she asked, pulling her feet out of the water and quickly yanking down her skirt so that it covered her wet legs.

"You and your beautiful cow. What is her name?"

"Her name is Céleste." For some reason the fact that he wanted to draw Céleste as well as her made her laugh. She liked that he thought Céleste was beautiful.

"Allow me to introduce myself. My name is Jean-François Millet. I am an artist," he said, extending his hand. She stood and shyly offered hers in return. His hand was huge and strong. It felt as if it was capable of crushing walnuts, but he held her hand as gently as if it were a newly hatched bird.

"I am hopeful your grand-mère will consent to have you and Céleste pose for me. What, may I ask, is your name?"

"My name is Berthe Bovary," she said. "What do you mean, pose?"

"I will sketch you for a painting that I will complete later."

A drawing, a painting, an artist. It all sounded very exciting.

"I don't think my grand-mère will consent. She doesn't believe in art. She says it's a waste of time." Berthe sighed.

Monsieur Millet laughed. He had a wonderful laugh that came from deep inside his chest. Just hearing it made her smile.

"She may very well have a point. But come, show me to her house. Perhaps I can convince her to let me steal you away for a few hours even if it is all a waste of time."

"I'm sorry. She would never allow it. She would probably beat me for even talking to you."

Berthe picked up Céleste's wet lead rope and pulled her away from the water and up the grassy slope. Once on higher ground she quickly glanced back at the artist, giving him a shy smile before hurrying away.

Madame Leaumont came bursting in the next day with exciting news.

"There is a famous artist who is painting our countryside," she said, her gray hair spilling out of her bonnet. Her pitted cheeks were flushed with the exertion of walking quickly up the road. "A famous artist. Here! Isn't it thrilling?"

Berthe felt a rush of anticipation, wondering if this was the man she'd met yesterday. Perhaps she would get a chance to watch him paint. She remembered how her mother had returned from one of her many trips to Rouen and had been filled with chatter about art. She had shown Berthe a miniature copy of a painting by an artist named Ingres. It was called *Une Odalisque*.

"I have been told that this painting resembles me. Isn't that absurd?" her mother had said, studying the painting.

Berthe looked at the small painting. It was of a pale naked woman whose back was turned to the viewer. Berthe didn't think it resembled her mother at all.

"Artists are people of great passion and vision," her mother continued. "My friend, Monsieur Léon, has the soul of an artist even though he is just a clerk."

"Does this painting belong to him?" Berthe asked.

"Only the truly wealthy can afford to have great art on their walls. Monsieur Léon can barely afford curtains," her mother said with a laugh.

"But, Maman, we have paintings," Berthe said.

"You silly girl, those are only poor, pitiful copies," said her mother.

"And who is this famous artist?" Grand-mère Bovary asked. She was sitting at the kitchen table repolishing the silver that Berthe had just polished that morning.

"Monsieur Jean-François Millet."

"I've never heard of him," Grand-mère said, as if she carried a list of famous artists in her head.

"Oh my, yes. He's very celebrated. His paintings sell for thousands," enthused Madame Leaumont, clearly happy to have one over on her friend. Berthe kept scrubbing the same spot on the floor over and over. She didn't want to miss a word. "But," Madame Leaumont continued, "the curious thing is what he is painting."

"And what is that?" Grand-mère Bovary asked, showing as much disinterest as she could and still keep the conversation going.

"Oh, odd things like peasants cutting hay and sowing seeds, and taking naps in the field. He even did a drawing of René Laforge's old horse spreading manure."

"I never heard of anything so ridiculous." Grand-mère Bovary threw down her polishing rag.

"And René said that the artist has paid him handsomely for his time," Madame Leaumont said, picking up the cake cover to see if there was anything to nibble on.

"If he's so important what is he doing painting peasants and old horses? Why isn't he in Paris painting with the other famous painters?"

Madame Leaumont had no answer.

"What a waste of time! Art is for the rich and they are welcome to it," Grand-mère Bovary said, swiping at a fly with her
dish towel. And then as if noticing Berthe for the first time, she
said, "Don't just stand there; get Madame Leaumont something
to drink. She must be thirsty after her long walk."

"Oh, I'm not thirsty," responded Madame Leaumont. "But if
you have a bit of cheese and bread, I've eaten nothing since early
morning." She patted her round belly as if it were a favorite pet.

"When you're done fetching Madame Leaumont something
to eat you might want to take notice of the dust in my bedroom.
It is so thick that I woke up in the middle of the night half choking to death," instructed Berthe's grand-mère.

Why stop at half? Berthe gave a deep sigh and picked up her
dust rag. She wished she hadn't even heard about the artist and
his great paintings. It was just a reminder of how drab and dull
her life was as the days stretched out before her in gray dust.

As she was sweeping the courtyard the next morning, the geese
kept getting in the way and Berthe grew frustrated with having
to sweep around them.

"Go away, you silly birds," she said, brandishing her broom.

"But I have just arrived, mademoiselle." She looked up.
Monsieur Millet had appeared out of nowhere. She blushed and
straightened the kerchief on her head.

"Oh, monsieur, I didn't expect you." For a big man, he was
very quiet.

"May I help myself to some water? The day is already quite
hot."

"Oh, yes, by all means," she said, handing him the well dip-
per. He leaned over the well, which stood in the center of the
courtyard, and inhaled deeply. "Ah, the smell of good clean
country water."

Through an open window Berthe could see her grand-mère sitting at the kitchen table tallying figures in her accounting ledger. She hated to be disturbed when she was doing her books, as she called it. Berthe went to the window and cleared her throat.

"I'm busy," the old woman said without looking up.

"Grand-mère, Monsieur Millet is here to make your acquaintance," Berthe said, twisting the broom handle.

"And why should I care?" she said, still not looking up.

"Monsieur Millet is the famous painter that Madame Leaumont spoke of."

Madame Bovary put down her pen. Berthe could see that despite herself she was impressed, art or no art.

"Well, don't leave him out there to melt in the hot sun. Show him in."

"Ah, already we are making progress," Monsieur Millet said. He smiled, touched her on the shoulder, and then followed her into the house.

"And what may I do for you, monsieur?" her grand-mère said after Berthe had introduced them.

Monsieur Millet took off his hat and held it in his hands. He may have been a famous artist but Berthe could see he was quite skilled in handling women like her grand-mère.

"I would like your permission to sketch your granddaughter and her cow," he said in a soft voice.

"The cow is mine," Madame Bovary said, obviously not wanting to miss a chance to claim ownership. "And Berthe has many chores and responsibilities. She has no time to pose for pictures."

"I will gladly pay you for her time," Monsieur Millet said, winking at Berthe. She smiled and ducked her head. It was as if they had a special secret between them. Although she wasn't quite sure what it was.

"Oh? And how much will you pay?" asked her grand-mère, her voice rising a notch.

"Would three francs a day be acceptable?"

"That's six days a week?" Madame Bovary asked, taking up her pen to calculate. Monsieur Millet nodded. "That comes to eighteen francs a week. But it is quite absurd. Why would you want to paint her? She is just a peasant girl." Berthe felt as if she had just been slapped. Her cheeks grew hot.

"That's exactly why," explained Monsieur Millet. "Peasants are what I paint."

"And you sell these paintings, monsieur?" Grand-mère Bovary asked, not bothering to conceal her skepticism.

"Yes, thankfully. Although, to be honest, my formal portraits have been more in demand. But my great passion is the countryside and the people who toil here."

"Well, Berthe must finish her chores before she does any posing for you," the old woman said, narrowing her eyes at Berthe.

"Oh, I will not interrupt her chores. In fact, that's what I want to capture: Berthe doing her usual work around the farm. Here," he said, taking a money pouch out of his vest pocket, "let me pay in advance."

"Leave us, Berthe," her grand-mère ordered. An unusual smile brightened Madame Bovary's face.

Berthe returned to her chores. She was sure that as soon as she left, her grand-mère would try and bargain with Monsieur Millet and he would change his mind about painting her.

A short time later, Monsieur Millet came out of the cottage. "Tomorrow we begin." He looked closely at her. "You know, mademoiselle, that you are quite beautiful. Even more than your captivating cow," he said, tipping his straw hat. Berthe blushed. No one had ever told her this before. It had always been her mother who was beautiful. It was her mother's beauty that had taken up so much space in their homely little house—almost as if it were another child. It had to be bathed, pampered, and dressed and, most of all, noticed. *Beautiful* was not a word Berthe would ever have used to describe herself.

Monsieur Millet was smiling broadly and Berthe's stomach did a corresponding flip of excitement. She turned her back to him and bent to pick up a stone. She was so nervous that she lifted the stone to her mouth and was about to bite into it when she realized it wasn't an apple. She hurried into the barn in an effort to escape her embarrassment.

"*À demain,*" Monsieur Millet called out after her.

Berthe was surprised to see the artist waiting in the courtyard first thing the next morning when she went out to milk Céleste. He had a small canvas stool with him which he set up in the corner of the barn. He took out a sketchbook and a box of charcoal and immediately began to sketch her.

"Where are your paints?" She had assumed that being a famous painter he would of course be working in paint. She had already envisioned her image surrounded by a beautiful gilt frame. She thought of the few elaborately framed copies of paintings her parents had owned before her father's creditors took everything. She remembered the frames being almost more beautiful than the pictures they held.

"These are just sketches," Monsieur Millet explained. "The painting happens much later." Berthe was disappointed, particularly when she looked over his shoulder at what he had drawn. It was a series of rough lines that ran back and forth to create a fuzzy image of her. And the cow that was supposed to represent Céleste was far too thin.

"Well," he asked, as he smudged the black lines even more with his little finger, "what do you think, Mademoiselle Berthe?"

"I think you should keep working on it," she said, folding her arms across her chest.

He laughed so loud and hard that she feared he might fall off his stool. She felt great pleasure that she had amused him. She couldn't remember ever having done that before. It gave her a curious sense of power. She began to relax and enjoy posing without worrying about what to say or how to act. Some time later he stopped sketching.

"Why do you live with your grand-mère? Where are your parents?" he asked.

"They are both dead."

"Oh, dear girl. I am so sorry." His brown eyes filled with sympathy. She had a sudden urge to throw her arms around this strange, warm man. She imagined following him about the countryside, carrying his little camp stool, helping him find interesting subjects, perhaps even learning to sketch herself. He would teach her all about art and painting. She was a good student and would be eager to learn.

Berthe had been fascinated by the practice of medicine but her father had always been too busy to answer her many questions. If he wasn't rushing off to patients he was too preoccupied in his clinic trying to wrestle with a difficult medical problem.

There was one day she remembered distinctly. He rushed into the kitchen where she was helping Félicité peel the potatoes.

"I believe I have discovered a cure for clubfoot," he announced.

"Oh, Papa, how exciting. What is clubfoot?" But he was gone before she could get an answer. Then she remembered the stable boy, Hippolyte, and how he hopped around town, thrusting his badly curled foot in front of him. Her father spent weeks talking the poor cripple into letting him operate on his foot. Berthe had stood by hoping to catch a view of her father's inventive surgery, but he shut the door in her face.

That afternoon Millet followed Berthe to the river and sketched her as she let Céleste drink. She noticed he was now using different colored papers with the black charcoal. She looked over his shoulder as he completed the sketch. Again she saw no likeness between the figure of the woman and herself, or between the scrawny cow and Céleste.

"And this will someday become a painting?" she asked, shooing a fly away.

"Yes, it will be a very beautiful painting," he said, as he worked the crayon over and over the buff-colored paper. He added three more cows, his hand moving quickly.

"But there is only one cow," she said.

"It is called taking artistic license, Mademoiselle Berthe," he explained, holding up the paper and squinting his eyes. He picked up a piece of red chalk and gave her a rose-colored top instead of her coarse cotton shirt. Then he quickly added a long pole in her hands. Something she would never have carried with Céleste, as it would have frightened the cow.

"If you keep adding things that aren't there, why do you need someone to model for you? Why don't you just draw out of your own imagination?"

"An artist uses his imagination but his inspiration comes from the world around him," he said, putting down the sketch. "Without the real world I would have nothing to say with my pictures." The way he spoke to her, as if she was someone worth talking to, made her think of her father again. After he had performed the surgery on Hippolyte's foot he had been so very proud. And so sometime later she felt encouraged to ask him about his most successful patient.

"Papa, how is Hippolyte's foot? He must be very happy to be able to walk so well." Her father stared at her for a long moment, his expression one of great distress. Then he walked out of the room without uttering a word. How was she to know that the patient had developed gangrene and lost his entire leg to amputation?

"You are able to create your own world," Berthe said to Monsieur Millet. She suddenly felt very bold and bright.

"That is exactly it, Mademoiselle Berthe. How well you understand. We all have the ability to create our own world, *n'est-ce pas?* Which is probably why I became an artist in the first place. But one doesn't have to be an artist to accomplish this. One need only have the gift of a rich imagination." He looked at her for a long moment, then turned back to his sketch. He took his thumb and softened the edges of the largest cow. "I actually prefer drawing to painting. Drawing seems to free my imagination. The only reason I paint is so I have something to sell. No one will spend good money on mere drawings. But I believe that one day my drawings will be more appreciated than anything I paint." He straightened his back with a groan. "Ah, I think that's enough art for one day. Tomorrow then, mademoiselle?"

"Yes, tomorrow." Berthe smiled over her shoulder as she pulled Céleste after her. She felt as if tomorrow were an eternity away. How wonderful it was to be able to take your imagination out of your mind and put it on paper. In Berthe's fantasy Monsieur Millet would hire her away from her grand-mère and she could spend the rest of her life modeling for him and discussing questions of art and creativity.

Monsieur Millet became Berthe's shadow, and she grew used to him following her everywhere with his bag of art materials and his stool.

One day he stopped her on the way into the house. She was carrying two heavy pails of water she had just filled at the well.

"Wait, stay there," he said, grabbing his sketch pad and a Conté crayon from his shoulder bag.

"But, monsieur," she protested, "these are heavy. Can't I empty the water from them?"

"That is exactly what I want to capture: the weight of the water, your arms straining, the painful look on your face. *The Peasant Labors,*" he said, as if to give his drawing a title right then and there.

"I cannot hold these any longer," she said, lowering the pails to the ground so quickly that half the water spilled out.

"Oh, I am sorry. How thoughtless of me," he said. He put his sketch pad on the ground and laid his crayon on top of it. "Here, let me ease the ache." He placed his hands on her shoulders and began gently kneading the muscles. It felt strangely soothing and yet she pulled away. "My apologies. Was I being too rough, mademoiselle?"

"No, no," she said, lifting the pails again. "I'm fine." Her face was burning but he didn't seem to notice.

"You are a wonderful model, Mademoiselle Berthe."

"But I don't understand, monsieur. Why do you only make sketches of me doing boring chores?"

"Ah, but there is great dignity in your labor. Don't you see that?"

She shook her head. She thought him slightly mad. This was a life of drudgery she longed to escape, and here was this man devoting his very considerable talents to capturing it on paper.

"My father and grandfathers were farmers," he said. "I was

supposed to take over the farm in Gruchy." He had a faraway look in his eyes. "The soil there gave forth more stones than it did wheat. In the end, they gave me their hard-earned savings and off I went to study art. And I never returned to the land. So I paint the country and the people as a way of honoring my origins and repaying my family."

Berthe liked the idea of doing work that had dignity. It certainly made her feel better about the blisters and sore muscles she had developed since coming to her grand-mère's farm. She liked the way the artist spoke to her as an equal. She assumed this was because he knew nothing of her mother's reputation.

Monsieur Millet sketched Berthe endlessly. Milking Céleste, churning the butter, carrying water from the well, herding the geese to the river, and resting against a haystack during the heat of the day. He even came by one evening to sketch her while she did her mending by lamplight. She missed him when he wasn't drawing her.

Her grand-mère, who didn't like Berthe to spend two minutes alone with Renard, had absolutely no problem with the fact that she spent many hours each day with Monsieur Millet. The fact that he was paying her handsomely for Berthe's time certainly helped overcome any objections she might have had. And then there was the man himself. Her grand-mère was not immune to his dark good looks and his considerable charm. Making the acquaintance of Monsieur Millet had somehow changed Madame Bovary's opinion of art in general. Every morning when he arrived at the farm she would engage him in conversation.

"Ah, Monsieur Millet, how goes the painting?" she said, straightening her apron with one hand while she smoothed away the stray ends of her hair with the other.

"It goes well, madame," he replied each time, not bothering to explain to her that he was sketching, not painting.

"And Berthe, she is behaving herself?"

"She is the perfect model," he responded.

"You let me know if she gives you any trouble. She has a temper, that one. She gets it from her mother."

"I can always take a stick to her," Monsieur Millet said, with a wink in Berthe's direction.

Her grand-mère didn't appear to know if he was joking or not. Fortunately, she let the matter of Berthe's behavior drop.

"If you ever need a more womanly figure to pose for you, I might be persuaded," her grand-mère said coyly.

"Thank you, Madame Bovary, I may well ask you to do just that."

Grand-mère Bovary smiled happily.

A few weeks later Monsieur Millet made good his word to Berthe's grand-mère. He arrived early one morning and stood in the kitchen doorway. Berthe was throwing grain into the courtyard for the chickens and geese. It was already quite hot. Mist rose from the fields. The smell of hay and pigs and apples all mixed together in the wet morning air.

"Madame Bovary, I want to avail myself of your generous offer," he said to her grand-mère.

"You need only say the word, Monsieur Millet." Berthe hated the idea of her grand-mère taking her place as Monsieur Millet's model. She kicked at the dirt with her heavy clog. The chickens and geese scattered in alarm.

"I need two more figures for a drawing I am working on. Perhaps you and your friend Madame Leaumont would accommodate me?" Berthe threw down the empty feed bucket. Her grand-mère was too taken with Monsieur Millet to notice this show of temper.

"I cannot speak for Madame Leaumont, but I'm sure she will consent. And I myself would be honored. What should we wear?" she asked, tilting her head in an almost coquettish manner.

"Just wear your plainest, most comfortable clothes," he answered. "You will speak to Madame Leaumont for me?" He picked up his drawing materials.

"Of course."

"Shall we say the day after tomorrow?" He tipped the brim of his straw hat.

"As you wish, monsieur," she said, making a small curtsy.

Two days later Berthe's grand-mère and Madame Leaumont stood in the farmyard awaiting the arrival of Monsieur Millet. They were dressed in their very finest clothing. Madame Leaumont wore a blue satin dress with a lavish bow-trimmed bodice, and a matching bonnet trimmed in black velvet with a jaunty black plume affixed to the side. Berthe's grand-mère was wearing what looked to be a crimson ball gown. It had a huge hoopskirt decorated with jet beads and scallops of black lace. The bodice was so tight she seemed to have difficulty taking a deep breath. Instead of a hat she wore a feather headdress with a curled upsweep. She had donned black lace gloves, and kept her skirts slightly lifted to avoid the manure and soiled hay that covered the ground. Where in the world had they acquired these gowns? Berthe wondered.

"Berthe, fetch a broom and clean this up," her grand-mère said, indicating the area where she stood.

Berthe opened her mouth to say something but thought better of it. What was she going to say? This was her grand-mère's house, her grand-mère's world for that matter. And now she was stealing her granddaughter's only pleasure.

"Isn't this exciting?" enthused Madame Leaumont. "We're going to be in a famous painting."

When Berthe returned with the broom, Monsieur Millet was standing by the front gate shaking his head and laughing.

"Oh, my dear ladies, this will never do. No, I'm afraid it won't do at all."

"What's the matter?" demanded Berthe's grand-mère. "This is my very best frock."

"Exactly the problem," he said. "I said to wear something plain and comfortable. You hardly look comfortable, my dear lady. Although I must say, you both look extremely elegant. Far too elegant to appear in my humble sketches."

"But we are to be painted, are we not?" protested Madame Bovary.

"First the sketch, then the painting," explained the great artist. "If you please, go and change into the plainest dresses you own, and, Berthe, if you will, fetch some soiled linens and washing paddles."

Berthe fought hard to keep the smile off her face. Monsieur Millet, in his constant quest to capture the hardworking countryside, was about to sketch laundry day. She expected her grand-mère to refuse to change, and was surprised and more than a little disappointed to see that she was going to comply with the artist's request.

Madame Leaumont borrowed an old dress from her friend and both of them changed and dutifully followed Monsieur Millet down to the river. He carried the washing paddles and his bag of art supplies. Berthe came after, carrying a huge basket of laundry.

She could see that her grand-mère was already beginning to worry about what the "modeling" entailed. Madame Leaumont, being of cheerful nature, just followed along, happy to be included in this new adventure. When they reached the edge of the river Berthe dropped the heavy basket of laundry.

"Good, good. Now, ladies, if you will please do the laundry while I capture your noble exertions for all time."

Grand-mère Bovary opened her mouth to protest and then closed it. His phrase "for all time" caught her imagination and she no doubt pictured herself hanging in the Louvre in Paris.

They made a glorious picture: the three of them laboring over the laundry in the river. Berthe's grand-mère was making a valiant effort of beating the sheets against a rock, her face red, her breathing labored, and sweat soaking the top of her home-spun dress. Poor Madame Leaumont struggled to keep up. And Berthe had the most enjoyable hour since first arriving at her grand-mère's house.

After thirty minutes of scrubbing, washing, and rinsing, Berthe's grand-mère straightened, dropped a sheet into the water, and said, "I hope you have your sketch, Monsieur Millet. Come, Claudine." She turned to Madame Leaumont. "That is enough of this . . . this . . . art." Leaving the wet laundry, the two women climbed the slope to the house.

At supper that night Berthe's grand-mère was so furious she could hardly eat.

"Who in the world will want to buy a painting of women doing laundry in a river? I believe that Monsieur Millet must be slightly demented. If it weren't for the fee he is paying me for your time I would tell him to take his sketches and go elsewhere."

"Why are you letting that old man follow you around?" Renard asked Berthe one morning as she poured Céleste's milk from the bucket into the copper jug. She lifted her chin and flung her gold braid over her shoulder as though it were a fine feather boa.

"I pose for him," she said. "He is an artist and I am his model. Besides," she added, "he's not that old." She wiped the outside of the jug with the corner of her apron.

"He must be at least forty," Renard said. He knocked a piece of loose shingle off the wall of the barn.

Berthe ignored him, hoisting the copper jug onto her shoulder and steadying it with the leather strap. Renard walked over to Céleste, draped his arm around the cow's neck, and whispered in her ear.

"Céleste, can you tell me why she likes an old man better than me?"

"Don't talk to him, Céleste. He's a stupid boy." Renard laughed. He pulled a piece of straw from Céleste's bundle and, walking behind Berthe, tickled her neck with it. She brushed it away with her free hand, taking care not to dislodge the milk jug.

"If I were an artist I would paint grand ladies. I wouldn't follow a poor farm wench around while she does her stupid chores," he said. His smile had disappeared.

"You don't know anything about it," she said, narrowing her eyes. She liked that he seemed jealous. It made her happy.

"He's not interested in you as a model. He wants something else," said Renard, staring at her intently.

"What are you talking about?" She turned quickly and some of the milk sloshed onto her arm. "It's art, and you're too ignorant to understand." She pursed her lips in a show of disdain.

"You're the ignorant one. Ignorant and ugly."

She was stung by his words. They were friends—why was Renard being so cruel?

Holding back tears, she turned and stomped out of the barn without another word. She didn't want to show him that he could so easily hurt her. The happiness she had felt only moments before had vanished.

CHAPTER 5

Homespun

RENARD WAS SPREADING MANURE OVER HER GRAND-MÈRE'S SMALL vegetable garden when Berthe and Monsieur Millet returned from an early morning sketching session. Berthe was still smarting from Renard's cruel comments of the day before.

She had so wanted him to like her, to be her friend. But she had let down her guard and he had taken advantage of it. Suddenly she had an idea. She would show Renard just who was ignorant and ugly. She pulled the artist aside and whispered in his ear.

"Monsieur Millet, wouldn't Renard make a wonderful subject for you?" She knew that Millet loved the humble farmer, and who looked more humble at that moment than Renard, ankle deep in cow dung?

"Brilliant," said Millet. He set down his stool and bag of art materials and, being careful not to step in the manure, approached the working boy.

"Excuse me, young man," he said, wiping his brow with his

handkerchief. Renard pretended not to hear him and continued working his rake.

"A moment of your time, kind sir," the artist said.

Renard looked up, scowling.

"What is it?"

"Will you allow me to sketch you?" The artist pulled at his beard, waiting for a reply. Berthe turned away so that Renard would not see her smiling. She knew he was about to become Monsieur Millet's next model. *Oh, how he will hate that.* "I will be happy to pay you for your time. All you have to do is continue what you're doing."

"You want to draw me shoveling *merde*?" Renard said.

Monsieur Millet nodded. To Berthe's great disappointment, instead of being offended Renard threw back his head and laughed long and loud.

It was a beautiful drawing. Monsieur Millet captured Renard's strong body leaning against a pitchfork as he seemingly dreamed the day away. In the background, the artist sketched just the barest indication of sapling trees and two bowed figures turning over the soil to work in the manure. The drawing had such a feeling of reality that Berthe could almost imagine one of the figures yelling, *Renard, stop your dreaming and get back to work.*

Monsieur Millet used him for many more sketches. The artist liked to talk as he drew. And he conversed with Renard on all kinds of farm topics.

"So, how do you think the harvest will be, come fall?" At first Renard didn't answer but Millet persisted in his efforts to engage the young man. "I see you keep your scythe in good condition. How often do you sharpen it?"

"My father has a fine stone that his father left to him. It takes only a minute to put an edge on my blade," Renard said, stroking the flat side of the scythe with his thumb.

"You're quite a strong young man. I can see that by the thickness of your arms. I wager you can lift a horse." Millet flexed his arms.

"Maybe a small cow," said Renard, laughing. Berthe found herself laughing too.

One beautiful fall morning when the sky was a brilliant blue and a cool breeze blew over the fields, Monsieur Millet asked Berthe to do her afternoon milking on a hilltop which overlooked the ocean many miles away. It was a good half hour's walk from her grand-mère's farm.

"Today I work in pastels," he said, unrolling a piece of pale blue paper that he affixed to his drawing board.

"Pastels?" she asked, looking up from Céleste.

"Colored chalks," he explained. "I found an old box. It's been so long since I've worked in color, I am afraid I will have lost the knack." He gazed up at the sky as if measuring its blueness. "But if there was ever a day that called for color, this is it."

The sketch that day took much longer than usual. Monsieur Millet asked her to stay seated on her stool long after she finished her milking. Céleste was perfectly content munching away at the thick grass.

"Done," he said finally, sighing. Berthe rose and moved to peer over his shoulder.

"Oh," she exclaimed, clapping her hands, "it's beautiful."

The drawing captured the brilliant green of the grass, the turquoise of the water, and the blazing blue of the sky. Céleste was the glorious centerpiece. Her end-of-the-summer sleekness shone in the brilliant sunshine. But Berthe was disappointed in how she herself looked in the picture, in her plain black skirt, blue homespun kerchief, and dowdy white cap.

"Why couldn't you at least put me in a pretty dress?" she asked. "I look so hideous." She thought about Renard's remark. She knew she wasn't ugly, but as her mother had always told her, "Clothes can make all the difference." She glanced down at herself. "I hate these things," she said, yanking the itching kerchief off her neck and pulling at it with both hands as if to tear it into shreds. She was feeling strangely weepy, almost as if the beautiful day was working against her.

Millet drew the kerchief from her clenched fingers.

"Look at this carefully," he said, "and tell me exactly what you see."

"I see horrible, scratchy cloth," she said, the corners of her mouth turning down.

"And what do they call this cloth?"

"Homespun."

"Yes," he said. "Homespun. Spun at home. It's a beautiful word for a beautiful material. It is made from the wool of lambs, carded and then spun and made into thread and finally woven into fabric."

"I don't care how it's made, it's still ugly." She stood with her hands on her hips.

"Dear Mademoiselle Berthe, don't you see?" he said, lightly touching her cheek with one finger. "This is fabric that comes from the land, from the hard work of human hands. That is what makes it so beautiful. Hold it up to the sun and pull it taut."

She grudgingly did as he told her. The sun shone through the material and she could see a crosshatch of lines that were not unlike those in Monsieur Millet's drawings.

"This is the beauty of texture. The fine lines that make up the fabric of everything around us," he said. As she continued to gaze through the material she saw a flock of geese fly past the golden sun. Slowly, she replaced the kerchief around her neck.

"Look around you. Look at the soil we stand on." He bent down, scooped up a handful of earth, and poured it into her hands. It was filled with pebbles, dry clumps of dirt, and bits of straw. "From this comes that," he said, pointing to an apple tree heavy with yellow fruit. "From that shaggy sheep over there comes the thread of the wool to make a kerchief to keep the sun from baking your beautiful skin." He lifted her hands, wiping the dirt from them. "These dear callused hands bring forth the sweet milk of Céleste. And from the crude heavy lines of my rough sketches will hopefully come a beautiful painting one day."

Millet had, just by the magic of his words, managed to transform Berthe's mood and lift her heart. She did love the countryside. It had been a great comfort to her since moving in with her grand-mère. The first thing she did every morning when she got up was to look out her small window at the lovely fields. She was always filled with gratitude for the beauty that surrounded her. It was the closest she came to saying her morning prayers.

"This is the most important thing I can teach you: the coarser the texture, the sturdier the weave; the rougher the life, the greater the reward. I believe this with all my heart, Mademoiselle Berthe. Your days may be difficult now but the gift of hard work will serve you well. Cherish the calluses and the blisters, see the dignity in the sweat of your labors, and always, always honor the homespun."

Berthe vowed then and there never to forget what Monsieur Millet said. She could only imagine what a joy it would be to put all her energy and effort into something she actually loved doing. Something creative and beautiful like Millet's art. That, she thought, would be a dream.

"Monsieur Millet, how did you know?" she asked, as she moved Céleste to a new patch of grass. The cow was growing fat and happy from all the posing she was doing.

"How did I know what?" He tilted his head back to study his sketch and then made a few quick corrective smudges with his little finger.

"How did you know you could make a living by your art?" She picked up a piece of Conté crayon from the box and began to roll it between her fingers.

"Oh, I didn't know. In the beginning I survived by doing portraits for very little money. But that allowed me to continue my studies. And then I began to do the drawings that got me not only great attention but much grander prices."

"What kind of drawings?"

"I'll bring some tomorrow and show you. But what about you, Mademoiselle Bovary? You must have a special talent. I mean beyond taking such good care of Céleste."

"I like to sew," she said simply. "But I don't believe it's a talent. Everyone can sew. It's just a skill one learns." She shrugged her shoulders.

"The difference between a skill and a talent is in the eyes of the beholder." Groaning, he got up from his stool and handed her a piece of the heavy paper. "Here, you sit and draw for a change. I'm getting too old for this, I fear."

"Draw what?" she asked, looking up at him.

"Whatever comes into your pretty head. Just not the cow. I've had enough cows for one day."

She closed her eyes and saw a field of flowers and over it the cross-hatching of the homespun. She quickly sketched what she had seen in her mind's eye and handed it to Monsieur Millet.

"Ha! I knew it. You do have an eye. And that, my dear Berthe, is a talent."

The next day Monsieur Millet brought a small black portfolio with him.

"These are some of the drawings I spoke of." He untied the black ribbons that held the case closed. Inside was a stack of rough sketches. They were drawings of women in various poses without a stitch of clothing. Berthe quickly closed the portfolio, her face flushed with heat.

"Don't be embarrassed, mademoiselle, they're just sketches." He chuckled.

"But the women are naked!" she said.

"That's how the artist studies the human body," he explained.

"But this is not how people walk around," she said. "Decent people wear clothes."

"It has nothing to do with decency." He laughed. "When I draw peasants working in the field I have to know how their legs support their bodies, how their arms work, how their backs lean into the labor. The human form is the foundation of everything I paint. I must be intimately acquainted with its workings. You see a naked figure. I merely see shapes and shadows."

She nodded her head. As he explained them, the nude sketches made sense. Still, it had been a shock to see so many different naked bodies. She thought of her mother. How she used to study herself in the full-length mirror, turning this way and that as if to reassure herself that she was still beautiful. It seemed to Berthe that her mother's loveliness had brought her nothing but heartache.

"I want to sketch you this way, Berthe."

"Without any clothes? Oh, no, monsieur, I couldn't." She ducked her head down so that he wouldn't see her beet-red face.

"I understand your shyness. I won't force you to do anything you don't want to. But this is art, Berthe. And I will be happy to pay you," he said.

She lifted her chin. "Pay me, not my grand-mère?"

"You."

"In sketches or in money?" she asked, her serious expression relieved by a small smile.

He had already given her two rough sketches: one of her milking Céleste and another of her sitting at the spinning wheel pretending to spin. But whereas Berthe loved his sketches, she desperately wanted, needed, prayed for the money. Because she knew money, if not spent, could beget money. Money could grow. Money could become a way out of this life and through the front door of a fabulous new life. She had seen how money worked. She had watched as Monsieur Lheureux had taken her mother's money and put it in his pocket. And his store on the rue Forchette had grown and prospered. She remembered walking by his once-humble shop with Félicité the maid. He had taken over the house next door and doubled the size of his business and his adjoining living quarters.

"Hmm, I see Monsieur Lheureux is putting your family's money to good use," Félicité had remarked.

Monsieur Millet ran his fingers through his thick beard and stared down at her through narrowed eyes.

"My, my, I have a bargainer to boot. Yes, mademoiselle, I will pay you in real money."

"How much?" she asked too quickly.

He thought a moment and then said, "Twenty francs. That is what I pay in Paris for professional models."

"I don't know..." She chewed on the end of her braid.

Berthe had grown to trust the artist. He spoke to her in a

kind and patient way that her own father never had. He made her feel as if she mattered in the world. But it was her body that gave her pause. Recently she felt as if her body wasn't her own anymore. Was she prepared to now hand it over to the world of art? She remembered the miniature painting her mother had shown her so many years before. The woman in *Une Odalisque* had no clothes but she hadn't seemed naked at all.

"You will think about it?" Millet asked. She nodded.

She felt a trill of anticipation mingled with fear. This is what models did, she reasoned. They took off their clothes and let famous artists capture their images for all time. Remembering Renard's words, she knew that Millet would not ask someone ignorant and ugly to model naked.

In fact, he made it sound like an honor. It was an honor, wasn't it?

The next afternoon Berthe drove the geese down to the river. Monsieur Millet found her there. It was a sweltering hot September day and the water looked cool and inviting. She sat on the riverbank and watched as the geese swam about.

Millet sat a way off, sketching quietly.

"Do you have a family?" she asked.

"Indeed I do. I am the proud papa of nine children."

"And where are they?" She threw a stone into the river. It barely missed one of the geese, who honked indignantly. She was stalling for time. What had seemed like a perfectly fine idea a day before now seemed more than a little threatening. She didn't want Millet to think she was a silly, naïve girl. She desperately wanted to keep modeling for him even if it meant having to do something that wasn't entirely comfortable.

"They are all at home with my wife," he said. "I have a home not far away, in Barbizon."

"You are able to feed such a large family with your painting?"

"Almost," he said, chuckling. "My wife is very good at making the soup stretch."

"Is she beautiful, your wife?" Her cheeks burned. She felt jealous of a wife and family she had never even met.

"My Catherine is the most beautiful woman in the world," he said, getting off his stool. He rummaged around in his bag. "Here, I have a drawing of her." He took out a small sketchbook and showed her.

She saw a woman with a sweet, soft face; she looked too young to be the mother of nine children. Her thick dark hair was parted in the middle and held in a loose chignon. She had long lashes, thick eyebrows, and a small upturned nose. Her mouth was soft and small with an upper lip that protruded slightly over the lower.

"She looks very nice," Berthe said, shoving the sketchbook into his hand.

He laughed. "Oh, I would never describe her as 'nice.' She has a terrible temper, my little Catherine," he said, as though it was something that brought him pride. "So, Mademoiselle Bovary, have you thought about my proposition?"

"No," she lied. She had thought about nothing else since he first asked her. "If you pay me I will be a professional model?" she added abruptly.

"Mademoiselle Berthe, I believe that you will be whatever it is you make up your mind to be," Monsieur Millet said, smiling.

"Then, in that case, I will be your model." She squared her shoulders.

She rose and went behind the nearest tree. Once there, she quickly took off her skirt and blouse, her pantaloons and chemise before she could change her mind. She left the blue kerchief on her hair. For a moment she stood, letting the warm summer air caress her skin. Never in her life had she been totally naked outdoors. She looked down at her body. It was as if it belonged to someone else. She had breasts. What had been the mere beginnings of growth a few months before were now bona fide breasts with large pink nipples. She suddenly realized that she had all the makings of a woman's body. She felt as surprised as if she had suddenly sprouted wings. For a minute she forgot to be shy and looked down with pride at her new body.

"Come, Berthe, the light is fading," Monsieur Millet called. She stepped out from behind the tree.

"Lovely," he said. No one had ever used that word to describe her.

Suddenly she was overcome with shyness. She quickly sat down by the water's edge, holding her legs close to her chest. She hid her face in her arms. If she couldn't see him, she reasoned, then he couldn't see her. She thought about how Renard had caught her with her shirt off that day in the courtyard and here she was sitting in front of Monsieur Millet without a stitch on. Why didn't she feel the least bit of shame?

"Very good," he said in a quiet voice. "Just hold that pose, if you will." He hummed as he sketched. And after a long while she began to relax. She looked up and she saw that he was totally engrossed in what he was doing. Every now and then he would glance at her. But it was as if he wasn't really seeing her. She was just a form, a figure of shadows and shades.

"Monsieur Millet, I have to move," she finally said. "I am getting quite stiff."

"Oh, my apologies. Of course. Just change to whatever position is most comfortable for you."

She extended one leg out so that her foot rested in the water.

She bent the other leg and leaned back on both her arms. Her entire body was now exposed to the sun, the air, and Monsieur Millet's Conté crayon.

There was a cool breeze blowing off the water. She looked down at her nipples, which had become hard and pointed. It seemed so odd that these pink nubs were meant for nursing babies. She felt a strange ache between her legs, a sudden pull that made her want to touch herself there. She wondered if the artist could tell that she was feeling these sensations. Had he noticed that her nipples had suddenly grown points? She glanced over at him, but it was almost as if she didn't exist. She was simply a part of his landscape.

He spent four days sketching her. Each day she grew more and more comfortable in her posing. "I will make a beautiful painting from these sketches," he said, late one afternoon. "One day you will hang in a museum."

"Oh, no," she exclaimed. "What will Grand-mère say?" The thought of her grand-mère seeing her naked granddaughter hanging in a public viewing place threw her into a panic.

"She will never know. I promise you. No one will know it is you."

"I guess it's a good thing that you are not very skilled with likenesses," she observed. Millet chuckled.

The sun was beginning to set and there was a chill in the air.

"I'm getting cold, Monsieur Millet," she said finally.

"Just a few more minutes," he said. It was almost dark by the time he put his sketches away. She got dressed, hating the feeling of the rough, heavy material against her skin. In a matter of minutes she had gone from artist's model back to farm girl.

"You are a very good model, Mademoiselle Berthe."

"I'm late. My grand-mère will kill me," she said as she hurried on ahead of him. She still had Céleste to milk and the dinner to make.

"Don't worry," he said, following behind her. "I'll take care of your grand-mère."

Once indoors, he made a big show of putting four five-franc pieces on the kitchen table. "Your granddaughter earned every centime," he said. Berthe's fingernails dug into her palms. *That is my money*, she thought. *What are you doing?*

"Oh, Monsieur Millet, you are far too generous," Grand-mère Bovary simpered. Berthe could tell she was counting the money from where she stood six feet away.

"Consider it but a small tribute to you and your lovely granddaughter." Millet winked at Berthe.

Her grand-mère swooped down and picked up the four coins, putting them in the Quimper vase that stood on the oak sideboard. This was where she kept the money she earned from selling eggs and cheese.

"But, Grand-mère, that's my money. I earned it." Berthe's voice trembled.

"And your room and board? When was the last time you paid anything for that?" She turned and smiled at Monsieur Millet. "Your work is going well, monsieur?"

"Yes, I believe I am almost done with this series," he said.

Why doesn't he say something? Berthe wanted to scream. *He told me he would pay* me, *not her.*

"Perhaps I may see some of your sketches," Grand-mère said, smoothing her hair.

"They are still too rough for your cultivated eye," he said.

Berthe couldn't sleep. She felt betrayed by the man she had learned to trust. In the middle of the night, she crept down to the kitchen. She couldn't stop thinking about the money her grand-mère had stashed away. *It's not really stealing. It's my money. I earned it.* And if she only took some of it her grand-mère might not even notice. At least not right away. She tiptoed over to the sideboard and slipped her hand inside the Quimper vase. It was empty. Her grand-mère had taken the money and hidden it somewhere else. Did she think somebody was going to steal it? Of course; she was that somebody.

The next day the skies opened up and the rain came down in sheets. Berthe realized that the bad weather would keep Millet away and she felt a great disappointment. She needed to see him and ask him about the money. Berthe's grand-mère had gone into town in the covered wagon with Madame Leaumont. *To spend my modeling money,* Berthe thought. After finishing her house chores she went into the barn to clean out Céleste's stall and spread fresh hay. Renard ran in after her. He took off his leather hat and shook it at her, showering her with water.

"Stop it," she cried, tossing her head. "You've got me all wet."

"You won't melt," he said, collapsing onto a pile of new straw. "Come, sit down beside me." He patted the space next to him.

"I have my chores to do." She picked up the pitchfork and began removing the soiled straw from Céleste's stall.

"You have time. Your grand-mère's not even here. I saw her drive into town with Madame Leaumont." His blue eyes seemed to attract all the light.

"And don't you have work to do?" she asked, her hands on her hips.

"Not on a day like this," he said, smiling. "Come, we'll play a game."

"What game?" she asked.

"First, lie back and close your eyes." She did as she was told. "Now, take off your pantaloons."

She sat up abruptly. "What?"

"Why are you being so shy? You took off everything with Monsieur the Artist."

"You saw me?" Her face burned.

"Of course I saw you. I saw everything," he said, grinning.

"But that was for art," she protested.

"And this is for fun. Come, Berthe, I won't hurt you. I promise." His voice was soft and pleading. He gently tugged at her skirt. "You'll like this game, you'll see."

"Why do I have to take off my pantaloons?"

"It's part of the game. I am a physician and I've come to cure you," he said. For some reason the idea of Renard being a physician made her laugh loudly. Renard stood to leave.

"You care more about that hairy old artist than you do me. I can see you are in love with him," he said angrily.

"I am not," she shot back. Berthe was confused. She didn't want him to leave. Had he spoken the truth about Monsieur Millet? The artist paid her such fine attention. He had said she was lovely. She did feel affection toward him, of what sort she wasn't sure. But at the same time, she hadn't meant to hurt Renard's feelings. She liked him, with his thick corn-colored hair and summer-blue eyes. Perhaps she even loved him a little as well.

"Wait, Monsieur le docteur. Please, what is my ailment?" she asked. He turned and smiled.

"I won't know until I complete my examination," he said, using a deep authoritative voice. "Now lie back and be still." He reached under her skirt and unbuttoned her pantaloons.

"Yes, monsieur," she said, trying hard not to giggle. Her heart was racing.

He lifted the skirt of her homespun dress and pulled it over her head.

"I can't see," she protested.

"Ah, but I can." He spread her legs apart with his hands. "Madame, you should have come to me sooner. This is very serious. Very serious indeed." She continued giggling. She was glad the skirt covered her face. Renard placed his fingers on either side of her sex. She thought of Monsieur Millet and how wonderful it felt to have him look at her and call her lovely.

"Oh, but you are so pretty," Renard whispered. She wondered how anyone could think she was pretty down there.

Then he began touching her lightly with one of his fingers. Up and down and up and down. The same pull between her legs that she felt when she was posing for Monsieur Millet came back, only much stronger. It was a sweet, strong ache in the very center of her being. It made her want to cry and laugh, all at the same time.

"Do you like this?" he asked. She nodded, afraid to speak. "Tell me you like it."

"I like it." Her voice sounded strange to her ears, soft and far away. For an instant a picture of her mother standing in the woods with her lover, her skirts raised above her hips, flashed before Berthe's eyes.

"And do you like this?" He pushed the tip of his finger inside her.

"That hurts," she said sharply, trying to push his hand away.

"I'm sorry," he said, but pushed his finger in a little farther.

"Stop." And he did. She immediately regretted asking him to stop. He began rubbing her sex lightly again with his fingertip. She felt as if she were magically divided into two halves, such was the sensation of his touch. The top half covered by her dress was having no part of this game. But the bottom half exposed to the cool, rain-wet air and to Renard's probing, playful fingers was experiencing a new and urgent pleasure.

"Does this feel good?" She nodded. "Say it," he demanded.

"Yes," she said, followed by a long sigh, "it feels good."

"Say, 'Thank you, monsieur, you saved my life.'" She repeated his words. "Now, give me your hand." She held out her palm. Something firm and silky and warm was laid in it. Renard cupped his hand over hers and guided it up and down. Up and down. Suddenly, the thing in her hand jerked and exploded into a sticky wetness. She wanted to look and yet didn't want to see at the same time. After a few moments, Renard pulled away and lifted the skirt of her dress off her face. She looked up at him. His cheeks were flushed and he was buttoning his breeches.

"Did you like the game?" he asked. She nodded.

"Good, we'll do it again, soon."

Berthe stood, wiped her hand on her kerchief, and shook the straw out of her skirt. She looked over at Céleste, who was munching away at her feed, ignoring them.

From that moment on, Renard took up residence in Berthe's mind. He seemed to fill a need, for someone or something that she had had as long as she could remember. She spent every waking moment thinking about him. No matter where she was or what she was doing, she was preoccupied with visions of him and of them together. She would have said it was love but wasn't she too young to be in love? She was not too young, however, for romantic fantasies.

Instead of saying her prayers at night she created scenes of herself and Renard in her imagination: walking hand in hand through the fields, wading in the river, sharing a lunch of apples and cheese, dozing in the summer sun, riding Jean-Luc, the huge Percheron, into the sunset and away, far away from her grandmère and Renard's family. She imagined a beautiful cottage at the top of a hill, Céleste grazing among the wildflowers and a pantry filled with all of Renard's favorite foods. And she conjured up a big wide feather bed covered with a soft white duvet. In her ever-expanding fantasy, the cottage grew into a country mansion with many rooms and tall windows opening onto fields of sweet mowed grass. She fell asleep decorating each of the rooms of her grand home. It was all so innocent. Her romantic imagination was something she had inherited from her mother—a dangerous legacy of hopeless love.

Some days later as she was posing for Monsieur Millet she caught sight of Renard coming across the field, the sun glinting off his golden hair. Her stomach twisted in a knot and her heart began to beat faster.

Even Monsieur Millet seemed to notice the change in her.

"Mademoiselle Bovary is dreaming." He was sketching Berthe in the act of using the long-handled baling rake to pull the hay into a bundle for tying. The artist always insisted on authenticity.

"Why can't I just pretend to be raking?" she asked, growing weary from the continual pulling.

"Because I need to see the body in motion," he said. "Now slide your hand further down the handle. There, that's it. And stop dreaming of your boyfriend," he said, nodding in Renard's direction. "Concentrate on the work at hand."

How did he know she was dreaming of Renard? she wondered. Did her thoughts actually show on her face? She bowed her head and began to rake with exaggerated sweeping movements.

"All right, Berthe, you can put down the tool. This is apparently not your day to be my muse. Come, it's time for me to show you the results of your labor. We will tell your grand-mère I am taking you to my home in Barbizon."

Berthe was surprised when her grand-mère agreed to let her accompany Monsieur Millet to Barbizon, which was over an hour away. As they bumped along in his dogcart he pointed out the fields and workers.

"Look over there." He pointed off to his left. "What do you see?"

"Nothing," she replied. For, in fact, they were passing by empty fields. It was after the harvest and the harvesters had finished building the huge haystacks that stood in the early afternoon sun. Sheep grazed in the stubble that was left of the fields. Beyond the flat mowed plain she could see the red rooftops of the village of Barbizon.

"Art is everywhere, my dear. Unless we have the ability to see it, this is nothing more than an empty hay field on a warm autumn day." They drove on for a long time in silence. She squinted her eyes trying to see the haystacks and the surrounding fields as he did. "You understand, Berthe, the artist's life is a thankless one." He sighed. "I work in a world of ignorance and indifference. Nobody sees and nobody cares. Sometimes I wonder why I even bother."

"Because you love it?" she volunteered. He laughed, put his arm around her shoulders, and gave her a squeeze.

"As good an answer as any," he said.

"And because you are well paid for it," she added, fixing him with a stern gaze.

"Ah, she brings up the subject of money, my little goose girl. I know, you are angry that I gave your grand-mère your modeling money. Don't worry. That was just to pacify the old woman. Here." He reached in his vest pocket and handed her a small pouch of coins. She emptied them out in her hand and counted them—one hundred francs. Closing her fist around the coins, she smiled broadly.

She expected Monsieur Millet's family to live in a grand house with many rooms surrounded by manicured gardens. Consequently, she was surprised when they stopped in front of an ambling laborer's cottage at the edge of town. A plump, pretty woman emerged from the low doorway. Berthe recognized her from the portrait the artist had shown her. It was his wife, Catherine.

Monsieur Millet jumped out of the dogcart and threw his arms around her as if he hadn't seen her in weeks. She cuffed him playfully on the head.

"Don't play the grand lover with me, monsieur. You cannot expect a meal in the middle of the day when you told me you would be gone until sunset."

"Ah, Catherine, my Catherine, I could not bear to stay away from your soft embrace any longer." He began nibbling on her neck. Berthe felt suddenly and painfully jealous.

"And who is this?" Catherine asked, looking over his broad shoulder at Berthe, her brown eyes glinting.

"Don't you recognize my muse, my milkmaid, my newest inspiration?"

"All your muses look the same to me, Monsieur *Chef d'oeuvre*. Come, don't just stand there. Bring her in." They entered the cottage. It was as humble on the inside as it was on the outside. There were three low-ceilinged rooms: a studio, a kitchen, and a bedchamber. How could nine children fit in this humble shack? Berthe wondered. As if reading her mind, Monsieur Millet opened a door in the far corner of the bedroom and showed her a narrow hallway that led to the rooms he had added to accommodate his huge family.

"Back here is where we keep the herd penned," he said. "And speaking of them, where are *mes enfants*?" he asked his wife.

"Your youngest is sleeping in the kitchen, in case you didn't notice, and the others are out in the back laying waste to the fields." She gave Berthe a sharp look. "Jean, give the poor girl something to drink. She must be thirsty after being dragged through the dusty countryside." Monsieur Millet obeyed his wife as if she were his mother and he were one of her many children. He poured Berthe a mug of cold water from an earthenware pitcher, then tilted the pitcher and drank down the rest of the contents.

"Jean," his wife scolded, "you have the manners of a pig."

"I know." He laughed and then, snorting like a pig, he grabbed at her skirt. She moved easily out of his reach. For some reason, the sight of their obvious happiness made Berthe want to cry. "Now I will give Mademoiselle Berthe Bovary the honor of a private showing of one of my masterpieces." He beckoned to Berthe. "Come, and bow your head. You are about to enter the hallowed halls of a great genius."

She followed Millet into his studio. The large room was very bright, with many windows that faced south and looked out onto the fields. She saw Millet's "herd" of children, all sizes and ages, playing on a haystack. The studio smelled of oil paint and turpentine. Canvases leaned against the wall, their painted sides hidden from view. On an easel in the corner stood a large unfinished painting of three peasant women picking up the sparse remnants of harvest. It was a beautiful picture composed of soft blues, rosy pinks, golden sun-drenched fields.

"Well, mademoiselle. What do you think?"

"It's quite . . . quite beautiful. And very sad," she said, tilting her head.

"Beautiful and sad. Very good. You understand what I'm trying to say in my painting."

Madame Millet stood in the doorway, her hands on her ample hips.

"All that is well and good, but you neglected to tell your muse how profitable this painting is. My impoverished painter can sell this for five thousand francs," she announced proudly.

"Five thousand francs," Berthe gasped. "For a painting?" She couldn't believe her ears. The painting wasn't even framed.

"Who knows? If people keep buying Jean-Francois's work, perhaps one day we can give up this hideous life and go back to Paris."

"And what would I paint there?" he asked. "Ladies with big hats and little dogs?" He made a face. "You know I can't do that, Catherine. My inspiration is here in the country. I would die in Paris."

"Oh, fool. You wouldn't die. You would just be rich, your children would get a decent education, and I, well, I would be able to rest my poor overworked back for once." She glared at him before turning to leave. Monsieur Millet seemed not to be bothered by his wife's angry outburst. It was obvious he had heard it all many times before. He continued to gaze with great satisfaction at the painting of the three peasant women. He pointed to the bent figure in blue that dominated the right side of the canvas.

"Now that, my dear Berthe, is an overworked back," he said. "One can feel her pain."

Berthe studied the figure. It was true. From the curve of her back and the way she leaned over to rest the weight of her upper body, Berthe could almost feel the pain and stiffness even in her young bones.

"I call it *The Gleaners*," Millet said. "Do you know what a gleaner is?"

She shook her head.

"A gleaner is the poorest of the country poor. The person who picks the field after the harvester is gone. Theirs is the most meager of livings. They live off the charity of those who are too poor even to be charitable." He directed her attention to a stack of sketches of the same three figures in slightly different poses. "I have been drawing them for years."

She thought about what Madame Millet had said. Why in the world would one choose this depressing subject matter when you could paint beautiful ladies in big hats? she wondered. She stole a glance at Monsieur Millet. He was staring at his painting as if looking for something hidden in the brushstrokes.

"You know, I may not sell this after all," he said finally. "I do believe it is my very best work. I'm not sure I can ever surpass it." He pulled at his thick beard.

"Won't Madame Millet be very angry if you don't sell it?" Berthe asked.

"Oh, yes." He laughed. "I should say she would be. She has these strange notions about children needing to eat. Can you imagine?" He gave her one of his big smiles in which the ends of his mustache tipped upward.

"But, Monsieur Millet, how lucky you are. Someone wants to give you large amounts of money for something you made with your own hands. I can't imagine anything better," Berthe said, hugging herself.

At that moment, Madame Millet rushed into the studio. Her cheeks were flushed with excitement.

"Monsieur Boulanger is here to look at your work. He rode the whole day from Yonville. That's over eighty kilometers," she whispered, quickly untying her apron.

"Who is that?" Monsieur Millet asked.

"Where is your head? I told you. He wrote you weeks ago. He is very rich and very eager to buy one of your pieces. Perhaps more than one. And now he is here. Surely you can bear to part with one of the thousands you have sitting here gathering dust." She turned on her heel and hurried out of the room.

"My wife worries too much about commerce. She has a difficult time understanding the artist's needs. If only we hadn't had quite so many children," he sighed.

It was difficult for Berthe to pay attention to what he was saying. The name Boulanger was suddenly ringing in her head. This couldn't be the same Monsieur Boulanger who came on his huge black horse to take her mother riding every afternoon for months. The Boulanger who had lifted her mother out of her dull, routine existence and filled her with something like fire. The man who had broken her mother's heart. He couldn't possibly be the same man. Could he?

Chapter 6

Monsieur Boulanger

BERTHE WAS SEVEN YEARS OLD WHEN RODOLPHE BOULANGER entered the Bovary home and her mother's life. He was a tall, handsome man in his early thirties with dark, deep-set eyes, thick eyebrows, and very curly black hair, which he wore tied back with a grosgrain ribbon. His skin was very white and although he was clean-shaven, the blue of his beard shadowed his cheeks. He had brought his manservant for Berthe's father to treat.

"I have no idea what ails the fellow. He has been poorly for the past two weeks," he explained to Dr. Bovary.

"I will bleed him and soon he'll be right as rain," her father said. Berthe had seen bleeding done a few times before and thought nothing of it. She sat on the hearthstone watching as her father made a small cut on the inside of the man's arm. Deep red blood ran down the servant's arm into a porcelain basin. The poor man began to grow faint and Berthe's father called out for his wife to assist.

It was a hot day in August and Berthe's mother wore a pale

yellow dress with three flounces. The tightness of the waist offset the wide skirt. As she bent down to put the basin of blood underneath the table, she caught the dress with her knee and it pulled the fabric down, exposing the top inches of her ivory bosom. Monsieur Boulanger could not seem to tear his eyes away from her neckline.

"Your wife, sir, is quite beautiful," Boulanger remarked to Berthe's father when her mother left the room.

"I am sorry to say that she is not feeling herself these days. She is pale and without energy."

"She should ride," pronounced Boulanger. "I find the exercise very beneficial."

"Unfortunately, we have no proper mount for her."

"Allow me to offer one of my horses," said Boulanger.

Later at dinner, when Berthe's father mentioned Monsieur Boulanger's offer, her mother demurred.

"Oh, no, I couldn't," she said. "Besides, I have no riding habit."

"Then you must have one," Charles Bovary answered. And that was that. A riding habit was immediately ordered from Monsieur Lheureux, the draper.

A few weeks later, Berthe watched her mother dress for her first ride with Monsieur Boulanger. Getting ready to go riding turned out to be a very involved process. First came the corset, which Félicité fastened loosely. Then cotton socks. Then a pair of very ugly cotton drawers, the kind that boys wore. Over the drawers her mother put on a pair of black equestrian tights that reached all the way to her ankles. Then the black calfskin riding boots with buttons that fastened on the outside to prevent chafing, Emma explained.

She buttoned up a white cotton shirtwaist with an ascot

stock that fastened with a pretty gold pin. And then finally the riding habit itself. It was made of a heavy material of dark forest green. The jacket was single-breasted and tightly fitted. The skirt, which opened in the back, was long and meant to drape down so that only her boots showed. She donned a black derby that was held around her chin with a strap of elastic. Attached to it was a veil which she lowered over her face. Finally, she pulled on a pair of soft black calfskin gloves which fastened on the side with two clasps.

Berthe was fascinated by the wonderful intricacy of her mother's outfit. She reached out to touch the fabric of the skirt. It was smooth and silky.

"So many clothes," Berthe sighed.

"Yes, I'm already exhausted"—her mother laughed—"and I have yet to get on the horse."

"When I go riding will I have a riding outfit?" Berthe asked, looking up at her mother.

"I doubt that you'll need a riding outfit as you are minus the horse. And I doubt that your father will be purchasing one for you anytime soon." She smoothed the veil under her chin.

Berthe heard hooves on the cobblestones outside. Monsieur Boulanger had arrived astride a huge black horse, leading a lovely dapple-gray mare behind. Emma Bovary took a final look in the mirror. Her cheeks were flushed and her eyes flashed with excitement. She was so beautiful at that moment that Berthe wanted to reach up and hug her, but Emma was in too great a rush and moved out of her daughter's reach.

"Wish me luck! Your mama is going riding." Picking up the leather crop from the top of the bureau, she hurried out of the room, her long riding skirt sweeping the floor behind her.

Berthe ran to the window and looked out. Monsieur Boulanger got off his horse and tied it to the post. When her mother came out he put his two hands together so that she could step into them and onto her horse.

Berthe had never seen her mother so happy. She waved frantically but her mother didn't see her. Instead she smiled down at Monsieur Boulanger, who was tightening the girth on her horse's saddle.

That was the first of many rides. And they did seem to have a curative effect on her mother's health. Her cheeks took on more color; her hair and eyes took on a new luster; and she began to eat with an increased appetite.

"I told you the riding would do you the world of good," Charles Bovary said. He was very pleased with her improvement.

When her mother wasn't out riding with Monsieur Boulanger, she was shopping. She spent long hours at Monsieur Lheureux's shop. She came home with all sorts of lovely things: the softest leather gloves, embroidered chemises, rose-scented soaps, and silk stockings.

It was during these times that Berthe felt closest to her mother. She would sit at her mother's feet as they went through her purchases.

"Just feel this chemise. Have you ever felt anything so soft?" her mother said. Berthe ran her fingers over the delicate white fabric. It was edged in intricate lace and threaded with pink satin ribbons.

"It's beautiful, Maman." Berthe held it up to her nose. "It smells like roses."

"One always keeps a perfumed sachet with one's underthings," her mother explained. She showed Berthe how to put on kid gloves by gently working them on one finger at time. How to use tissue paper to keep dresses from wrinkling. How to tell if a dress has been properly made.

"Look at the buttonholes." Berthe gently poked her little finger through one of the buttonholes. "They must be stitched all around with good silk thread, and the hems must be finished with silk binding," her mother continued.

Whereas some children remember a mother's kisses, Berthe held in her mind the memories of a mother's dresses. Emma Bovary would read to her daughter from the pages of *La Corbeille*, her favorite fashion journal, as if it were a much-adored fairy tale. In many ways, for her it was.

"'A dress of gray silk with three narrow pinked flounces at the bottom. Each flounce is edged with a row of blue pinked silk just peeping below the gray,'" she read in a dreamlike tone. "'There is a broad band of blue silk which is sewn next to the top flounce. The sleeves are trimmed in blue silk and the body of the dress is buttoned to the throat with blue buttons.' How perfectly lovely," she murmured.

For winter, Madame Bovary preferred soft shawls made of cashmere, and for summer fine merino or grenadine, embroidered with tiny flowers and decorated with finely stitched bands of silk. And then there were the satin undergarments and peekaboo lace corsets that her husband probably never laid eyes on. He barely noticed what his wife was wearing on any given day. Had he opened her armoire he would no doubt have been stunned by the vast array of garments he found inside.

Berthe loved to sit inside her mother's armoire and feel swaddled in the soft muslins and summer satins. She thought this must be what heaven was like, surrounded by clouds of fragrant fabrics. She understood that beautiful things made you feel beautiful and therefore somehow lovable. Silks could wrap you in loveliness, kid gloves caressed your hands, combs swept your hair up in soft folds, earrings not only graced your ears but they lit up your eyes as well. People could move in and out of your life. But beautiful things would stay forever. Or so it seemed, until her mother lost everything.

"Monsieur Lheureux extends credit to Madame Bovary like a spider extending the hospitality of its web," Félicité muttered as she put away her mistress's recent purchases. Berthe didn't know what credit was but she certainly knew what spiders were. She was deathly afraid of them. Someone once told her that the bite of a spider could kill. She felt a momentary fear. But then she thought Félicité was just being silly. How could her mother's beautiful purchases hurt her?

One day Berthe's mother brought home a riding crop with an elegant silver top.

"Oh, Maman, how beautiful," Berthe said, caressing the intricately engraved handle.

"Shhh," Emma said, "it's a surprise."

"For Papa?" Berthe asked, her eyes widening.

"No, for a special friend." Her mother smiled. It made Berthe uneasy. It was as if her mother were a stranger with a secret that her daughter would never know.

But Berthe knew who the special friend was. Everyone but her poor papa knew. Her father was too busy trying to keep up with her mother's growing expenses. He was gone all day and on call at night for emergencies that took him many miles away. Sometimes his work took him as far as his mother's farm and he was forced to spend the night there. He was much too tired to pay attention to what his wife was up to.

Berthe, on the other hand, never stopped paying attention. Her mother was an endless source of fascination to her. One beautiful blue summer day she even followed her out the back door, across the grass meadow, over the cow bridge into the woods on the other side of town. She stayed far behind her. If Emma Bovary had known her daughter was following her, Berthe would have received a sound thrashing.

Over her arm her mother carried a large wicker basket which Berthe thought must be a picnic lunch. The girl kept well back and hid behind the occasional bush or the trunk of a tree until her mother stopped at the edge of the stream. There she stood for a moment as if waiting for something. Berthe found a lovely resting place among soft grass and lilies of the valley, where she could lie and watch her mother without being seen.

Suddenly there was a sound in the thicket. It was Monsieur Boulanger leading his huge black horse. Berthe wondered where her mother's horse was. Weren't they going riding? she wondered. He tied his horse to a branch and walked slowly up to her mother. The smile on her face was one that Berthe had never seen before. Then Emma slowly leaned her body against his as if she couldn't stand on her own. They put their lips together. Berthe saw Monsieur Boulanger slip his tongue into her mother's mouth. She gasped, then quickly clamped her hand over her mouth lest she cry out again and risk embarrassing both her mother and herself. She had never seen her parents kiss like that. Never. Then she closed her eyes. Somehow she knew this was something she was not supposed to see. But she couldn't keep them closed. She couldn't stop staring. This was the most wonderful, awful, exciting, and terrifying thing she had ever witnessed.

Boulanger lifted up the skirt of Emma Bovary's summer frock, and Berthe was stunned to see that underneath her many petticoats her mother was naked. The sun shining through the trees dappled her pale white thighs. She held up her skirts while Boulanger ran his hands lightly over her smooth, round bottom. His hand moved around to her front, and he began to touch her with his fingers. Berthe heard her mother moan. She thought he was hurting her, but then she saw the look on her mother's face. Her eyes were closed and she looked blissful.

Berthe stumbled out of the wood, heart racing. What was her mother doing? Why did she seem so happy? In her confusion she ran headlong into a tree, scratching her forehead on the rough bark.

"You naughty, naughty girl. Where have you been?" Félicité asked, shaking her roughly. "And what in heaven's name did you do to your face?"

"I was with Madame Homais," Berthe said. Lies came easily to her even then. "Please, please, don't tell Maman," she begged. But of course she knew Félicité wouldn't, for fear of getting into trouble for having let the girl out of her sight.

That night she lay in bed and the unsettling thoughts about her mother and Monsieur Boulanger returned. Why had her mother forgotten to wear her underwear? And why had she smiled at such an invasion? It was Félicité who finally told her the truth about Monsieur Boulanger after Madame Bovary screamed at Félicité one morning.

"You've torn my best chemise. Just look at it. This can't be repaired. I will have to throw it away." She waved the garment in Félicité's face.

"But, madame, this is your oldest chemise. Look, the cotton is worn thin. I can't help it if it tears easily."

"You have the hands of a field worker, Félicité." The maid snapped her mouth shut and didn't say another word for the rest of the day. As she was putting Berthe to bed that night she finally spoke.

"Your mother has no right to talk to me that way. Who does

she think she is? Having an affair in broad daylight. She's nothing more than a wicked adulteress."

Before Berthe could ask what an adulteress was, Félicité explained. "She allows Monsieur Boulanger to have his way with
her without regard to her reputation or the reputation of her
poor husband." Whatever that meant, Berthe was convinced it
was a sin.

One day Berthe was playing behind the water trough in the
courtyard. She looked up and saw her mother in the upstairs
window. She watched as Emma placed a small piece of paper in
the shutter and then disappeared from view. Berthe felt a wave of
excitement run through her. Was it some sort of signal? Every so
often her mother would reappear in the window. She was looking for someone.

Suddenly, Monsieur Boulanger appeared in the courtyard.
He threw a small pebble up at the window. Within moments her
mother rushed out the door and into his arms. Neither one of
them could see Berthe sitting on the ground behind the trough.

"Take care, someone might see," he told her mother, gently
pushing her away.

Berthe was stunned at the sight of her mother crying, her
shoulders shaking with huge sobs.

"I can bear it no longer!" she cried.

"What do you want me to do?" Boulanger said, looking
down at her.

"Take me away," she beseeched. "Carry me off...I beg of
you!" She pressed her lips against his mouth.

"But..." he began.

"But what?" her mother cried, holding on to the lapels of his
coat.

"Your little girl! What about your child?" said Monsieur Boulanger. There was a long silence and then Berthe heard words that she never imagined she would hear from her mother's mouth.

"We'll take her with us, of course." Berthe wanted to run out and throw her arms around her mother. She wanted to bury her face in her mother's skirt and never let go. Her mother did love her after all!

Just then Félicité called from the kitchen window.

"Madame, have you seen the child?"

Her mother quickly pulled away from Monsieur Boulanger and ran into the house. Berthe stayed behind the trough for a long time until she knew it was safe to come out.

She hugged herself, thrilled beyond belief. They would go off with Monsieur Boulanger, travel the world in beautiful clothes. But then she thought about her poor father. He would miss his wife and perhaps his daughter as well. However, what with his work, he seemed to have so little time for either of them, she reasoned.

Over the next few weeks her mother radiated a beauty and happiness Berthe had never seen before. Berthe was happy, too. Knowing that her mother loved her enough to take her away with her filled her days with untold joy.

Her mother became totally preoccupied with preparing for their trip. She spent even more time with Monsieur Lheureux.

One rainy afternoon the shopkeeper brought a new stylebook and swatches to show to her mother. Berthe played quietly in the corner with her doll while he and Emma discussed her wardrobe.

"And I need a traveling costume," she said.

"Ah, very good, madame," replied Monsieur Lheureux, taking out his leather order book.

"I want it done in blue-gray velvet," she said. "The jacket must be fitted to a point in the center with closing hooks and eyes. I want satin piping along the seams. And a lace collar. The sleeves should be tight on the upper arms but fuller at the bottom."

"Excellent. A pagoda sleeve." Monsieur Lheureux nodded, busily taking notes.

"Yes, exactly," said Emma, appearing pleased that her sleeve had such an exotic-sounding name. "As for the cloak," she continued, "it must be a light color and trimmed in the same blue-gray and lined in gray silk. And oh, yes, it must have a hood."

"A burnoose style," said Monsieur Lheureux, ever the authority on the very latest fashions.

Emma Bovary smiled and nodded. "And I need to purchase a small trunk."

"So, Madame is going on a trip," Monsieur Lheureux said, one eyebrow raised.

"No. But I have never had a proper traveling costume or luggage. A lady must have luggage," said Berthe's mother, fanning herself with her ostrich feather fan. "Oh, and tell the luggage maker to be sure and line the trunk."

She was in such a happy mood that Berthe summoned up the courage to speak.

"Maman, can I please have a travel costume, too?"

Her mother glared at her.

"What in the world do you need a travel costume for? You're not going anywhere, you silly girl." She turned back to Monsieur Lheureux. "She's such an acquisitive thing."

Berthe felt a sharp ache in her throat. She realized her mother had lied to Boulanger. She was going away with him but leaving her daughter behind. Despite all her preparations, all her mother's late-night needlework, adding cross-stitching and drawn-thread work to her linens and nightgowns, she had never once taken out any of Berthe's garments to have her mend them or make them more beautiful.

Berthe wanted to cry out. She wanted to beg her mother to take her, just as her mother had begged Monsieur Boulanger weeks before. But somehow she knew it was useless.

It was not long after that Rodolphe Boulanger's servant delivered a beautiful basket of the largest apricots Berthe had ever seen. In the basket was a letter with Emma Bovary's name on it. Berthe's mother saw the basket, quickly snatched the letter, and disappeared upstairs into the attic. Félicité gave Berthe one of the apricots to eat. Beautiful as it was to the eye, the flesh of the fruit was pulpy and strangely without flavor or sweetness.

Moments later, they heard a loud thump. Something had fallen over in the attic.

"Stay here," Félicité commanded and ran up the stairs. Berthe heard her knocking on the attic door.

"Madame, madame, are you all right?" There was no answer. It was not until hours later that Emma Bovary came down the stairs. Her hair was disheveled and her eyes were red and swollen. Bloody scratches ran up and down her arms. Berthe was frightened at the sight. How had she come to injure herself so?

At that moment her father arrived home. He smiled, delighted to see the basket of apricots on the kitchen table.

"From Monsieur Boulanger's orchard?" he exclaimed. "How very kind. And what perfect fruit. Here, my dear," he said, extending one of the apricots to his wife. "Have one." Shaking her head violently, Emma Bovary drew back as if he were offering her a rat. Then she put her hand up to her brow and simply crumpled to the floor. Berthe knelt by at her mother's side and began to cry. Her father, too, was alarmed.

"Call Homais," he shouted to Félicité.

The chemist came at once. He opened a small bottle of strong-smelling liquid and Berthe's mother revived. Her father breathed a huge sigh of relief, but Berthe couldn't chase away the feeling that something awful had happened that morning, something she couldn't quite grasp. She bit down hard on her lower lip, hoping she could make it bleed, hoping someone would take notice.

"Oh, my darling one, you are all right," her father said, clasping her mother's hand. "How you frightened your daughter. Here, give her a kiss." He thrust Berthe toward her mother. Berthe stretched out her arms to embrace her, but Emma pushed her away.

"No. No, I want no one," she cried, turning her face aside.

There followed a long period of illness. Emma took to her bed, had the curtains drawn, and all but stopped eating. Her father was beside himself. He couldn't determine the cause of his wife's sickness. He thought that perhaps the apricots had somehow caused her sudden collapse. Monsieur Homais seemed to concur, explaining that some people were very sensitive to certain foods. Perhaps Madame Bovary was allergic to the fruit. Between these two men of science, it was a wonder that Berthe's mother didn't perish right then and there.

Winter came and her mother hadn't improved. Berthe was sent to stay in the house of her old nurse, Madame Rollet. When she returned in the spring she discovered a stranger, a mother she barely recognized. Emma Bovary wore her black hair in a simple chignon, and she was dressed in a dark gray cotton dress and cotton stockings without a hint of decoration. She looked for all the world as if she were the housemaid, not the mistress of the house. And her demeanor had gone through an even more startling transformation.

She had lost her spirit, her energy, and her passion for life. She spent a great deal of time praying every day, something her daughter had never seen her do before. Neither she nor her husband had been churchgoers. Monsieur Boulanger was not seen again, but Berthe knew without a doubt that he was the cause of her mother's great sadness. It was only much later that his name was even mentioned, and that was only when her mother was desperate for his help. Help that never came.

And here was Rodolphe Boulanger, eight years later. The very same man with the same thick, curly hair, but now with a touch of gray at the temples. The same dark eyes that stared both at you and through you. The same lopsided smile. Berthe kept her head lowered for fear he might recognize her. How she hated him. She hoped that Monsieur Millet would refuse to sell him a picture and send him away. *Show him that his wealth doesn't mean anything. Make him feel small just as he made my mother feel.*

Monsieur Boulanger removed a thick leather wallet from his coat. "Well, Monsieur Millet, I come prepared to buy. I just pray you won't take advantage of the fact I am so enamored of your work."

"I regret, Monsieur Boulanger, I have nothing to sell," said Millet, stuffing his hands in the pockets of his smock. Berthe almost laughed out loud. She turned her head so that they wouldn't see the smile spreading across her face.

"What? Your wife wrote me that you had many paintings." Boulanger's gaze took in the entire studio and the canvases stacked against the walls.

"My wife sometimes gets carried away with her desire to increase my sales, promote my reputation, and fill our coffers."

"But what about that one?" Boulanger said, pointing to the painting of *The Gleaners* that stood on the easel.

"Oh, I'm afraid that has already been spoken for."

"You have others," Boulanger said impatiently. Clearly, he was a man used to getting his way.

"My paintings are not for sale at this time," Millet said with a sweet stubbornness. "But I would be more than happy to sell you some of my sketches."

Berthe thought about her mother. How happy she would be if she could see the great Boulanger being denied something he desired. She wanted to throw her arms around the artist for not falling prey to the wishes of this entitled man.

"I don't want sketches. How can I hang sketches in my gallery?" said an exasperated Boulanger. "I have traveled all day to pay my respects and any amount of money for one of your paintings. How can you deny me?"

"Dear sir, it is very difficult for me to part with my paintings. They are like children to me. I look at them as being in a state of growth. In constant need of correction and improvement."

"But, monsieur, you must make a living. You have a family to feed, do you not?"

"Ah, methinks you have spent too much time corresponding with Madame Millet. 'Feeding the children' is one of her favorite refrains," he said, laughing and patting his stomach. Boulanger was not amused.

"Perhaps I should take my money to the artist Corot. I think he would be more than glad to sell me his work."

"Never heard of him," said Millet, shrugging his shoulders.

"I'm surprised you haven't. He, too, paints the countryside. But with much greater use of color. His landscapes are greatly admired for their lack of pedantry."

This seemed to give Monsieur Millet pause. He scratched his heavy beard.

"What do you think, Berthe? Should I sell this gentleman

one of my paintings?" Feeling her face and neck go red, she ducked her head down further.

For the first time Rodolphe Boulanger looked her way. She held her breath, hoping and praying he wouldn't recognize her. At the same time she wanted him to know exactly who she was. She wanted to remind him of how he had destroyed her mother. But as soon as he spoke she lost all her courage. "This must be one of your beautiful daughters," Boulanger said, bowing slightly.

"No, this is my beautiful model, Mademoiselle Berthe Bovary."

Berthe gasped.

"Bovary, Bovary," Boulanger repeated. "I used to know a Bovary in Yonville. Are you any relation?"

She shook her head. "No, monsieur," she said breathlessly. She lowered her eyes again but she could feel him studying her.

Meanwhile, Millet turned three of the canvases that had been leaning against the wall around so that they could be viewed, and to her great relief Boulanger immediately lost interest in her.

One canvas showed an exhausted man leaning all his weight on a hoe. The second was a beautiful depiction of three large haystacks beneath a stormy sky. The third was a very small painting of a boy chopping wood.

"Wonderful," exclaimed Boulanger. "I will take all three. How much do you want for them?"

Millet thought a moment. "Perhaps I should let my wife negotiate. I am at a loss when it comes to money matters."

"I will give you one thousand francs for all three," said Boulanger quickly.

"One thousand is a fine price," Millet said, smiling. "But, of course you mean for each one." With a rush of delight, Berthe suddenly realized that this was all a clever ploy. Monsieur Millet was turning out to be an even better salesman than his wife.

"Three thousand francs! You appear to be as talented a bargainer as you are a painter, Monsieur Millet." Boulanger laughed. "All right. Have them wrapped and I will send my man for them."

Smiling, Millet began to carefully wrap the paintings in cloth, tying them with soft cord.

As he was leaving Boulanger turned to Berthe and said, "I recall that my friends the Bovarys had a young daughter. She would be about your age. Her mother was a very beautiful woman." He reached out and lifted her chin with one finger. She bit the inside of her cheek as his dark eyes studied her face. "And I can see why Monsieur Millet has chosen you to model for him." Berthe felt sick to her stomach as she turned away. "When you have completed the paintings of Mademoiselle Bovary," he said to Millet, "I hope you will let me have the first viewing."

CHAPTER 7

The Rake

WHEN BERTHE RETURNED FROM MILLET'S HOUSE RENARD greeted her as if she'd been gone for weeks. He grabbed her hand and pulled her into the barn before she could even tell her grand-mère she was home.

"Where have you been?" he demanded.

"You sound just like my grand-mère." She laughed. She was happy to see him. He was nothing like Monsieur Boulanger, who had seduced her mother and then abandoned her without a thought. No, she could tell Renard cared about her. Perhaps he even loved her. If he did love her then she would certainly love him. Yes, it was really all so simple. They could pledge themselves to this love. Nothing would ever come between them. She felt herself grow warm inside. She was immediately transported to the beautiful mansion in her mind.

She stood in the open French doors greeting Renard as he returned from a hard day's labor. For even though they weren't poor, he continued to labor in the fields because he believed in hard work, particularly as an example for their young children. How many children? Three—no, five. And how the peasants looked up to Berthe and Renard. Renard, because he still insisted on getting his hands dirty in the fields, and his beautiful wife the very devoted mother of their five flawless children. What a lovely home she kept for them. Granted, she had maids to help her with the housework, but nobody could manage a household like she could. And while Renard taught their children the value of honest labor, she instructed them in the finer things in life: furniture, art, music, and, most especially, fine fabrics and well-made clothing.

"I went to Monsieur Millet's house to see his paintings. He is truly a wonderful artist. You should see the colors, Renard. He makes the countryside—"

Renard stopped her words with a kiss. And he kept kissing her. Long, strong, very grown-up kisses. She couldn't catch her breath.

"Your Monsieur Millet is just a dirty old man," he said finally. "He is up to no good, painting dirty pictures of naked girls." He reached up under her skirt and she began to giggle. And soon the giggling stopped and she became aware of their breathing, of their two bodies. The barn, the farm, and the rest of the world seemed to fall away.

"Oh, Berthe, Berthe," he breathed into her ear. She could feel him harden against her leg. She longed to touch him. As if reading her mind he guided her hand with one of his while with the other he unbuttoned his breeches and gently curled her fingers around his sex.

Berthe sensed her grand-mère's presence before she heard the scream.

"Mon Dieu!"

They jumped apart. Her grand-mère stood in the doorway, backlit by the late afternoon sun. Berthe couldn't see her face but she didn't need to. She felt her fury.

"You harlot! You whore! Curse of your mother's womb!"

Renard ran out of the barn. Berthe's grand-mère didn't even turn as he hurried past her. It was as if he didn't exist. Her rage was focused totally on her granddaughter. She looked around wildly for something to beat Berthe with. Her eyes landed upon the rake and she reached for it. The old woman's eyes bulged and her face turned a terrible purplish red.

"I'll beat the devil out of you if I have to kill you doing it," she screamed.

The old woman lifted the rake, but Berthe ran past her and into the woods. Her heart felt as if it were leaping out of her chest. Not stopping until she found her favorite spot by the river, she slumped down against the big oak tree. She had hoped Renard would be there but he was nowhere to be seen. What should she do? Where could she go? She knew she couldn't face her grand-mère. Dropping her head in her hands she felt deeply ashamed. Was her grand-mère right? Was she a harlot and a whore? She had let Renard touch her and she had touched him. Her mother's life had been ruined by just this kind of touching. She cried until she ran out of tears and her eyes were almost swollen shut. Finally, exhausted, she fell asleep.

She awoke a few hours later. The sun had set and it was growing dark. She was hungry, cold, and sore. She knew she couldn't go back to her grand-mère's. She was terrified of the woman's fury. She vaguely remembered where Renard's house was and made her way slowly over the bumpy, harvested fields in that general direction.

She was practically penniless, pitiless, and now homeless. All she had in the world was the hundred francs Millet had given her to model. It was hardly enough to live on. The image of Monsieur Millet's painting, *The Gleaners,* came to her. She realized her life was not unlike the wretched women he had portrayed. She shared their misery and poverty because, like them, she had not even the scanty remnants of a life to pick up.

She stumbled along until she came upon a low farmhouse. Could this ramshackle house be where her beautiful Renard lived? She knocked on the rough-hewn door. A tired-looking woman answered. She appeared almost as old as Berthe's grand-mère. She was stooped over by the weight of her breasts, which hung down practically to her waist. In the dimly lit room Berthe could see several children playing with stones in front of the fire.

"Excuse me for intruding, madame, but does Renard live here?"

"Who are you?" the woman demanded.

"My name is Berthe Bovary. I am the granddaughter of Madame Bovary."

"She owes us money," the woman said curtly. "She is always so slow in paying. Just when I think it will never come, she manages to cough up the few francs to pay my poor boy."

"Is he here?" Berthe said, wrapping her arms around herself.

"Renard is in the barn. Tell him supper is almost on the table. If he doesn't come in soon, there will be nothing left." Renard's mother slammed the door.

The barn was a crumbling affair that looked as if it would fall down with the next strong wind. The roof sagged in the middle and there were holes in the siding. The light of a small oil lamp gave the interior a warm glow.

She heard them before she saw them. There was the sound of rustling hay. Renard was on the barn floor bent over a neighbor girl. Her plump white legs were wrapped around him, her skirt hiked up above her waist. They were moving up and down making animal-like noises. The girl looked over Renard's shoulder and gave Berthe a broad grin.

"Renard, I think your sweetheart is here." He lifted his head from her bare bosom, turned, and smiled at Berthe.

"Ah, Berthe, come here. Join us." Berthe stood with her mouth agape. At first she felt like laughing. Was this a game they were playing? Then she felt the heat of a blush rise up her face. That was when she realized what it was she was seeing. She was aware of the fact that she had been holding her breath. She let out a sudden "Oh!" and stamped her foot hard on the dirt floor. She felt tears starting down her cheeks and she furiously wiped them away. They were not going to see her cry. Filled with an emotion she had never before experienced, she suddenly wanted to strike out, to beat Renard with a stick. She wanted to scream at the top of her lungs. And finally she did:

"You horrid pigs!" She turned and ran out of the barn.

How could he turn out to be so opposite of who she had thought he was? She had thrilled at being touched and touching him. It was something that was just between the two of them, she had thought. How dirty she felt now. How could someone who had made her feel so happy and alive and so appreciated make her feel like the lowest thing on earth? Love wasn't supposed to be this way. She ran quickly along the old cow path, not bothering to look where she was going. Suddenly, she tripped and fell face forward onto the stone-covered path, coming down hard on her hands and knees. She sat there waiting for the pain to go away. Her hands and knees were bleeding.

She remembered her mother reading aloud from one of her favorite books, *Pride and Prejudice.* How even when things weren't going well between Darcy and Elizabeth, they treated each other with respect and well-chosen words. And in the book's end, after so many painful pages of misunderstandings, their elegant love had won out. That was what Berthe had grown up expecting from life, just as her mother had. How terribly, terribly wrong they both had been.

Berthe stood and limped slowly toward her grand-mère's house. She stopped and drew in a deep breath. She realized she would have to apologize to her grand-mère for what the old woman had witnessed between her and Renard. At this moment she began to see her grand-mère's side. The old woman had been shocked. She had a right to be angry, Berthe reasoned. From now on she would learn to live by her grand-mère's rules. After all, she was providing a safe home for her granddaughter. Berthe would show her that she was grateful to have a roof over her head. Her mother and all her rich fantasies had not been able to provide that. The least Berthe could do was respect her grand-mère and honor her way of life.

The oil lamp was still burning in the kitchen. *Grand-mère must be waiting up for me to give me my beating.* She took a deep breath and made herself ready to receive what she knew would be a terrible punishment. She almost welcomed it. It might help to deflect her thoughts from the awful pain inflicted by Renard.

"Grand-mère, I'm back," she called out. "And I'm sorry," she said, hoping to smooth the way with an apology first. Her grand-mère was nowhere to be seen. She walked over to the pitcher on the kitchen table, took the corner of her apron, and dipped it in the water. She sat down at the table, lifted her skirt, and bent over to dab at her bleeding knees. Her eyes caught sight of a clog on the floor at the other end of the long kitchen table. Her grand-mère never went anywhere without her shoes. Berthe got up and walked to the end of the table. Her grand-mère hadn't gone anywhere. She was lying flat on her back on the kitchen floor. Around her lay torn pieces of paper. They were the two pictures Millet had once given her.

"Grand-mère, what's wrong?" she cried, falling to her bruised knees. She quickly picked up the old woman's hand. It was quite cold. "Grand-mère, wake up, wake up." She shook the old woman's shoulder gently at first and then with greater urgency. Her grand-mère's body moved back and forth as she pushed at it. Her face was a grayish white and her mouth was slack. Berthe realized with a sudden start that her grand-mère was dead. She thrust her hand in her mouth to stifle a cry of horror. Falling back on her heels, she shut her eyes as if that would block out the sight of the dead woman. She opened them again and began to sob. Her mother's death came back to her in one painful flash.

Emma Bovary's solution to the mess in which she'd found herself after a failed love affair and a mountain of debt turned out to be painfully simple. Sneaking into Homais's pharmacy, she managed to find and ingest a great quantity of arsenic.

And then she came home and began the long, agonizing process of dying.

Berthe stayed in her room alternately crying and praying. She desperately needed someone to come and comfort her but they were all too busy with her mother to bother about the girl. Her mother's dying went on for days. She prayed that her mother would recover, mouthing over and over the meaningless prayers she had heard her mother chant in the days after Boulanger abandoned her. When she paused for breath, she heard her mother's agonizing screams coming from the bedroom. Wild, gut-wrenching, ear-piercing cries of pain. She heard Félicité's steps rushing up and down the stairs. If she could have, she would have stolen her father's horse and the dogcart and gone far, far away. No one would have missed her, and she wouldn't have had to hear those horrible screams.

After a night of howling, all was quiet. Morning came and Berthe thought her mother must have died. But no, she was still dying. Days passed. The screams continued, but each hour they grew weaker and weaker. Late one night Berthe heard a tap at her door. It was Félicité.

"Your mother has asked for you," she said. The maid's eyes were red and her auburn hair had come undone. Her normally spotless apron had yellow stains all up and down the front.

Berthe huddled in the corner of her bed and shook her head.

"You must come," she said, stretching out her hand. "She needs to see you." Berthe pulled back farther into the corner. Félicité reached out and grabbed the girl's arm and dragged her off the bed and out of the room.

Berthe was not afraid that her mother would die, because she knew by then with great certainty that she would. What she feared was actually witnessing the agony she had only heard the past few days.

The door opened onto the bedroom, which was in a state of great disarray. There on the bed, her head thrown back, was Emma Bovary. It was a terrible sight. Gone was any trace of the beautiful woman she once was. Her skin was white and waxen, her black eyes sunk into her head like pits. Her lips were colorless, cracked, and covered with a strange thick coating. Even her black hair had lost its luster; it lay spread across the embroidered pillowcase like something that had been dead for many years.

The smell of vomit, of strong soap, and of lavender scent filled Berthe's nostrils. The room was ablaze from candles on the table, on the mantel, and at the bedside. It was like the beginnings of a ghastly celebration. Emma Bovary's head turned, and her eyes locked on to Berthe standing by the side of her bed.

Félicité leaned against the girl as if to prevent her escape. Charles Bovary stood at the head of the bed, his hands holding on to the bedpost as if to keep himself from falling over. The fearsome creature reached out her hand to grab at her daughter's. Berthe knew her mother wanted to kiss her farewell. She may have even wanted to show her daughter that she loved her. But it was too late for that. Far too late.

"Berthe, dear, here is your mother. Give her a kiss," her father said softly. She did as she was told. Her mother's skin was dry as paper. The mother whose touch she had once craved, whose beauty had so enchanted her, whose love she had longed for was gone. Berthe opened her mouth to speak, yet nothing came out but the sobs of a grief-stricken child. Félicité led Berthe back to her room. She tried to comfort the distraught girl but nothing she said could stop her tears. Berthe never saw her mother again.

Berthe placed her grand-mère's cold hand on her unmoving chest. After smoothing her hair from her forehead, she stood up. Death had become a regular occurrence in her life. This was the third time she had lost someone in less than two years. She was now truly and totally an orphan.

CHAPTER 8

Another Move

As it happened Berthe's grand-mère was buried on the very day that Berthe turned thirteen. No one knew it was her birthday. So, of course, there was no celebration. There was no one left to celebrate. No one even looked her way. Berthe stood apart from the few mourners, hugging herself tightly. She felt that if she didn't hold on to herself she might evaporate into the air.

As she watched the last shovelful of earth fall on her grand-mère's simple pine coffin she allowed herself to hope that a new future lay before her, one with new possibilities, perhaps even a better life. That thought was her birthday gift to herself.

Berthe had always believed her grand-mère was exaggerating about the poor state of her finances. After all, Berthe reasoned, grand-mère had the farm. But, as it turned out, she hadn't overstated her money problems. She was hugely, hopelessly in debt. Financial ruin seemed to run in the Bovary family. Everything, even Céleste, was to be auctioned to pay off what she owed. Once again Berthe was going to be without a home.

Her first thought was to appeal to Monsieur Millet. Immediately after her grand-mère's small funeral, she begged a ride to his home in Barbizon. He was in his studio adding delicate dabs of paint to the sky of another haystack painting very much like the one that Monsieur Boulanger had purchased. His wife was busy cleaning his brushes.

"Ah, Berthe, my deepest condolences. Your grand-mère was a difficult woman, but still a loss is a loss." He stepped back from the canvas, squinted his eyes, and tilted his head first to the left and then to the right. "What will you do now?" he asked, chewing on the end of his paintbrush as he scrutinized his work.

"That is what I have come to talk to you about, Monsieur Millet."

"Yes, yes, I am happy to offer any advice," he said. He took a step toward the painting and quickly added a few more strokes. "You must forgive me. Monsieur Boulanger is purchasing this painting for a friend. He is coming to pick it up this morning and I wanted to fix the sky."

Boulanger! That hateful, horrible man! Her skin crawled as she remembered the way he had looked at her. The hooded eyes, the full wet lips curled in a half smile as if he thought himself the most irresistible man in the world. A chill of fear and disgust ran through her. She had to ask Millet her question, but she must hurry so she could leave before Boulanger got there.

"This is what happens when you sell your soul." Millet sighed and began adding dark gray tones to the clouds. "My good wife doesn't understand this. Before long, I will be turning out hundreds of haystack paintings and then they will want me to do haystack wallpaper, and then there will be a great demand for my peasant paintings, only they will request that I put happy smiles on the workers' faces. Trust me; this will be the ruination of my art."

"Oh, hush up, Jean," his wife said, placing the clean brushes back in a ceramic jar.

"What do you think, Mademoiselle Berthe, do they look like clouds to you?" he said, ignoring his wife as he studied the painting.

"Yes, monsieur, they are very cloudlike. It feels as if it is about to rain."

"Ah, good, good." He turned to his wife. "You see, Catherine, Mademoiselle Berthe appreciates my talent." His wife snorted. "Now, my dear, how can I be of service?"

She was afraid to ask and afraid not to.

"I was wondering if in exchange for posing and helping Madame Millet around the house and with the children, I could perhaps come and live with you."

"What a splendid proposition! I don't see why not, do you, Mother?" he said, smiling broadly. A frown brought Madame Millet's eyebrows together in one uninterrupted line.

"Are you mad? We already have nine mouths to feed," she said, her arms folded across her chest.

"And what is one more?" the artist said, shrugging his shoulders.

"One more is ten, you idiot!" she snapped.

"Ah, what a clever woman I have! You see, Berthe, that is why she keeps the accounts and I just do the painting." He laughed and leaned over to kiss his wife on the cheek. She merely scowled and moved away.

"And I had to marry an artist. To think, at the time I thought it was just a passing phase," she said.

"You did not, you wicked woman," he said, patting her on the bottom.

Madame Millet went over to the window and peered out. "Oh, Monsieur Boulanger is here!" As she hurried to greet him,

Berthe frantically searched the room for another way out. Her heart was beating as hard as if she were running a race. She had trouble catching her breath. There was only the one door. She moved into a dark corner of the room hoping Boulanger wouldn't see her.

"I don't like to have a canvas moved before it dries," Millet said. "These art collectors are always in such a hurry to collect their art. As if it will spoil if they don't get it hung in time." He had already lost interest in Berthe and her plight.

Boulanger entered and went immediately over to the easel. Berthe was relieved that he hadn't so much as glanced in her direction. Holding his chin, he stood and gazed for a long time at Millet's latest painting.

"I'm not completely happy with the sky," said Millet, approaching the painting with an upraised paintbrush.

"Leave it," said Boulanger. "It is perfect. My friend will be delighted, I assure you."

"I just don't know," said the artist, shaking his head and twirling the paintbrush in both his hands.

"It's one of the best paintings you've done," countered Boulanger.

"Really?" said Millet, one eyebrow raised.

"You are a genius, Monsieur Millet," said Boulanger, slapping the artist on the back.

"You are too kind, sir," said Millet, smiling broadly.

As the two men studied the painting, Berthe inched toward the door. She wanted to avoid Boulanger at all costs. She was almost out of the room when Monsieur Millet seemed to remember her.

"Ah, Berthe, where are you going?" Berthe felt as if she had been caught stealing. All the air went out of her. Millet turned back to Boulanger. "Monsieur Boulanger, we seem to have a problem on our hands. Perhaps you can be of assistance. It appears that Mademoiselle Bovary here has found herself in a difficult situation. As you may or may not know she has not only just lost her grand-mère but it seems her home as well. Unfortunately, as my dear wife points out, *chez* Millet is already bursting at the seams. But I had a thought," he said, tapping his head as if to indicate the area in which his thought took place. "Is it possible that she could obtain room and board from you, in exchange for housework of some kind?" As Boulanger turned his hooded gaze toward her, Berthe felt a chill run through her entire body. He shook his head and smiled as if she were an errant child who had somehow managed to get herself into yet another fix.

"Why, what a splendid idea," he said. "She would be most welcome. I'm sure my housekeeper can find some useful work for her."

"How very generous you are, monsieur," said Madame Millet, who had been hovering in the doorway. "She is a very lucky girl."

"No!" Berthe said, louder than she meant to. She clamped her hand over her mouth.

"What?" Madame Millet exclaimed. "Where is your gratitude? Beggars can't be choosers."

"I am not a beggar!" Berthe shouted.

"But, child, certainly there are worse things than living under Monsieur Boulanger's very gracious roof," Millet said soothingly. "This is the perfect solution to your dilemma, is it not?"

"I think Mademoiselle Bovary is afraid of me for some reason." Boulanger chuckled. "Rest easy, mademoiselle, I do not devour young girls."

Without another word Berthe turned and fled.

"Come back, you ungrateful little wench!" she heard Madame Millet call after her.

As she walked quickly down the road that led from Millet's house, she heard the sound of a horse cantering behind her. She knew without turning around that it was Monsieur Boulanger. She took a deep breath and told herself not to panic, not to run, and not to act afraid. *He can't hurt you,* she said to herself, but she didn't believe a word of it. For of all the misfortunes that befell Emma Bovary, it was letting this man in her life that finally killed her in the end.

Boulanger trotted past her on the road, then stopped and turned the horse in front of her, blocking her way. She looked up, heart pounding. The sun was behind his head and she couldn't see his face. He dismounted quickly and grabbed her arm before she could get away.

"You are being very silly, mademoiselle. How do you imagine you are going to manage without a home?"

"Leave me alone," she said, trying to pull away as he squeezed her arm tighter.

"You know I loved your mother very much," he said, more kindly than she expected.

"Did you?" she asked, remembering the note in the basket of apricots, her mother's red eyes, and the months she spent suffering from her broken heart. "Then why did you leave her?"

"But, dear girl—" He laughed. "I fear you are too young to understand. She was a married woman with a family. A young daughter. It was impossible. Let us get back to the problem at hand. You have no place to go. I offer you my home with no strings attached. Don't be a ninny," he said, bringing his face within inches of hers. Berthe kicked him hard in the shin, wrenched her arm out of his grasp, and ran into the thickest part of the woods.

"You foolish, foolish girl," he shouted after her. "You're just like your mother."

I am not just like her, Berthe thought as she pushed her way through the thick branches. *I would never let you hurt me like you did her.*

She had run out of options. She could not go back to the Millets'. And she certainly didn't want to take the chance of ever running into Monsieur Boulanger again. The money Millet had given her for modeling was not enough to pay for room and board indefinitely. She realized suddenly that Millet had used her just like everyone else. He had gotten all the sketches he wanted out of her and she was left with nothing but one hundred francs.

As a last resort, she called upon her grand-mère's friend. She sat in a rickety chair in Madame Leaumont's dingy kitchen. The evening was growing cold and Madame Leaumont had put the last leg of a broken side table into the fire. Berthe drank weak tea from a chipped cup. This was the first time she had been to Madame Leaumont's house. She had never realized how impoverished she was. *However does this old woman survive?* Berthe had known the minute she entered the kindly woman's home that there would be no help forthcoming from this poor widow.

"Oh, dear, I would take you in if I could, my child," the old woman said, "but I barely have enough to feed myself. Your grand-mère was always so generous with me, giving me milk and cheese whenever I needed it. I had no idea she was in such poor straits; otherwise, I would never have taken anything from her."

The old woman hesitated and then tapped her chin with the tip of her crooked forefinger.

"There is someone. Your grand-mère has an older sister who lives in Lille. They had a falling-out and haven't spoken in years, but I'm sure she would welcome you. She is a Bovary, after all."

Berthe packed her few things. With the money she had

earned from Millet she was able to pay for her transportation to the town of Lille, where her father's aunt, Charlotte Bovary, lived. It was a day's journey by train. She didn't bother to write her great-aunt that she was coming. She was, after all, Berthe's only recourse. Why write to ask for permission when she had no place else to go? she reasoned.

Following in the Bovary family tradition, Great-aunt Charlotte was living in a pauper's shack, having had a reversal of fortune many years before.

"You say my sister left you nothing? And her son, the great doctor? Nothing?" she asked only minutes after Berthe introduced herself. She was a woman in her seventies or eighties, almost bent double with age, and Berthe had difficulty seeing her face. She had to address her comments to the top of her great-aunt's white head.

"There was nothing to leave," Berthe said. The old woman shook her head sadly. She seemed unsurprised. Berthe looked around the single dismal room and saw that there were three narrow beds lined up side by side, in addition to an old table and chairs. Berthe's great-aunt followed her gaze.

"My tenants," she explained. "They pay me a paltry sum but it's what I live on." She gave Berthe a cup of tea and apologized for having no milk or sugar to go with it.

"Unfortunately, as you can see, I am in no position to even offer you a bed." She wrapped her thin, torn shawl tightly around her shoulders and tilted her head back to peer up at Berthe. Her eyes were sad and watery and the wrinkles on her face had wrinkles of their own.

First her mother, then her father, next her grand-mère and Madame Leaumont, and now this poor distant relative. Was there nowhere she could turn?

"I will find work," Berthe said, with far more confidence than she felt.

"Ah, yes." Her great-aunt brightened visibly. "There is plenty of work at the cotton mill. They are always looking for strong young girls. And they will give you a place to sleep and meals. I'm so sorry, my dear, that I cannot be of more help."

"Don't worry, I'm sure I can find something," said Berthe, a tremor in her voice. "I'll be fine."

"I know you will be. And if you think of it, dear, you might send something extra to your old auntie from time to time."

Berthe bit her lip, then she saw the expression on the old woman's face. She was actually looking at Berthe with a hopeful smile. She truly expected her to go out into the world and make a success of herself.

The old woman laid a wrinkled hand on Berthe's face and patted it gently. Suddenly, Berthe felt a surge of real confidence. She took a deep breath and squared her shoulders.

She was thirteen years old, certainly old enough to make her own living. Now that she was on her own, maybe her life would get better. She knew it could not get any worse.

PART 2

Rags

CHAPTER 9

The Mill

LILLE, 1854

BERTHE WAS DIRECTED BY A STRANGER TO RAPPELAIS ET FILS, which was situated next to the river at the very edge of town. The town itself seemed like a city compared to Yonville. The four- and five-story buildings were squeezed tightly next to one another as if huddled against the cold. There were no yards, no grass, not even the sign of any soil, just street after street of rectangular cobblestones. To see the sky, Berthe had to tilt her head and look up. People, dressed in warm clothes and good leather boots, hurried by as though they all had somewhere very important to go.

As she walked along the winding narrow streets she began to grow excited about her new life. It seemed fitting that she would end up working in a mill that made fabrics. She thought of her mother and how proud she might be to know her daughter could actually earn a living working with cotton, the soft material they both loved. Berthe knew she had a talent for sewing and needlework, and she had no doubt that the mill owners would recognize that and give her a job that fit her abilities. She didn't know how a mill operated but she assumed they would have a need for a seamstress or an embroiderer or certainly someone with "an eye," as Monsieur Millet had said. She tried to remind herself not to dream up things that hadn't yet happened, but she couldn't stop herself. This did seem like the whole new beginning of a much better life.

At the end of the street was a river, and sitting alongside it was an enormous brick building that appeared to Berthe to be as long as a train. Its many large windows were opaque and seemed to be coated on the inside with thick dirt. The entranceway to the mill led into an open courtyard. Draft horses stood waiting patiently by two wagons filled with bales of cotton.

"Excuse me," Berthe said to a man who carried a huge bale of cotton on one shoulder, "I am looking for the *patron*. I am interested in acquiring a position," she said in her best formal French.

"A position! A position!" The man laughed, spraying Berthe with saliva. He wiped his eyes and face with a dirty rag with one hand. Then he indicated a small wooden door in the side of the building. "Ask for Monsieur Roucher. He's the one to see about a position. And while you're at it ask him for a nice hot meal and a bath. Let me know what he says."

Berthe entered the building. It was dark and musty; the air was filled with white particles. She could hear and even feel through the soles of her feet the movement of machinery somewhere in the mill. It took a minute for her eyes to adjust, and then she spotted a closed doorway. The sign on the door read *Office*. She knocked.

"Come in and it better be important," called a voice from inside.

Monsieur Roucher was a thin bent man in his fifties. The skin on his face was stretched tightly; his cheekbones were prominent and hard-edged. He was seated at a tall desk making notes in a thick ledger. Berthe cleared her throat. He looked up.

"What do you want? I'm busy," he snapped.

"I'm looking for a position in your mill, sir," Berthe said.

"We have no positions here. We only have work. Hard work," he said, scowling.

"I'm used to hard work, sir. I'll be happy to do any job you have for me," said Berthe, lifting her chin.

"Oh, you will, will you? We shall see about that." He got up from his stool, took Berthe by the shoulders, and turned her slowly around as if to make sure she had all her working parts. Then he pulled a slip of paper from a pile on his desk and handed it to her.

"Take this and give it to Madame Lisette, the owner of the boardinghouse at seventeen, rue de la Côte. This will tell her that you are to be provisionally employed by Rappelais et Fils. She will give you a bed and a meal. The money for your room and board will be deducted from your wages. Make sure you are back here Monday morning at six sharp. Don't be late on your first day or you will start off with a beating. And there won't be a second day. Now off with you." He turned back to his desk.

Berthe prepared to leave and then stopped.

"Excuse me, sir."

"What is it now?"

She took a deep, shaky breath.

"What will my pay be?" she asked. He looked down at her over his half glasses as if he couldn't comprehend her words. She was anxious to start her savings. She had already planned what she would buy with her first pay. She longed for a pair of real leather boots like the kind she had seen people wearing on the streets of Lille. Winter had arrived and the air was cold and damp. Her feet felt like blocks of ice in her wooden clogs.

"You'll get what you earn and not a penny more or a penny less. And if that's not good enough for you, well, there are plenty of others waiting for work."

It was almost dark by the time Berthe arrived at 17, rue de la Côte, a large six-story stone house on a street with similar houses. There was no light coming from any of the windows and Berthe wondered if anyone was home. She rang the bell and waited several minutes. The blustery wind blew up her skirt and her toes ached with cold. She kept one hand under her shawl but the other one holding her small valise felt frozen on the handle. Finally, a small door opened. An extremely fat woman stood in the doorway.

"Yes, my dear. What can I do for you?"

"Madame Lisette?" asked Berthe.

"The very one," boomed the woman.

"I am here for a room," Berthe said, handing Madame Lisette the slip of paper. The woman studied the paper and then looked up at Berthe, her small eyes squinting through the darkness.

"Get in here so I can better see you," Madame Lisette said, opening the door wider.

The door opened onto a courtyard and Berthe was immediately assaulted by an all-too-familiar smell. The entire courtyard was covered with high mounds of manure. She felt as if she were back in the country.

"My dowry," said Madame Lisette, laughing loudly. "Have you never seen dung before?"

"I come from my grand-mère's farm," explained Berthe.

"Good, then you are used to it. My boy Lucien collects this

from the streets and sells it to farmers for fertilizer. I'm never one to turn up my nose at a little supplemental income." She led Berthe through another door and they were inside a large kitchen with two long wooden tables set end to end. A small but very hot fire was burning in the fireplace. Hanging over the fire was a huge iron kettle of what Berthe assumed was soup. It smelled slightly of cabbage, carrots, and dirty feet.

"Welcome to the house of busy hands," said Madame Lisette grandly. "You're very fortunate. Tonight is special soup night. Dinner is served every evening at ten P.M. If you're late you don't eat. No exceptions. The privy is in back of the house. This, as you can see, is our kitchen." There was an old gray cat asleep on top of the table. At first Berthe thought she was dead until she lifted her head and looked at Madame Lisette through half-closed amber eyes.

"And here is our grand *salle à manger*," she said, opening the door of another room. It was dark and dingy and smelled of rotten onions and cat urine. The room was long and narrow with most of the space taken up by two more rough pine trestle tables, the kind that were used for outdoor picnics. "Now, follow me and I will show you to your *boudoir.* The dormitory rooms are all full but I have a nice spot on the fifth floor. You'll be with Hélène. She'll show you the ropes. But take care, *chérie,* she is a terrible thief."

Berthe followed the woman's broad bottom up five flights of stairs. Madame Lisette had to stop every few steps to catch her breath. On the top floor, she pushed open a door and moved her large frame aside so that Berthe could see the room. It was no bigger than a closet. There were two wood plank beds lined up inches apart from each other. Bags and boxes were stashed away underneath one of the beds. Both beds were covered with a jumble of clothes and gray woolen blankets. More clothes hung from hooks on the walls. The room was freezing. They had left what little heat there was five flights below.

Berthe suddenly longed for the clean country air and her grand-mère's immaculate farmhouse. She felt suffocated by the smells, intimidated by her new surroundings. Who were these people she would be forced to share a roof with? She had difficulty understanding Madame Lisette. Was she joking or serious? Was the girl she was to share a room with really a thief?

"I like my guests to keep things neat," Madame Lisette said. She bent down and with both arms gathered up a huge pile of clothes and dumped them on the bed with the bags and boxes stashed beneath it. Then she separated two woolen blankets from the pile, folded them neatly, and placed them on the foot of the empty bed. Berthe noticed that the sheets and pillowcase were either dirty or gray from the lint of the blankets. "The rest of our little family is at work. You will meet them all soon enough. Rent is four francs a week payable every Friday. But you don't have to worry about it. The mill takes it out of your wages and pays me directly. The cost includes a hearty supper pail to take to work and a hot dinner every night," she added as if to justify the amount.

"But, madame, I'm not even sure what I'm getting paid at the mill."

"They didn't tell you?" Madame Lisette turned to look at her, hands on her hips.

Berthe shook her head.

"How old are you, dear?" the woman asked.

"Fourteen," Berthe said.

"Ah, good. You will probably get about seven francs a week. I believe the beatings are free." Berthe felt a wave of fear run through her. Madame Lisette threw back her head and laughed and laughed. Finally, she caught her breath and wiped her eyes with a lace hanky she had pulled from her sleeve. "You can hang up your gowns in the armoire," she said.

"What gowns?" Berthe asked, confused.

"What armoire?" Madame Lisette answered back, again roaring with laughter. Her bosom shook so much Berthe thought it would slide off her chest onto the floor.

"One has to keep laughing. There is too much in this life to cry about," the woman said, chortling to herself as she left.

Berthe took her small valise and placed it on the empty bed. A smoking oil lantern dimly lit the crowded room. She opened her bag and unwrapped the picture of the beautiful white tulle dress, which she'd carried from her home in Yonville to her grand-mère's, and from her grand-mère's to here. She examined the details, analyzing how the seams were put together, how the flounces were attached. She wondered if pearls might not have been more elegant than the crystals. The woman in the illustration was standing in a beautiful ballroom, glancing over her right shoulder as if someone was approaching. Was she waiting to be asked to dance? What kind of music was playing? This was certainly a gown that called for a waltz.

What a joke. What a fool you are. Dreaming of dresses and dancing in ballrooms while you're living in a smelly hovel.

She looked out the small window. There were tile roofs and chimneys of all shapes and sizes as far as she could see. She had never experienced a view like this. The panorama gave her a feeling of being both above the city and part of it at the same time.

For a moment her fears were forgotten and she was infused with a new energy. The sky was tinged red-orange with the last light of the setting sun. This wasn't a town, it was a city. And despite feeling cold and frightened, she was filled with a great excitement. She had a job. She would be earning a living. She

would be working with fabrics, beautiful fabrics, the kind her
mother pored over at Monsieur Lheureux's shop. And if she
worked hard enough perhaps they would increase her salary. No,
not perhaps, for certain. She had no idea what her job would be
but she was sure she would excel at it. She would be the best
worker in the entire mill. And they would see her value and the
seven francs would grow to fourteen and then twenty and soon
she would be the proud owner of soft leather boots and a new
dress with braid around the collar and jet buttons . . . and a bonnet with black ostrich feathers.

She yawned then, overcome with a great fatigue. She had
traveled a long way in a very short time. She lay down on the
bed, closed her eyes, and within moments drifted off to sleep.
She was awakened by the sound of heavy footsteps pounding up
the stairway.

Berthe opened her eyes. Once they adjusted to the dim light
she could see the figure of a very tall, very broad-shouldered girl
standing over her bed. Berthe sat up and backed into the corner
of the bed.

"What do you think you're doing in my room?" demanded
the girl.

"I'm supposed to share it with you," Berthe shot back. She
fought hard to keep her voice steady and strong.

"Sez who?" asked the girl, leaning in closer, bringing her face
to within inches of Berthe's. Her breath smelled of onions.

"Madame Lisette." Berthe sat up and swung her legs over
onto the floor.

"And what is this?" the girl asked, snatching at the drawing of
the dress on Berthe's bed.

"That's mine," said Berthe, reaching for it. "Give it back."
There was something about Berthe's tone that made her comply.

"Who wants your filthy drawing," she said, dropping it on the floor. "And what are you doing with a picture like that?"

"It's one of my mother's dresses." Berthe carefully folded up the drawing.

"Oh, and who's your mother, the Queen of England?" Clutching her stomach, the older girl doubled over with guffaws. Suddenly she stopped. "You touch any of my things and I'll kill you." She shoved aside a pile of clothes and sat down on the opposite bed. Her rust-colored eyes were the same color as the freckles that exploded across her face, and she had blood-red hair that seemed to want to fly away from her head. It was barely restrained by the single fat braid that hung down to the middle of her back. Her legs were so long and skinny her stockings rumpled around her ankles. She wore a tattered gray dress that came to her knees and an apron of the same color over it. Her large hands were bruised and covered with welts.

"Why would I want to touch your dirty things?" said Berthe. The girl seemed to think this over.

"Make sure that you don't," she said, swinging her legs up on the bed. "Just remember, this was my room first."

Berthe had no idea what possessed her to talk back to the bigger, older, and angrier girl, but somehow she sensed that if she didn't assert herself now she would be very sorry later. She took a deep breath and said, "Well, now it's *our* room, isn't it?" The other girl glared at her.

There was the faint sound of the dinner bell and without a word the tall girl rose and clomped downstairs. After a few minutes, Berthe followed her.

Her first impression of the people seated at the long trestle tables was that they were asleep. They sat with their heads bowed or resting on their hands while bowls of soup were distributed. Berthe guessed that most of the residents were around her age— anywhere from twelve to sixteen—though some seemed as young as ten. There were a half dozen older women and men as well. Madame Lisette stood at the head of one table ladling soup out of the big pot.

"Ah, *mes enfants,* tonight I have outdone myself. This is my most superb soup yet. However do I do it, you ask? How does one spin gold out of hay? The recipes for all my soups shall remain a secret. They will die with me."

"Now, that will be a day to celebrate," someone whispered.

"Who would want the recipe for this swill?" another mumbled.

Madame Lisette paid no heed. She looked up at Berthe in the doorway. "Ah, here is our newest member. Hélène, introduce your sister to her new family."

"She's no cursed sister of mine," snarled the redheaded girl from her seat at the far end of one of the tables. She was squeezed in between two smaller girls who never looked up from their bowls.

"Sit here next to Monsieur Ratatouille. He will take good care of you." Madame Lisette indicated a spot next to a young boy whose face was almost buried in his soup bowl. When he glanced up, it took everything Berthe could do not to gasp. She understood why Madame Lisette had called him ratatouille. His face was a mass of painful-looking red eruptions. He quickly looked down again.

"*Bonsoir,*" said Berthe, picking up her spoon. The boy didn't answer. She peered down at the bowl of soup in front of her. She touched her spoon to the surface and a film of grease parted to reveal strange pieces of what appeared to be vegetables with a few chunks of what might have been sausage. It smelled abominable.

But she was famished and she couldn't afford not to eat. At the far end of the table in front of Hélène was a basket of bread. Berthe summoned up her courage.

"Pass the bread, *s'il vous plaît*," she called out.

Hélène ignored her. One of the girls sitting next to her started to lift the basket. Hélène's hand came down hard on the girl's wrist.

"Girls, girls," sang Madame Lisette. "Please let's not squabble. There's plenty of food to go around. More soup anyone? Don't be shy. I have half a full pot here."

"You're welcome to give it to the pigs," the boy next to Berthe whispered.

Berthe was more than a little intimidated by Hélène. But she knew from her experience with her grand-mère that she couldn't let the girl bully her, especially when it came to getting enough to eat. She stood, walked down to the end of the table, reached over, and tried to pick up the basket of bread. Hélène's hand held it down. A silent but serious tug-of-war ensued until with her other hand Berthe knocked over a pitcher of water. The water ran off the table and directly onto Hélène's lap.

"Why, you little snake!" Hélène shouted. She jumped up and brushed the water off her lap. Berthe picked up the breadbasket and returned to her place at the table. All eyes were upon her.

"Now you're in for it," the boy with the bad skin mumbled into his soup.

"She doesn't scare me," said Berthe. But her hand was shaking as she picked up a piece of hard bread.

Immediately after the meal she went straight up to bed. She lay there for a long time afraid to shut her eyes for fear she would be attacked in her sleep. But finally, the hot soup and the long hours of travel did their work and she drifted off to a dreamless slumber.

She awoke late the next morning and looked over at the other bed. It was empty. Hélène was nowhere to be seen. Where had she spent the night? And then Berthe had a wonderful thought: Perhaps the girl was as afraid of Berthe as Berthe was of her.

It was Sunday. She had the whole day before her. There was nothing to do until she started work early Monday morning. Berthe squirmed underneath the gray blankets. She desperately needed to urinate. She leaned over and looked under the bed. There was no chamber pot. She would have to go down all five flights and out the back to the privy in order to relieve herself. She just hoped she could hold it until then.

She dressed quickly, putting on the few clothes that she hadn't slept in. The water in the pitcher had a thin sheet of ice. She broke the ice with the handle of her hairbrush and poured the water into the washbowl. Then she wet the corner of her flannel and quickly scrubbed her face.

Madame Lisette met her at the bottom of the stairs.

"Ah, off to church, Mademoiselle Bovary?" she asked.

"No, madame. To the privy," said Berthe. Madame Lisette laughed.

"Well, sometimes nature calls even before God," she said. "The cathedral is down the street on your left. You've missed the early mass but the next one is at ten o'clock."

"Thank you, madame." Berthe didn't care to explain that she had no interest in church, that her parents had never taken her, and that the only so-called religious instruction she had ever received was from Félicité, whose version of the Eighth Commandment was revised to read: Thou shalt not steal unless when absolutely necessary.

"Of course this is my day of rest as well," Madame Lisette said, "so my family have to fend for themselves when it comes to supper. We'll have a nice hot Sunday soup tonight. There is a *boulangerie* across from the church. Their prices are not too dear." Just hearing the word *boulangerie* caused Berthe's mouth to water. She remembered the meal from the night before and realized her stomach was empty. She had one franc fifty in her purse left over from her train ticket. But that would have to last until she received her first wages.

After her visit to the privy, she left the boardinghouse and walked down the street toward the church. Before she had gone a few steps her feet began aching. Her toes were so stiff she felt they were about to snap off. There was an old newspaper in the gutter. She picked it up, folded a few pages, and stuffed the paper inside her clogs. But within minutes her feet were as cold as ever.

Across the street, warm lights and irresistible smells were coming from the *boulangerie.* Berthe crossed over and stood for a long time gazing at the window. Doily-covered plates held pastries: *mille-feuilles* oozing with custard, tiny jeweled tartlets topped with gleaming raspberries and peaches, a mountain of Chantilly cream studded with chocolate profiteroles, and a majestic towering glazed *croquembouche.* She inhaled the delicious aromas: toasted almonds, vanilla, and cinnamon. She had never in her life seen such an array of delicious desserts. In the corner of the window, almost hidden like plain stepsisters, were the freshly baked baguettes, brioche, and flaky croissants. Berthe swallowed hard. The woman inside beckoned to her.

Berthe entered, knowing she couldn't afford to spend even a small sum on such treats.

"What can I offer you, mademoiselle?" said the woman behind the counter.

"Oh, nothing, madame," said Berthe. "I was just admiring your display."

"Come now, my pastries cannot be admired merely with the eyes. They are made to be eaten. Try one."

"I'm not hungry, thank you, madame. I just had my breakfast," said Berthe, trying to swallow the saliva that kept gathering in her mouth. *Get out of here before you drool all over the woman's floor.*

"Here, have a slice of my *tarte aux pommes.* I'll cut you a small piece. People swear it is the best they've ever had."

She handed Berthe a thin wedge of the tarte on a piece of paper. It was in her mouth before she knew it. Berthe wanted it to last forever. But the pastry was so light and so perfectly baked that it melted away. The creamy rich custard slipped down her throat followed by the tender cinnamon-laced apples and light flaky crust. Berthe practically swooned from the richness of it.

"Good, yes?" the woman said. Berthe nodded, still savoring the sweetness. "I normally charge ten centimes for that. But it is a slow day. I will let you have it for five." Berthe felt the tart start to come back up. She coughed.

"But, madame, I have no money. I thought…" The woman's smile vanished. Two cherry-red spots appeared on her cheeks.

"You thought what? That I give away my pastries to any street urchin who walks in the door? Get out of here and don't come back." The woman turned away and began rearranging the fruit tarts on a sheet of bakery paper. Berthe wanted to explain herself but could find no words. On her way out she snatched another slice of apple tart off the tray.

"Why, you little thief!" the woman yelled after her. Her heart racing, Berthe took off down the street as fast as she could run. Once she realized the baker wasn't coming after her, she slowed to a stop and caught her breath. She wrapped the tart in the piece of paper the woman had given her and put it carefully in her apron pocket.

It was not an auspicious beginning for her in her newly adopted home of Lille, she realized. Now she could never go back to that shop or even to the church across the street. Just as well, since she was probably already damned to hell for being a thief, unless Félicité's eighth commandment was in fact true.

Another part of her knew there was no such thing as hell; there was just her life as she endeavored to live it. She controlled her own destiny. She took the apple tart from her pocket and ate it in three quick bites. She decided there would be much more where that came from. But how, and from where, she didn't know.

Berthe spent the rest of the day slowly walking the streets, drinking in the sights and sounds and smells. She was so entranced with everything she saw that she forgot about her cold feet, her hunger, and her loneliness. She devoured the city with her eyes. She came to a street of shops, one more glorious than the next. The first shop was a *parfumerie*. She thought of her mother's lavender scent. Before her were shelves and shelves of the most beautiful bottles, a set of three cut-glass crystal bottles encased in an ornate gilt caddy, a hand-enameled egg-shaped white opal glass held by a small golden figure of a woman, a sky-blue opaline bottle decorated with a gold filigree collar. She could only imagine what incredible fragrances they held. She moved on to Madame Marnault's Couturier next door. In the window was an evening dress modeled by a headless form. Its skirt filled the entire window. Berthe immediately felt a wave of pleasure. She eagerly read the calligraphy on the white card in the corner of the window:

"This elegant ball gown is made of silk. The underskirt is composed of white glacé silk, ornamented at the bottom with four puffings of pink silk, each puffing being edged with quilled silk ribbon. Additional fabrics available. Inquire within." She wondered how much a dress like this would cost. What would it feel like to wear it, to dance in it? To have all eyes on her? She would love to one day own a gown like this. Even more, she wished to be able to create something just as beautiful. Personally, she felt the quilled silk edging was a little too much. She gave a deep sigh and moved on.

Next to the dressmaker's shop was the shoemaker's shop. Affixed to the side of the building above the door of the shop was a large wooden boot. On the boot were the words *M. Gregoire Beautiful Boots Elegant Footwear.* Berthe studied the shoes in the window. There were high boots, short boots, boots with narrow lasts. Boots made of silk and lace, boots embroidered with metallic thread. Boots with buttons, everyday boots with laces. Boots with elastic gussets that could be easily slipped on or off, fancy opera boots made of brocade and satin, and boots of soft, supple-looking leather on sturdy heels. M. Gregoire was certainly a master of boots. This is where she would come to purchase hers.

She imagined what the new boots would feel like. She looked down at her clumsy clogs. She tried on the satin opera boots in her imagination . . . Then what to go with this footwear? She envisioned herself in the pink silk ball gown. She lifted the heavy flounced skirt as she put the toe of her satin opera boot on the first step of her carriage. *Her* carriage, not a public vehicle. She heard the sound of the many crinolines whoosh as she sat back against the velvet cushions. She took a deep breath and inhaled the lily of the valley perfume she had so delicately placed on her wrists and behind her ears. Her ears, from which pearl and diamond chandelier earrings swung gently back and forth. She yawned, bringing her white kid-gloved fingers to her mouth. It was so boring being so rich and beautiful with no one to admire her, no one to kiss her hand, no one to inhale the scent from her long white neck, no one to admire her slim ankle and small satin-clad foot. In her vision, her foot had begun to ache, to throb with pain and cold. Oh, that shoemaker had gotten her measurements all wrong. She would have to take the opera boots back.

She looked down and was momentarily surprised to see she was still wearing a pair of clumsy wooden clogs.

CHAPTER 10

First Day of Work

IT WAS ALMOST FIVE O'CLOCK AND JUST GROWING DARK WHEN Berthe returned to Madame Lisette's boardinghouse. Where was everyone? she wondered. The tables were set with bowls and spoons awaiting the Sunday evening meal. She heard movement from upstairs. Slowly people entered the kitchen yawning, rubbing their eyes, and looking as if they'd just gotten out of bed. That was when she realized that was exactly where they had been all day. In order to stay warm and forget about their hunger the entire houseful of workers had spent their one day off in bed under the covers, dreaming no doubt of warmer weather and better meals.

Then she saw the soup. It was the same soup as the night before but with pieces of turnip added. Berthe bit into one of the turnips. It was barely cooked. It took all the strength in her jaws to chew it.

"I can't wait until we can go back to cold oatcakes," mumbled the boy with bad skin. Suddenly there were shouts from the other end of the room. Two of the men were throwing wild punches at each other. Neither one had managed to land any-thing above the shoulders of the other.

"Gimme back my bread, you thieving scum," panted one man.

"Ain't yours. It's my portion. You already got two pieces, you foul-smelling pig."

"Why are they fighting?" Berthe asked the boy.

"Oh, those two they's always stealing bread from each other. It happens almost every night. All depends on the temperature outside. The colder it is the more they go at it. I think they just do it to work up a sweat. Get theyselves all warm. It don't hap-pen in the summer, I can tell you that," said the boy.

Madame Lisette walked around checking people's bowls. She bent over and picked up random pieces of uneaten turnip.

"Waste not, want not. Finish your *potage*," she said to Berthe "or there won't be no chocolate soufflé for you." Berthe now knew better than to take the bait. "You going to be needing that?" asked Madame Lisette, pointing to a piece of turnip on the side of Berthe's bowl.

"No, madame, you can have it."

Madame Lisette picked up the turnip and dropped it in her pot.

"Excuse me, madame, is it possible to get another blanket for tonight?" Berthe asked. The landlady tilted her head as if Berthe had posed a philosophically complex question.

"I gave you two blankets, didn't I?" she finally said.

"Yes, madame, but the room is quite cold."

"That cannot be. You are on the top floor. And as everyone knows, heat rises. You receive all the heat from the rest of the house. It should be quite warm. And if it isn't you can always throw another log onto the fireplace."

Berthe didn't bother to remark that there was no fireplace. Seeing that Berthe was not going to respond to her joke the landlady said again, in a louder voice, "You can always throw another log onto the fireplace." The room burst into delayed and somewhat forced laughter. "Yes, take the roasted mutton off the spit and throw another log onto the fire." Madame Lisette gave Berthe a little poke in the arm. "You are not laughing, mademoiselle," she observed.

"No, madame, it's not funny. It's cold." Berthe felt her cheeks flush with irritation.

"This is the coldest winter in memory," said Madame Lisette, as if it was a fact to be proud of. "Except for last year. That was the coldest winter in memory." Everyone laughed again. "My dear girl, you must learn to laugh more. Laughter is what warms the body and satisfies the soul."

"Just like the pissin' soup," someone shouted.

"Watch your filthy mouth," Madame Lisette said to no one in particular. "Well, dear mademoiselle, tomorrow is your first day of work. So be sure to get a good night's sleep."

"As if that will make a bloody difference," someone said. A few people laughed. Others were too tired to even look up from their soup bowls. Berthe had never seen a group of more exhausted people. Even the farmworkers at the end of harvesttime hadn't seemed so enervated. She suddenly worried: *Am I up to this work?* But of course she was. She would be working with fabric, wouldn't she? It was what she was meant to do.

Berthe was surprised to see that there was again no sign of Hélène either at supper or when she entered their room some time later. She took off her clogs and got into bed.

Her teeth were chattering. It was too cold and she was far too nervous about the next day to sleep. Maybe Madame Lisette was right about the laughing. She tried it.

"Ha ha ha ha." She pushed the air out of her lungs. And soon she began to feel warmer, albeit a little foolish. Just as she began to fall asleep, she heard Hélène stumble into the room. She was moaning and groaning. At first, Berthe tried to ignore her but the moaning continued.

"What's the matter?" Berthe said, sitting up.

"Nothing. Go to sleep," came the slurred reply. Berthe lit the oil lamp. She gasped. Hélène's face was covered with bruises. Her upper lip was split and swollen. She was spitting blood into a dirty rag.

"What happened to you?" Berthe asked.

"Leave me alone," Hélène said, falling back on the bed. As she lay there, she unwrapped a napkin. In it were four soft white rolls. She took one and began eating it, chewing gingerly on one side of her mouth.

"Where did you get those?" Berthe asked.

"I stole 'em from our dear landlady, Madame Private Pantry," Hélène snarled.

"Who?"

"How do you think our Madame Lisette got so fat? Not by eating oatcakes. She's got a secret larder filled with food."

"Did she beat you?"

"No, her watchdog of a son beat me. But I bit him hard. And I can tell you"—she held up the roll—"this was well worth it. And don't be looking at me. You're not getting any of this. You can steal your own."

"I already have," boasted Berthe. "I stole an apple tart from the *boulangerie* across from the church." She felt that Hélène was looking at her with new respect. Perhaps they could be friends, she thought.

It seemed Berthe had just closed her eyes when the morning bell rang from downstairs. She lifted her head and peered out the window. It was still dark outside. After a hurried breakfast of watered-down coffee and stale bread she was given a supper pail which contained her ration of oatcake—oats with a dollop of fat covered by boiled milk and water.

She followed the other children and adults down the hill toward the cotton mill. She had a hard time keeping up with them as they hurried along the street. Her clogs kept slipping off her feet. She had felt breathless and anxious from the moment she had opened her eyes that morning.

Roucher, the mill manager, was standing in the doorway of his office watching the workers file in. He stopped Berthe.

"Bovary, come here." He handed her a piece of paper and a pen. "Just put your mark here."

"My mark?"

"Put an *X* here," he said, pointing to a space at the bottom of the page.

"You mean my signature?"

"Oh, fancy that, she knows how to sign her name," he announced to the workers as they filed past.

She signed her name at the bottom, then summoned up her courage and said, "Can I please read what I signed?" He was taken aback. Berthe was proud of the fact that she had been reading her mother's books since she was a small child.

"It's nothing. Just a standard work agreement. Do you want to get paid?"

"Yes, sir."

"Well, then don't be wasting your time reading what doesn't concern you," he said, snatching the paper out of her hands.

"And you don't need to be going around boasting about the fact you can read and write. We don't need any of your airs here. Now for the rules." He motioned a group of workers who were just entering the mill to stop where they were.

"But, Monsieur Roucher, we be late," said one of the girls.

"I said, now for The Rules," repeated Roucher in a louder voice.

The workers recited in unison:

"Do not leave your workstation without overseers' permission.

"If you are late you will not be paid.

"Workers who produce poor quality work will be discharged.

"There will be no talking except what is necessary to the work.

"Those who fail to obey the orders will be punished."

"Well done," said Monsieur Roucher. "Now, stop dawdling and get to work." He turned back to Berthe. "Bovary, go inside and report to Clothier, the Master Carder."

Once inside Berthe was amazed at the size of the factory, a long, high-ceilinged space that seemed to go on forever. As large as the room was, it was crowded from end to end with what Berthe took to be spinning machines. She was assaulted by the odor of rancid animal fat. This was not at all how she expected the factory to smell. She had expected the scent of the lavender sachet her mother kept hanging in her armoire. And where were the lovely fabrics? All she saw was spool after spool of dirty white thread. The noise in the room was deafening. She had to shout the words "Monsieur Clothier?" to one of the workers. He pointed out Clothier, who stood on a high wooden platform. From his vantage point the Master Carder could view the activity on the entire floor. Berthe stood at the base of the platform and looked up.

Noticing her for the first time, he bent down and shouted, "See Marnet. He's the Overlooker. He'll show you what to do." Clearly, the Master Carder was too exalted a position to have to deal with training a new hire. Clothier pointed to a man who was wiping down the parts of one of the machines with a greasy rag. Berthe made her way over to him. There were several men who seemed to be in charge of maintaining the machinery, and they turned from their work to ogle her. A few of them whistled.

"Ooh, là là! What a beauty," shouted one.

"Enjoy it now. Your looks won't last long," said another.

Marnet was a huge man who was missing part of his right arm up to the elbow. With his left hand he dipped the rag into a bucket of what turned out to be just what it reeked of: animal fat. Berthe assumed there was a nicer part of the factory where they made the finer fabrics. The smell was beginning to nauseate her. She couldn't imagine working in this odorous room.

"Come here, miss. Tell Marnet your name," the one-armed man said.

"Berthe Bovary," she said, trying not to breathe through her nose.

"Ever done this kind of work before?" he asked.

She shook her head. Her stomach seemed to have dislodged from its moorings and was nervously moving about as if looking for a place to re-anchor.

"Ah, I got me an authentic virgin," he roared. Some of the men snickered. Marnet led her through the narrow aisles between the machinery. His stump was wrapped thickly in rags and he used it almost as if it were a hand, pushing levers and gears, wiping down machine parts, occasionally giving the young workers a friendly pounding on the head.

"Don't cross him or he'll stump you," one of the older boys said as they walked by.

"This ain't no game," Marnet said, suddenly getting very serious. "This here's your life's work." He stopped and turned to her.

"Here comes the grand indoctrination," someone announced.

"Every time we get someone new, he acts as if he's the bloody heir to the cotton throne," remarked another.

"Do you know how long I been gainfully employed at this here fine establishment?" Marnet asked Berthe, gesturing with his good arm to the large room around them.

"No, sir, I have no idea." Her mouth was dry and her eyes felt as if they were made of tissue paper.

"Twenty-nine years, come this February. There's not a day that goes by that I don't thank my lord Jesus Christ for the honor. It's what's kept bread in me mouth and allowed me the glorious life I have today."

"He calls this a life?" shouted a boy next to her who was unwinding tangled thread from a bobbin.

"He thinks he's one of the *fils*," said someone else. Clearly Marnet heard the other workers' comments but he acted as if he didn't care. He was too caught up in his own somewhat uneven rhetoric.

"I would give me right arm for Rappelais et Fils." He looked down at his stump as if noticing it for the first time. "Uh-oh, looks like I already did," he said, roaring with laughter. He tapped Berthe's shoulder with his foreshortened arm. She pulled back in horror. "Follow me, Mademoiselle Beautiful Bovary, and you shall see the wonders of cotton-making revealed before your very eyes." Her head had already begun to ache from the loud clatter and whirring of the machines slamming back and forth as he led her over to one of the huge contraptions.

"This here is the carding machine. After the cotton gets beaten up the carders line up the fibers to make them easier to spin. You got to watch your hands here. I can surely testify to that." He waved his stump merrily. "These rollers have lots of small teeth that get closer and closer together and that makes a sliver, which is this here." He held up a thick rope of fibers. "Now slivers get separated into rovings. And rovings is what we got to deal with. This here is the roving." He showed her a long thin strand of cotton which was about the thickness of a pencil. "This here spinning machine takes the roving and twists and turns it into yarn." Marnet motioned her to follow him through the huge, noisy, greasy-smelling mechanical structures.

Berthe noticed that no one looked up from his or her work. They seemed chained to their machines. Even the men and boys who had previously looked at her with admiration were now intent on their work. She felt as if she were walking through someone else's nightmare. Even in her wildest imagination, she could never have dreamed up this factory.

"Here you got the spinning area. These glorious machines take the roving off their bobbins and feed 'em through more rollers so that the roving gets to be the same size yarn. Then the yarn gets twisted and twisted and rolled onto the spinning bobbin. After that you got the plying," Marnet said, pointing out yet another machine. "The plying gets done by pulling the yarn from two bobbins and twisting it together in the opposite direction that it was spun in. Then after all that spinning and plying it goes to a warping room. And this, *chère* Mademoiselle Bovary of the soon-to-be-cotton-making Bovarys, is where you come in."

They came to another large area where there were racks and racks of bobbins set up to hold the thread that was ready to go onto the loom for weaving.

"Now the warping and the weaving and the thread count—that's for another time. Too much information will fill your pretty head with lint. The important thing is this—" Marnet held up a large bolt of plain cotton muslin. "Feel it," he said.

Berthe ran her fingers over the white rough-textured fabric. She hated the feel of it. How hideously different this was from the smooth fabric she had expected.

"Of course, this isn't the fine stuff. That's in another factory. We just do the basics here. But it's a God-given, glorious trade. One that will keep you fat and happy for years to come."

Berthe looked around the room. None of the workers looked fat or happy. She had never seen a sorrier-looking group of people. Young girls and boys her age, and even smaller children, seemed to almost be swallowed up by the work. Their clothes were rags at best, their hair limp and dull, their complexions a sickly gray. And their bodies, especially those of the older children, seemed crippled by some unknown disease. Their spindly legs had turned inward at the knees; their elbows were enlarged and knobby; and their hands were swollen and red. Her job, as Marnet outlined it for her, was simple enough, but it was the final blow to her fantasy of work.

"They say you can read and write. I guess that means you can count as well. Alls you got to do is count the finished bobbins, mark 'em down in this here ledger when they been filled with the thread." He handed her a ledger and a pencil and then indicated a small stool in the corner. "If you just do your job, which I must say is a blessed easy one for a beginner, mind your p's and q's, don't make no trouble, and don't listen to the rest of the hordes, you'll do just fine." He gave her head a friendly tap with his stump and he was off.

She sat and watched and counted while others made the bobbins. After a few hours her back and legs hurt from sitting hunched over on the small stool. She wished she could move around like the others. Halfway through her tedious and endless first morning, she heard a terrible scream from the room next door. Berthe held her breath. She waited for the sound of another scream but it never came. She found the absence of the second scream even more frightening. Her breakfast rose up in her throat and she thought she might be sick all over the floor.

Marnet rushed up to Berthe.

"Good news, Madame Brilliant Bovary, you've got a promotion and on your first day," he said breathlessly. "Come with me." She followed him to the room next door. "I am pleased to announce that you are hereby promoted to Piecer," he announced.

"What is that, sir?"

"A position of great responsibility is what that is. A Piecer leans over the spinning machine to repair the broken threads. We usually give this job to the smaller ones, but you look to be fast on your feet and light with your fingers. Though watch out for that wheel there, or you'll be minus a few."

This didn't seem like a promotion to Berthe. Quite the opposite.

"Just thank your lucky stars they didn't make you a Scavenger," whispered a small girl at the machine next to her. "Although you are far too big for that."

"What's a Scavenger?" asked Berthe, not taking her eyes off the moving machinery.

"There's one there," said the girl, pointing to a small figure who scurried underneath the moving machine like a mouse after cheese. "Only the very littlest ones can be Scavengers. Their job is to sweep up the loose cotton from underneath the machinery," the girl whispered. "It's quite scary down there under the moving machine, and then of course you breathe in all that dust and lint. It's by far the worst job."

"And this is a good job?" Berthe asked.

"Dunno. I just started myself. They had two accidents this morning, so they're short on Piecers. It's a position of responsibility," she said, echoing Marnet's words.

"Du Croix, come here," Marnet shouted across the room. "I am putting the virgin in your hands. Show her how to do her job."

Du Croix turned out to be none other than Hélène. She scowled at Berthe.

"Get someone else to show her. I have to sleep with the bitch. That's bad enough."

"Dearest Du Croix, I know Christ the Lord gave you a mouth but he don't mean you to use it in defiance of your superiors, me being the most immediate one. Get over here and do your job, or I'll give you a good what for with my trusty stumpy."

Hélène grudgingly showed Berthe the ropes, or threads to be precise. How she had to stand with her right foot forward and her right side facing the frame in order to mend the broken threads. Berthe was to stay in that same position and keep sliding sideways to the right and then to the left, never stopping, always in motion. She was to mend a break immediately by tying the two broken ends together in a simple square knot before the thread was lost in the machine. Clearly, Hélène had put in her time as a Piecer. She demonstrated the job effortlessly.

"Just keep doing this until they tell you to do something else," Hélène said, going off to her own job. It was tedious, backbreaking work. After a while, the weight of her body resting always on her right knee created an ache deep down in Berthe's hip bones. The air was filled with clouds of lint. It went into her eyes and up her nose. She began sneezing and coughing. She longed for the fresh air of her grand-mère's farm.

"You'll get used to it," the girl next to her said. "In about two weeks your lungs will be lined with the stuff and it won't hardly bother you anymore."

When the bell rang for supper Berthe was shocked to see that many of the girls couldn't straighten up. They were permanently bent over, their backs curved into the shape of the letter C.

Her oatcake was covered with a fine layer of dust. A little boy sitting next to her had something different and offered to split half of his supper with Berthe. The boy's supper was a potato pie with a piece of boiled lard. It was so thick with fat it was hard to swallow. But compared to her dry oatcake, it tasted delicious.

"What's your name?" Berthe asked.

"Antoine," said the boy. He was very small, about half her height. He had pale blond hair that stuck out of his head every which way like stalks of wheat. His face had a gray tint and looked as if it hadn't been washed in a year.

"How old are you?" Berthe asked.

"Eight going on nine." Pieces of oatcake flew out of his mouth. "You took my job, you know."

"I don't understand."

"I was hoping to get promoted to Piecer. They usually give that job to the smaller ones like me. And I could do it. I know I could. I been practicing. I could tie those knots with me eyes closed." He sighed. "I was so hoping to get out from down under."

"Down under?"

"I'm a Scavenger," he said.

"Oh," said Berthe remembering what the girl had told her about the job of Scavenger.

"Sometimes I forget about the machine and lift me stupid head and it pulls out me hair." He touched the back of his head.

"It hurts like the devil, I can tell you that. And I get that cotton dust in me throat and it tickles and tickles, and I can't stop me coughing. When I saw Violette get hurt I was happy 'cause I thought I was next in line to do her job. I don't know why they gave it to you. You're way bigger than me and you're brand-new. You don't know nothing," he said matter-of-factly.

"That's true," Berthe assured him. "Do you want me to say something to Monsieur Marnet?"

He shook his head. "It won't do no good. Once they make up their minds they don't like to change. The problem is I'm the best Scavenger they got."

"How long have you been working here?" she asked. He looked at her as if her question made no sense.

"Since I was small. Since me folks up and died." Her heart went out to him. *Poor little orphan.* And then it hit her: That's what she was. But of course, they were probably all orphans here. What else could they be to work in this awful place? The boy glanced into Berthe's supper pail.

"You gonna eat the rest of that potato?" he asked.

"No, you can have it," she said, handing him the cold greasy lump.

"Wait until Easter Sunday," he said.

"Why, what happens then?" asked Berthe.

"We get cheese and brown bread for supper," he said, his eyes lighting up. "And a whole extra franc."

"Tell you what, come Easter you may have my cheese."

"You're joking!" His eyes grew wide.

"No, I hate cheese. My grand-mère made cheese on her farm and I never liked it."

Five minutes later the bell rang again and everyone went back to their workstations. With a wave of his hand, Antoine was gone.

By the end of the first day her hands were bleeding. Her eyes and throat burned and she couldn't stop coughing. She was dizzy with fatigue. How she missed the farm. Céleste, the geese, the sweet smell of new-mown hay. She looked around her. Berthe realized that other than the few men who kept the machinery in repair there were no older people working at the mill. They were mostly children. Rather, not children, but strange gray creatures with bent backs, bowed legs, and dead eyes.

As she trudged home, a figure came up beside her.

"Don't spend your money all in one place." Berthe looked up in time to see Hélène rush past her.

"What?"

"The seventy-five centimes you earned today. Not bad for slave wages." Hélène laughed as she hurried on. Berthe's tired mind focused on the number seventy-five, blocking out the word *centime*. For one split second she felt gratified by this enormous amount. It took a minute to register that seventy-five centimes was just short of a franc. At seventy-five centimes a day she was earning less than the seven francs a week Madame Lisette had predicted would be her pay. Then she realized that the rest of her wages had gone to pay for her room and board.

She thought back to the day before and her excitement about starting her first job and earning her first wages. She passed by the dress shop she had seen that day. She turned her eyes away from the ball gown in the window. She couldn't bear to be reminded of the luxury that was so far out of her reach. She hardly remembered walking the rest of the way home. She was too tired for dinner and went straight up to her room and fell into bed.

On the second morning she woke with every bone in her young body aching. By the end of the day she felt as if she had been doing this work her entire life. On the third day, her index finger became tangled in a twist of thread and she almost lost the tip of it before freeing it. Her nights were filled with the endless repetition of her daily work. In her dreams she ran up and down the long track tying and retying knot after knot of broken thread. On the fourth day she began to hallucinate, seeing patterns of flowers and leaves appear on the dirty white cotton. The fifth day melted into the sixth and on the seventh day she didn't just rest, she collapsed. On the second Sunday she forced herself to get up. Hélène slept on, her mouth open, her red braid draped over the edge of the narrow bed. As tired as she was Berthe desperately needed to get out, to breathe in the relatively fresh air of Lille. The streets held the only possibility of distraction from what was now her dreary working life.

But today the cold was too much even for her. Her feet and face ached from the bitter wind and she was forced to return early in the afternoon.

Upon entering her room, she discovered Hélène going through the contents of her valise. The big girl seemed totally unembarrassed at being caught.

"What are you doing? Those are my things." Berthe stood in the doorway, her hands on her hips.

"Of course they are. It's your bag, ain't it? And here's your very own mother's fancy froufrou," Hélène said, holding up the illustration from Berthe's mother's fashion magazine.

"Give that to me," Berthe said, trying to grab it out of the other girl's hands. Hélène backed away, waving the paper above her head as she danced in place.

"A fancy lady goin' to town needs a wiggle in her gown," she sang, swinging her hips. Berthe suddenly reached out and grabbed Hélène's long braid. Using all her weight, she yanked back with both hands, knocking the bigger girl off balance.

"Ooowww, let go!" screamed Hélène. She fell back on the floor pulling Berthe with her. She grabbed Berthe's neck and began choking her. Berthe felt her throat closing and she struggled for air. Swinging wildly with her fists she landed a sharp blow directly on the bridge of Hélène's nose. "Why, you little thug." Hélène let go of Berthe's throat and clutched her nose. Blood poured out between her fingers. Berthe had never hit anyone or anything in her life. She was astonished at what she had done.

Hélène pushed herself up with one hand and looked around for a weapon to hit Berthe with. They both saw the umbrella at the same moment, but Berthe got to it first. She raised it above her head and was about to beat Hélène on the shoulders, but changed her mind. Hélène was trying to protect herself with one arm while the other hand was still occupied with staunching the flow of blood from her nose. Berthe reached into her apron pocket and pulled out a clean rag.

"Here, wipe your stupid nose," she said.

"I don't want your filthy rag," snarled Hélène.

"You're bleeding all over the floor," Berthe pointed out. "You're going to slip and fall in your own blood and break your ugly neck."

"What do you care?"

"I don't. But I don't want to have to drag your big fat body down the stairs."

Hélène seemed to consider this for a moment.

"You could push me out the window," she said, suddenly grinning.

"What if you land on some poor bystander? Then that would be murder," observed Berthe.

"Wait till Monsieur Roucher walks by and you can push me out then. It would be my great pleasure to flatten the bugger like a pancake." Berthe tried to keep from laughing. Hélène removed the rag from her nose. It had stopped bleeding. She threw the rag on the floor and yanked the umbrella out of Berthe's hands. Berthe stood ready, her hands raised and clenched into fists. Suddenly, Hélène began to laugh.

"Oh, you're scaring me," Hélène said between guffaws. "I give up. I surrender. I'm your prisoner." She laughed and laughed until Berthe put down her fists and began laughing herself. "I can't afford to have you as me enemy. You're much too dangerous. So, starting today, I'll be your friend."

"I don't want you as my friend," Berthe said. "You're a thief."

"Well, it takes one to know one," said Hélène. And they both laughed. Hélène reached under her bed and pulled out a cloth bag. From the bag she removed a large paper book. "Do you want to see something hilarious?"

Berthe recognized her mother's favorite ladies' periodical, *La Corbeille.* The very same journal that Emma Bovary had spent hours poring over. She felt a pang in her stomach.

"Where did you get that?"

"I borrowed it from Madame Lisette. She'll never notice it's gone. She has a whole stack of these." She sat down on her bed and opened the periodical. "Have you ever seen anything so ridiculous? Just like that fancy picture of yours." She pointed to an illustration of four women dressed in ball gowns. They were strangely shaped figures with unnaturally long necks and arms, and no shoulders to speak of. "Where do they think they're going all dressed up like that?"

"To a ball or to the opera or to some other formal evening engagement," said Berthe knowingly.

"But ain't this dress the silliest thing you've ever seen?" Hélène said, singling out one of the gowns. "How can you even sit in something like that?"

"I don't think they do sit," Berthe said. "I think they probably just dance the night away." She read the description from underneath the illustration. " 'An evening dress of white silk with two skirts. The lower one having a flounce of lace, headed by a puffing of silk caught up at regular intervals with delicate sprays of crimson salvia.' "

"Saliva!" cried Hélène, doubled over with laughter. "Caught up in saliva!"

"*Salvia,*" corrected Berthe. "It's part of the mint family."

"Oh, ain't we the educated one," Hélène sniffed.

"My mother had lots of these periodicals," explained Berthe.

"And she read them to you?"

Berthe nodded. Her mind was suddenly filled with memories of her mother. Berthe knew she had her mother's affinity for clothes. She could tell just by looking at an illustration in *La Corbeille* which gowns were overdone, which ones had the right lines to flatter any figure. *Perhaps we are not so very different, after all.*

She remembered watching as her mother got dressed to go for the first time to the opera at Rouen. This was almost a year after the end of her affair with Monsieur Boulanger. Attending the opera had been another idea hatched by Berthe's father and Monsieur Homais in an effort to raise her mother's poor spirits. Her mother had ordered a new evening gown particularly for the occasion. As with the riding costume, it was hard to tell if she was more thrilled about the event or what she was to wear to it.

Getting ready was a process that took her well over an hour. She seemed unaware of Berthe's presence, as the child sat in the corner watching her. Emma Bovary removed her silk *peignoir* and stood naked before the large gilt mirror that hung in the corner of her bedroom. Berthe's eyes widened. She had never seen her mother without clothes. Emma turned this way and that, admiring her reflection. Berthe was struck by how different her mother's body was from her own. Is this what she would look like when she grew into womanhood? she wondered. Was it even possible? She looked down at her own flat, narrow chest covered by her white pinafore. Her mother's heavy breasts were laced with tiny blue veins and crowned with large pink nipples. She had pearl-white skin, long slender arms and legs, and a triangle of thick dark hair where her legs joined. She slipped the *peignoir* back on and called out for Félicité to come help her with her coiffure.

Félicité followed Madame Bovary's precise directions, combing the sides of her hair high on top of her head, fastening it into a topknot, and then creating individual curls so that they cascaded down her long white neck. Finally, she pinned the salvia at the top of each individual curl. The purple blossoms shone like jewels against her mother's dark hair. Berthe closed her eyes. The fact that her mother was even allowing her to be in the same room while she dressed filled her with conflicting feelings of gratitude and shame. Awe and fear.

Emma Bovary put on an ivory-white chemise and slipped into a pair of matching bloomers. The chemise was trimmed in the finest Belgian lace and strung throughout with ribbons that tied in the front. Then the hoop petticoat and an overpetticoat that had an elaborate hem of green satin ribbon leaves and vines dotted with pink rosettes. And, at last, the dress: a bottle-green satin with a fan front bodice, short-capped sleeves, and a four-tier flounced skirt. The bodice was cut very low and Emma's bosom swelled above it. She slipped her feet into pointed satin shoes which had been dyed the same green as the dress. Finally, she picked up a pair of long kid gloves and draped a white cashmere shawl around her shoulders.

"Well, how do I look?" Berthe's mother asked, as she turned slowly, her white arms outstretched.

"Oh, Maman, you look so very beautiful," Berthe whispered.

And she did. Berthe had never seen her look so lovely. She remembered reaching out to touch one of the flounces on the huge billowing skirt.

"Don't," her mother said, pulling the skirt away, "your hands are filthy." To this day Berthe could remember every ribbon, every rosette of her mother's gown but she could not, for the life of her, remember one kind word or one single kiss.

As the girls continued to thumb through *La Corbeille,* Hélène made fun of every page. Berthe tried to explain to her why the dresses were so beautiful. For some reason it was very important to her to make Hélène understand the importance of high fashion.

"Look at the detail on this skirt. And the lace. How exquisite!"

"They look like elephants dressed in hot-air balloons," said Hélène.

"The bigger the skirt, the more slender the waist appears," explained Berthe.

"The bigger the skirt, the bigger the buffoon."

"You know, this is what we do for a living," Berthe said.

"What?" exclaimed Hélène.

"Making fabric. Fabric becomes fashion. It's what Rappelais et Fils is all about."

"Stop!" Hélène screeched with laughter and clutched her stomach. "You're killing me."

Berthe had a sudden inspiration. "Come with me. I want to show you something," she said, putting on her cloak. It was still light out.

"It's freezing. I ain't going anywhere." Hélène pulled her blankets around her.

"Please, it will only take a few minutes. Besides, the walk will warm you up."

"Is it something we can steal?"

"Perhaps," said Berthe. Hélène needed no further encouragement.

They stood in front of Madame Marnault's Couturier staring at the white ball gown.

"Do you see how the tulle gives the flounces a shape and stiffness that they wouldn't have if they were made out of just plain silk?"

"What I see is a stupid dress behind a glass window of a shop that's locked up tighter than Madame Lisette's pantry. This is what we're supposed to steal?"

"We don't steal the dress. We steal the idea, the inspiration of it."

"Oh, I see. We take the idea and turn it into a ball gown made out of Rappelais et Fils's hideous cotton. Bovary, you're crazy. I'm going home. It's almost time for our disgusting Sunday night dinner." Hélène stomped off.

Berthe suddenly saw the humor of two factory girls clothed in rags, looking at a ball gown that they would never be able to afford even if they combined their wages for the next twenty years. Smiling to herself, she followed Hélène back to the boardinghouse. *And yet I can see myself in that dress. If I can see it then there must be a way for me to have it. I just have to find the way.*

CHAPTER 11

A Visitor to the Factory

MONTHS PASSED. BERTHE GREW USED TO THE ROUTINE OF FAC-tory life. Her hands became tougher and she found that she wasn't as tired at the end of the day. She enjoyed Hélène's company and learned not to let the older girl's temper intimidate her. They each had an unspoken respect for the other.

She felt a growing pride in the fact that she was earning her own way. Granted, the sum they paid her was hardly enough to live on, but still she was taking care of herself. It was something her mother never would have understood.

One Tuesday, the mill workers were all in a froth. Monsieur Rappelais himself was coming. It was one of his twice-yearly visits to the mill.

"He's a very busy man," Marnet explained to Berthe. "He's got many factories besides this one. And he's coming all the way from Paris to make sure everything is up to snuff. He's a great man, is Monsieur Rappelais. He truly cares about his workers."

"He does?" said Berthe. She found that hard to believe given the deplorable mill conditions.

"Oh, yes. You'll see. It be an honor and a privilege to work for such a fine man."

Sometime during that day when the breaks in the thread seemed to happen every two minutes Berthe became aware of someone watching her. Out of the corner of her eye she saw Monsieur Roucher, the manager, and another much taller man in a dark coat and top hat. She moved quickly up and down the frame tying the broken ends. She tried to ignore their stares, but her movements became stiff and her fingers clumsy.

"You there, come down," Roucher called.

"But, sir, I cannot. I must attend the breaks."

"Du Croix, take over for the girl," he called out to Hélène, who was just passing by with a basket of spools. "Step down at once." Berthe did as she was told. She thought she was in trouble. She stood before the two men, her hands clasped behind her back.

"Do you know who I am?" the tall man asked. He was a distinguished-looking gentleman in his late fifties. He had a strong cleft chin and bright deep-set eyes, a prominent but well-shaped nose, and a high, elegant forehead. His muttonchops were full and well trimmed and his thin mouth turned up at the corners as if he was thinking of something amusing. Berthe could smell the wonderful fragrance of pine wafting from his clothes.

"No, sir. Yes, sir. You are Monsieur Rappelais et Fils," she said, flustered.

"Well, I am not the *et Fils*. The *fils* happen to be away at school. And what is your name, mademoiselle?"

"Berthe Bovary, monsieur."

"You are doing an excellent job, Mademoiselle Bovary. What do you think of our wonderful cotton?"

"Actually, I prefer silk." She had no idea why she said what she did. Monsieur Rappelais threw back his head and laughed loudly.

"Perhaps one day you will visit my silk mills in Lyon and tell me what you think of the fabric we make there. How long have you been employed at Rappelais et Fils?"

Berthe looked at Roucher as if he had the answer. He shrugged his shoulders.

"About two months, sir," she finally said.

"Only two months?" His bright eyes burned into her face. She looked down at her feet. He picked up one of her hands and turned it over as if it were an important part of the machinery that had come loose. "Well, you have very good hands, mademoiselle. Perhaps too good for this kind of work." He ran his thumb gently up and down the calluses on her fingers. She wanted to jerk her hand away but was afraid to. He dropped her hand, then, with one finger, lifted her chin and studied her face. "Quite extraordinary," he said to Monsieur Roucher. "A real beauty."

"Yes indeed, Monsieur Rappelais," muttered Roucher. Berthe felt herself go cold all over. She hated the special attention the owner was showing her. What did it mean? What did he want? She wished she hadn't opened her mouth at all, especially about preferring silk. Would he hold that against her? It seemed wherever she turned there was some new danger. She was nervous for the rest of the day and her stomach could not hold the little food that had been provided.

At the supper break, a bell was sounded. Everyone grew very quiet. Monsieur Roucher stood on a wooden box and spoke in a loud voice.

"As you all know, we are honored today to have our own beloved Monsieur Rappelais here to cheer us on and share his words of wisdom. May I speak on behalf of the entire establishment, sir, when I say how much we appreciate your taking the time to grace us with your presence. It gives us encouragement, strength, spurs us on to even greater—"

"Yes, thank you for your kind words, Monsieur Roucher," interrupted Monsieur Rappelais. Roucher quickly stepped down and Rappelais took his place on the box. He looked around the room, seeming to take time to observe each individual face. "I want to talk to you good people about an important subject: factory reform. There are some who have accused mill owners such as myself of being indifferent to the plight of their workers. I am here to tell you that is not the case with Rappelais et Fils. You may or may not be aware of the reforms that I have made in all my mills. As of last year there are no children under the age of nine employed by Rappelais et Fils." Berthe saw Antoine and another boy his age nudge each other. "And like our neighbors in England, we have reduced the number of hours that children under thirteen may work, from sixteen hours a day to nine." There was a distinct grumbling coming from the back of the room. It did not go unnoticed by Monsieur Rappelais. "If there is anyone here of that age who is working longer hours than you are supposed to, please raise your hands."

Berthe started to raise her hand to explain that there were much younger children working much longer hours but Hélène, who was standing next to her, held it fast.

"Don't be an idiot," Hélène whispered.

"And I have asked Monsieur Roucher to make sure that strapping is kept to a minimum and only done when there is just cause. Has anyone here suffered unfair punishment? Raise your hands." Again not one hand was raised. "Well, I am well pleased with your work. And as a reward, come this Christmas you will all receive a sausage for your supper. And an extra franc in your pay." The entire room applauded loudly. Berthe's mouth watered at the very thought of sausage. "And that will be in addition to your Easter bonus." Applause filled the room once again.

"Christmas is eleven months away," whispered Hélène. "By then half of us will be dead."

"Are there any questions? Any complaints?" asked Monsieur Rappelais. "Good, good. Back to your work."

The next morning Roucher stopped Berthe on her way into the mill.

"Bovary, in here," he said. She followed him into the dark office. She stood quietly as he took a seat behind his tall desk and peered over his glasses at her. Was she in trouble? Was she going to be fired? She kept her shaking hands hidden behind her. She didn't want to show Roucher how frightened she was.

"You are a very lucky girl. You have a new job this morning. As I recall you can read and write."

"Yes, sir." She bit her lower lip.

He handed her a ledger and a pencil.

"Go out to the courtyard and mark down every bale of raw cotton that gets unloaded. Copy down the numbers that are written on the tags attached to each bale and give me a report at the end of the day."

"But what about my piecing job?" She somehow felt she was being demoted. Counting bales of cotton seemed far less important than repairing broken threads.

"This is by order of Monsieur Rappelais himself. I have already given your job to someone else."

"To Antoine? He can do the job. He's even been practicing. And he wants it badly."

Roucher laughed. "Antoine? He's my best Scavenger. And they're not easy to find, or to keep. Why don't you let me man-

age the mill? You just attend to your bales of cotton, mademoiselle."

The job was easy. She sat on a stool in the courtyard marking
down bales as they were unloaded. The air was clean and free of
the rancid smell of fat and the suffocating lint. At the end of the
day she took the book in to Roucher. He glanced at her neatly
written list.

"Can you do sums?" he asked. She nodded.

"Enter the bales that were delivered today to those in this
book," he said, pointing to a ledger that sat atop a high desk,
"and then add up the total for the week. I'll check your figures
over to make sure you don't make any errors."

The next morning Monsieur Roucher put her to work again
adding more figures in the ledger.

"Your penmanship is quite satisfactory," he said, peering over
her shoulder.

"Thank you, Monsieur Roucher," she said, not lifting her
head from her work.

"Let's see if you can take dictation," he said.

"Dictation?"

"I will dictate a letter and you will write down exactly what I
say." He put a quill, a bottle of ink, and a heavy piece of cream-
colored stationery before her.

He dictated a letter to one of his cotton suppliers. It was a
long letter filled with numbers and weights and dates of delivery.
When he was finished, he took the paper from her and read it.

"No errors and no ink spots. Yes, you will do."

To her amazement she had been promoted to office work.
She was thrilled with her rapid advancement. She wondered if
this came with a raise in pay. She decided not to push the point
until she had really proven herself to Roucher. But despite her-

self, she began to calculate an imagined increase in pay into her meager budget. Even if it was only a few centimes she knew she would be that much closer to her new boots.

Hélène did not share Berthe's happiness in her sudden promotion.

"What did you do to make him give you that job?" she demanded as they walked home.

"I didn't do anything," protested Berthe. "He needs someone who can read and write and do sums to help him in the office."

"He never needed help before. He spends half his day sleepin' in his chair. I seen him. He ain't exactly overworked, the weasel. Why does he suddenly need your stinkin' services? Think about it."

"I don't know," said Berthe. "But I thought you'd be happy for me."

"Why should I be happy for you? It don't make my life any easier, do it?"

"Maybe I can talk to Monsieur Roucher about getting you a better job. I'll have his ear, after all."

"That's not all you'll have, I guarantee. Listen, Mademoiselle High-and-Mighty, don't get ahead of yourself. Roucher's going to want something from you. Something you might not be wantin' to give to the slimy bastard. Or to his equally slimy employer."

"I don't know what you're talking about," said Berthe. "I think you're just jealous."

Hélène walked off ahead of her. They didn't speak for the rest of the night.

Berthe couldn't help but notice the other workers giving her dirty looks. The weather had warmed and she took to eating her supper in the courtyard rather than endure the black glances and barbs from the rest of the employees. One day, while she was sitting in the courtyard about to eat her supper, Marnet the Overlooker passed by.

"Well, if it ain't the queen of the cotton bales." He made an exaggerated bow. "Don't you want me to taste that first to make sure it ain't been poisoned?" he asked, pointing to her supper pail. Remembering her mother's gruesome death, she was startled by the suggestion of poison.

"Why would it be poisoned?" she asked.

"With all the grumbling and resentment goin' on about your sudden and spectacular advancement in this here fine establishment, especially after loyal employees have worked their fingers to the boney-bones for years just to get an extra centime and a kind word from the master? It rankles, it does. Course, I ain't talking about myself. I'm well pleased and wonderfully grateful for me place of privilege in this company. But bein' in the position I am, I do know what's going on behind the scenes, so to speak. I got me ear to the grindstone. Do you get my drift?"

"I think so," said Berthe.

A week later Monsieur Roucher greeted her with a big smile when she arrived for work.

"I have just this morning received a communication about you from our beloved Monsieur Rappelais," he said, holding up the letter as if to offer proof. "In his infinite generosity he is offering you, Mademoiselle Bovary, a position in his household in Paris."

"What position?" Berthe asked. For some reason her stomach twisted into knots.

"The position you are to fill is that of upstairs maid." Roucher folded the letter carefully as if it were the Holy Grail and replaced it in its envelope. "Don't tell me. The next thing you will want to know is what your salary will be." He laughed.

"What *will* my salary be?" she asked, lifting her chin.

"You are truly the most arrogant girl I have ever had the misfortune to meet," exploded Roucher. "You should be down on your knees kissing my feet for just being the bearer of these glad tidings. I really don't know why Monsieur Rappelais is interested in such an ingrate. But it is not my place to question my superiors. Finish your work today and be ready to leave tomorrow."

"Thank you, Monsieur Roucher, but I need to think about it." She felt a drop of perspiration run down her back.

"What?" he exclaimed. "Are you mad? You have to think even for a second about working in a grand household in the most beautiful city in the world?"

"Paris is so far away," Berthe said.

"You *are* mad. There are at least one hundred girls who would jump at this chance. Ha! I would even take the job myself had he offered it to me."

"Still, I must think about it," she repeated. "You cannot just ship me off against my will, can you?"

For a minute he scowled at her, saying nothing.

"You must give me your answer tomorrow. The very idea of making Monsieur wait upon your reply is . . . is . . . unheard of," he sputtered.

Berthe walked home pondering the proposal from Monsieur Rappelais. She was filled with so many conflicting feelings. Why would a man so powerful and rich as Monsieur Rappelais have the slightest interest in her? She couldn't answer the question and it filled her with a great unease. And Paris was a long way off. It was a huge cosmopolitan city, the capital of France, the home of over a million people. She was distrustful of this sudden opportunity, this unexpected stroke of good luck. It seemed to her that there was something dangerous lurking behind it. She remembered the way Monsieur Rappelais had looked at her, how he had held her hand.

She had already experienced so much upheaval in her life. She was just starting to feel at home at the boardinghouse, her friendship with Hélène was growing, and she now had work that she liked and was good at. The idea of yet another move to another city filled her with fear. She longed for some security and stability in her life.

But as always, despite her doubts and fears her imagination and fantasies took over: Monsieur Rappelais had taken one look at her and realized she was the daughter he had always longed for. Berthe knew he had sons but had no idea if he had any daughters. Still, she was not one to let facts interfere with her daydreams. She felt certain he was merely using the guise of needing a maid to get her to Paris. Once there he would tell her the truth: He wanted to formally adopt her. He would love her better than any child had ever been loved before. He would educate her at the finest schools. She would learn to play the piano. And the violin. How to sing in Italian, and paint in oils. She would get to decorate her own room with its six floor-to-ceiling French windows which looked out onto a terraced garden of flowering bushes and rare roses.

Oh, but first, as his beloved daughter, she would have to acquire a new wardrobe. "No daughter of mine can be seen dressed in rags," said Monsieur Rappelais. "Come, we will visit the dressmaker before we do another thing." Her mind filled with hoopskirted dresses, trimmed in lace and ribbon, and feathered bonnets and soft shoes. "You will never want for anything, my darling daughter," Monsieur Rappelais said as she tried to decide between the yellow satin shoes with buckles and the blue ones with bows. And she would grow up in this lovely, loving home, wearing a different gown every day, and she would meet and fall in love with a wonderful man even richer than Monsieur Rappelais and they would live in a grand house and her husband would love her and they would make a family, a perfect family who would live beautifully dressed and happily ever after. She was so immersed in her thoughts and her wonderful fantasy future that she almost stumbled over Antoine, the Scavenger, who was trudging slowly ahead of her.

"Oh, Antoine," she said, touching his shoulder, "I didn't see you." He stopped and turned to look at her. He was crying.

"Why the tears?" she asked.

"Monsieur Marnet strapped me today."

"Whatever for?"

"He caught me sleeping under one of the spinning machines. I don't mind the strappin'," he said, "but he's dockin' me wages. I got to work extra hours to make it up. Only, there ain't so many hours in a day." He sighed.

Berthe desperately searched her mind for something to say to cheer him up but she could think of nothing. She brushed his blond hair away from his face. She didn't even have a crust of bread to give him. She reached into the pocket of her apron. There was a filigree button. She remembered that she had taken it from her mother's sewing basket so many years before. She carried it around with her as a good luck piece. She had all but forgotten about the good luck part. It had just become a habit to carry it around with her. She handed it to Antoine.

"What's this?" he asked, studying the button.

"It's one of my mother's buttons. Put it in your pocket. It will bring you luck."

"Really?" A brilliant smile lit his dirty face. "Thank you, mademoiselle. I've never had a good luck piece before." He said it as if this were the single cause of his miserable life until now. As he walked away he had a small bounce to his step.

Hélène was sitting cross-legged on her bed. On the blanket in front of her was a pile of coins. She quickly covered them with the blanket when Berthe walked in.

"You'll never guess!" Berthe said. "I have been offered a job with Monsieur Rappelais in Paris."

Hélène began laughing. "I knew it! That's how come you landed such a plum job in the office. It weren't because of your reading, writing, and countin' abilities, as fine as they may be. The *Grand Patron* was just getting ready to catch you in his web."

"I don't understand."

"Course you don't. You're an ignorant country bumpkin. Did you think you were the first silly girl Monsieur Rappelais has taken a shine to? Oh, he prefers 'em stupid *and* young, like you. Mariette, the last mill girl who went to work for him, was never seen nor heard of again. She was only twelve and as thick as a board. Naturally she thought she had died and gone to heaven when he moved her to his house in Paris. Poor thing. They say that he kept her locked up in a room in the cellar, tortured her day and night, had his way with her, and when she finally escaped she were so destroyed she jumped into the river Seine and drowned herself." Hélène yawned and stretched her arms over her head. "Well, congratulations, you are about to be ruined for life," she said cheerfully.

"He's offered me a job," said Berthe weakly. "As upstairs maid."

"Ha! Don't you think Paris is filled with maids, upstairs, downstairs, in between stairs? Why do you think he picked you out of all the girls in the world?"

"I don't know," said Berthe, frowning.

"Because you ain't got no family. Because you're a useless orphan. Because there is nobody in the world who cares whether you live or die. Because you are dim-witted and dumb beyond belief. And because he probably has a taste for copper-colored hair, big bosoms, and skinny legs."

As tired as she was, Berthe tossed and turned all that night. She knew Hélène was right. Monsieur Rappelais had no good reason to offer her the position. She was better off staying where she was. She so liked to live in her fantasies she found that she didn't trust reality at all. And after talking to Hélène, she certainly didn't trust Monsieur Rappelais's intentions.

"I am afraid I will have to refuse Monsieur Rappelais's offer," Berthe said to Roucher the next morning.

"This is preposterous!" he shouted. "Utterly preposterous. Monsieur Rappelais will not be pleased, I can assure you of that, mademoiselle." Berthe started to take her seat at the desk. "What do you think you're doing?" asked Roucher.

"I was going to finish copying yesterday's sums into the ledger," explained Berthe.

"I don't believe so," said Roucher. "If you're too stupid to accept a perfectly fine position in Paris, then you're much too ignorant to work in my office. No, I think your talents are far better suited elsewhere."

She was back where she'd started, at the spinning machine tying knots in broken thread.

CHAPTER 12

A Den of Thieves

UNFORTUNATELY, BERTHE WAS NOT QUITE BACK WHERE SHE started. The fact she had the temerity to turn down the mill owner's offer of work in his Paris home did not sit well with Roucher or Marnet the Overlooker. She was reprimanded over and over again for doing sloppy work and was given an extra cleanup job that shortened her lunch hour. Marnet seemed to hover over her and every knot she tied as if hoping to provoke her into making a mistake. She was more exhausted than ever. But she was angry as well. They could pile on the work and the criticism as much as they wanted. Somehow she would not just survive this time, she would prevail. She would show them what she was made of.

"Why dontcha get yourself a pair of decent shoes," Hélène asked one Sunday as she watched Berthe inserting newspaper into her clogs.

"As soon as I get through paying for my carriage and four," Berthe said, not looking up.

"Don't be mouthy with me," Hélène shot back. "I was just making a friendly suggestion."

"Come, I'll show you the boots I'm going to buy when I've saved up enough," Berthe said in an effort to make amends. It was a pleasant day. The early March sun warmed the dingy streets. There was a feeling of spring in the air. The two girls walked arm in arm, enjoying the mild weather. Berthe was glad of Hélène's company. It made the long, hungry Sunday easier to get through.

She pulled Hélène toward the shoemaker's shop at the end of the street. Berthe was surprised to see that it was open on this Sunday. Hélène gazed up at the sign.

"What does it say?" asked Hélène. Berthe couldn't imagine what it was like not to be able to read a simple sign.

"M. Gregoire. Beautiful boots. Elegant footwear," read Berthe.

"Maybe he's got a pair of ugly boots he's willing to part with."

"Ugly or not, I have no money."

"Let's just go in and see what they cost," said Hélène, pulling Berthe after her. A bell rang as the girls entered the shop. A man was hammering small brass nails into the bottom of a high riding boot.

"What do you want?" he asked rudely, glancing at the two girls before returning to his work.

"What do you think we want?" Hélène said. Berthe tried to pull her out of the shop, but Hélène ignored her. "We're here to buy a pair of lady's boots for my friend." She turned to Berthe. "Which boots did you have in mind?"

Berthe pointed to a pair of black leather boots with thick sturdy heels.

"Let me see your money first," said the shoemaker.

"Don't you worry about our money. We got ourselves good

jobs. We get paid every Friday. Let my friend try on those boots to see if they fit," said Hélène.

"It doesn't matter if they fit or not. I can make boots to fit any foot." He picked up one of the boots Berthe had pointed out, and caressed it. "These particular boots were made for a poor lady who died. I can let you have them for a very good price."

"First let her try 'em on," repeated Hélène. She made Berthe sit down on the one chair in the store. Berthe curled the toe of her woolen sock underneath her foot so that the shoemaker couldn't see the hole. The boots were made of soft, supple leather that had a deep, lustrous sheen, as if it had been buffed for hours. She laced up both the boots, carefully tying bows at her ankles, then she gazed down at her feet. The boots felt wonderful, as if they had been made for her.

"How much are they?" Hélène asked, all business.

"They are custom-made of the finest Italian calfskin. I can't part with them for a cent less than twenty-five francs."

"Did the dead woman give you payment on them?" asked Hélène.

"No, why do you ask?" said the shoemaker, stroking his long mustache.

"Well, seein' as they were custom-made for a dead woman they carry some bad feeling with them. They just happen to fit my friend here perfectly, so I am thinking you could do a bit better with the price. That's what I'm thinking. What are you thinking, Mademoiselle Berthe?"

"I was thinking exactly the same thing," agreed Berthe. The shoemaker continued caressing his mustache.

"All right, you may have them for twenty francs. That's as low as I am willing to go. Take it or leave it." Berthe looked down at the boots.

"Can I buy them in small payments?"

"Of course you can, dear mademoiselle. I am always happy to accommodate my customers when it comes to payment." Berthe got up and searched her purse for two francs, which she handed to the shoemaker. He took out a ledger and made an entry in it. "I will pay you more on Sunday next," she said, turning to go.

"Wait a bloody minute," he said. "You don't think you are going to walk out of here with my beautiful boots? You'll get them when you give me the rest of the price." He held out his hand for the boots. "Don't worry, I will keep them safe and sound." Berthe hated taking off the boots, but she slowly unlaced them and handed them back to the shoemaker. Then she slipped her feet back into the hateful, hurting clogs.

As they walked away from the shop Hélène began laughing.

"What is so amusing?" asked Berthe, who at that moment felt like crying. She wondered why she had given the shoemaker her last two francs when she didn't know when or if she would ever get the remaining eighteen to pay off her debt on the boots.

Hélène reached under her cape and drew out a pair of lady's elegant evening shoes.

"Oh, no," said Berthe. "What have you done? He'll know who took them. Now I can never go back there. I've lost my two francs."

"Don't be an ass. Course you can go back. He's got your money. And he's holding the boots for you. When you do go back, just deny everything. Or blame it all on me. Your friend, the thief."

"What are you going to do with those?" asked Berthe, pointing to the evening shoes.

"Sell 'em, of course. Unless you happen to be needing 'em for the opera."

"I'm afraid they won't match my dress," said Berthe. Hélène crowed.

Berthe felt a warmth that came from deep inside her. It was almost a physical thing that bubbled up within her, up and up until it reached the corners of her mouth and she smiled. She had a friend. She liked Hélène's bigness and brashness, her strength and her fearlessness. She even liked the fact that she was a thief.

She wondered why she found it so easy to forgive Hélène for taking things that didn't belong to her and that she certainly hadn't earned. And yet she felt nothing but contempt for her mother's rapacious ways.

"Wake up," Hélène whispered to Berthe a few nights later.

Berthe sat up, rubbing her eyes.

"What time is it?"

"It's one in the morning. Come on. I'll show you how to earn some spendin' money."

"How are we supposed to make money in the middle of the night?"

"Just get your clothes on. I'm gonna give you lesson number one in lifting."

"What's lifting?"

"Copping, pilfering, stealing, you nincompoop. C'mon, time's a-wastin'."

"I'm not going anywhere," said Berthe, pulling the covers over her head and turning toward the wall. "It's freezing out there."

"You want those boots, dontcha?"

"This is insane," mumbled Berthe, as they hurried through the shadowy streets.

It was very dark and very cold for March. The air felt like ice against her face. They walked through the more commercial area until they came to a residential one. It was a quiet street of elegant townhouses, fronted with small gardens surrounded by wrought-iron fences. All the windows were dark. The only light came from the gas street lamp on the corner.

Berthe certainly wasn't against the idea of stealing. She had a history of minor theft herself, she thought, thinking back to the items of food she had taken in the past. But when she saw what Hélène had in mind to steal she was appalled.

"Here, give me a hand," Hélène whispered as she bent down and pulled at a cast-iron birdbath. "I had me eye on this beauty for some time." The birdbath featured a plump naked cherub with tiny wings who held on to the pedestal as if afraid someone was going to make off with it in the middle of the night. A hummingbird was perched precariously on the cherub's shoulder. "This bugger is even heavier than it looks. No wonder they didn't bother nailing it down. It weighs a ton," grunted Hélène.

Berthe picked up one end of the birdbath.

"Heavens," she gasped, "I don't know if I can carry this."

They lugged the birdbath through the streets, stopping to rest every few blocks. Hélène carried the heavier end with the bowl. Berthe hoisted the pedestal.

"What are we going to do with this?" she panted.

"Sell it, what do you think?" Hélène shot back.

"Who's going to want to buy a stolen birdbath in the middle of the night?" Berthe asked, rubbing her aching back.

"Shut up and lift," commanded Hélène. Berthe's whole body strained with the weight of the birdbath. Several times she tripped on the uneven cobblestones and almost dropped her end. Fearing arrest, she began to compose a plea of mercy for herself and, as an added gesture of generosity, for Hélène as well.

Please, spare us. We meant no harm. It's just that we were hungry. Poor. Starving. She couldn't finish her defense. She was too terrified to think.

They came to a part of town that was composed of small factories, blacksmiths, and one small building with a sign that said: *Foundry.*

Hélène knocked on the dilapidated door. A large burly man opened it. He wore a heavy leather apron and leather sleeve guards.

"Got yourself a pretty little helper, I see," said the man. His skin was almost as black as his beard and his eyes gleamed red. Berthe took a step back from the doorway.

"Yeah, well, I'm trying her to see if she works out," said Hélène.

"So what you got for me today, missy?" He lifted the birdbath a few inches off the ground. "Hmm. Good and heavy. I'd say about ninety kilos."

"And I'd say about ninety-seven," corrected Hélène. "I'd also say put it on the bloody scale."

"She's always questioning me," he said to Berthe. "After all this time, you'd think she'd learn to trust me. Do I look like the kind of person who's gonna cheat a hardworking girl out of a few centimes?" Berthe thought he looked exactly like that kind of person. "All right, bring her in and put her on the scale." Berthe was immediately hit with the heat of the blazing foundry fire and the smell of the melting metal. It was a small but efficient operation. One huge cauldron held the metal to be melted over a white-hot coal fire, while in another corner of the room Berthe could see the forms that would take the liquid metal and turn it into uniform machine parts.

The man helped Hélène lift the birdbath onto a huge scale.

"Oh, she's got an eye, she does. Ninety-seven kilos on the dot. All right," he said, scratching his head, "ninety-seven at twenty centimes a kilo, that makes..."

"One franc, ninety-four centimes," answered Berthe.

"Oh, now I see why you brought the skinny one along."

"Round it out to two francs," said Hélène.

"I ain't rounding out nothin', you greedy slut."

"It's a beautiful piece . . . it's got to be worth far more than two francs," said Berthe.

"One franc, ninety-four centimes," he repeated. "And it don't matter if it's the Emperor's crown, it just gets melted down with the rest of the junk."

When they got back to the boardinghouse, Hélène counted out twenty-five centimes and gave them to Berthe. "Here's your share. It adds up, you'll see," she said as she collapsed on her bed. Berthe was wide awake.

"It seems like a lot of work and a big risk for not much money," observed Berthe.

"You're so smart. What do you suggest?"

"Why not steal from inside the houses rather than outside?"

"Because they would hunt you down and put you in jail for that, me thieving friend."

"Well, they would put you in jail just as quickly for stealing things from the outside of a house," observed Berthe.

"They don't care about an odd item here and there. They puts it down to vandalism," said Hélène, closing her eyes. Within moments, she was snoring.

Unlike Hélène, Berthe did not want to be a thief for the rest of her life. But desperate times required desperate measures. Thus, a few weeks later, Berthe came up with the idea of the department store. Since she was already immersed in a life of crime, she reasoned, why not make their efforts more profitable.

"Why not? I'll tell ya why not," said Hélène. "We couldn't even get ourselves into a fancy place like the Galeries Napoléon.

They'd take one look at ragamuffins like me and you and arrest us just for trying to cross the bloody doorstep."

The Galeries Napoléon was the finest store in Lille. A six-story glass and steel structure with a majestic dome skylight, it was one of the first stores of its kind built outside of Paris. Hélène and Berthe stood admiring it one night on their way home from dropping off a small but extremely heavy garden bench at the foundry. "And besides that," Hélène continued, "they ain't open on Sunday, which if you consult your social calendar, happens to be the only day we got off." Berthe was silent. She stared at the dark building, imagining all the luxurious goods that lay beyond her reach. The term *kleptomania* had just been introduced into French society. Berthe had read a story in Madame Lisette's Sunday paper about a wealthy woman who was accused of taking three pairs of gloves because "she was overcome by a tremendous need to put them in her purse."

"Madame X was clearly suffering from kleptomania, an illness that left her weak of mind and not responsible for her actions," explained her lawyer. She was released with no formal charges brought against her. According to the article, kleptomania was a result of the introduction of the large dry goods stores to French society.

"The display of so much appealing merchandise tends to confuse the lady shopper," one well-known physician was quoted as saying.

"That's what we'll be," Berthe told Hélène after reading her the newspaper story. "We'll be kleptomaniacs. If wealthy ladies can get away with it, then so can we."

"Klepto sounds all right," observed Hélène, chewing on her fingernail, "but I ain't sure about the maniac part."

One Friday morning they arrived at the mill to discover the fire wagon blocking their entrance. A fire had broken out in the early morning hours. They were told to go home and report for work as usual the next day.

Berthe clapped her hands. "This is the day," she said to Hélène.

"The day we don't get paid," said Hélène, kicking a piece of manure out of her way.

"No, the day we begin our careers as kleptomaniacs. The problem is, they'll never let us in dressed like this," Berthe said, looking down at her homespun dress.

"Oh, don't worry, me dear, I've already figured that out," said Hélène, pulling her down the street. When they got to their room Hélène reached under her bed and drew out a cloth sack. Inside was a very elegant navy blue dress with black jet beads down the front, and black lace ruffles.

"Where in the world did that come from?" asked Berthe, stroking the fabric.

"From our landlady's armoire. It's stuffed with dresses."

"She's bound to miss it." Still, Berthe was impressed with her friend's audacity.

"Stop fretting; I'll return it as soon as we're done with it. Here, put it on."

The dress was far too big for Berthe, but Hélène was able to pin it so that it looked as if it almost fit.

"And here—" She removed a blue velvet bonnet from the bag.

"What about shoes?" asked Berthe.

"You can wear my boots. But just for today," said Hélène, bending down to unlace her boots.

"What happens if Madame Lisette sees me in her dress?"

"Don't worry. Today's her market day. She'll be gone all day."

"And what will you wear?"

Hélène pulled a clean apron from under the bed and put it on.

"You'll be the grand lady and I'll be your humble servant girl."

"Excellent," said Berthe, lacing up the boots.

"One more thing," said Hélène. She handed Berthe a pot of rouge. "A spot of makeup to make you look older."

"I already feel like an old woman. I'm so tired I think I could sleep for a million years."

They watched from the corner as elegantly dressed women went in and out of the department store. It was a beautiful spring day and the sun glinted off the large windows.

"Just behave naturally," said Berthe, barely moving her lips.

Hélène shot her a look as if to say, What do you mean by "naturally"?

"Better just follow me," Berthe corrected. She took a deep breath, straightened her bonnet, and strode into the store, head held high, chin tilted upward like one of the wealthier women of Yonville. The same women who had looked down their noses at Berthe and her mother on market day. Hélène followed two humble steps behind. Once inside, Berthe fought the temptation to gape. Everywhere she looked tables were stacked high with beautiful things. She glanced up. The glass rotunda shone high above the main floor. Rising up around the rotunda were six open floors that looked down on the main floor. From where she stood she could see shelves and shelves of hats and gloves, shawls and lingerie. The air was filled with scents: roses, lavender, and lilies of the valley all blended together. It was intoxicating.

The main floor was crowded with women, so many women that their big bell skirts crushed together. There were women trying on gloves and hats, holding glassware up to the light. Women dabbing perfume on the insides of their wrists, attaching earrings to their ears. On Berthe's right was a table covered entirely with bolts of lace. Next to that was another table heaped high with rich velvets, and beyond that a table laden with huge bolts of brocade fabric. Berthe felt she had entered another world—a dream world. So many beautiful fabrics, so within her reach. She didn't want to be seen dawdling without purpose, so she walked over to the table on which bolts of lace were piled. She fingered the end of one. A salesman was busy with several other women, unrolling lace for them to examine.

"I'll be with you in a moment, mademoiselle," he said, glancing at Berthe.

"I'm in no rush, monsieur," said Berthe, her heart racing.

"Do you have any of the Belgian lace in colors?" asked a woman in a cranberry-colored dress with matching bonnet.

"Yes, madame, I have some lovely yellow and gold. It's in the back. I'll fetch it at once," said the harried salesman.

Out of the corner of her eye Berthe watched as the woman turned away from the table, lifted her skirt, and stuck a small bolt of Chinese silk from an adjacent table up under her petticoats. She quickly lowered her skirt and turned back to examine the bolts of lace on the table.

"Did you see that?" whispered Berthe.

Hélène nodded. "I'd like to see how she's going to walk out of here with *that* stuck between her legs."

Berthe and Hélène moved away from the lace to another table which featured kid gloves in every length and color. As with the lace, there were a large number of women crowded around trying on gloves.

Berthe put on a pair of white opera gloves. The leather was as soft as butter and they fit her perfectly. Her rough hands felt all the rougher inside the soft leather. The lone glove salesman was being inundated by requests at the other end of the table, so Berthe carefully pulled off the gloves finger by finger as she had once seen her mother do after attending the opera in Rouen. She looked around her quickly, then folded the gloves and handed them to Hélène, who put them in the pocket of her apron. Berthe breathed a sigh of relief. It was all so easy. *Too easy.* They moved on to the evening bag section. The bags were jeweled and beaded affairs, too small to hold anything but a lady's hanky, yet beautiful to behold. Berthe was able to slip two of them down the front of her dress.

"It's time to go. The marquis will be waiting," Berthe announced to no one in particular. She turned and, without glancing back to see if Hélène was following her, glided out of the store, her knees knocking together beneath her long skirt.

"The marquis," laughed Hélène, when they were out on the street. "Bugger the marquis." A few passersby glanced at her and she ducked her head, retreating to her position two steps behind Berthe.

"Two purses and a pair of gloves. We did well," said Berthe, admiring the booty later in their bedroom. "But who are we going to sell them to?"

"Don't worry. I have the perfect customer," said Hélène, putting the stolen goods into the cloth sack and slipping it in the already crowded space underneath her bed.

After dinner they knocked on Madame Lisette's door.

"Oh, my lovelies. Do come in. What can I do for my two darling girls?"

Berthe did all the talking.

"Madame Lisette, we have come to conduct some business. We thought perhaps you might be interested in purchasing a few items that happened to come into our possession."

Hélène laid the gloves and two purses on Madame Lisette's settee.

"Well, will you look at this," said the landlady, picking up one of the purses and examining it carefully. "You say they 'came into your possession,' dear hearts. How did that happen, if I might be so bold to ask?"

"It don't matter none," Hélène shot back. "You're either interested or you ain't."

"I don't have that much use for evening bags or opera gloves. But then if the price is right I might be convinced." She pulled on one of the opera gloves and held her arm out, admiring it. "What were you thinking as far as a fair price?" she looked at Berthe.

"Twenty francs for everything," said Berthe.

"Oh, no, that's beyond my humble means. And please forgive me for saying this, but if there's the slightest possibility of this being stolen merchandise . . . well . . . I have my reputation to think of, not to mention you girls. I couldn't live with the idea of you spending time in jail. Oh, the very thought . . ."

"Eighteen francs," Berthe interjected.

"Twelve," countered Madame Lisette.

Berthe nodded and Hélène held out her hand.

Madame Lisette paid them the money. The two girls left, encouraged by the landlady's last words.

"If any more pretty things happen to fall into your possession, you'll come to me first, all right, girls?" They now had a convenient outlet for their stolen goods. All they needed was more merchandise. But how were they to get it when they had to be at the mill every day, all day? It was Hélène who came up with a solution.

"You stay home sick one day. I'll tell Monsieur Roucher you were puking the whole night. Course they'll dock your pay. But we'll more than make up for it in what you can steal from the Galeries. And they ain't gonna fire you. They have enough trouble finding fools to work there. I ask you, what's the worst that can happen to you?"

They held on to the "borrowed" dress from Madame Lisette. Berthe stayed home from work the next day. In the afternoon she again went to the department store. It was another very crowded day at Galeries Napoléon. She focused only on small and expensive items. She managed to bring home six pair of gold-framed pince-nez, five pair of kid gloves in varying lengths and colors, three beaded evening bags, two crystal necklaces, and four bottles of French perfume. They took the goods to Madame Lisette later that night.

"Well, it looks as if you girls could have your rent paid up for the rest of the year," she said. "I'll tell the mill to stop deducting from your pay."

"We want the cash," said Berthe.

"We may not be here for the rest of the year," added Hélène.

"Oh, my, aren't we coming up in the world. Well, my little ladies, let's not forget who provided comfort and shelter to you two lost souls from the very beginning."

"Not to mention the soup," said Berthe. Madame Lisette gave her a look.

They made a total profit of forty francs.

"I can finally get my boots," Berthe said happily.

Unfortunately, she got something else quite unexpected the next day.

CHAPTER 13

The Boots

"Report to Clothier," said Monsieur Roucher when she arrived at work the next morning.

The Master Carder stood next to his platform as if waiting for her. He was slapping a heavy leather strap across his palm.

"Ah, the ailing Mademoiselle Bovary. Be so kind as to take the position," he said, indicating a wooden bench to his right.

"What? I don't understand," she said, taking a step back.

"Absenteeism for whatever reason is punished by twenty strokes of the strap. It's in the rules."

"Not the rules that I heard," she protested, thinking back to her first day and the group recitation of the mill rules.

"Them's the written rules. This here's the unwritten rules," he said. "Now, bend over."

She wasn't sure which hurt more, the strapping or the public humiliation of being strapped. Clothier had everyone stop work for the two minutes it took to administer the punishment.

"Remember when you were talking about the worst thing that could happen to me if I missed work?" she said to Hélène as they walked home that night. Hélène nodded, unable to look Berthe in the eye. "Well, it seems you forgot to mention the strapping."

"I didn't want to worry you," she said. "You needed to have a clear and free mind."

"Thanks ever so much," Berthe said, scowling.

On Sunday she went to see Monsieur Gregoire, the shoemaker.

"I've come to collect my boots. Here are the eighteen francs," she said, handing him the money.

"What boots?" He scratched his head.

"The ones I gave you two francs for as a down payment," Berthe said, frowning.

"Oh, yes, of course. But I'm afraid the price has gone up since last we spoke," he said, bringing the black boots out from underneath the counter. "These gorgeous boots are now thirty francs."

"But you told me they were twenty. We agreed on a price. You can't go back on your word." She stamped her foot.

"All my prices have gone up, mademoiselle. Owing to the high cost of materials as well as to the losses I suffer as a result of theft," he said, giving her a meaningful look.

She realized then that he suspected but didn't know for certain that she and Hélène had stolen the evening shoes. She decided to call his bluff.

"You made an agreement. Either you give me my boots for the price we agreed upon or I will report you to the local *gendarmes*. I'm sure they wouldn't look kindly on a successful shop owner such as yourself doing a poor girl like me out of a pair of boots." She felt short of breath as she delivered her speech.

The boots felt wonderful. The leather squeaked as she walked. She threw her wooden clogs into the first refuse bin she passed on her way home.

Now that she had her boots Berthe put aside the idea of shoplifting. Thieving didn't require talent, just nerve. She had bigger goals beyond how to get her next meal or her next pair of boots. She wanted to make beautiful things. She remembered the thrill of being able to create original flowers out of simple colored thread when she first learned to embroider. She remembered the satisfaction of creating clothes for her doll, how she loved making the small even stitches, keeping the seams straight, seeing the garments come to life. She thought back to how much pleasure she had gotten from transforming the homespun dress at her grand-mère's farm. Even the sketch she had made for Monsieur Millet that day in the field had given her a glimpse of what she could do. What she should do. She needed to hold on to the belief that she was meant for something more respectful than stealing, more creative and challenging than tying knots in a cotton mill.

Still, over time, she became better and better at her job at the mill. She could almost anticipate the threads breaking before they did. She developed a method of moving up and down the spinning machine and quickly tying the broken threads without breaking her stride. Soon, she became lost in the rhythm of the work and in her daydreams.

Late one afternoon she was distracted by Antoine ducking under the carriage of her machine to pick up the loose cotton. She still hadn't gotten used to the sight of his small body so dangerously exposed to the heavy moving machinery. He kept himself as close to the floor as possible. Using a short-handled broom, he swept the fallen cotton out as the knitting machine passed noisily back and forth over his head. The look on his face told her he was in a constant state of terror. It was only minutes later when she heard the cry.

Antoine had apparently lifted his head too high. A piece of his curly blond hair was caught up in the moving wheel.

"Help! Help me!" he yelled out in terrible pain and fear.

"Turn off the machine!" Berthe screamed

"Turn off the machine! Turn off the machine! Someone turn off the bloody machine!" echoed one of the men who had been tightening the bolts on a nearby spinning machine. Antoine reached up a hand in an effort to untangle his hair from the hold of the revolving machinery. Berthe ran to the boy. His hair was being ripped from his scalp, and his scalp was being ripped from his head. Blood was running out all over his face. The next thing that happened was too horrible to imagine. The machine caught his hand and then his arm and kept moving forward. His shrieks of pain filled the air. Berthe grabbed his foot, but he was being pulled in the opposite direction.

"Turn it off! Turn off the machine!" she cried.

"For Jesus' sake, man, stop the machine!" shouted Marnet the Overlooker.

The Master Carder quickly climbed down from his platform and pulled a lever, but by that time it was too late. The poor boy lay under the machine, his arm mangled beyond recognition, his face frozen in agony and horror, blood pulsing out onto the floor. He was already dead.

Berthe continued to hear the clack-clack of the machinery before her brain registered the fact that all the machines had been turned off. The sound of the silence was almost as deafening. With a cold efficiency, two of the men removed Antoine's poor broken body, washed the floor, and cleaned the machine. The Master Carder bade everyone to return to work. Berthe, numb, stepped back to her position by the stretch of threads. As she did, she noticed something on the floor near where Antoine had lain. She bent down and picked it up. It was the filigree button she had given him for good luck. Some luck, she thought, as tears poured down her cheeks.

"You ain't comin' to dinner?" Hélène asked that night.

"How can you eat?" Berthe shook her head. She lay in bed, the gray blankets pulled up to her chin. She felt a great guilt and responsibility. She had taken Antoine's place as Piecer, forcing him to return to a job that had ultimately led to his death. She didn't know how she had even managed to finish the day as the boy's cries of pain kept echoing in her mind.

"Well, with Madame Lisette's soup, it ain't easy. But when you're hungry, anything'll do."

"No, I mean how can you eat after what happened to poor Antoine?"

"What?" Hélène scoffed. "You never saw a bit of blood before?"

"My father was a doctor. I've seen blood. But not coming from one little boy."

"One *stupid* little boy," said Hélène. "I had that job when I first started. It was a piece a cake. Alls you had to do was keep your head down. I used to take myself nice naps underneath the machinery. Course every once in a while I got a beating for layin' down on the job, but it was worth it."

When Berthe finally drifted off to sleep shortly before dawn she had a dream. She was at the mill, working as a Piecer. Her job required her to tie the braids from one small girl's head to another girl's. Then she bade the two children to lie down side by side, and she pulled a lever. Seconds later the platform on which they were lying moved forward into a machine that contained many sharp teeth. The little girls were turned into long shredded strips of flesh, which were then woven into bolts of blood-soaked fabric. The entire process went on without a sound. In the dream she wondered why there was no screaming. Someone should be screaming, she thought to herself. And then she heard it: a high-pitched, horrified "Noooooooooo!" She awoke to the sound of her own voice.

"Can we have a bit of quiet?" grumbled Hélène. "You been moanin' and yellin' for the past hour. How'm I supposed to get any sleep?"

Berthe had the same dream with slight variations every night for the next week. Finally, she knew she had to get out of the mill. Her fear of hearing the screams of another injured child or being hurt herself overwhelmed her during the day and haunted her even in her sleep. More and more she began to dread going to work.

She looked under her narrow bed. There were her beautiful new boots. And next to them the picture of her dress. She unfolded the paper and stared at the illustration.

She remembered not so very long ago how excited she had been about beginning her job at the mill. She had actually thought she would be making beautiful things out of cotton. She forgot for a moment the drudgery of her job at Rappelais et Fils and her imagination took her to a vision of owning her own mill. She would control the manufacturing of the fabric from beginning to end. And her mill would not make just plain cotton but she would weave fantastic fabrics of silk and satin in every imaginable color. And she would free all the workers from their awful servitude. She would give the poor children shorter hours, more food, a longer supper break, real sweets, and lots of money at Christmas, Easter, and even All Saints' Day. Berthe sighed. It was a grand dream, but one that would have to wait for another day.

Stop dreaming, you fool. Nothing was going to happen unless she took action and made a change. She suddenly made a decision. The boots were a reminder that better things and another life was possible. No one ever should have to live—or die—like Antoine.

"Excuse me, Monsieur Roucher." It was during the supper break the next day when she tapped on the manager's office door.

"What is it? Why aren't you eating your supper?" He glanced at his pocket watch. "You only have three minutes left."

"I was wondering if the position is still open." She shifted her weight from one foot to the other.

"What position is that?" He turned back to his ledger and entered several numbers in a column.

"The one in Monsieur Rappelais's household in Paris."

"Oh." He chuckled. "I very much doubt it. Half of Paris would give their right arm to work in that distinguished house." Berthe shuddered at his reference to right arms. "No, I'm sorry. She who hesitates is—"

"Could you please write and ask if it is still available?" she interrupted him. "Please, monsieur." She hated the idea of having to beg him.

"Who do you think I am, your personal secretary?" he barked. "You already have a perfectly fine 'position,' Bovary. One that you will not keep very much longer if you keep dawdling and wasting both my time and yours. Now, get back to work."

Berthe started to leave and stopped.

"I had understood that Monsieur Rappelais wanted me to work as a maid in his household. I think he would be very annoyed if he were to discover you were unwilling to inform him that I had accepted the position." She smiled sweetly.

"You had your chance," he hissed, leaning forward in his chair. "I recall you turned it down."

"Well, I changed my mind," said Berthe, still smiling. He glared at her. "You'll write the letter, then?" He didn't answer. His face was red.

"Actually, I can write him myself. I *can* write, you know," she said, squaring her shoulders.

"I'll write your cursed letter. Now, get back to work." He yanked open a drawer and pulled out a piece of stationery.

Within a week she had the answer. She was to proceed to Paris immediately.

The morning Berthe was to leave she woke to the sight of Hélène lacing up Berthe's new boots.

"What are you doing with my boots?" Berthe said, rubbing her eyes.

"I'm stealing them, what do you think?" said Hélène, not looking up.

"But I thought I was your friend. How can you steal from a friend?"

"I'm a thief. That's what thieves do," Hélène said, non-plussed. She finished lacing the boots, stood, and bounced on the toes of her feet as if testing them out.

"Give me back my boots, or I will turn you in to the *gendarmes.*"

Hélène looked down at the boots fondly. "You can get others when you're in Paris. At least leave me something to remember you by," she said.

"My boots, if you please," Berthe said. She held out her hand. Hélène sat down, slowly unlaced the boots, and kicked them across the floor toward Berthe.

"Well, good luck to you, then. I s'pose you'll be having your choice of footwear livin' the grand life in Paris."

"I suppose I will," said Berthe.

"Think of your old friend once in a while, will you?" Hélène said, flashing a smile. "Maybe I'll come and visit you one of these days, and you and me can make a run of the fancy shops. Pick us up a few things."

"You take care," said Berthe, hugging her.

"No, you take care," said Hélène, returning the hug. "You're the one walkin' into the Devil's den."

PART 3

Into the Fire

CHAPTER 14

The Convent

ROUEN, 1856

BERTHE HAD TURNED SIXTEEN YEARS OLD A FEW WEEKS earlier and was now starting over again for the third time. The carriage that was to take her to Paris had a one-day stopover in Rouen to change horses and pick up new passengers. *Rouen,* she thought as she stepped down from the carriage. Then it came to her. This was the place her father had been sent to school as a young boy. She remembered him telling her how he was dragged away from the fields he loved in order to be educated. It had been his mother's wish that he achieve his place in the world as a professional man. Berthe had the feeling that once he had embarked on this "city life" he had never been completely happy again.

Berthe was seeing for the first time where it all began for her mother and father. It was in nearby Tostes where her father first laid eyes on his bride-to-be at her father's farm. The Ursuline convent in the town of Rouen was where Emma Bovary had been schooled.

"It was at the convent where I spent two of my best years,"

Emma had once told Berthe. "It was a wonderful place for a young girl. I would have been happy to spend the rest of my life there." Berthe had a difficult time imagining her mother locked away inside a nunnery. Suddenly, she wanted to see the place that had been such a source of joy for her mother.

The convent wasn't difficult to find. It was a sixteenth-century two-story stucco structure surrounded by an ivy-covered wall located near the center of town. The tall arched doorway made it seem both inviting and intimidating. Instead of going directly in, Berthe followed the vaulted cloister path that bordered the garden. The garden was abloom in tender white peonies. Setting down her valise, she was bending to inhale the delicate fragrance when she heard a voice behind her.

"May I help you, mademoiselle?" It was a young nun. She seemed hardly older than Berthe herself. Her round pink face was made even rounder by the stiff white bandeau and coif. Her eyes shone like two bright coins as if Berthe's unannounced visit was a cause for celebration.

"My mother once attended school here and I..." Berthe said, struggling for more of an explanation.

"Oh, then you'll want to see Mother Superior. Come," the nun said, easing Berthe over her awkward hesitation.

Berthe followed her into the convent itself. Instead of the dark interior she expected she was surprised to see how light and airy the hallways were. The smiling nun led her to a large vaulted room. One wall was taken up by huge gold-framed oil paintings. On the opposite wall were French doors that opened out onto the garden. At the end of the room was a shoulder-high fireplace. On either side of the fireplace were two huge double doors.

"Wait here," the nun said. "I'll fetch Mother. You can put your valise in the corner."

"I don't want to disturb her," said Berthe, nervously fingering the fringe of her shawl.

"She likes being disturbed."

While she waited for the Mother Superior, Berthe studied the paintings. One was more distressing than the next. She read the title plates underneath each picture. *The Martyrdom of Saint Stanislaus,* a poor figure in full armor apparently newly slain by a sword. *The Penitent Mary Magdalene,* a beautiful woman clutching her breast, looking as if she had just lost her last friend on earth. Christ appearing to Saint Anthony during his Temptation. Again anguish, pain, and fear. Christ himself appearing to Saint Peter on the Appian Way, bent under the weight of an enormous wooden cross. And Christ on the cross, thorn-crowned, head bowed, bleeding from nail-pierced hands and feet. But the final painting gave Berthe some relief. It was of a young Jesus dressed in long white robes and holding a baby lamb in his lap. How handsome and happy he seemed.

An elderly woman in a nun's habit entered from the doorway on the left of the fireplace. She approached Berthe with open arms, spreading the folds of her habit as if they were wings. A wide toothless smile lifted the wrinkles of her face.

"Why, it's dear Mademoiselle Rouault," she lisped. "Why aren't you in Chapel?"

"No, Mother, I am her daughter, Berthe." The Mother Superior clutched Berthe's hand with cold, clawlike fingers.

"Her daughter, of course. I'm afraid my age has robbed me of my senses," she said, peering up at Berthe's face from underneath her coif. "I remember your mother well. Always reading a book. And never the right book," she added, chuckling.

Berthe, of course, had the same memory of her mother always reading. Once, as a very small child, she tried to climb onto her mother's lap to literally squeeze between Emma and the book she was so engrossed in.

"Not now; they are slaying the dragon," her mother had said, turning the page as she pushed Berthe away.

"Didn't she have to read the Bible?" Berthe asked.

"I'm afraid Sir Walter Scott *was* her Bible," the Mother Superior said, smiling and shaking her head. "She was not our usual student. No, in all honesty, she really didn't belong here."

"But my mother always said this was the happiest time of her life," said Berthe.

"I'm not surprised. Oh, she loved it here. But not as most of our girls love the convent. She loved the beautiful trappings. Not the spiritual benefits. No, she was certainly not suited to the life of seclusion and meditation. She was far too free a spirit, that one."

Berthe looked around the room, taking in the stained-glass windows, the mosaic floor tiles, the ornately carved mahogany window frames and moldings. "You know what she once said to one of the sisters?" the Mother Superior continued. "She said that this was a waste of a grand home on a God who wasn't here to enjoy it. Can you imagine? She was a handful. But we did love her spirit. We were sorry to see her go," she said, gazing up at Jesus and the lamb. She turned to look at Berthe. "And how is your beautiful mother? Still with her head in the clouds?"

"Actually, all of her is in the clouds now, Mother. She died over three years ago."

"Oh, I am sorry." The old nun crossed herself. "So you have come here to make a pilgrimage to where your dear mother attended school?"

Berthe nodded. "I am on my way to Paris, but when the coach stopped in Rouen I remembered that my mother's school was here and I thought..." Suddenly, Berthe's voice broke with an unexpected emotion. She could never understand why her husband's and daughter's love hadn't been enough for her mother. But this place, this convent had clearly made Emma Bovary feel loved.

"Of course, it is only natural that you would want to visit the places that were meaningful to your mother," said the Mother Superior, patting Berthe gently on the shoulder. "But wait, if you want to learn more of her you can talk to Madame Blanquet. She was here when your mother was an adolescent and she still does our linens every month. She can tell you all about your mother as a young girl. Between you and me, I believe she is the one responsible for corrupting her," she said with a laugh.

Carrying her valise, Berthe followed the Mother Superior down a long passageway into the basement of the convent. The stone walls gave off a cold, musty smell. In the dim light she could make out an old woman sitting at a table that was piled high with folded linens. She was mending a hem on a pillowcase.

"Madame Blanquet, you will never guess who I have here," said the Mother Superior in an overly loud voice. The old woman looked up, a confused expression on her face. "Here is our dear Mademoiselle Rouault's daughter, Mademoiselle Bovary. Do you remember Mademoiselle Rouault from so many years ago?" she said. "Well, I'm sure you both have much to talk about. Come and see me before you leave," she said to Berthe.

Madame Blanquet put down her sewing. Berthe thought she must be almost one hundred years old. The hands that held the mending were so bent and thickened with arthritis and age that Berthe wondered at the fact that she could even hold a needle. Her watery eyes seemed almost sightless.

"Mon Dieu, it is my *chère* Mademoiselle Rouault. Come sit down. Where have you been, you naughty girl?"

"Madame, I am Berthe Bovary. Emma Rouault was my mother."

The old woman stretched out her knobby hand and grabbed Berthe by the chin, turning her face this way and that. "Ah, yes. Now I see. The hair is a different color. And how is your mother? Your naughty, naughty mother?"

"She is dead," Berthe whispered, again embarrassed by the sudden emotion she felt. Her mother's presence in this place was almost unendurable.

"Of course she is dead," said the old woman, nodding her head and smiling. "She must have died tragic and young, with her hair spread out upon her pillow and a red rose clutched to her breast. Am I right?"

"She did die young." The words stuck in her throat. Berthe didn't want to recount the gruesome details of her mother's agonizing death.

"How she loved all the tragic tales of romance. All those beautiful ladies and their handsome lovers. They always die young. Sit down. Here, you can help me with my mending. Your mother had a fine hand with a needle. The thread and needle are somewhere in the basket. Take care you make the stitches small."

Before she knew it, Berthe was repairing the edging on a pillowcase with tiny, even stitches.

The cotton was so worn and soft it almost felt like silk. For how many years, how many heads had lain on this same pillowcase? She held it to her nose and inhaled the clean smell. Perhaps her mother's head had once rested on this very fabric. She thought about the cotton mill for the first time since leaving it and remembered what a terrible price was paid in making this simple material.

She was suddenly aware that the old woman was talking to her.

"She even made up her own wonderful stories," Madame Blanquet was saying. "She would tell me about how one day a handsome young man would come and take her away and lock her in his beautiful castle and dress her all in gold and silver and leave her there until she told him she loved him. Everything was a fairy tale. She even invented sins to confess to the priest. I told her that her imagination would get her into trouble one day. But how I did love listening to her. Here, dear, let me see your work." She reached out her hand and Berthe placed the pillowcase in it. The old woman brought it up to within inches of her eyes. "Fine work, just like your mother," she said, running her fingers over the stitches. They sat for a long while stitching in the dim light. Finally, the old woman stopped and touched Berthe's hand.

"I just remembered, I have a book of your mother's," she said, reaching over and pulling out a drawer in the long table. She took out a faded red leather-bound volume and handed it to Berthe. "This was her favorite. The Bible never had enough plumes and passion for her taste." Berthe took the book and studied it. It was entitled *Sense and Sensibility* by "A Lady." It was an English novel translated into French. On the inside first page was an illustration, covered by tissue paper, of two ladies in high-waisted dresses of the Regency period standing under a huge oak tree. Off in the distance could be seen an enormous mansion with a meandering path that led up to it. One woman peered at a small miniature painting while the other looked on. The caption underneath the illustration read: *"Be so good as to look at this face."*

"She used to read this to me while I sewed, and when she left the convent she gave it to me. You may as well have it. I can't see the words anymore, anyway. The sisters never did know what to do with her. Luckily, it was decided that she had to go home and take care of her father when her mother died."

Berthe reached out and touched the old woman's gnarled hand. "It's the first time I've heard about my mother as a young girl. Thank you for sharing your memories, Madame Blanquet."

"My memories are all I have left to share," said the old woman.

Berthe took leave of Madame Blanquet and found her way back to the main salon. She was surprised that there had been nothing but kind words for her mother.

"Mother Superior asks that you wait until she finishes her evening prayers," said the young sister who had first greeted her earlier in the day.

Berthe sat down on a wooden chair and opened the book. She noticed that there were lightly penciled underlinings of what must have been her mother's favorite passages. She closed the book. She couldn't bear to read it now. She made an effort to push her mother's presence from her mind. The closeness she felt to her was almost too painful to bear.

As she sat in the great room with the gold light of the setting sun coming through the windows, Berthe thought how wonderful it would be to stay here, to study, to read, to sew small stitches in old soft cotton and to just be at peace. Suddenly she had an idea. She would beg the Mother Superior for a job in the convent. She would do the wash, cook, clean the rooms, anything as long as she could make this her home.

If she could just live here she would do it differently from her mother. She would follow the rules. She would even try and dedicate herself to the Father, Son, and Holy Spirit. She would learn humility and obedience—something for which her mother obviously never had a talent.

The Mother Superior entered from a doorway at the end of the room and seemed to almost glide across the floor before Berthe realized she was standing at her side.

"Mother Superior, let me stay," said Berthe, standing up. "Give me a job. I'll work hard to earn my keep."

"Oh, my dear." Mother Superior took Berthe's hands and

smiled kindly. "We can't possibly take you in. Our sisters do all the labor, with the exception of Madame Blanquet, who takes care of the linens. We keep her on because, well, where is she to go at her age? But the convent is no place for you. Oh, no. I need only take one look at you to see that you are your mother's daughter. You belong in Paris. That's the life for a beauty like you. Go and be happy. And may our Lord Jesus Christ protect you," she added, making the sign of the cross over Berthe.

Berthe felt as if this was more of a warning than a blessing. Her shoulders sagged and all the breath went out of her. Again, she was being pushed toward a life she hadn't chosen, one that she felt was fraught with danger. She wrapped the book in a shawl, carefully placed it in the bottom of her bag, and took her leave.

CHAPTER 15

A Palace in Paris

BERTHE STOOD IN FRONT OF 11, RUE PAYENNE, AND STARED UP at the enormous three-story stone house. She thought she had never been so nervous. Underneath the heavy homespun skirt her grand-mère had given her, her legs felt weak.

The first two floors were composed of tall many-paned windows; the top floor had smaller round windows topped off by a copper-trimmed mansard roof. It was hard to imagine that this was someone's private home. Hesitating, she lifted the heavy bronze knocker and tapped it lightly on the double door. A pretty raven-haired girl dressed in a maid's uniform opened it immediately. Tears were streaming down the girl's face and her cheeks were flushed and splotchy.

"Oh, I . . . I'm sorry, I'm Berthe Bovary."

"I know who you are," the girl snapped, opening the door wider. She pulled up her apron to wipe at her tears. "Stay right here." She pointed to a spot on the floor. "I'll tell Madame you have arrived." She turned and went quickly up a huge spiral staircase.

Nothing had prepared Berthe for her first glimpse of the interior of the house. The walls were covered in a rich cerise damask. The floor was polished marble.

A huge crystal chandelier hung in the center of the hall. On the walls above the staircase hung ornate gilt-framed oil paintings of serious-looking people in fancy dress and complicated hair arrangements.

Berthe caught a glimpse of herself in the elaborately framed mirror that hung over a delicate tapestry-covered bench in the entranceway. She looked frightened. She *was* frightened. What was she doing in this place? The shock of coming here from the dingy mill life in Lille was almost more than her nervous stomach could bear.

The house smelled of furniture polish and fresh flowers. She waited for a long time. The longer she waited the more nervous she became. She didn't know the first thing about being a maid. She thought about Félicité, their old maid. But she was more like a member of the family. She did the cooking, the wash, and the cleaning, but she did all these household chores in her own simple country way. Berthe looked around. This was definitely not a simple household. The Rappelais home was, as far as she could see, a veritable palace.

The dark-haired young maid finally returned. Her tears had dried into white streaks.

"Madame will see you now," she said, blowing her nose. Berthe followed her up the long staircase, keeping her eyes lowered. They walked down a wide hallway, the walls of which were covered in blue damask and hung with more paintings of even more severe-looking people in formal dress. The maid knocked on a door at the end of the hall.

"Entrez," said a soft voice. Inside, everything was red—warm blood-red. The paneled walls were covered in red and gold silk,

as were the chairs, the chaise, and the bed. The canopy over the bed was hung with heavy red brocade embossed with beautiful gold and silver palm leaves. Madame Rappelais was sitting at her secretary, writing. She looked up and smiled.

"Leave us, Mariette," she said.

"But, madame," wailed Mariette, her tears starting anew. *Mariette?* Wasn't that the name of the girl Hélène told Berthe about, who was supposed to have drowned herself in the Seine?

"Mariette, compose yourself, dear," Madame Rappelais said quietly. "Now go and tell Madame DuPoix that the new girl has come, and make sure her room is ready." Madame Rappelais was a beautiful woman, with the whitest, creamiest skin Berthe had ever seen. Her silver-blond hair was worn in a simple upsweep with side curls that just touched her high, elegant cheekbones. She had a lovely aquiline nose, clear gray eyes, and her full soft mouth turned up at the corners as if she was about to burst into laughter. She wore a pale blue-gray satin gown, trimmed in off-white lace. She was quite slender except for an ample bosom which swelled up and out of the top of her dress.

"Well, Mademoiselle Bovary," she said, looking Berthe up and down, "you come highly recommended by my husband. I trust his judgment implicitly, which of course is why you are here. He knows how much I appreciate beauty. And you are quite the beauty, my dear." Berthe blushed and lowered her head. "You will replace Mariette, who has, up until today, been my lady's maid."

Berthe understood now why the girl Mariette was so upset. She had been fired from her job. Berthe wondered what she had done to incur her mistress's disapproval.

"But, madame..." Berthe twisted her fingers together.

"Yes, my dear?" said Madame Rappelais, already turning back to her correspondence. Berthe forced the words out.

"I have no experience as a lady's maid."

"Don't worry. My housekeeper, Madame DuPoix, will show you everything you need to know. She is an excellent teacher. And you seem like an intelligent girl. I am sure you will pick up your duties in no time. Now, you must be tired after your long journey. Why don't you settle in? Madame DuPoix will show you your room." Berthe was dismissed.

Madame DuPoix escorted Berthe to the top floor. She was a tall woman who held herself as if she had a pole running down her back. She had smooth olive skin, a full down-turned mouth, and a long, elegant neck. She wore her brown hair pulled painfully back into a tight little bun. Berthe thought she could be quite beautiful if she smiled.

"Tomorrow we will begin your training," she said, leaving Berthe alone in her room. It was a bright, spotless room with a large, quilt-covered iron bed, an armoire, a washstand, a writing table, and a chair. Berthe went to the window and opened it. It looked out onto a magnificent manicured garden. It was a soft spring day; the smell of lilacs filled the air. Overcome with gratitude, she began to cry. Finally, her life had taken a turn for the better. She had been given a new chance in a beautiful home with a beautiful and kind mistress.

She opened the armoire. In it was a long black maid's uniform and a starched white pinny with simple frills. She put her few things away, then unwrapped her mother's book. She lay down on the soft bed. Opening the book to one of the underlined passages she read:

> "And yet two thousand a year is a very moderate income," said Marianne. "A family cannot well be maintained on a smaller. I am sure I am not extravagant in my demands. A proper establishment of ser-

vants, a carriage, perhaps two, and hunters, cannot
be supported on less." . . .

"Hunters," repeated Edward—"But why must
you have hunters? Everybody does not hunt."

Marianne colored as she replied, "But most peo-
ple do."

"I wish," said Margaret, striking out a novel
thought, "that somebody would give us all a large for-
tune apiece!"

She woke the next morning to the sound of rain clattering on the slate roof. It was still dark when there was a knock on the door. It was Madame DuPoix.

"Before we begin let me explain about Mariette, because you will of course wonder why she lost her position. And it behooves me to tell you, so that you avoid the same mistake." She folded her arms across her chest. "One of the gardeners saw Mariette in the stable kissing young Bernard, the footman. The gardener told me and of course, as my duty as housekeeper, I informed Madame. Bernard was let go and Mariette demoted to downstairs maid. And that is that." Something about the delivery made Berthe wonder if Madame DuPoix was telling the truth. She remembered what Hélène had said about Monsieur Rappelais having his way with the maid. Was this what had actually happened to Mariette? Anxiety gripped her stomach. She pulled her shawl tighter around her shoulders.

"I advise you not to become too friendly with Mariette," Madame DuPoix continued. "She is not a happy girl. She is, however, very fortunate that Madame is loyal to a fault. She rarely gets rid of anyone. We girls all ultimately become a part of her family."

"You were her lady's maid?" Berthe had a difficult time thinking of Madame DuPoix as a girl.

"That was my first position in this family," she said. Her mouth tightened into an even thinner line. "I was not much older than you. Of course, I was trained properly before coming here. My mother was a lady's maid before me." She looked Berthe up and down and sniffed. Madame DuPoix clearly found her wanting.

"I don't understand why Madame Rappelais wants me to be her lady's maid. I know nothing about what's involved," said Berthe, straightening her pinafore.

"It's quite simple," said Madame DuPoix. "You have the look."

"Oh." Berthe had no idea what that meant but again she felt a wave of apprehension run through her entire body.

"Now get dressed and come down to the kitchen," Madame DuPoix said, glancing at the small golden watch pinned to her starched white pinafore. "The day is getting away from us."

The kitchen was an enormous room, hung with heavy copper pots and pans and long-handled ladles and spoons. Madame DuPoix introduced Berthe to the cook, Madame Brobert, Jeanine the scullery maid, and Madame Croisset the laundress, all of whom were sitting at the long, scrubbed pine table, dipping their bread and butter into steaming bowls of *café au lait.*

"Sit down, dear," said Madame Brobert, filling a bowl with coffee and hot milk and passing it to Berthe. "Help yourself to the bread and butter. You look as if you could use a bit of fattening up." Madame Brobert was a round, happy-faced woman with curly white hair that peeked out from underneath her starched cap.

Berthe tore off a piece of bread from one of several long

loaves on the table. The bread was warm, as if it had just come out of the oven. She spread the butter and took a bite. It was crusty and chewy, and the butter sweet. She had not tasted anything as delicious since leaving her grand-mère's farm. She ate quickly but had difficulty swallowing. As comforting as the food was, the knot in her stomach prevented her from fully enjoying it. She was filled with trepidation about the work she was to do, about what Madame Rappelais expected of her, and mostly about Monsieur Rappelais and what had been his real motive for bringing her here.

"Ah, good," said Madame Brobert, watching Berthe consume the bread. "I was afraid we had a non-eater. Never trust anyone who doesn't love their food is what I always say. Now, hurry up and finish, ladies. The men will be coming in for their breakfast."

Berthe followed Madame DuPoix up the back stairs. "This is Monsieur Rappelais's bedroom," she said as they passed by.

"Where is Monsieur Rappelais?" asked Berthe nervously. "I haven't seen him since I arrived."

"Monsieur is visiting his silk mills in Lyon." Berthe suddenly felt relieved.

"Silk is all Monsieur really cares about," Madame DuPoix said sharply. "It is his only passion."

She opened the door adjacent to Madame Rappelais's bedroom, and Berthe followed her in.

"This is Madame's dressing room," she whispered. "Keep your voice down. She is still asleep." The dressing room was mirrored from floor to ceiling. In between the mirrors were panels of red and silver brocade wallpaper. There were built-in closets hidden by hand-painted doors. One entire wall was taken up by a set of five burled maple armoires. "Your responsibilities are to clean this room, the bedroom, and the bath. You are to keep everything tidy and dusted, aired and in perfect order. And that means everything. Your first job is to sweep the hearth in here and build a small fire on cold and inclement days. Do it quickly." Madam DuPoix watched closely as Berthe did as she was told. She felt stiff and self-conscious. She worried about making a mistake in front of the critical eyes of this stern, stiff woman. Of course this was not the same as making a mistake on the dreaded mill machine. She was not about to have her arm torn off. But still, she was nervous.

The housekeeper nodded stiffly in approval. "Next, go through the clothes that Madame has discarded from the night before." She bent and picked up a beautiful plum-colored satin dress. "Check to make sure the clothes are clean." She pointed to a line of mud at the hem of the dress, then opened a cabinet drawer and removed a soft merino cloth. "All your cleaning supplies are here." She rubbed the hem of the dress with the cloth and the mud disappeared. "Never take a brush to a silk dress. As the season changes you need to be aware of the different treatments for the lighter materials. And never assume that you know how to clean a certain item. Always ask me first if you're in doubt. For now we will go through what we have here."

She picked up a velvet and silk plum-colored bonnet with black ostrich feathers at the brim. "Dust bonnets with a light feather plume to remove every speck of dirt. All this should have been done the night before, but I see that Mariette was too upset to finish her duties. If the bonnet feathers are damp hold them in front of the fire for a few minutes."

Madame DuPoix showed Berthe where the dress should be hung in one of the huge armoires. There were three armoires just for dresses: summer dresses, winter dresses, and ball gowns. Berthe gasped at the sight of so many elegant gowns. Her mother would have thought she had died and gone to heaven.

There was even a separate armoire just for bonnets. The house-keeper picked up a pair of beautiful brown kid boots that had been flung in the corner. "These are kid," she said, holding them up for Berthe to inspect. "They must be wiped off with a sponge soaked in milk. Later, I will give you the recipe for boot black-ing. Madame has over thirty pairs of shoes and boots."

Thirty pairs for just one pair of feet!

Madame DuPoix looked around the dressing room to make sure everything was in its place. She glanced down at her watch and sighed, and Berthe suddenly realized that her training was an added burden to Madame DuPoix's already full schedule. "Next, you must prepare for the dressing of Madame." She said this as if they were preparing for the coronation of the Emperor. She pulled open one of the built-in drawers in the wall and care-fully removed a set of lingerie. She laid the finely embroidered, white-ribboned, lace-edged chemise and bloomers on the chaise longue. "In the winter you must warm them first by holding them in front of the fire." Berthe felt overwhelmed. How could she remember all this? If only she could take notes. "Today is Monday, Madame's day to go calling. And because of the in-clement weather you should lay out one of her warmer spring frocks, a pair of sturdy boots, a light short cape, and, of course, her umbrella." She opened one of the armoires and turned to Berthe. "Pick one," she said. Berthe stared at the endless line of long, elaborately trimmed, full-skirted dresses, mostly in pastel shades. She tentatively touched the sleeve of a black silk dress embroidered with tiny red flowers and felt a small thrill. How she wished she could own a dress like this.

"Wrong. That's a dinner frock," said Madame DuPoix. Berthe felt her face flush. She had already failed her first test. Madame DuPoix removed a dove-gray dress with puffed sleeves and black velvet piping running in several rows around the entire skirt. From another armoire she unfolded a wire cage hoop-skirt and crinolines.

Then she turned her attention to the dressing table.

"Look at this mess," she exclaimed. There was face powder everywhere on the mirrored tabletop. She replaced the silver lid on the crystal powder pot, took the powder brush and shook it out over the fireplace. She carefully placed the silver-handled brush and comb set side by side and moved by minuscule inches the perfume bottles, the pillboxes, and a beautiful hand mirror so that everything lined up exactly. *How can one person own so many beautiful things?*

"Now it's time to draw Madame's bath." The bathroom adjoining the dressing room was as large as Berthe's bedroom, if not larger. Her mouth fell open. She had never imagined even in her most fantastic dreams that there were bathrooms such as this. The room was filled with a soft light that seeped through the translucent pale green drapes. The drapes covered the tall windows that looked out onto the wet green garden. A huge gilt-framed mirror was set into the wall and framed on either side by gilt sconces. The washbasin was white marble set into a carved, hand-painted cabinet. The gold handles for the hot and cold water were in the shape of dolphins. The faucet was a swan with a long, elegant neck. The enormous white bathtub had four clawed golden feet; the handles and faucet matched those on the sink. Madame DuPoix turned the faucet and hot water steamed out.

Berthe was amazed. Where did the hot water come from? She was not about to ask. She didn't want to display her ignorance any more than she had to. The housekeeper opened a tall cabinet, removed a large white towel, and hung it over a needlepoint chair in the corner. She tested the bathwater with her elbow, then added some bathing salts from a silver and crystal container and a splash of lilac bath oil from an exquisite cut-glass carafe. Finally she straightened up and announced: "And now it is time to wake Madame." Berthe's stomach did a turn. It was one thing to be instructed by this stern woman, quite another to have to deal directly with the mistress of such a grand house.

Berthe followed her into the darkened bedroom. Madame DuPoix pulled the heavy damask drapes aside. It was still dark and rainy outside. Madame Rappelais lay in the exact center of the enormous high-canopied bed, her head on a stack of small white embroidered pillows, her hands crossed over her bosom. It was as if she were laid out for burial. Berthe felt a twinge of horror.

"Good morning, madame," said Madame DuPoix quietly.

"Oh, goodness me, is it that time already?" said Madame Rappelais. A satin and lace sleeping mask covered her eyes. "Where is my beautiful Berthe?" she asked, yawning. Berthe reddened with embarrassment.

"She is right here, madame."

"And you have shown her everything she needs to know?" she said, removing the mask and smiling at Berthe.

"No, not everything, madame. We have only just begun."

"Run along, Madame DuPoix. I can instruct her in the rest."

"But, madame, you shouldn't have to—"

"I would enjoy teaching her," interrupted Madame Rappelais. "You may go. You have enough to do as it is."

Berthe dreaded being alone with her employer. Why was she afraid? Her mistress seemed so kind and patient.

"Yes, madame," said Madame DuPoix. She curtsied and then backed out of the room as though she had just ended an audience with the queen.

"You can make up the bed and tidy around here while I take

my bath," Madame Rappelais said to Berthe, sitting up and sliding off the bed.

She disappeared into the bathroom. Berthe made the bed, fluffed and refluffed the pillows, straightened the items on Madame's secretary, opened the window slightly to air the room, and then was at a loss as to what to do next. As cool as the day was, she felt the perspiration run down her back.

After some time Madame Rappelais emerged from the bath wearing a beautiful Chinese kimono.

"Come into the dressing room," she said, "and we'll do my hair." She sat at the dressing table, picked up the silver-handled brush, and handed it to Berthe. "Not too rough; I have a very sensitive scalp." Her hair was long and lustrous. It fell down her back in thick, heavy waves. "Just a simple hairstyle will do for a day like this," she said. Showing Berthe what she meant she pulled her hair up and back then twisted the long locks into a spiral bun at the top of her head.

Berthe had a sense of *déjà vu*. She remembered watching Félicité dress her mother's hair before she went riding with Monsieur Boulanger. She had sat in the corner enjoying Emma Bovary's welcome change of spirits. As if noticing her daughter for the first time, her mother turned from the mirror.

"Well, what do you think?" she asked.

"I think you're a princess, Maman." Her mother beamed at her and for that one split second, Berthe felt almost loved, or, at the very least, accepted. It was a moment she never forgot.

Madame Rappelais picked up the hand mirror and examined the back of her head. "Now a few pins and that's it." With shaking hands, Berthe placed the hairpins carefully so that they didn't show. Then she pulled down a few stray curls around her mistress's face. "Very good," Madame commented, turning her face this way and that. "You see, it's not so difficult. For the evening, of course, it's another matter entirely. But I shall have a professional hairdresser come and give you a few lessons. You won't need many. I see you have a real knack."

"Shall I fetch your breakfast, madame?" Berthe asked, beginning to feel slightly more at ease.

"If you ever hear me asking for breakfast in my bedroom, call the doctor immediately. No, I like to eat sitting up at a proper table in the dining room. I cannot bear getting toast crumbs all over my lovely bedroom. You've had your breakfast?"

"Oh, yes, madame, hours ago."

"Well then, I suppose it's time to get me dressed. Can't you see I'm totally helpless?" She laughed.

Madame Rappelais stood, untied the kimono, and let it drop to the floor. Berthe was suddenly flustered. She simply stood there and stared in shock.

"My dear girl, have you never seen a naked woman before?"

"No, madame," Berthe stuttered. Of course this wasn't true. She had seen her mother naked, and her grand-mère, the memory of which caused her to shudder. And she had certainly seen the naked half of Renard's neighbor as they embraced in the barn. But Madame was a virtual stranger and her employer to boot.

"Well, don't just stand there gawking, get my clothes before I catch my death." Madame patiently showed Berthe how to dress her. How tightly to pull the corset. How to put on the cage hoop followed by the crinolines. How to attach the band of her petticoats around her waist with a strong safety pin.

"My friend the comtesse de Léon once lost her petticoats at a ball. She was being twirled around by her much younger husband when they fell to her feet and almost caused her to break her neck." She showed Berthe how to make sure the sleeves of her gown fell nicely over her arms, how the folds of the dress should be arranged over the petticoats so that they fell into graceful waves. She instructed her how to tie the sash in a bow and then secure the bow with a pin on the inside.

Berthe remembered how new clothes had always seemed to lift her mother's moods. Madame Rappelais seemed unmoved by the whole experience of dressing in a beautiful gown. But of course, her spirits were already good. And why shouldn't they be? Berthe thought. Her mistress's life already seemed a delicious dream.

"What about jewelry, madame?" she asked.

"No, I never wear jewelry during the day. It's gauche." Berthe filed away that bit of information for future reference.

A knock sounded at the door.

"Madame, your breakfast is getting cold," said Madame DuPoix in an impatient tone that surprised Berthe. She was even more surprised by Madame Rappelais's reaction to her house-keeper's chiding. She laughed lightly and waved her hand.

"Oh, yes, yes. Don't nag, DuPoix. I'll be right down."

When Madame Rappelais went down to breakfast, the housekeeper took over Berthe's instruction.

"While Madame is at breakfast you are to finish with the dressing room and her bedroom. I will only show you this once, so pay attention. I see you made the bed already." DuPoix glanced at the bed and shook her head in disgust as if it were covered with bird droppings. "You did it all wrong. Madame likes her coverlet turned down." Berthe's face flushed. The house-keeper placed the brocade slippers precisely, so that only the toes peeked out from underneath the high bed. "The windows should stay open for at least an hour to air the room." She showed Berthe where the carpet sweeper, feather duster, and dustpan were kept in a small closet built in next to the fireplace. From this same cabinet she took a jar that contained moist tea leaves and threw them about the floor.

"The tea leaves keep the carpet smelling sweet. Now you may sweep them up. Dust each individual piece and make sure you move everything. Madame Rappelais hates dust. It makes her sneeze. Empty all the water pitchers and refill them with fresh water. And empty the slops into the slop pail and take it down. Mariette will dispose of them with the rest of the household waste. Polish the furniture with lemon oil. Keep track of everything in the closet—the polishes, the soaps, the toiletries—and let me know what requires replacing. Find out what her evening plans are so that you make sure what she wishes to wear is ready and in perfect repair. Do you sew?"

Berthe wanted to say she was an experienced piecer, that she knew how to tie knots in broken thread, but she decided against it.

"I did some sewing as a girl," she said. She was not about to overstate her skills to this woman.

"Well, you had better practice because your job requires you keep Madame's wardrobe in good repair. You must check her stockings to see if they need mending, and her hems, and the edging on collars, and of course repair all the lace. Madame is an easy mistress. Far too easy in my opinion. But I am the housekeeper and my job is to make sure that you do your job even if she doesn't seem to care as much as she should." She scowled. "So always remember, I am watching you."

Berthe spent the next hour dusting, sweeping, and polishing. The room was filled with small objects of incredible beauty. Tiny jeweled pillboxes, small framed portraits of beautiful ladies in lavish dresses, silver candelabras and bud vases. Everywhere she turned there was another lovely piece to admire.

In the bathroom, she inhaled the many delicious scents, from

Madame's creamy vanilla soap to the lavender-scented towel that she hung on a rack to dry. On a gold-plated tray fastened to the side of the huge bathtub were several crystal bottles of bath oil. She lifted one, removed the crystal stopper, and inhaled the contents. Lilies of the valley. How well she remembered the intoxicating smell of those tiny white, waxy flowers.

It was this same sweet fragrance that was connected to the day she hid and watched her mother and Monsieur Boulanger touch each other in the woods. She remembered it as if it were yesterday. The picture of Boulanger's dark hand against her mother's white sun-dappled buttocks suddenly came back to her. And along with it, her mother's moan, her thighs opening, his fingers probing.

"It is a lovely fragrance, *n'est-ce pas?*" Madame Rappelais stood in the doorway of the *salle de bain,* smiling. Berthe was so startled by the sudden appearance of her mistress that she dropped the crystal bottle; it shattered into tiny shards all over the marble floor.

"Oh, oh! Oh, madame. I am so sorry! Oh please, forgive me..." Berthe burst into tears as she dropped to her knees to pick up the pieces.

CHAPTER 16

The Master Returns

"Hush, child, it is nothing. Just take care not to cut yourself cleaning up the glass." Madame Rappelais reached down and squeezed her shoulder. She smiled and left the room as if there was nothing more to be said. Berthe had expected anger and berating. Such unexpected kindness left her feeling oddly uneasy.

As she bent down to clean up the mess, the tears continued to spill down her cheeks. She thought of her mother and how she might have reacted to Berthe's breaking the beautiful crystal vase. She would have been furious. How very different Berthe's life might have been if she had had a mother like Madame Rappelais. She vowed to fulfill Madame's every wish to the very best of her ability. Nothing would stand in the way of her doing a perfect job for her perfect mistress.

Over the next few weeks the endless backbreaking hours spent in the cotton mill began to seem like a bad dream. Apart from the hustle and bustle of the Rappelaises' kitchen at breakfast, it was as if Berthe was in an elegant new world of her own.

And for most of the day she was able to avoid Mariette, who gave her dirty looks every time they passed in the hall.

She spent much of her time going through Madame's wardrobe, examining each gown for detached lace, a loose hem, a frayed bow. She caressed the rich fabrics and marveled at the fine detailing of every dress. She reorganized the long dresses by color so that the result was a range of hues from the darkest to the palest pastels, not unlike Monsieur Millet's palette of Conté crayons.

Madame Rappelais surprised her one afternoon while Berthe was peering inside the sleeve of a particularly elaborate satin ball gown to examine the stitches.

"You are interested in fashion?" asked Madame. Berthe dropped the sleeve and quickly turned to her mistress.

"No. Yes. I'm sorry, madame, I was just wondering how the lace was attached."

"Then you are interested. All the better. Come with me." Berthe followed her into the bedroom. "The more attention you pay, the better you can serve me. I want you to make a study of these," Madame said, pointing to a stack of large journals that sat atop a marble end table. Berthe immediately recognized her mother's favorite fashion periodical. "Your job is to keep abreast of the latest fashions. When a trim or a button or a feather changes in *La Corbeille*, it must change in my closet. I can't be running to the dressmaker every two minutes for these things. Do you think you can do this?"

"Oh, yes, madame. I used to look at these books with my mother. She loved fashion."

"And where does she live, your mother?"

"She passed away some time ago, madame."

"A pity. She would be very proud of her daughter."

"Thank you, madame." Berthe tucked the stray strands of her hair back in her cap and readjusted her pinafore.

"This afternoon, I shall send you to the dressmaker to place an order for me. I must make a decision on my summer visiting dress. Which do you think?" She held up two lengths of fabric. One was a lemon yellow silk with black threads shot through. The second was a linen in the palest of pale blue.

"Oh, madame, I don't know..." said Berthe. Before she could stop herself she reached out to touch both fabrics.

"Of course you do. You have an opinion. I want to hear it." Madame Rappelais peered closely at her.

"Well, madame," said Berthe, taking a deep breath and forgetting her anxiety, "this would make a beautiful dress." She pointed to the blue linen. "It has a lightness to the material that the yellow doesn't. But more important, the color is a perfect complement to your eyes."

"I told you," said Madame Rappelais, looking pleased. "You know more than you say and much more than you think, young lady." She draped the blue fabric over Berthe's shoulders and then stood back and studied the effect. "The blue suits you as well. You are quite the loveliest thing. But I suppose you know that." Berthe shook her head, her face crimson. "Oh dear, now I've embarrassed her. Being beautiful isn't a crime, you know." Madame Rappelais laughed and pulled the fabric away from Berthe. "You may go, my dear."

"Monsieur returns tonight," sighed Madame Rappelais when Berthe woke her mistress the next morning. She lay in bed for a long time without removing her eye mask. Berthe's heart sank. It was the thing she had been dreading since she arrived *chez* Rappelais. She had yet to work out how she was going to handle his advances. Even though the story about Mariette jumping into the Seine proved to be false, she was certain the other part of the story must be true. Why else had he brought her all the way from Lille, if not to seduce her?

She didn't want to leave this lovely house. Was she to give in to his lecherous advances? Should she quietly do his bidding? Was that the price she had to pay for this new life? She remembered his long dry fingers on her cheek. His clever eyes taking in every detail of her face. And what if she said no? Undoubtedly, that would be the end of her wonderful job. She suddenly felt clammy all over.

She couldn't risk being fired. Would they send her back to the mill? She couldn't go back. She would rather starve on the streets of Paris than risk life and limb in that place.

She remembered Renard's caresses in the hayfields. Would Monsieur Rappelais want the same thing? Or would he want to mount her as Renard had the neighbor girl? She felt dizzy and nauseated.

That night, after she had laid out her mistress's *peignoir,* pulled back the bedcovers, and sprayed the sheets with *l'eau de cologne,* Madame Rappelais appeared in the doorway.

"Berthe, my dear, my husband requests your presence. He's in his bedroom."

"But I . . ." She felt her whole body go cold. And yet there were beads of perspiration running down her back.

"It's very late. Please don't keep him waiting. *Bonne nuit,*" said Madame Rappelais. She raised her arms above her head, yawned, and slipped into bed. Berthe felt as if she were being fed to the lions. She stood there for a moment wanting to ask Madame what was expected of her. But her mistress was already snoring lightly.

Berthe tripped on her own feet as she made her way slowly down the long hallways to Monsieur's bedroom. She thought she was going to be sick all over the Oriental runner. She took a deep breath before knocking lightly on the door. There was no answer. Perhaps he had fallen asleep. She knocked a second time, hoping against hope that he wouldn't answer.

"Entrez," came the command. She opened the door and stepped inside. Monsieur Rappelais's back was turned to her. He stood before a long table that was stacked with bolts of material. He was wearing a beautiful green and blue silk brocade dressing gown and elegant velvet brocade slippers. Berthe immediately noticed that his legs were bare. *He's naked underneath his robe,* she realized with a start. He turned around and smiled.

"Ah, the beautiful mademoiselle from the mill. Come in, come in. Tell me, how do you like your new job?"

"Very much, monsieur. Thank you," she said in a barely audible whisper.

"And the mistress? She is not too demanding?"

"No, sir, not at all."

"Ah, good. Good. Now I need you to do something for me, my dear. Look at these fabrics. Are they not exquisite? They come from my mills in Lyon. You see, cotton is my bread and butter. But silk, silk is my caviar and champagne. Look at the detail of this." He unrolled a bolt of cloth. "Is this not the most delicious fabric you have ever seen?" It was a heavy silk of yellow and white flowers upon a royal blue background with a design of ivy intertwined with golden *fleurs-de-lis.*

"It is very beautiful, monsieur." Her fingers hesitated over the cloth. She was afraid to touch it.

"Now, mademoiselle. Take off your clothes." He said it so matter-of-factly, Berthe wasn't sure she had heard him correctly.

"What?" She backed away.

"Just do as I say. Don't be shy." He tutted impatiently.

"But, but, sir...I...I..." she stammered, twisting her apron string round and round her hand.

"Please, it's late and I'm very tired. I want to see how these fabrics drape." He unrolled another bolt of cloth—a pale blue and cream satin with a design of red roses and blue ribbon. Berthe was sure it was a trick. When he had her completely naked and there was no escape, then he would pounce on her. The fact that Mariette was still working in the Rappelais household just meant that rather than throw herself into the river Seine she had decided to swallow her pride and shame and continue to work for the man who had ruined her life. "I haven't got all night, mademoiselle," Monsieur Rappelais said, frowning at her.

Berthe took a deep, shaky breath and untied her apron. Then she removed her dress and with trembling hands, carefully laid it over a brocaded chair. She stood shivering in her cotton chemise and underpetticoat. She willed herself not to cry. During all this time Monsieur's attention was elsewhere. He was rolling and unrolling bolts of cloth, one on top of the other. He commented to himself about each one.

"Too heavy, too formal, too fussy." Finally selecting a bolt of cloth, he turned and looked at Berthe. "Ah, let's try this, shall we?" He draped a plum-colored silk with raised black brocade over her and stood back to admire the effect. "*Parfait!* Just *parfait!* This is lovely on you. You should always wear eggplant. You have the most exquisite coloring. Like a peach. This is not an easy shade to wear. I wager there are not three women in all of Paris who can do it justice. Well, we'll let Monsieur Worth worry about that, shall we? Take that off. And let's put this on." He unfurled a bolt of light green chiffon and swept a length of it over Berthe's bare shoulders. "Oh, marvelous! So delicious I could eat it." As he turned around, the sash on his robe came undone, and Berthe saw something that so shocked her she gasped aloud.

Underneath his dressing gown, the distinguished Monsieur Rappelais was wearing a woman's black lace corset and garters and nothing else. The garters, unattached to stockings, dangled freely.

"Oh, monsieur!" said Berthe, covering her eyes and turning away.

He looked down.

"What? Oh, sorry," he said, retying the robe. Was this the man who was going to ravage her, to take away her virginity? What exactly was he going to do to her? "Now, which do you like better, this or this?" He held up two different lengths of crimson silk. "Here, feel it against your skin. This has a much heavier heft to it and I think it would be lovely as a lining for a cape. What do you think?"

She suddenly realized that he was, in fact, far more interested in the fabric than he was in her. She felt the fear begin to leave her.

"I like this one," she said, tentatively touching the heavier silk. "But this," she pointed to the second, "would make a lovely underskirt."

"Ah, yes, very good. Very good. Come here, I want to show you something." She stiffened again. He led her over to a stack of books on another long table. They were filled with small swatches of silk: silk in every conceivable color, every conceivable design. "This is what makes my job so very difficult. How to choose what to manufacture from all of these. How to know what the ladies will want." He sighed. "Silk is what dictates the look of the day. Silk changes, it innovates, it leads the way. Fashion follows ever so slowly. Fashion is what hangs in your armoire. Silk is what dresses the future." He turned to look at her. "Do you understand?"

Berthe nodded. He reminded her of Monsieur Millet. The artist's speech about texture came back to her: "The coarser the texture, the sturdier the weave; the rougher the life, the greater the reward... Always honor the homespun." Here was another man passionate about fabric—but, ironically, exactly the opposite kind of material. Berthe found Rappelais's words and his enthusiasm as exciting as she had found Millet's. As the evening progressed, she forgot all about the fact that her employer was wearing a corset underneath his dressing gown. It suddenly didn't matter.

"Now, look at this," Rappelais said, carefully removing a swatch from the book and holding it up to the light of the chandelier. "This is going to be in great demand."

"How very beautiful," said Berthe. The fabric was a deep wine silk with gold threads woven to create a raised design of grapes and grape leaves.

"The world is moving into darker solid colors," explained Rappelais, "but florals and fruits will always be in vogue. This fabric is very dear. Of course, none of this would be possible without that genius Jacquard. You have heard of Jacquard?"

Berthe shook her head.

"Oh, *mon Dieu*," he said, slapping his face. "I must take you in hand, mademoiselle. There is much to learn. Luckily, I am a brilliant, inspired teacher. My wife, unfortunately, cares nothing about the making of silk. All she is interested in is the wearing of it." He peered at her closely. "You are not tired, are you?"

"No, monsieur." Her body ached with fatigue, but her mind felt unexpectedly alert, ready to absorb all he had to offer.

"Good. Very good. Sit down." He indicated a chair. He poured them each a small glass of liqueur. "I thought I had found a pearl for my wife and I ended up with a diamond for myself." He laughed. "Do you remember telling me you preferred silk as you stood in the middle of my cotton mill?"

She nodded, taking a small sip of the liqueur. It burned her throat but tasted deliciously of pears.

"I thought to myself then: This is a girl who is not afraid to declare her love of the more luxurious things in life. There is nothing in this world more important than silk. And my wife tells me that you also have an eye for fine fashion. Is that correct?"

"I think so, monsieur."

"So let us continue. In 1804, Joseph-Marie Jacquard invented a loom which used a belt of pattern cards that were punched with various holes designed to create a patterned weave. The result was that the Jacquard weave replaced the need for humans who had to spend long hours hand-pulling the old-style looms. It is because of his invention that we have brocades, brocatelle, and lamé such as these." He showed her various fabric samples to illustrate his story. "In the beginning, because the Jacquard loom was putting so many workers out of work, there was a great deal of sabotage of these looms. But that was years ago. Now there are over four thousand Jacquard looms in Lyon alone." He yawned and stretched. "Well, even if you're not tired, mademoiselle, I am exhausted. Next time, we'll discuss the beauty of brocade and the threat of the new blends."

Thus began her education in the history and manufacturing of silk. Berthe began to dream of another sort of job: working alongside Monsieur Rappelais, helping him choose and perhaps even design fabrics. Could she earn her living this way? Why not? To think of it: making money doing something she loved. Not having to depend on a husband or some other man to support her, the way her mother had. Now, that was a dream worth dreaming—one that Berthe reasoned her mother never even imagined.

The following afternoon, as Berthe was helping Madame Rappelais dress for an outing, Monsieur appeared in the doorway.

"Well, I am pleased to say that your Mademoiselle Bovary has the eye for fabrics and a mind eager to learn more," he said. "Finally, someone who can appreciate my talent."

"I'm happy you're pleased, my dear," said Madame Rappelais, as she handed a comb to Berthe to place in her hair. Monsieur Rappelais bowed to both of them and left the room. "I hope my husband isn't boring you to death," she said to Berthe.

"Oh, no. Not at all. I love learning about the making of silk."

"Well, take care that he doesn't monopolize you. And don't forget your place," she said with mock sternness. "Your place, my little mademoiselle, *is with me.*"

Monsieur Rappelais spent the next two weeks grabbing Berthe whenever she had a spare moment, to have her model the newest silks and to explain to her the origins of some of the lavish designs.

"These are some of my most successful creations," he said, proudly handing her a book of swatches. The book contained page after page of designs: daisies, lilies, bouquets of roses entwined with ribbons, laurel, oak leaves, exotic birds, and bees. The latter, according to Rappelais, were a favorite of Napoléon's. Berthe turned each page slowly, touching every swatch.

The time came that Monsieur had to again make another trip to Lille and Lyon. "From the sow's ear to the silk purse," he said to Berthe. "I spend only one day at Lille because what is there to say about cotton? It is what it is. My presence is more important in Lyon. They are after me to start making, forgive the expression, blends. These hideous department stores have created a demand for fabric that the great unwashed can more easily afford."

"The great unwashed?" Berthe frowned. She was poor, but certainly not unwashed.

"Perhaps I put it too harshly," Rappelais said, noticing her expression. "But my point is that silk was created for a certain class of people. And unfortunately, these blends are getting better and better at masquerading as the more expensive fabrics."

"But, monsieur, if a less expensive blend could be made wouldn't that benefit everyone? Why shouldn't less fortunate women be able to own beautiful gowns as well as wealthy women?"

He looked at her as if a frog had just emerged from her mouth.

"We just can't have everyone wearing silk, my dear! You have to understand, the fabrics I manufacture are embroidered by hand and finished by hand. They are expensive to buy because they are expensive to make. Can you imagine how a woman of means wearing an exquisite gown would feel if she saw her maidservant wearing a cheap replica of the same thing? Why, she would feel terribly cheated. I am not in the business of cheating the rich. We must maintain our standards, or society as we know it would crumble!"

Though she couldn't say it aloud, in her heart Berthe reflected that if she ever had the chance, she would see to it that every woman, rich *or* poor, could have the pleasure of dressing well. Then, as her mother always said, the world would be a prettier place. It was not such a terrible idea, after all.

CHAPTER 17

The Bath

SEVERAL WEEKS HAD PASSED SINCE MONSIEUR RAPPELAIS HAD departed for his mills. Before leaving he had given Berthe the book of swatches. "Here," he had said, handing her the heavy leather-bound book, "you may borrow it and study it at your leisure." His only interest in her seemed to be as a potential student of fabric and fashion, and as a model. She was relieved not to have been molested by the strange old man, just as she was happy to be serving Madame Rappelais. At least with her there would be no sudden surprises.

"Oh, I am desperate for a nice, long bath," said Madame Rappelais, coming home after a long day of shopping.

"Shall I run the tub for you, madame?"

"Please, and, Berthe, make it good and hot. Shopping leaves me feeling *dégoûtante*." Berthe ran the water, adding the bath salts and a splash of lavender oil. She took two thick white towels and hung them on a rack near the fireplace. The evening was cold and rainy, so she built a small fire. She pulled back the duvet, fluffed and smoothed the feather pillows, straightened and scented the sheets for the second time that day. Then she went into the dressing room and removed a fresh nightgown and Madame's favorite *peignoir*. After laying the nightclothes on the bed, she went downstairs and fetched a pot of tea and a few biscuits from the kitchen. Madame liked something hot and sweet before turning in for the night. Berthe found that she enjoyed observing the details of Madame's routine. It gave her a sense of security and order.

She lit the oil lamp next to Madame's bed and placed the book her mistress had been reading on the bedside table, surprised to see that it was *Emma* by Jane Austen, a book her mother had read. But why, she wondered, would a fabulously wealthy woman like Madame Rappelais be interested in a story about a well-to-do family? To Emma Bovary the whole point of a book was to give her a glimpse of another world, a world otherwise out of her reach. Why would Madame Rappelais want to read about a lifestyle that she herself was already living?

"Berthe, can you come here, please?"

The request startled Berthe. With a last glance at the book, she walked across the room and knocked on the bathroom door. She had never before entered while Madame was taking her bath.

"Entrez," called Madame Rappelais. She lay in the tub surrounded by fragrant soap bubbles. Her silver-blond hair was swept up in a topknot. The hot water had turned her skin a rosy pink.

"Ah, Berthe, dear, my back needs a good scrub. Would you be so kind?"

"Yes, madame." Berthe picked up the soft sponge and rubbed it against a bar of the vanilla-scented soap. Madame Rappelais sat up in the bath and leaned forward.

"Don't be afraid to scrub hard," she said, smiling over her wet shoulder. Berthe kept her eyes averted. "Ahhh, yes, that feels wonderful." She sighed. "Now the front, but lightly, very lightly." She leaned back, rested her head against the edge of the tub and closed her eyes.

Now Berthe couldn't help but see her mistress's full, red-nippled breasts. She rinsed the sponge and soaped it again and tried not to wonder why tonight of all nights Madame Rappelais couldn't wash herself. She gently brought the sponge around her shoulders, the tops of her arms, and then, finally, across her breasts. She felt her face flush with warmth. She didn't know where to direct her gaze.

Suddenly Berthe felt a hand on the back of her neck pulling her down. Madame Rappelais's gray eyes were inches from Berthe's. She pulled Berthe even closer and kissed her softly on the mouth.

"Madame!" Berthe pulled away, wiping her mouth with the back of her hand.

"Don't be afraid," whispered Madame Rappelais. "I'm not going to hurt you. I would never hurt you, dear child. Quite the contrary, my sweet, lovely girl." The next kiss was longer. And, if possible, even softer. Berthe's lips seemed to fit perfectly against Madame's generous mouth. And then Madame's tongue slipped between her lips. Berthe was torn between a desire to pull away and a desire to immerse herself in the warm scented water with her beautiful mistress.

"Take off your clothes, dear. Take them off now," Madame Rappelais instructed softly.

"But I . . ." Berthe drew back, her wet hands nervously pulling at her pinafore.

"I know they must have taught you how to follow instructions in my husband's mill. Just do as I say and all will be well." Berthe suddenly understood the threat that lay underneath the words. And yet Madame Rappelais was smiling kindly as if she were teaching a slow child.

Trembling, Berthe kept her head lowered as she took off her pinafore and her dress. She lowered her petticoats to the floor. She felt as if she were not connected to her body, as if some power had taken over her every move. The next thing she knew she was kneeling by the side of the tub and they were kissing again. Madame's soft fingers danced across one of Berthe's nipples and then the other until they stood out sharp and erect. She knew she should hate this woman for what she was doing, but her mind had gone somewhere else. She had stopped thinking altogether. Only her body was present.

Madame leaned down and with the tip of her tongue licked around and around the perimeter of Berthe's breasts, ignoring the silent pleas of her erect nipples. *Please, touch us, please kiss us, please bite us, please, please.* Finally, when Berthe thought she would die from need, Madame's tongue lightly tipped the end of her nipple and with the other hand she continued to caress Berthe's other breast. Then she began suckling on Berthe like a hungry newborn baby.

"Get in," she said huskily, "and I'll show you what to do." She made room for Berthe in the tub. Berthe slipped in beside her. At first the water felt too hot, but then her skin adjusted to it and the warmth embraced her. "You are so delicious. So young and delicious," breathed Madame Rappelais. "Do you know how beautiful you are? Of course not. Kiss me."

Berthe gave herself up completely. She kissed her mistress again and again. She wanted never to stop. "Kiss this," Madame Rappelais said, pointing to her breast. Berthe lowered her mouth to the perfect breast and began to kiss it, lick it, and then finally suckle it. She thought, incongruously, of her mother at that moment, and she began to cry. Madame Rappelais appeared not to notice.

They caressed and kissed each other until the water turned cold and Madame Rappelais began laughing.

"Oh, it's freezing," she said, stepping quickly out of the tub and grabbing a thick towel. "Get out, *m'enfante*, or you'll catch your death." She wrapped Berthe in the other towel and dried her off as if she were a baby. And then, as if only moments before they hadn't been wrapped in each other's arms, she smiled and said, "Sleep well, Mademoiselle Bovary. I'll see you in the morning." She left Berthe standing on the wet marble floor, her head spinning with confusion, her body aching with desire.

The next morning, Berthe went downstairs to the kitchen to get her breakfast. She felt as if everything that had happened in Madame Rappelais's bathtub was written all over her face. Fortunately, no one seemed to notice. Everyone treated her exactly the same, except Mariette. She was ruder than usual to Berthe. Did she sense something?

"Hurry up with the butter, Bovary. You're not the only one at this table," she snapped. "Hush your mouth, Mariette," scolded Madame Brobert. "There's plenty for everyone. You take as much as you want, dear." Mariette scowled and reached across the table to grab the butter. When Berthe got up to take her dishes over to the washing sink, Mariette stuck out her foot and Berthe tripped over it. Later, on the back stairs as she was carrying down the sheets for the laundress, she ran into Mariette once again.

"You think you're special. You're not special. Just wait and see. She'll tire of you just as she did of me." Berthe suddenly realized why Mariette had been crying that very first day. She hadn't just been demoted to downstairs maid. She had been rejected as Madame's lover. No wonder she had acted at the time as if her heart had been broken. It had.

Berthe's stomach was tight with tension when she went to awaken Madame. She didn't know how to behave. She didn't know what was expected of her. And she was afraid. Afraid that Madame would start up with her again. Afraid that she wouldn't. What should she do? Should she wake her mistress with a kiss? Should she keep her distance? She needn't have worried. Everything was as if last night had never happened. Madame Rappelais was her usual self, if not somewhat distant. She acted exactly the same as she had before the bathtub incident. Berthe began to wonder if she had dreamt it.

She felt relieved and, at the same time, disappointed. But she knew enough not to say anything. She was a servant, after all. She must be prepared to do her mistress's bidding, whatever that might be.

CHAPTER 18

Family & Friends

A WEEK WENT BY WITH NO FURTHER SIGN FROM MADAME Rappelais that anything had passed between them. Berthe felt herself turn red with embarrassment every time she was in Madame's presence. She was much relieved when Monsieur returned from his trip. Ironically, she felt much safer in his company now than with his wife.

Monsieur Rappelais was exhausted, and unhappy with one of his new fabrics.

"What do you think of this?" he asked Berthe. It was an unusually simple pattern of orange vines and white baby's breath against a deep blue background. Berthe frowned as she caressed the heavy silk.

"I know. It's boring," he said.

"Oh, sir, it's beautiful . . . but . . ."

"But what? Say it."

"It has no . . . how to describe it . . . anchor. Nothing holds the eye."

Rappelais tilted his head and squinted. "Yes, I see what you mean. But I am sick to death of tulips and roses."

"What about stars?" she said, turning to Monsieur Rappelais. "Stars?"

"Large stars scattered throughout, and then you could weave the ivy vines around them." She picked up the pen from his desk and quickly drew her idea on a scrap of paper.

"Brilliant. Yes, stars. I've never used stars before. But why not? It's all out of nature." He patted her on the shoulder. "You have the gift, mademoiselle." Berthe flushed with pleasure. The dream of working on fabrics with him suddenly seemed very real.

"Ah, the geniuses hard at work," said Madame Rappelais as she entered the room.

"Perhaps not genius," chortled Monsieur Rappelais, "but we are certainly hard at work. I hope I'm not being too piggy with Mademoiselle Berthe's time, my dear."

"Actually, you are being very naughty about her. I don't understand why you need her so much." She pursed her lips petulantly and turned to Berthe. "Dear, go into my dressing room and see about cleaning my shoes, if you will." As Berthe left, she heard Madame tell her husband: "The boys are coming home the day after tomorrow, for a week."

"So soon?" was Monsieur's only response.

The next day the house prepared itself for a weeklong visit from the *fils*. Madame DuPoix put all the small breakables away or on high shelves. She had Mariette roll up the smaller Orientals.

"They like to slide," Madame DuPoix explained to Berthe, pointing to the polished marble floors. Mariette draped the silk damask couches and brocade chairs with muslin covers. Madame Brobert, the cook, began baking up a storm. The household in general was acting as if preparing for the invasion of the Huns.

The boys, Roger and Raoul, nine and eleven, arrived around noon the following day. They tore through the house as if it were a gymnasium. They climbed on Madame Rappelais's bed with muddy shoes and jumped on and off her delicate sofas and chairs.

"You bad, bad boys," Madame Rappelais said in a faux angry voice. She seemed not to care what they did as long as they showered her with kisses. She indulged their every whim. Berthe felt uncomfortably jealous of the affection that Madame Rappelais showered on them. That evening when Monsieur returned from the shops, he greeted his sons with a stiffness and formality that Berthe found surprising.

"And how are the young gentlemen? Are your studies progressing well?" The boys all but ignored him.

In the middle of the night Berthe was awakened by a knock on her door. She opened it, surprised to see Monsieur Rappelais holding a candelabra in his hand.

"I'm so sorry to wake you, mademoiselle. But I'm afraid I need your help. Please, will you come with me?" She found her shawl and followed him downstairs to his room. "My wife is fast asleep. Otherwise I would have asked her assistance. You see my difficulty," he said, taking off his dressing robe. Underneath it he was wearing a crimson ball gown, without the usual crinolines. He turned his back to her to indicate what his problem was. One of the satin buttons was caught in a twisted button loop and it couldn't be unfastened. "Please, if you would be so kind." Berthe stifled a giggle and nodded, then released the button. "As long as you're back there, perhaps you can manage the rest for me. I'm not as limber as I used to be." She unbuttoned all the buttons and the dress fell to the floor. She quickly turned her back.

"I'm decent," announced Monsieur Rappelais. She turned around. He had put his robe back on. "My little hobby is sometimes more trouble than it's worth. Ah, well, *bonne nuit,* mademoiselle, and thank you."

The next morning, while Madame was taking her bath and Berthe was making her bed, the two Rappelais boys burst into their mother's bathroom. It was then Berthe discovered that everyone knew about Monsieur Rappelais's odd penchant for women's clothing.

"Maman, why does Papa wear ladies' dresses?" Roger, the younger boy, asked.

"You know, darling, that's part of his business."

"But why must he wear the dresses?"

"I expect because he likes to. Your papa cherishes beautiful things. That's one of the reasons he's so successful."

"When we grow up and take over the mills will we have to wear ladies' dresses?" asked Raoul, the oldest. He was a beautiful boy with hair and coloring much like his mother's.

"When you grow up you can do whatever you want to do, dear boy. That's the joy of being grown-up, isn't it?"

It hit Berthe then that these boys would grow up to take over their father's business. But they would not follow in his tradition. No, they showed little interest in fabrics or fashion. And it was unlikely that they would ever entertain the idea of her joining the Rappelais firm. In their eyes she was nothing but a maid. Not just in their eyes, she reminded herself, but in reality as well. And with that her dreams frayed, like so many threads, right before her eyes.

After a week the boys went back to school.

"Well, now that they're gone, the house can return to normal," Madame DuPoix sighed with relief. *Normal* was not a word Berthe would have chosen.

That night, after supper, Monsieur retired to his room and his beloved fabrics.

"I am expecting a Monsieur Bonlit at ten o'clock. Please show him up to my bedroom when he arrives," Madame Rappelais instructed.

"Yes, madame," said Berthe, hanging up Madame's dress.

"Ah, not even a look of surprise at my late-night company?" said Madame, smiling at Berthe. "You are turning into a true sophisticate, my Mademoiselle Bovary." She laughed.

At exactly ten o'clock, Berthe heard the knocker on the front door. She hurried downstairs. Mariette was just opening the door. A handsome young man in top hat and coat stood before them.

"Monsieur Bonlit to see Madame Rappelais," he announced.

"This way, monsieur." Berthe took his coat and hat and handed them to Mariette, who for once looked amused instead of angry.

"How does it feel to be replaced so soon?" she whispered. Berthe ignored her.

She led Monsieur Bonlit up the stairs. She could feel his eyes on her back.

"And how is your mistress this evening?" he asked.

"I am sure she is quite well, monsieur." She knocked on Madame's door.

"Come in," the voice sang out. Madame Rappelais reclined on her chaise longue in a silk dressing gown of the deepest blue embroidered with long-tailed birds of every color. Her blond hair fell in loose waves over her shoulders.

"Ah, René, what a surprise," she said, extending her delicate hand to be kissed. "Dear Berthe, can you fetch a bottle of wine and perhaps some nice fruit from the kitchen? I think Madame Brobert will have left it out."

"Yes, madame." Berthe quickly exited the room.

The man was still in Madame's bedroom the next morning. Berthe could hear their soft laughter as she straightened up the dressing room and readied Madame's clothes for the day. Her sons barely gone, her husband still asleep in his bedroom at the end of the hall, and here was the lady of the house in bed with a man she wasn't married to. Was this what Madame meant by sophisticated?

It was time to wake up her mistress, but clearly she was already awake. Berthe stood at the door not knowing what to do. She took a deep breath and knocked, three sharp raps.

"Yes, Berthe, come in," Madame called out. Berthe entered. "Monsieur Bonlit was just going."

"Not before I ravish you once more," laughed the young man, reaching up to tweak Madame's breast.

"René, you forget yourself," Madame said indignantly. Her indignation rang false considering the fact that she was totally naked and sitting astride the young man. Her face burning with embarrassment, Berthe left them to their tumbling and went to run Madame's bath.

That night a different man showed up at the same time as Monsieur Bonlit had the night before: a Monsieur Folinger, who knew his way up the stairs without having to be shown. He seemed in a great hurry and took the steps two at a time.

What kind of marriage did the Rappelaises have? Berthe knew nothing about how the upper class conducted their conjugal relationships. The only thing she had to compare it with was her own parents' marriage, and she had never even seen them embrace. Her father had occasionally placed a kiss on the top of her mother's head, but his wife's reaction to his gesture of affection had been one of annoyance and distaste. Then once again she remembered watching her mother in the woods with Monsieur Boulanger. That had certainly been passion. But was it love? Weren't you supposed to marry for love? She thought about the Homaises and the Millets and their many children. She'd assumed that children were evidence of passion *and* love, but was that true of the Rappelaises? Theirs appeared to be a marriage that had produced two children without the benefit of either passion or love.

Madame Rappelais wasn't the only one entertaining guests. A few days later Monsieur Rappelais announced to Madame DuPoix, "I am expecting Monsieur Worth on Saturday. He will be here for lunch and will possibly stay for dinner."

"Worth is coming on Saturday?" Madame Rappelais clapped her hands. "Finally. I must see him. I have new ball gowns to order."

"He is coming to see me, my dear. We will discuss next year's fabrics. It is business."

"You always monopolize the poor man. You never leave any time for me," she pouted. "He is the only one who understands how to dress me. I am lost without him."

"But you have your regular dressmaker."

"My dressmaker makes dresses," replied Madame Rappelais. "Monsieur Worth creates gowns."

Rappelais said nothing for a minute. And then, "Yes, well, let us do our business and then you may have him for what time remains."

Saturday arrived and with it a torrential rainstorm. Monsieur Charles Worth arrived in the late morning dripping wet and speaking French with a strange accent, not to mention an odd usage.

"The rain is making many cats and dogs," he announced to

Berthe as he handed her a large carpetbag and followed her up the stairs to Monsieur's bedroom.

"I'm sorry, sir. I'm not sure I understand," Berthe said, turning around to glance at the strange man as he huffed and puffed his way up the stairs.

"French is not my virgin tongue," he explained to Berthe. "But I know it like the back of my foot." With all the fuss that Madame and Monsieur had made over his visit, Berthe had expected a person of great stature or beauty. To her surprise, he was a homely man. A high pale forehead was framed by tight auburn curls, over which he wore an odd black skullcap. His mustache grew down both sides of an already down-turned mouth. His eyes followed the same line as his mustache: They slanted downward and gave his face the look of a sad hound. Perhaps to overcome his less-than-impressive looks, he was dressed in a wildly inventive way. He wore a full coat of green and blue brocade over a jacket of red Chinese silk. Underneath that was a flowing white silk shirt that tied in a huge bow at his throat.

"Monsieur Worth is here," Berthe announced outside Monsieur Rappelais's bedroom. The door flew open.

"Come in, dear friend, come in." Rappelais embraced Monsieur Worth after kissing him twice on both cheeks. "Dear Charles, you look wonderful. Just wonderful." He fingered the fabric of Worth's coat. "Ah, I see you've made good use of the brocade." Worth made a *pirouette*, his arms held far out from his sides.

"Stunning," exclaimed Monsieur Rappelais. "I adore the way you've used the extra material in the back. It has a lovely swing to it." He suddenly seemed to remember Berthe, who was just turning to go. "Oh, Charles, I want to introduce you to Mademoiselle Bovary. She is new to us. And she has, I must say, an excellent eye for *les textiles*."

"And she has quite the beautiful *façade*," said Worth, holding Berthe's chin and turning her face slowly from side to side. She tried to smile.

"You must excuse Monsieur Worth. He thinks his French is perfect. No one can correct him. I don't even try anymore."

"What's wrong with my French? I speak like an indigent. You French think you invented language. It is we English who gave you the gift of words. Name one French poet that is equal to our Shakespeare. Just one."

"Baudelaire," offered Monsieur Rappelais.

"Never heard of him," said Worth. "But enough of this. Come show me what you have brought me from Lyon."

Berthe started to excuse herself.

"No, no, you stay here. We need you," said Worth. "One cannot envision the fashion mode without the mannequin."

They spent the next hour draping Berthe with various fabrics. One was more beautiful than the next.

"Now what about this?" Rappelais asked, draping a heavily embroidered cloth of red roses and small yellow birds over Berthe's shoulder. Both men studied the fabric for a long moment.

"I don't know," said Worth, shaking his head. "It doesn't shriek to me for some reason. What do you think, mademoiselle?"

"It's awfully heavy for a dress," said Berthe finally. She felt weighed down by the material. "Perhaps it would be better on a piece of furniture."

"Of course. She is right," said Worth, clapping his hands. "We are to dress ladies, not chaises longues." He wagged his finger at Monsieur Rappelais.

"Oh, dear Charles, don't mock me." Monsieur giggled, flapping his hand in his friend's direction. "Finally, the *pièce de résis-*

tance," announced Rappelais with a flourish. "I have something very exciting to show you. Close your eyes, my dear."

"If I close my eyes how can I see, you ignorant fig?" said Worth. Both men laughed uproariously.

Monsieur Rappelais picked up a small package and unwrapped it. "*Voilà!*" he said. It was a piece of silk of the deepest, richest purple.

"Ah, this is the much-tooted work of the chemist Henri Perkin," said Worth, reverently fingering the fabric.

Monsieur Rappelais explained to Berthe, "A young English chemist has recently discovered that aniline extracted with alcohol could produce this royal color. He calls it *mauveine.* It is able to hold its color regardless of the number of washings or exposure to light. This is the favorite color of the Empress Eugénie. Everyone will want it. And given the amount of fabric that goes into each dress, he will be a very rich young man. He has fallen into a pot of gold."

"More like a pot of purple. Now every woman regardless of her statuary will be able to dress in the royal manner," said Worth.

"That would please our Mademoiselle Bovary," said Rappelais. "She believes that we should be providing ball gowns to scullery maids, don't you, mademoiselle?"

"I do think beautiful clothes should be made more affordable," Berthe said shyly.

"Well, these new hideous department stores would certainly agree with you," sniffed Worth. "They want to reduce the prices of fabrics and trims and they even speak of selling synthetic blends." He turned to Rappelais. "They are trying to ruin me. How am I ever to become rich and famous and adored by the *crème fraîche?*"

"You mean the *crème de la crème,* my dear Charles," corrected Rappelais.

"As you say." Worth turned his attention back to the purple fabric. "What shall we do with this? It is so dense and depressing. So lacking in light. Rich as it is, it's not festive enough for a ball gown, I fear."

Berthe picked up a length of white silk tulle and draped it over the purple material, giving it a gauzy cloudlike effect.

"Brilliant!" exclaimed Rappelais.

"Interesting," said Worth. "I will steal this idea and claim it as my own. With your permission, of course, mademoiselle."

"As you wish, monsieur," said Berthe, feeling suddenly very pleased with herself and no longer shy.

"You see? She has real talent," Monsieur Rappelais proudly exclaimed, as if he himself were responsible for Berthe's ideas.

"She does have the eyeball," agreed Worth.

Madame Rappelais appeared in the doorway with her arms folded.

"Luncheon will be served shortly, my dears. That is, if you can tear yourself away from all this," she said, indicating the myriad fabrics that lay strewn around the room.

"No, no. First we must fit the new dress," commanded Worth. "It must be before luncheon. I want to fit the bodice at the smallest of your waistlines," he said to Madame Rappelais. He picked up his bag. "Come, mademoiselle," he said to Berthe, "you will assist me with the assassination of Madame's waistline." They proceeded to Madame Rappelais's bedroom.

Worth opened the large carpetbag on the bed and removed a dress carefully rolled in tissue paper. He held it up and shook out the voluminous skirt. The dress was made of the palest blue satin with an embroidered design of tiny blue hummingbirds hovering amid delicate bamboo leaves.

"Tighten Madame's corset until she can no longer breathe," he instructed Berthe.

Berthe pulled her mistress's corset as tight as she could, leaning back with all her weight. Then she helped Worth button Madame into the gown.

"But how ever can I dine in this? How will I be able to dance?" gasped Madame Rappelais.

"There will be no eating and no dancing in this gown," Monsieur Worth replied with a laugh. "And only the barest of breathing. But do not despair, dear madame. There will be a great deal of falling in love with the beautiful body embalmed therein."

He walked around her, scrutinizing every angle. "Wait, this will not do. Where are the breasts?" He plunged his hands down the front of Madame Rappelais's dress, pushing and prodding her bosom until it swelled up and over the bodice to his satisfaction. His fumbling seemed not to bother Madame at all.

"Ah, good. Good. Now fetch Madame's crinolines and hoop," he said. Berthe did as requested, and handed him the wire hoop, which he took from her with a flourish. "You probably didn't know that this is my invention, did you?"

"No, monsieur, I didn't."

"Be assured that I am the voice of all that is vain. I am the eye of the future of fashion. I am the hand of God encased in silk and lace. Isn't that right, my dear Madame Rappelais?"

"You are, indeed, the great master." Madame turned to admire her reflection in the mirror.

"One day I will wake up and decide no more big skirts. And *voilà,* there will be no more big skirts. I am thinking, in fact, of this..." He pulled the skirt back and bunched it behind. "As you see, the bottom is an entirely unexplored area of seduction." He turned to Berthe. "What think you, mademoiselle?"

"It seems an entirely new look," said Berthe.

"Of course it is. I am the original original." He chuckled to himself. "I shall call this creation the bustle. But enough genius for now. One has to spoon-feed fashion to the unfashionable. Too much too soon and they get constipated."

"You mean confused," corrected Madame Rappelais.

"Oh, you French and your precision for language," Worth said with a wave of his hand. "Constipated, confused—it is all the same to me. All this creativity is leaving me famished. Shall we lunch?"

"First, Berthe must get me out of this beautiful straitjacket," groaned Madame Rappelais.

Observing Worth at work made Berthe again aware of her longing. She wanted to change places with him. How she wished to be designing gowns instead of just tightening corsets. Feeling a sudden rush of impatience, she fought the impulse to tighten her mistress's corset even more, to squeeze Madame's middle until she passed out from lack of air.

What happened to the calm acceptance of Madame that she had talked herself into only days before? She had no right to be out of sorts. Wasn't life as Madame's lady's maid far better than any life she had had before?

CHAPTER 19

Lessons in Love

"THOSE POLES ARE FAR TOO RICH FOR THEIR OWN GOOD," Madame Rappelais said weeks later, returning early from a much-anticipated ball given by the Polish prince Adam Czartoryski at his home in the Hôtel Lambert. "The entire Île Saint-Louis is overrun by them with their strange names and even stranger accents." As Berthe helped her out of her new gown, Madame rubbed her ribs where the corset had left deep wedge marks in her skin. "I can't imagine what the ball cost Prince Czartoryski. You should have seen it. They put a parquet floor over the stone entranceway. There was an enormous tent with huge crystal chandeliers hanging down from the ceiling, three different orchestras played, and the champagne flowed like water. So ostentatious." She held her head in both hands. "Oh, Berthe, I'm so tired of all this, all these parties and these ridiculous people. The torturous dresses, this stupid house. And that husband of mine. He spent the entire evening fingering the fabric of everyone's dress." She fell back on the bed and Berthe could tell then that she was quite tipsy. "It's all so superficial, so meaningless," she moaned. "They only care about how one looks and what one is wearing."

She opened her eyes and looked up at Berthe.

"Nobody really cares about me or how I feel. Except you. You care, don't you, dear girl?"

Berthe nodded. She hadn't realized until this moment how very much like her mother Madame Rappelais was: spoiled, self-centered, and manipulative. "Come." Madame reached out and took Berthe by the hand. "Lie down, keep me company just for a few minutes."

"But, madame . . ." Berthe hesitated. "Madame, it's quite late and you have an early appointment with your jeweler tomorrow."

"I do?"

"Yes, madame." Berthe silently thanked her stars that she knew her mistress's schedule. She pulled the cover up to Madame's chin. Even before she left the room she could hear the woman snoring.

Berthe was intimidated by Madame's power and her position. She was resentful of the control Madame had over her. But mostly, she deeply feared her. Every day she worried that her mistress would try and get her into bed. Madame differed from her mother in one important respect. Whereas Emma Bovary's affairs had been the result of what Berthe believed was a genuine search for love, Madame Rappelais toyed with people; gaining their affection was nothing more than a game to her.

Each day brought something different from her mistress. Sometimes she acted as if Berthe were invisible. Other times she spoke to her as an intimate, even a daughter. Berthe was kept totally off balance. And always, Madame Rappelais took up all the air and the space in Berthe's life.

On the other hand, her relationship with Monsieur Rappelais continued to be thankfully the same. He had taken her under his curiously attired wing.

"I fear my business will fail when the *fils* take it over," he confided to Berthe one evening when they were going through one of Monsieur Rappelais's ribbon sample books. "They care nothing about the beauty of fabrics."

Berthe felt as if she could spend hours turning the pages of the heavy book. On every page was a small sample of ribbon trims, each one more beautiful than the last. "Black and blue. Those are the only colors my sons care about," muttered Monsieur Rappelais. Berthe looked up. "As in getting bruises," he explained. She laughed.

"You see this." He pointed to a page in the book. "We are returning to delicate patterns of floral tendrils and ribbon streamers and charming baskets. It's back to nature, just as I predicted," he said happily. He walked over to his desk and opened a package that had been delivered that afternoon from his cotton mill in Lille. He removed a cotton swatch and held it up to the light of the lamp.

"What is this abomination?" He handed the sample to Berthe. "Just look at the uneven spaces. I was going to give several bolts of this to the good sisters at Saint Sulpice." Berthe could see that there were slight irregularities in the weave. "You worked with these idiots. Where is their pride? Where is their sense of workmanship? What are these stupid, lazy people doing?" He paced around the room.

"They are probably taking long naps after their huge midday meal," said Berthe. She immediately regretted her words.

"What?" Monsieur Rappelais stopped and looked at her sharply. "What are you saying?"

She took a deep breath. She was compelled to go on.

"Monsieur Rappelais, the people at your mill work very hard."

"Well, of course they do. That's what they're paid for. But I don't pay them to produce garbage like this," he said, flapping the cotton in front of her face.

She wondered if she dare tell him how awful the conditions were at his mill. Her guess was that he had never had a conversation with someone who actually worked at the level she had.

"Monsieur, the working conditions at your mill are terrible."

"That's the way it is at all mills. Mine is no different. No better. No worse. I am providing people a way to earn a living."

"But you could make the hours shorter, the food a bit more plentiful. And you could hire older workers instead of such young children."

His mustache twitched. He was smiling.

"My dear Mademoiselle Softheart. I see you know nothing about running a mill. Why, if I did as you suggested I would end up in the poorhouse."

"Right along with the rest of your workers," she said quietly. He threw back his head and laughed. She forged ahead. "Monsieur Rappelais, I saw a young boy killed; pulled up by his hair and ripped to pieces by one of your machines."

"Unfortunately, these things happen," he said, crossing to the table and pouring himself a brandy.

"Well, they shouldn't," she snapped. And then she worried she had gone too far. Now she would be fired for certain. But Rappelais's attention had already strayed back to his sample book of ribbons and no more was said on the matter.

One morning after a night of trying to ward off Madame's advances, Berthe dragged herself into the kitchen for breakfast. She felt tired, dirty, and depressed. The idea of throwing herself into the Seine was not unappealing. Madame DuPoix sat at the long kitchen table doing her accounts. Madame Brobert, the cook, was at the stove stirring milk for custard.

Mariette smiled at Berthe and even more surprisingly handed her a bowl of coffee.

"You take it with three sugars?" she asked. Berthe nodded and accepted the steaming bowl of *café au lait*. The minute she brought it to her lips she saw something strange: a gritty white powder, barely visible, on the surface of the coffee. It all came back to her in a flash: her mother, the open black mouth, the endless dying, the scent of vomit. *Arsenic!* Horrified, she immediately slammed the bowl onto the table, causing some of the coffee to spill out.

"What in heaven's name?" Madame Brobert exclaimed.

"Poison," Berthe said. "She's trying to poison me," she gasped, pointing at the maid.

"I don't know what she's talking about. She's crazy," said Mariette, her face flaming red.

Madame DuPoix looked closely at the bowl of coffee, then drew back. "What have you done, you wicked, wicked girl?" she shrieked.

"Nothing, I did nothing," cried Mariette.

"I shall speak to Madame. But I think it's wise if you pack your things immediately." Mariette threw her apron to the floor and fled the kitchen. She was gone within the hour.

Madame Rappelais was strangely unbothered by the whole incident. If anything, she seemed amused.

"Jealousy is an ugly thing," she said, rubbing cream into her long white neck. "I know, I speak from experience. It can cause one to act in very rash ways. I hope you are all right, my dear girl," she said, turning and grasping Berthe by the hand.

"I'm fine, madame," Berthe said, pulling her hand away and hiding it behind her back. But she wasn't fine. She knew this woman cared nothing about her. And certainly less about Mariette. And what about her husband? She thought of Monsieur's deaf ear to the plight of his mill workers. It seemed as if this house held as much ugliness and selfishness as it did beauty. But where else would she go?

"Now Madame DuPoix has to find a replacement for Mariette. What a bother," Madame sighed, dabbing perfume behind her ears.

Berthe suddenly had an inspiration. "Madame, I have a friend whom I worked with in the mill at Lille," she said. "She's a very hard worker and I know she would love to come to Paris."

"Is she reliable?"

"Oh, yes, madame." Berthe firmly believed that if Hélène were given a good job she would learn skills that would enable her to support herself without having to steal. Besides, she longed for a real friend and ally in this place. For a moment she worried about what might happen to Hélène at the Rappelaises', but then she remembered that Hélène, of all people, could certainly take care of herself.

"Well, write to her and tell her she has a position if she wants it."

And it was as simple as that. Almost before she knew it, Hélène arrived *chez* Rappelais, tattered bag in hand, red hair swept up underneath a ridiculously formal black bonnet. Berthe wondered where she had stolen that from, but she was too thrilled to

see her old friend again to care. She introduced her to Madame
DuPoix, who seemed appropriately unimpressed.

"Madame was in such a rush to hire someone she neglected
to check your references," Madame DuPoix said with a sniff.
"May I see them, please," she said, holding out her hand.

"See what?" Hélène asked.

"Your letters of recommendation."

Hélène laughed. "She is my recommendation, ain't she?" She
indicated Berthe with a wave of her hand.

"I see," Madame DuPoix said dubiously. "Well, you may as
well show Mademoiselle Du Croix to her room."

As Berthe led Hélène up the stairs to the top floor, her
friend's eyes darted from the hand-carved oak banister to the
crystal chandeliers to the ornately framed portraits on the walls.
On the second-floor landing she stopped by an ornate gold in-
laid table. On it were a framed miniature painting of Madame
Rappelais, a mother-of-pearl vase, a jeweled pillbox, and a small
alabaster Cupid. Before Berthe could stop her, Hélène slipped
the Cupid into the pocket of her skirt.

"Stop it," Berthe hissed. "Put it back. You have a roof over
your head and a room of your own, the food is plentiful and delicious, and you are to be paid a decent salary. You don't have to
steal anymore."

Hélène looked at her as if she had said "You don't have to
breathe anymore."

She replaced the Cupid and picked up the pillbox instead.
She examined the jeweled top with one eye closed as if trying to
determine its value.

"Hélène!"

"I'm just looking, ain't I?" she said, smiling a wicked smile.
"There's no harm in that. Why else do they have all these lovely

things if they don't want people admirin' them?" She put the pillbox back on the table.

Berthe wondered for a moment if she hadn't made a mistake bringing Hélène to Paris. It was like escorting the fox into the henhouse.

"Hélène, please promise me you'll behave."

"I promise," said Hélène, solemnly crossing herself.

CHAPTER 20

Monsieur Worth Has Some News

BERTHE WAS SORTING SWATCHES BY COLOR AND DESIGN WITH Monsieur Rappelais late one night when there came a loud banging at the front door.

"Who could that be at this hour?" Rappelais asked.

Everyone was asleep. Berthe hurried down the stairs and opened the heavy front door. It was Monsieur Worth. He was in a state of great excitement. His skullcap was perched at an odd angle on his head and, instead of his usual elegance, his clothes looked as though he had been sleeping in them.

"I am in a renovation," he said in his usual battered French. "I must make words with Monsieur Rappelais. Is he up?"

"My dear friend, what's the matter?" asked Monsieur, rushing down the staircase, his silk robe flapping about him.

"I have the good hour," said Worth, collapsing on the chaise longue. "Please, a touch of brandy." Berthe poured drinks for both of the men. "I have finally made my proposal to Gagelin." Maison Gagelin was the fabric and dress accessories shop that had employed Worth since he first arrived in Paris. It was there that he'd met his wife, Marie Vernet, one of the young women who modeled shawls and cloaks for Gagelin's clients. "I thought he would love the idea of a partnership but he turned me down, the ugly radish."

"Oh, I am so sorry," said Rappelais.

"Don't be desolated. He is an idiot. The future is in ready-made dresses. You know that, and I know that, but Gagelin is too blind to see it. He has the stupidity of a mutton. He sees only the need to sell fabric and accessories. My brilliance is wasted there. It is not enough that I make beautiful dresses, that my *chère* Marie models them, and that the customers are clamoring for me to make more and more. No, he sees no reason to change. He doesn't see my genius as important. He thinks he can go on stealing my ideas, my soul. Can you imagine? He has refused me. Me, the heart and soul of his stupid rag business. Well, I thank him for giving me the foot in the bottom. I have decided this very night I will take my designs and open up my own shop." He fell back on the sofa, exhausted from his long speech.

"But, dear Charles," said Monsieur Rappelais, sitting down next to him and clasping his hand, "can you afford to do this?"

"Of course not. I am as poor as a church mousse. But I have been planning this for some time. I already have a partner lined up. My dear and very rich friend Monsieur Otto Bobergh has money coming out of his pince-nez. He has been begging me to allow him to invest a small fortune in my business. And you, Rappelais, you will give me an exclusive on all your most beautiful fabrics. We will leave Gagelin nothing but the ugliest scraps. And we will all live happily and wealthily ever after." He leaned forward and kissed the older man on both cheeks.

Berthe watched as Monsieur Rappelais gazed upon his friend with a look of utter adoration. She suddenly realized that, in his own peculiar way, he was in love with Charles Worth. "More brandy?" she asked. The two men nodded their heads and lifted their empty glasses.

"Just think," said Monsieur Worth, "all I have to do is design and make my dresses and then sit back. Women will come from all over France, from Europe, from the world. They will flock to my atelier for the honor of purchasing one of my creations. I will be famous. I will be ravished. Women will boast to their friends of owning an original Worth."

"Ah, my dear friend, indeed you are an artist. But permit me to remind you that as brilliant as you may be you are nothing without my fabrics. Textiles, as you know, are what determine fashion, not the other way around. It has always been this way."

"Dear Rappelais, what was always the way as you call it, will no longer be the way. Wake up, my dear strawberry. I can design several hundred dresses at a time and have them ready-made in my workshop. So my fashions and the demand for them will necessarily determine what fabrics you will, by necessity, weave."

"Dear Charles, fashions do change, but the fabric stays the same. A dress falls apart, falls out of fashion, but the fabric, the beauty of the design, the colors—those endure."

Berthe thought the two men would go on "dearing" each other to death until the sun came up. But finally, they seemed to reach a standoff.

Both men looked at each other. "Why are we arguing, *chèr* Rappelais? It is the old question: Which came first, the chicken or the olive? Fashion dictates fabric; fabric dictates fashion. Who cares? We are geniuses living in the fashion center of the universe. Which makes us..."

"...the most powerful men in the world!" they said simultaneously. They tipped their glasses and drank the brandy down as if it were water. Berthe felt her eyes closing. It was almost two in the morning and she was exhausted.

"Is there anything else I can get you gentlemen before I retire?" she asked.

"Stay," commanded Monsieur Worth. "This is a hysteric moment. We are creating the future of fashion here. And we need a witness to our great ideas. Please, take notes." And so Berthe picked up pen and paper and jotted down their increasingly drunken ideas. Hours passed while they talked and drank and argued. She longed for her bed. She still had to get up at the crack of dawn to prepare her mistress for the day.

"And perhaps one day Mademoiselle Berthe will come and work for me. She can model my dresses, along with my darling Marie." Berthe stirred in her seat. She felt a thrill of excitement. Could she be a model? To think of actually wearing the beautiful fabrics she loved. And then perhaps she could even begin to design a little . . . She shook herself to stop that sort of dreaming. It seemed every time she fantasized about her future something would happen to dash her hopes.

"She is not going anywhere. I need her here," answered Rappelais, almost as if reading Berthe's mind.

"Isn't it wonderful to be fought over by two talented and soon-to-be-world-famous gentlemen?" said Worth.

Almost as wonderful as it would be to be fast asleep in her own bed, Berthe thought.

CHAPTER 21

Madame Has a Surprise

As the weeks passed, Rappelais and Worth came to rely on Berthe more and more. At the same time, to no small relief, Madame Rappelais seemed to lose all interest in her as a bedmate. And Hélène, remarkably, seemed to take to her new position. But with her light-fingered friend in the house, Berthe knew not to relax her guard entirely. Still, she had begun to experience an unfamiliar sense of contentment.

Madame arrived home late one morning, her face flushed with excitement, carrying a small flat package about fifteen by eighteen inches in size. It was carefully wrapped in brown paper and secured by twine. Without removing her cape she instructed Berthe to follow her up to her bedroom. She shut the door and turned to Berthe.

"Close your eyes," she said. "I have a wonderful, wonderful surprise." Berthe did as she was told. She heard the ripping of paper. And then: "You may open them now."

Berthe gasped. Madame Rappelais held in front of her a

lovely painting of rich browns and greens. In the background one could see a gaggle of white geese making their way through the trees to a small stream. And in the foreground was a figure clearly recognizable as Berthe, wearing... *nothing but a blue kerchief on her head.* She sat with one leg bent and the other held straight out, her white foot dipping into the slowly swirling water. The sun shone warmly on her back and shoulders, and on her budding breasts. Berthe felt her cheeks turn hot. How had Madame managed to find the one thing that could so publicly shame her?

"Where did you get this?" she croaked, barely able to get the words out.

"At Monsieur Jean-François Millet's studio, where else?" Madame laughed with delight. "You can imagine my surprise when, upon viewing some of his work, I suddenly recognized my very own Mademoiselle Bovary as naked as a newborn baby. I, of course, insisted he sell it to me. Poor man had no choice. I do think this is one of his better pieces, and not just because I know the subject so well. Most of his work is so relentlessly rural and peasantlike. Why didn't you tell me you modeled for the great Millet?"

"I didn't think it was of any importance," Berthe said through gritted teeth.

"Well, Monsieur Millet certainly thought a great deal of it. This painting cost me a bloody fortune. Aren't you the lucky one? To be immortalized by a famous artist. Now, where do you think I should hang it?" Berthe felt a growing panic. *She couldn't. She wouldn't.*

"Oh, no, madame. Please, please don't hang it."

"It's art, my dear. That's what it's for. To be hung and admired. Let's see, should I put it downstairs in the gallery or on the wall going up the stairs where all the Rappelais ancestors hang? That would liven up the relatives a bit, I think."

She held the small painting out at arm's length and peered at it through half-closed eyes. "No, you certainly don't belong with all of Monsieur Rappelais's ugly ancestors. I think I shall put you here, right over my dressing table, where we can both appreciate it. I'm not sure I like the frame but that can be easily changed." She placed the painting on the floor next to the dressing table. "By the way, I told Monsieur Millet that you were in my employ. He was so pleased to hear that you were in Paris. I have invited him to dinner next week. The two of you shall have a grand reunion. Do you own a dinner dress?"

Berthe wanted to strangle her. "Madame, I am your maid! I can't possibly attend your dinner party."

"Of course you can. If I say you are invited then you will be there. Besides, we don't want to disappoint Monsieur Millet. It will be a small, intimate affair. Just us art lovers."

Does she want to humiliate me in front of everyone? She can't be that cruel. "But, madame, I don't belong—"

"And you think I do?" Madame Rappelais laughed harshly. "You have no idea where I come from, do you? I was born outside Lille. My father was a dairy farmer who lost all his cows to disease. I went to work in the mill just as you did. And like you, I caught the eye of Monsieur Rappelais, who at the time was married to the first Madame Rappelais. When she died he brought me to Paris, dressed me, educated me, impregnated me twice, and has kindly left me alone ever since. The question of whether I *belong* has never come up."

"I had no idea, madame." Berthe was taken by surprise. She marveled that this woman had the ability to keep her always off balance.

"Why would you?" she said, smoothing her upsweep.

"But, madame, I can't ..." She twisted the skirt of her apron, feeling powerless.

"Don't you dare spoil my evening," Madame Rappelais said sharply, her eyes flashing. And then, as if a storm had cleared, she smiled sweetly. "When the time comes we'll find you something nice to wear."

CHAPTER 22

La Grande Fête

WHEN MONSIEUR RAPPELAIS HEARD ABOUT THE PAINTING, HE studied it for a long time then exclaimed, "*Merveilleux!* Painted by Millet himself." He turned and looked at Berthe. Her face was scarlet. "Why, you're famous, my dear girl. Of course this calls for a celebration. Mademoiselle Bovary will be our guest of honor. How perfectly delightful. I shall invite Monsieur Worth as well. The two artists should get along swimmingly. It will be a veritable *grande fête.*"

Berthe was almost more terrified of the Rappelaises' *grande fête* than of anything she had encountered in her life. She had no idea what went on at a formal dinner. She had helped Madame DuPoix set the table on one occasion and couldn't believe the amount of cutlery and the number of glasses each person required. With which fork or spoon did one begin? Did one actually eat or just pretend to eat? And far worse than not knowing the proper etiquette, she realized she was being paraded out as a novelty, a piece of entertainment. She felt sick to her stomach with nervousness as the night of the dinner drew near. She hoped and prayed that the painting would stay in Madame's room.

"I feel quite ill, madame," she said, holding her stomach an hour before the dinner was to begin.

"I don't care how you feel," said Madame Rappelais with a hard, bright smile. "You look beautiful and that's all that matters." She had dressed Berthe in one of her own gowns, a lovely pale blue silk. The skirt had a pattern of full-blown roses and foliage and the long tight sleeves were trimmed in lace. Madame had combed Berthe's hair into a simple upsweep and given her a pair of sapphire earrings.

Madame glanced at the gold pendant watch pinned to her breast. "Oh my, look at the time. Now we must get me dressed and ready. We can't have the lady's maid outshine the lady, can we?"

When the guests arrived at exactly eight o'clock they were ushered immediately into the dining room and the double doors were closed.

"Stay here and wait until I announce you," Madame Rappelais whispered to Berthe in the hallway. "It will be a lovely surprise."

"Oh, madame, please don't make me. I don't want to be a surprise." Ignoring her pleas, Madame put a finger to her lips and then swept into the dining room.

Hélène was helping to serve. When she caught sight of Berthe dressed in Madame Rappelais's beautiful gown she could hardly keep her eyes in her head.

"Mon Dieu," Hélène exclaimed. "What are you doing? If you're gonna steal it, don't parade around in it first, for heaven's sake. They'll throw you in jail, you little fool."

"Madame Rappelais has loaned me this dress for tonight,"

said Berthe, nervously fingering her earrings as she waited for her cue.

"What? Why?" Hélène's mouth fell open.

"I am to be a surprise guest at her dinner party," Berthe said with a sigh.

"This is too perfect! You can steal the silverware!" said Hélène, clapping her hands. "I helped Madame DuPoix set the table. There is so much silver they'll never notice a few spoons here and there. Does this dress have pockets?" She pulled at the full skirt.

"Hélène! You've lost your mind. I'm not stealing anything." But Hélène wasn't listening.

"There are also tiny salt and pepper shakers by each place. Or wait, I have a better idea—the silver napkin holders! No one will miss those." Suddenly, Madame DuPoix appeared. She wore a starched white serving apron over her black dress.

"Hélène. To the kitchen! It is time to begin service of the meal." Madame DuPoix's eyes narrowed as she regarded Berthe dressed in the elegant gown. "I understand from Madame that you are to be seated at dinner. Mind your manners—what few you possess," she hissed.

Just then the dining room doors opened and Madame Rappelais announced in a bright voice, "And now, for the guest of honor: our very own, very original Goose Girl." She pulled a reluctant Berthe into the room. Monsieur Millet stood up.

"*Incroyable.* It is! My goose girl, all dressed up!" he exclaimed, holding out his huge hands. His beard and mustache were as thick and shaggy as ever. His wife, seated next to him, peered over her pince-nez as if trying to place Berthe.

On the other side of the long table sat Monsieur Worth and his swan-necked, elegant wife, Marie. Both smiled broadly at the wonderful surprise. Monsieur Millet rushed over to Berthe, clasped both her hands, and kissed her four times on each cheek.

"My beautiful Mademoiselle Bovary, how you've grown. And even lovelier than I recalled. You remember Mademoiselle Bovary," he said to his wife.

"Ah, at first I didn't recognize her dressed," said his wife, setting aside her pince nez. Everyone laughed and Berthe turned an even brighter shade of red. She could feel herself perspiring under the heavy gown. She looked first at Madame Rappelais and then at Monsieur, pleading with her eyes to be excused.

Instead Monsieur Rappelais stood and pulled out a chair for Berthe. But Berthe continued to stand, still hoping for a last-minute reprieve.

"Sit," commanded Madame Rappelais, as if speaking to a dog.

"Yes, please, mademoiselle, sit down," said Monsieur Worth. "It's not often we have the honor of dining with the subject of a famous painting." That was when Berthe noticed that the painting of her hung above the long mahogany buffet. She felt doubly exposed, having the painting of her there for all to examine: her young breasts, the beginning of her pubic hair, her naked body. Added to that was the agony of wearing a dress that wasn't hers, in a room in which she didn't belong, with people who were far above her in social standing. She wanted to die, to disappear. *Maybe I could faint or have a fit.* If she had an eye-rolling, mouth-foaming, limb-thrashing fit it would distract from her shame and embarrassment. But then she realized that the fit would only bring her new shame and embarrassment. So she sat down and began to count the minutes, hoping the evening would soon be over and she would be safe back in her room.

"How very nicely you've developed since I painted this,

mademoiselle," Millet said, standing by the painting. He ran his forefinger along the breasts to prove his point. Everyone laughed.

Berthe flinched as if she herself had been touched.

"Yes, I would say the development merits another portrait," said Madame Rappelais, smiling wickedly at Berthe.

"Madame Rappelais is right. You must come and model for me again," said Millet. "I have a studio on rue Jacob."

"But how will you paint her without all the poultry, *mon chèr*?" asked Catherine Millet with a gleam in her eye. Again everyone laughed.

"My wife was a model as well," Monsieur Worth offered. "That was how I met her."

"But never with geese, and never ever without my clothes," chimed in Madame Worth. To Berthe's continued humiliation, the room exploded into guffaws. She hated being the object of ridicule, particularly in front of Monsieur Worth. She had hoped one day to impress him with her willingness to learn about the world of fashion and the creating of beautiful gowns. Now even his elegant wife was making fun of her.

It seemed to Berthe that the whole idea of a dinner *à la russe* was to use as many dishes and as much glassware as possible. To begin, there were six different glasses and nine pieces of flatware at each place. She realized that, with the exception of Hélène, Madame DuPoix had hired a new staff to serve. It was certainly not the first time the servers had managed a dinner of this magnitude. They moved in and out of the dining room like a well-rehearsed dance company, never missing a step or soiled plate. The food was always served from the left and removed from the right, the drinks poured from the right and removed from the right.

Berthe felt as if she were onstage in the middle of a ballet performance surrounded by a corps de ballet waiting for her to make the first graceful *jeté*. And there she stood, or rather sat, never having taken a ballet lesson in her life.

First came the soup course with sherry carefully poured into each cut-glass goblet. The soup plate, soupspoon, and sherry glass were removed and the fish course came next, a pale poached salmon on a fish plate with a fish fork, a fish knife, and white wine. The first entrée, the terrapin course, followed in a pot accompanied by a terrapin cup and lid, a butter plate, and a terrapin fork. The second entrée was a ramekin course with ramekin fork and plate. Berthe suddenly remembered her meager dinners at Rappelais's cotton mill. Her fingers had been her only utensils, a tin pail her dinner plate.

As luxurious as the food was, she was far too nervous to eat or certainly to speak. She felt dazed by the constant arrival and removal of food, wine, and utensils. Things moved along smoothly enough until she saw Hélène slip a serving spoon in her apron pocket. Berthe sat forward suddenly, knocking her glass of claret onto the floor.

"Oh, I'm so sorry!" She watched helplessly as the wine soaked into the Persian rug.

"Don't be sorry," said Madame Rappelais, clearly annoyed. "Just don't let it happen again."

Hélène had paused at the swinging door which led into the kitchen as if to say, *Thank you for the excellent distraction.* Just at that moment Madame DuPoix came through the door carrying a large bowl of puréed peas and carrots. The door hit Hélène hard on the side of the head and she let out a yelp. Luckily, DuPoix managed not to drop the bowl of purée. She glared at Hélène, who fled the dining room holding the side of her slightly bleeding head.

"Tell us about your latest work," Monsieur Rappelais said, turning to Millet. Berthe, in an effort to show great interest, turned toward the artist, placing her chin in her hand and her elbow on the table. Unfortunately, her elbow landed in the middle of her puréed peas and carrots. She quickly extracted her arm, but not before Madame Rappelais shot her a venomous look. Berthe hid the soiled sleeve in her lap. Then she looked down and saw with horror that the stain on the sleeve had soiled the skirt of Madame's elegant gown. She fruitlessly swiped at the stains with her napkin.

"Leave it, Berthe," Madame hissed. Berthe took a long drink of her wine.

Then came the sherbet course with sherbet spoon, and the game course with new plates, utensils, and new wine.

Berthe realized, with the sort of insight that only comes too late, that unknowingly Madame Rappelais had given her the chance of a lifetime: to meet with Monsieur Worth across a dinner table, to have him view her as something more than a lady's maid, perhaps to see her as someone who might be worthy of hiring one day. But so far Berthe had failed miserably. She looked down. Hélène was at her feet soaking up the spilled claret with a serviette.

"Keep up the good work," Hélène whispered, reaching up and slipping a set of miniature salt and pepper shakers into her pocket.

The asparagus course was served. Then the cheese course. New flatware was brought and new wineglasses were put out. The table was cleared and crumbs were swept away to make room for the sweet course: chocolate mousse and ice cream. Was this finally the end? wondered Berthe. No, apparently not. There was still the fruit with fruit knife and fork, fruit plate, and new wineglass. And last, but not least, the finger bowl, followed by coffee. Berthe could only imagine the condition of the scullery maid Jeanine's hands after tonight.

She tried to take a deep breath, but the stays of Madame Rappelais's borrowed corset cut deep into her sides. By this time, the novelty of Berthe's presence had worn off and she was thankful to be ignored as the other guests conversed.

Madame Rappelais exuded enough charm for the entire room. When she turned her attention to Millet, Berthe began to relax and enjoy her wine.

"Monsieur, it is such a great honor to have you sitting at my table. I have admired your work for a long time."

"I assure you, madame, the pleasure is mine," said the artist, bowing his head modestly.

"I am planning a grand ball for my birthday, and I would dearly love for you to paint a mural in my ballroom in honor of the occasion. Needless to say, I would pay whatever you ask."

"My dear Madame Rappelais, I regret I am not a mural painter. I find it far too time-consuming and I need to conserve my energies for my paintings."

"He fails to mention the condition of his decrepit back," added his wife.

"It's true, as my wife so ungallantly points out: Murals are a young man's work." Millet smiled lovingly at his wife. He seemed to welcome any kind of attention from Madame Millet, even of a negative nature.

"Oh, but, Monsieur Millet, you are not so old," ventured Berthe. The words were out of her mouth before she knew it. Everyone laughed at her comment. But this time they were laughing with her, not at her. She took another sip of wine. Perhaps the evening would not be a complete disaster.

"*Je suis désolée,*" said Madame Rappelais, sulking. "I had so wanted to have a depiction of Greek mythology on the ceiling. I have seen something similar in Madame Chanteloix's house on the rue d'Arbre."

"Scenes of Greek mythology are definitely not my milieu." Millet chuckled. "However, I do have a young apprentice I can recommend to you. He has great talent. I am sure he can create a beautiful mural for you."

"I suppose one must learn to accept compromise in these things," sighed Madame Rappelais.

"I shall send him to you tomorrow. His name is Armand de Pouvier."

"Do you think he can have it done in time for my birthday in two months' time?"

"Aside from being greatly skilled, he works very quickly," Millet assured her.

"You can't work too quickly for my dear wife," said Monsieur Rappelais. Madame shot him a look and then laughed her delightful laugh, fanning herself repeatedly with her black ostrich fan. Berthe marveled at her charm and sociability.

"Monsieur Millet, may I ask you something about your wonderful work which has been troubling me?" said Worth, popping a chocolate truffle in his mouth.

"Why, of course, ask away." Millet rubbed his hands over his silk brocade vest as if making sure it still covered his expanding belly.

"Why do you dress your subjects in such pitifully ugly rags? Their apparel is devoid of color, style, and beauty."

"But Monsieur Millet's paintings show the beauty of the countryside," explained Berthe. By now she had consumed three full glasses of wine. She was caught up in the conversation and forgot, for a moment, that she was only there as a novelty. Again, she was the recipient of one of Madame Rappelais's warning glances.

"Thank you, my dear," said Millet. He turned to Worth. "I am painting peasants, monsieur," said Millet. "These are the poorest of the poor, the lowest of the low. They barely have money to eat, let alone worry about what they put on their backs."

"But you paint the countryside and its people so beautifully. Why can't their clothes have a little more stool?" persisted Monsieur Worth in his questionable French. "What harm is a bow here, a touch of lace there, a bit of color, for heaven's sake? Isn't it the role of art and the artist to create beauty wherever he can? You do an admirable job of reflecting poverty. But I'm not sure I myself would want to have poverty hanging on my wall. It's so very depressing."

Millet took a sip of his wine and wiped his mustache. Berthe noticed that his wife had put her hand on his as if to restrain him. Finally, he said, "Well, Monsieur Worth, it's a good thing I don't have to rely on you for my livelihood. I am well aware that art and beauty are in the eye of the beholder."

Worth lifted an eyebrow and another truffle. "I hope you didn't take offense, monsieur. As a fellow artist I know that many times we are at the mercy of our critics."

"And what kind of art do you do?" Millet asked.

"Ah, well, you are looking at two excellent examples of my work," Worth said, indicating Madame Rappelais and Berthe. Millet seemed confused. "Oh, not the ladies," Worth said with a laugh. "The gowns they are wearing."

"You are a seamstress?" asked Millet, barely able to disguise his contempt.

"Ho, no, not a seamstress. I am a creator of gowns. A couturier. An artist whose medium is the finest silk and satin, the most exquisite lace and ribbon. My work immortalizes the female farm."

"Oh, yes, Monsieur Worth is an artist in his own right," Berthe said, nodding vigorously. Madame Rappelais glared at her, but somehow Berthe didn't care.

Millet snorted. "You sew dresses. That makes you a seamstress, monsieur. You are not an artist. You are a purveyor of goods. And gaudy ones at that," he said, indicating both the women's gowns in one sweep of his arm. "I take umbrage, sir. You sully the name artist."

"My gowns are works of great beauty. In fact, I am planning a show of my first complete collection," said Worth haughtily. "Women will come from all over France, from all over the world, to see it, to commission one of my pieces for themselves, and to pay greatly for the privilege. Therefore, I ask you, in what way is what I do any different from what you do?"

"Women are fickle. Fashions change. Silks fade. Brocades fray. My art is for all times. More important, I paint truth. I paint the peasants who labor in our fields, the soul of the common man. I celebrate the humble and hardworking! I honor the homespun! I stand for the common man and his endless labors on this bountiful earth!"

"Poppy poop," said Worth. "And how much did Madame Rappelais pay for this common man's vision of a naked nymph by the riverside?" Madame smiled weakly. "More than for one of my frocks, I would venture to say. You, my dear Monsieur Millet, claim a higher moral ground, a more elevated art form. You look down your nostril at my silks and satins. You are a purveyor of paint. Nothing more. Your work makes rich people feel superior to your poor painted folk. My work actually makes my patrons *look* superior. You hang your art on the walls of the wealthy. I hang my art on the walls of wealthy women. What is the difference, pray tell?" Worth twirled the ends of his mustache.

"But don't you see? Both of you are right," exclaimed Berthe, again forgetting herself and earning another of Madame's sizzling looks. She had failed to notice that she was the only one of the women participating in the conversation.

"Impossible!" both men answered at once.

"What a fascinating conversation we are having," said Monsieur Rappelais, lifting his wineglass in salute to the two men. "What would our dear Louis-Napoléon have to say about all this?"

"*Your* dear Louis-Napoléon, certainly not mine," snapped Millet. And therein followed a heated argument about the pros (Worth) and cons (Millet) of the Emperor Louis-Napoléon and his industrialization of France.

"You and yours have caused the death of the poor farmer!" shouted Millet finally.

"I have murdered no one. My feet are clean," said Worth, again reverting back to his uncertain French and raising his palms upward. "Let the peasants come to the city. They might as well starve here as in the country."

"Mark my words, there will be an uprising of the common man. Your beautiful art, as you call it, will end up torn, in useless tatters."

"Haven't we already had the uprising?" whispered a worried Madame Worth.

"Wait. We have here an opportunity to put this argument to rest. Mademoiselle Bovary happens to have come from humble beginnings in rural France to seek her fortune in Paris. Let's ask *her* what *she* thinks of all this," said Worth.

All eyes turned to Berthe.

"Well, mademoiselle, what think you?" said Monsieur Rappelais, trying to inject a bit of levity into what had turned into a cantankerous evening. "Can you shed some light on this discussion?"

Berthe took a deep breath and then, despite her previous fears, spoke her mind. "I think there is a tendency on all three of your parts to underestimate what you call the 'common man.' As if people of little means can't possibly understand the value of a fine painting or, for that matter, a well-designed gown! We understand quality and beauty just as much as those born to a grander lifestyle." Berthe clamped her lips shut and felt her eyes widen. Was it the wine? What else would have prompted her to speak so boldly?

"My, my," said Monsieur Rappelais, one eyebrow raised.

"Just look at you, young lady," Millet said, wagging a finger at Berthe. "All beribboned and besmirched in that ridiculous gown. You have abandoned everything I taught you. You have forsaken the homespun and the humble."

"But, Monsieur Millet, where is your homespun coat this evening? And look at your lovely wife. I see she is not wearing the rough woven material of the peasant woman," Berthe said, smiling sweetly, though she now knew for certain that she had gone too far—she could see it in Madame's eyes. *Why, oh why, couldn't I have kept my mouth closed?*

"Excellent point," said Worth. "Millet, you want everyone dressed in rags because it makes you feel both superior and holier-than-thou. Holier than thou. Holy, as in full of holes. Yes, you are definitely holier than *moi*." He laughed at his own pun. "That's very good, isn't it, my dear Marie?" His wife touched his arm with her petite hand and smiled at him.

Berthe swallowed heavily. "May I be excused, madame?" She started to stand.

"Stay," commanded Madame Rappelais, not looking at her.

The men, still debating, adjourned to the study for cigars and brandy. Loud voices could be heard coming through the closed double doors.

As soon as they had left, Madame Rappelais tried to encourage conversation between Madame Worth and Madame Millet, but it was like trying to tighten a fat woman's corset into a twenty-four-inch waist. Fashion was the first subject she introduced, but the two women seemed to be afraid to tread on that already dangerous ground. Finally, she turned the talk to their children and the ice was broken. The women traded stories of their offspring with ease and animation, seeming to forget Berthe entirely. She wondered why Madame Rappelais had insisted on her remaining. Her head was spinning from all the wine, and she desperately wanted to go to bed.

"They say children should be seen and not heard. I say they shouldn't be seen either," Madame Millet was saying. "I prefer they appear when they are fully grown and well married." The two other women laughed.

"Then why, in heaven's name, do you all have so many children if they are just things to be ignored?" Berthe burst out. "Isn't the whole point of being a mother to offer love and care to a helpless being? Do you have any idea what it's like to grow up with a mother who cares nothing for her child? One thing is certain: You don't deserve the children you've given birth to!" She jumped up from her seat. The three women stared at her, speechless, as she burst into tears and stumbled out of the room. *I'm through, done for, finished,* she told herself. *From the grande fête table back to the gutter.*

Once in her room, she tried to calm herself, to no avail. She had sealed her fate. She would be fired, if not tonight then certainly first thing in the morning. Where would she go now? This was what she got for thinking she had opinions that mattered, for mixing up the fantasy of who she wanted to be with the reality of who she was.

She cleaned the stains from the gown and hung it in

Madame's armoire. Then she turned down the bed. She heard her mistress's footsteps. She closed her eyes and held her breath, waiting for the inevitable ax to fall. She opened them in time to see Madame Rappelais fall upon the bed, her huge skirt rising a foot as she did so.

"Artists," Madame groaned. "Heaven spare us." And with that, her mistress promptly fell asleep.

CHAPTER 23

Yet Another Artiste

MONSIEUR MILLET KEPT HIS PROMISE AND SENT HIS YOUNG apprentice two days later to discuss the painting of a mural for Madame Rappelais's birthday ball. Berthe was called to the ballroom, where Madame Rappelais was speaking in a highly animated voice to a tall young man facing away from Berthe. He stood with his legs apart and his hands clasped behind his neck.

"Ah, Berthe, you're here," said Madame.

The young man turned. He had dark curly hair that fell over his forehead, halfway down his strong neck, and over the white collar of his shirt. His face was all angles; the jawline seemed almost sculpted. He was clean-shaven but with a bluish tint indicating a heavy beard. His nose looked as if it had been broken at one time. It had a slight but somehow alluring crook in it. His bright blue eyes were wide-set, rimmed in dark lashes and shaded by heavy brows. He looked to be no more than nineteen or twenty, but he had a quiet reserve, an intensity about him that made him seem much older.

Berthe had seen handsome men before but he was different.

Something about his sheer physical presence pulled at the most inner part of her—his hands, with their long, strong, capable fingers; his height and breadth, the way he took up space in the room. It was odd, but all the furniture around him seemed to be slightly reduced in size.

Madame Rappelais was all atwitter, which made the young man's calm and quiet striking by comparison. The more silent he was, the more she seemed to feel the need to talk and explain her commission.

"I want you to hear this, Berthe, so if there are any questions from Armand here, you will be able to answer them in my place. Armand, this is my maid, Mademoiselle Bovary." Armand didn't so much as glance in Berthe's direction. His full attention was on Madame Rappelais.

"How do you do?" said Berthe, curtsying. His eyes barely flickered toward her. Berthe felt a flash of anger; she hadn't felt this ignored since she was a child sitting with her parents in the parlor.

"Armand—what did you say your surname was?" asked Madame Rappelais.

"De Pouvier, madame."

"Armand de Pouvier." She pronounced his name as though tasting each syllable and, as she did, she pushed her lips out provocatively. "Well, Monsieur de Pouvier, are you familiar with *Venus and Cupid with a Partridge,* painted by Titian?"

"Yes, madame, I have seen it in the Louvre."

"Well, that is what I want and there is where I want it," she said, pointing to the domed section of the ceiling from which the chandelier hung. "And I want it to be completed by my birthday, which is in two months' time. Can you do that?"

"Yes, madame."

"You're a man of few words, Monsieur de Pouvier. But I

imagine that is because you choose to express yourself in paints,"
she said, looking him up and down through catlike eyes. "As I
am not familiar with the mysterious workings of you master
painters, please explain to me how you will proceed."

"I will need to erect a scaffold, madame. You won't be able to
use this room while I work here."

"That is no matter. Now, about the painting itself. I want
you to make a few minor alterations to the original: I want my
face in place of Titian's Venus. As you can see, we have the same
hair color. Will you require me to pose?"

"No, madame. I can work from a miniature of you," said the
artist with a wry smile. For the first time since Berthe had entered the room, she thought that there might be something
about this Armand de Pouvier to actually like.

"As you wish," said Madame Rappelais, clearly disappointed.
"Now, I want the hills of Rome, if that's what they are, in the
background. But no partridge. I hate the partridge. And instead
of the boy Cupid, I want Cupid to be a girl."

"But, madame, wouldn't you prefer an exact replica of the
Titian? It is considered a masterpiece," he said, frowning slightly.

"That may well be, but I want my own masterpiece. Do you
have a problem with that, Monsieur de Pouvier?" she asked, her
eyes flashing.

"It is your ceiling, madame. And your money." Armand
shrugged.

"Ah, but you think I am a presumptuous dilettante, don't
you?" Madame said, tilting her head and trying to charm him
into a smile.

"I don't know you well enough to say. I just think you are a
woman who knows what she wants," he said evenly. "When do
you wish me to begin?"

Berthe hid her smile. This was the first time she had heard

anyone talk so confidently to Madame Rappelais—including Madame's husband. Even more amazing was the fact that her mistress seemed to be taking the young artist's attitude toward her in stride.

"The sooner the better," she said, peering over the top of her fan.

"I will build the scaffolding tomorrow and begin my sketch the next day."

"He's a cold one," Madame Rappelais remarked to Berthe once De Pouvier had left. "I hope he has the skill to accomplish this task." She gazed upward. "It would be awful if he ruined my ceiling just in time for my birthday ball."

Berthe suddenly imagined how wonderful it would be if he did ruin Madame's ceiling. If he painted something so atrocious, so incredibly ugly, that her birthday ball would be ruined, her ballroom would be the laughingstock of all her fancy friends. She felt the thrill of possibility. At the same time, she admired Armand de Pouvier for holding his own with someone as formidable as Madame Rappelais. He had the makings of a true hero in her eyes.

The next day, the young artist brought in long lengths of lumber and built scaffolding that allowed him to reach the ceiling. Madame Rappelais had gone out for a day of shopping, so after finishing her chores Berthe stood in the doorway of the ballroom and watched him work. She was impressed by his silence, his seriousness, and the air of brooding in a man so young. He must be either very sad or wise beyond his years, she thought. To her, he approached the embodiment of her dreams: someone who was making a living using his talent, and had already earned the support of a master like Millet. At the same time, she wondered why anyone who was doing what he loved to do would seem so somber.

That afternoon, using a thin stick of charcoal, Armand began to sketch out the mural. He continually referred to a miniature copy of Titian's original, which he kept by his side.

"Do you mind if I watch?" Berthe asked. He glanced over his shoulder at her but didn't answer. "How long do you think it will take you?" Again no answer. "Will the paint cover the charcoal marks?" The longer his silence, the more determined she became to extract an answer from him. "Are you a great admirer of Monsieur Millet?"

He glared down at her and finally spoke.

"I have better things to do than educate a maid about my work. My admiration of Millet is not necessary to do this job. And this is a job, not art. It doesn't require talent, just an empty belly and chronically empty pockets." He made broad slashing strokes with the charcoal.

"Well, at least I know that you can talk," Berthe retorted.

She turned on her heel and left the room, slamming the door behind her. She may have been dependent on her mistress for her livelihood but she certainly didn't owe this arrogant man anything, including her goodwill. *Who does he think he is? Just because he's handsome and talented doesn't give him the right to treat me like a servant girl.* And then she remembered: She *was* a servant girl. She thought about what he said about an empty belly and empty pockets. Why, he was as poor and dependent on work as she was. *We have much more in common than he realizes.*

Still simmering an hour later, Berthe carried a tea tray to the solarium, where Messieurs Rappelais and Worth were in conference over the selection of fabric for Madame Rappelais's birthday ball gown. The teacups clattered as she set the tray down harder than intended. Sun poured through the French windows, illuminating the men's heavy brocade coats. They were dressed far too warmly for the room, but Berthe knew that for them to shed their elegant jackets was tantamount to leaving their egos at the door.

"This will be an excellent opportunity for you to promote your new establishment, my friend," said Rappelais. "Therefore, you must pick the most incredible fabric. Something that will cause the guests to drool with envy."

"You're right. It must be truly redundant. Something never before seen," said Worth, fingering various swatches of cloth. "For the first time I feel a bit uncertain. I just don't know. Perhaps we should ask your wife."

"Are you mad? You know quite well that she has terrible taste. She thinks there is no such thing as too many bangles and baubles. It is you and I who have made her one of the best-dressed women in Paris. We're better off asking Mademoiselle Berthe here what she thinks."

Berthe bristled. Were they making fun of her? She was tired of being asked her opinion as if it were a novelty and then being dismissed as inconsequential in every other way. Both messieurs had told her on more than one occasion that she had an eye for fashion, a talent for suggesting tasteful combinations of fabric and design. She longed to be seen as a collaborator, an equal, not someone whose ideas they could take advantage of because she was a nobody. Just the same, she knew she still had much to learn from the men, and that she would have to be patient. She took a deep breath and squared her shoulders. For the first time, she told herself that this wasn't just a fantasy, a daydream out of her reach. She believed in herself, and she would not give up until she'd made a career—and steady income—for herself in the fashion industry.

Monsieur Worth was speaking to her, a worried expression on his face. "This is the most important occasion, because it will represent the debut of my new enterprise, as my friend Rappelais suggests. This must be a one-of-a-kind fabric for a one-of-a-kind dress. It must make a statement. So please, mademoiselle, stop furrowing and give us your opinion."

Berthe leaned over and calmly paged through the swatches in Monsieur Rappelais's sample book—embroidered satins and silks, gold lamés, brocades, intricately woven designs in every shade imaginable. She looked up and said, "What about something simple?"

"Simple!" both men exclaimed in horror. It was as if she had said, "What about something mud-splattered?"

"Do you remember the purple gown with the white silk tulle?" asked Berthe.

"Of course I do. It was one of my most inspired creations," said Worth, twirling his mustache. Berthe opened her mouth to remind Worth of her contribution to the design but instead sighed, realizing that her ego stood only as an emerging sprout in the shadow of his towering oak.

"I suggest that you design a silk gown in the palest pink possible. It is one of Madame's best colors. Drape it with the lightest white tulle and nothing else."

"Nothing else? No lace? No bows?" asked Worth, nervously biting the end of his mustache.

"No ribbons or embroidery? No crystals or pearls?" joined in Rappelais, one finger held to his lips in consternation.

"Nothing. Let her jewels be the only decoration. Her beauty will not have to compete with an overly ornate gown."

"It is a radical concept," said Worth, releasing his mustache and smoothing the damp end back into place.

"And it will be much talked about," said Rappelais.

Both men beamed at each other.

"Now all we have to do is convince Madame," said Worth, kissing Monsieur Rappelais on both cheeks.

"I would wait until the night of the ball if I were you," said Berthe.

"What about fittings?" asked Rappelais, blushing deeply thanks to Worth's gesture of affection.

"I already have all her measurements," said Worth.

And so it was decided. The Birthday Gown would be the simplest, most unadorned ever to grace Madame Rappelais's perfect form.

"She'll have a conniption, of course," said Monsieur Rappelais, rubbing his hands together.

"Of course," said Worth, smiling broadly. "She will give birth to a cat."

"But when she looks in the mirror, I believe she will be well pleased," said Berthe.

"You have the pink silk?" asked Worth.

"The palest of pale pinks, the color of a virgin's buttocks," said Rappelais, flipping through his sample book.

"That being decided, I am much relieved," said Worth. He took a seat at a small table, reached for the bowl of grapes, and began popping one after another into his mouth. "Unfortunately, the discussion of silk reminds me that I have some unpleasant news to impart to you, dear Rappelais. A purveyor of textiles came into the shop the other day. He mistakenly thought I would be interested in his wares; he talked of nothing but the great Louis Pasteur."

"We do owe him a huge debt of gratitude," said Rappelais

distractedly. "He did manage to save the silkworms by identify-ing the cause of the epidemic. He deserves a medal."

"Save your medallion until you hear the rest of it," said Worth. "Like all scientists he has become carried away by his own genie. Have you ever seen the way he dresses? I saw him at the opera the other night. He was wearing a black serge coat that was so old, the black had turned to chocolate brown."

"Get to the point," said Rappelais.

"The point is this," said Worth, taking a piece of fabric out of his coat pocket and handing it to Monsieur.

"A very mediocre piece of silk," said Rappelais, fingering the fabric. His lip curled upward in disgust, as if he were touching something repellent. "It's certainly not something I would ever manufacture in one of my mills." He handed the swatch to Berthe, who examined it carefully.

"But, you see, it is not silk at all. It is an impostor!" screamed Worth. He stood and began pacing the solarium, waving his arms as he did so. "And it is all the fault of that damned Pasteur."

"I don't understand," said Rappelais.

"It is not from worms but from the fiber of trees."

"Trees?" exclaimed Rappelais, jumping up and almost knocking over the small table. Berthe steadied it before it could topple over.

"As you know, Pasteur is working on trying to save the worms that threaten the silk industry. Another scientist, a Georges Audemars, became interested in trying to produce an artificial silk. And the result is what Mademoiselle Berthe is holding in her pretty mitten."

"The idea is as ugly as the fabric," sneered Rappelais.

"The good news is that at this juncture, it seems that the fab-ric is highly flammable." Worth rubbed his hands together rather gleefully.

"Another great addition to the world of fashion," Rappelais scoffed. "Dress flambé." The two men burst into laughter.

"It almost feels like silk," Berthe said, as she rubbed the fabric between her fingers and thumb.

She was sorry the minute she said it.

Rappelais stiffened. "Almost is not enough. It is cheaply made. And it looks that way. It's true Pasteur did save the silk industry. But why is he trying to undercut it by supporting this hideous faux silk? I don't care how brilliant a scientist he is. He's an idiot!"

"You know I always thought he was mad, ever since that whole rabies thing," added Worth, resuming his seat and holding out his cup for Berthe to fill.

"These scientists know nothing whatsoever about fabrics," said Rappelais, taking a pinch of snuff and inhaling deeply. "If they want cheap fabric, they should just wear *serge de Nîmes.*"

"What is that?" asked Berthe, filling Monsieur Rappelais's cup as well.

"It's a fabric made in Nîmes especially for the peasants. It is soft and durable and lasts forever," explained Monsieur. Berthe smiled at the thought, wondering if Millet knew that finally something had been created for the peasants to wear that wasn't the scratchy homespun he seemed to think was such a noble cloth.

"I would love to see Pasteur and his fellows at the Opéra all dressed in artificial silk and *serge de Nîmes,*" Worth chuckled.

"Let's see if that little fashion idea catches fire," said Rappelais. And both men burst into uproarious laughter.

CHAPTER 24

Watching Paint Dry

AS HER TUTELAGE UNDER THE TWO MEN CONTINUED, BERTHE'S confidence grew and along with it her feelings of security. But of course as one part of life grew sweeter another always soured.

She already regretted that she had ever recommended Hélène to the Rappelaises. She knew her friend was stealing things left and right. One afternoon she went into Hélène's room to search for the valuables she suspected had been taken. She got down on her hands and knees and lifted up the plain white bedspread covering the narrow iron bed. She pulled out Hélène's battered leather suitcase and opened it. Inside, wrapped in an old apron, were a half dozen Sèvres dinner plates double rimmed in gold with a bouquet of crimson roses painted in the middle of the white background. In addition, she found a sterling silver sifter, two sets of Cardeilhac silver flatware, a matching set of crystal vinegar and oil cruets, and finally, an elaborate Frenais Winged Sphinx butter dish. Not to mention the silver salt and pepper shakers and serving spoon Hélène had slipped into her apron pocket the night of the dinner party.

"Are you looking for something in particular, mademoiselle? If you don't see what you like, I can easily get it for you." Hélène spoke from the doorway in a good imitation of a luxury shop proprietor.

Berthe jerked her head up.

Hélène watched unperturbed as Berthe placed each item on the bed.

"Close the door," Berthe hissed. "What are you doing with all of this?"

"I'm just keeping my inventory stocked." Hélène laughed. "I take things that ain't being used and hide them for a week or two. If Madame DuPoix notices something's missing, I manage to find it. If she don't miss it, I pawn it. I've already made one hundred twenty francs," she said proudly.

"Are you mad? Are you trying to get us both fired?" Of course the Rappelaises would assume she and Hélène were in on the pilfering together. Both of them would lose their jobs.

"It's just a few trinkets. They'll never miss 'em. They have more silver and stuff than they need."

"It's not your place to decide what they need and don't need," snapped Berthe.

"Who do you think you're talking to? You're as much a thief as I am."

"You promised me you would change!" Berthe cried. "Now you're ruining everything."

Her anger gave way to fear as her mind flew to the worst possible outcome—not only would she lose her position, she would surely lose the respect of Monsieur Worth, and with it all her dreams. If she had to go back to the mill she knew she would die. "Please, please, promise me you won't steal again," Berthe pleaded.

"I promise," said Hélène, a slight smile lifting the corners of her mouth.

Berthe realized a promise from Hélène was like a wish on a shooting star. It meant nothing.

"Promise on your mother's grave," she demanded.

"My mother ain't got no grave. She's lying at the bottom of some dirty river." Hélène laughed, and then she grew serious. "Why in the world would you find me a job in this house of treasures if it wasn't for me to steal? You know I'm a thief—and a very good one at that. But if it's your cut you're worried about, don't worry, you'll get your share," she said, reaching over and plucking at Berthe's starched pinafore.

"I don't want a cut!" Berthe shouted. "I just want to keep my job."

"Shhh!" Hélène put a finger to her lips. "Someone's coming."

Berthe held her breath and listened to the footsteps approaching on the stairs. Then she and Hélène quickly began shoving Hélène's booty underneath her bed, finishing just as the door opened. Madame DuPoix stood there with her arms folded across her chest.

"Mesdemoiselles, is this a tea party you're having?"

"No, madame," said Hélène. "We're just talking, catching up on old times."

"Hélène, you still have your chores downstairs and you, Mademoiselle *Bovary*," she said, underlining Berthe's surname, "I realize your duties are confined to Madame's needs, but I'm sure there is something more constructive you can do besides chatting with your friend in the middle of a workday." She gave them a look that said *I know you're up to no good. I don't know what exactly, but trust me, I'll find out sooner or later.*

"I were just telling my dear friend how grateful I am for this wonderful position," said Hélène. She twisted a piece of her loose red hair and refastened it under her white cap.

"You're going to have to do better than that, mademoiselle. I don't believe a word that comes out of your mouth. Perhaps your friend here can give you lessons in lying." Berthe started to protest and then thought better of it. "Madame Rappelais has a wonderful habit of picking up strays and installing them in her household. I, for one, have never understood it."

"And wasn't you also one of the strays, Madame DuPoix?" asked Hélène with an air of innocence. Madame DuPoix narrowed her eyes and then turned to leave. "Get back to work, girls."

While Madame was taking her nap or away visiting friends, Berthe split her time between keeping an eye on Hélène and sneaking looks at the painter's progress. She wasn't the only one who had developed an interest in art. The entire household seemed drawn to the young artist as to a fireplace on a cold winter's day. Whenever Berthe visited the ballroom it appeared someone else had already been there, evidenced by empty dishes, glassware, and remnants of food that had clearly been brought by the other staff to curry favor with the young man. Once, she came upon Monsieur Rappelais sitting in one of the upholstered balloon-back chairs sipping tea as he watched the painter paint.

"Takes my breath away," said Monsieur.

"Yes, it's going to be a beautiful mural," agreed Berthe.

"I meant the painter, not the painting." He laughed.

De Pouvier continued painting without looking down from the scaffold. But Berthe saw that the back of his neck had turned red at the comment—either with embarrassment or anger, she couldn't tell which. She wished that he would acknowledge her, if only so that she could tell him she knew how he felt about unsolicited compliments.

Another time, Berthe came upon Madame Rappelais sitting in the very same chair. She'd thought her mistress was out visit-

ing but apparently Madame had come home early. She was still
wearing her cape, bonnet, and gloves. She stared up at the mural
and didn't turn her head when Berthe entered the room.

"What a gift this is," she said dreamily, "the joy of witnessing
the artist in action; of seeing my vision become a reality. I could sit
here all day. I think, Monsieur de Pouvier, that when you are done
with this I shall commission you for a mural in my boudoir."

"As you wish, madame," he said stiffly.

Berthe couldn't help but feel empathy toward De Pouvier,
who seemed to be in the same predicament as she was—forced
to endure the flirtations of Madame Rappelais in order to keep
his job and his livelihood. She vowed to break through his cold-
ness by engaging him in conversation, and one morning, em-
boldened, she began another onslaught of questions.

"May I get you something to eat, to drink?"

"When did you first learn how to paint?"

"How do you know how to mix the colors correctly?"

"How long does it take for the paint to dry?"

She remembered this same need to ask questions of her father when he was busy studying his medical texts or writing up
a patient's case. There had been something about her father's intense preoccupation with other things that seemed to spur her
on and on.

"Papa, do I stop breathing when I sleep?"

"Why do you cut people to make them feel better?"

"Does that big thing growing on Madame Cornier's neck
hurt?"

"Does it hurt to die?"

He was always too busy or too tired to answer her, but still
she couldn't stop asking the questions. Invariably, he would lose
his temper as she knew he would.

"Berthe, for heaven's sake, leave Papa alone! Can't you see I'm busy?" She would cry and he would console her, patting her shoulder as he gently pushed her out of the room. It was that final caress that vaguely reassured her that he might, indeed, love her, after all.

The more silent the artist was, the more questions she asked. She knew she was annoying him but she resolved to prove to him that she was nothing like the patrons for whom he worked. She was determined to win him over.

"How did you meet Monsieur Millet?"

"Do you always work in oils?"

"Is French your native language?"

"Aren't you afraid of the scaffolding collapsing?"

"What happens if you make a mistake? How do you correct it?"

"Is it difficult to get your brushes clean?"

He climbed down from the scaffolding and looked up at the ceiling. It was as if she had never spoken. As he studied the mural, he wiped his brush upon the paint-stained rag that hung from his back pocket. Berthe watched the slow, measured movement of his hands. Blue, red, and green paints were all smeared on the rag, and on his smock. There was a streak of blue paint on one cheek, as if he'd brushed at a fly without being aware that he held a brush in his hand. He was totally absorbed in what he was doing. Berthe had certainly never felt that way while polishing her mistress's shoes or making her bed. What did it feel like to paint like him, to be totally immersed in your work? The only time she had experienced that lately was when looking at fabrics with Monsieur Rappelais.

She was brought back from her reverie by the sound of De Pouvier's voice.

"Don't you have anything else to do, mademoiselle?" he said without looking at her. "Can't you see I'm busy?"

"Oh, I see that you're busy," she said, pleased that she had managed to get him to speak. "But are you so busy you can't answer one question?"

"Yes," he said. He turned and continued to scrutinize the mural. His eyes narrowed as he studied the painting. *Was he looking at something he liked? Was it something he didn't like?* She longed to be able to see things through his eyes.

Finally, unable to evoke a response, she said, "I must say, monsieur, you are very arrogant for someone so young."

That did it. "And you are very irritating for someone so very . . . so very . . ."

"So very beautiful?" she offered. She found herself unable to keep quiet. "So very brilliant, perceptive, charming, talented, kind?"

Despite himself, he grinned. "So very *irritating*," he finally said. He climbed back up the scaffolding and began painting again. With her skirts swirling around her, she swept from the room, holding her head as high as her neck would allow.

She found herself thinking about Armand constantly. She lay awake at night picturing his long strong arms as they quickly sketched out the mural and how the cords on his neck stood out as he worked. She became more and more absentminded in her duties. One morning as she was pulling aside Madame's bedroom drapes, her mistress said, "Berthe, isn't there something you've forgotten?" Madame Rappelais was sitting up in bed, her arms crossed and a quizzical look on her face. Berthe shook her head in confusion.

"What, madame?"

"My bath."

"Sorry, madame. I'll run it right away."

"Your mind isn't on your work, my dear. That just won't do, will it?" Madame said, yawning.

"No, madame." It was her first warning. But despite all her efforts, her mind continued to wander back to thoughts of the young artist.

She felt drawn to him and yet hesitant, remembering how she had been so hurt by the farm boy, Renard. But Armand was older—and she was older, too. Did that change things, did it make it easier to trust someone? She liked to think that she had learned from her experience, but then she thought about her mother. She had a memory of Emma Bovary standing at the upstairs window for hours at a time, waiting for Monsieur Boulanger to arrive on his big black horse. When would he come? Would he come at all? What if he never came? She had a sense of her mother's whole life being one long wait for someone to come, for something to happen. Her mother had certainly not learned from her mistakes.

A few days passed and Berthe found herself again in the ballroom regardless of her promises to herself to stay away from Armand.

"Is Titian your favorite artist?" she asked, looking up.

"Why in heaven's name would you think that?" He stopped painting and looked down at her. She was startled for a moment that he'd answered her.

"I ... I suppose you would have to admire him in order to make such an excellent copy of his work," she said, shifting her weight from one foot to the other.

"I am merely copying a second-rate work of art. Titian is not someone I admire." He wiped his brush on a paint-covered rag and turned back to his work.

"But wasn't Titian considered a great master?" She felt herself growing annoyed again, but then Armand rewarded her with a thoughtful expression that made her heart beat quicker. His dark hair fell forward into his eyes, and he brushed it away, leaving yet another smear of paint on his forehead. She smiled her most charming smile.

"No one would question the genius of his technique," he said finally. He studied the half-finished mural through critical eyes. "He revolutionized the way oils were done at the time. His brush-strokes were among the boldest and most sweeping. He was the first to work in small patches of color that are best viewed from far away. From a distance his subjects appear alive. But Titian did not have the soul of an artist. He had the mind of a merchant. He was a greedy man who would pretend poverty in order to promote the myth of the starving artist. And he always claimed to be much older than he was. Thinking he would soon die, his patrons were manipulated into paying higher prices for his work."

"Is he dead now?" she asked.

"Oh, yes." He laughed, displaying charming dimples. "For almost three hundred years, the rogue."

"Then why are you so angry at him?" she said. He frowned, as though confused.

"I hate having to copy his work," he finally said. "I want to be painting my own art. I resent the fact that Titian is revered just because he painted reverential subjects. Though he did, in my opinion, paint one masterpiece. Are you familiar with his *Venus and Adonis*?"

Now it was Berthe's turn to be silent. She was suddenly aware of how dismally ignorant and uncultured she was. She shook her head, embarrassed for having lured him into a conversation that was totally beyond her comprehension.

"I'm afraid not," she finally said. Armand looked down at her in surprise.

"It's quite famous. Have you never been to the Louvre?" With one paint-covered hand, he pushed back the curls of his dark hair.

She shook her head again and felt herself blushing.

"You live in Paris and you've never been to its most famous museum? Quite possibly *the* most famous in the world."

She felt utterly humiliated. She wanted to tell him that she had been exposed to art, that she had even been the sometime subject of his very own master's celebrated paintings, clearly something he didn't know. But she sensed that he would not have been the least bit impressed.

"I am just a lady's maid after all," she snapped. "I know nothing except how to repair lace collars, polish boots, replace ribbons on bonnets, and run the bath for my mistress. I have no time for your precious paintings or famous museums." And with that she turned on her heel and, fighting back tears, rushed out of the room. Even as she left, she felt she had made this embarrassing exit one too many times.

CHAPTER 25

A Visit to the Louvre

ON ONE OF BERTHE'S RARE DAYS OFF SHE VISITED THE LOUVRE for the first time. If Armand had a favorite painting of Titian's she wanted to see it, to try to understand him better. His derisive "You've never been to Paris's most famous museum?" echoed in her thoughts. *I'll show you; I'm not a complete dolt.* She waited nervously outside for the Louvre to open in the Palais Royal; she untied and retied the ribbons of her bonnet so tightly that she had difficulty swallowing.

Are we all doomed to go through life desiring what we can never have? She pictured Armand working from his scaffold—literally above her, completely out of reach. How she admired the fact that he still held on to the dream of creating his own work instead of copying the work of others. She could see that this passion drove him. What exactly was driving her?

In 1852 Napoléon III had proclaimed himself Emperor of all of France. And wasting no time, he immediately turned his substantial energies to the "Nouveau Louvre." Over the next fifteen years, he would raze the last city structures within the Louvre-Tuileries precincts and finish the north gallery, effectively enclosing the Tuileries and Carrousel gardens. Later, at great expense, the imperial architects Louis Visconti and Hector Lefuel doubled the size of the wings of what was originally called the *Cour Napoléon*. This was the imposing structure that Berthe entered that day.

She felt as if she had suddenly been dropped in the middle of a foreign country where she didn't speak the language or understand the customs. But she refused to let her intimidation stop her. She was on a mission.

She walked quickly past one elaborate, gilt-framed painting and tall, imposing sculpture after another, until at the end of the long hall she came to an abrupt halt. A huge white marble sculpture of an armless woman stood in front of her. She gazed up at it, her mouth open. Where were her arms? Without arms she was unable to cover her breasts or reach down and grasp the drape that seemed to be slipping off her hips. Even though she was half clothed, she seemed more naked than naked. She appeared powerless and at the same time, incredibly powerful.

"She is something, *n'est-ce pas?*" a voice behind her said. Berthe turned to see a uniformed museum guard. He smiled, twirling the ends of his mustache as if he were a dandy about to ask either Berthe, or the statue, to honor him with the next dance.

"What happened to her arms?" Berthe asked.

The guard chuckled. "Ah, that is always the question. You're not the first person to ask." He cleared his throat and said, "In 1820 the beautiful lady was discovered on the island of Melos by a Greek farmer who found her while plowing a field. She was in two pieces. In her left hand was an apple, while her right hand held her robe from slipping further. Both hands were badly damaged, as was her *petit nez,* as you can see. A few days later the farmer told a French naval officer, a Monsieur d'Urville, about the statue. But the officer's captain wasn't interested in old pieces of marble. D'Urville, obviously an art lover, made sketches and upon arriving in Constantinople showed his sketches to the French ambassador, the marquis de Rivière, who sent a ship to buy it for his country. However, after fetching the lost lady there was a scuffle between the French sailors and some Greek bandits, who had suddenly decided the statue must be worth something. In the midst of the fight the statue was dragged across rocks to the ship, breaking off both arms. The sailors refused to go back and search for the pieces. And *voilà,* there you have it: the most famous armless woman in the world."

She tore her eyes away from the statue.

"Can you tell me where I may find the work of Titian?" she asked.

"Go down that hall," he said, pointing. "Turn right and keep walking for several miles until you get to the end of the long corridor, then turn left."

Berthe stood some distance away from Titian's *Venus and Adonis* and studied it for a long time. Unlike the romantic Venus and Cupid mural that Armand was replicating on the Rappelais ceiling, there was something about this work that made her feel as if she were intruding on a private scene. She recognized the figure of Venus, who was, as seemed usual in the world of art, totally naked. But it was Adonis who dominated the painting. Dressed in a rich orange tunic and holding on to three enormous hunting dogs and a staff, he looked as if he was far too busy to be bothered with the naked figure who clung to him. Venus was clearly begging him not to go hunting, to stay with her, to do with her whatever he had in his close-cropped curly head to do.

The sun streamed down through thick clouds onto the far-off hills. In the background, asleep under a tree, was a very plump Cupid. His bow and arrow hung high off an adjacent tree. Was that why Venus was unable to entice Adonis to stay with her instead of following his dogs? Berthe wondered. Was it because Cupid was asleep on the job? The expression on Adonis's face was not one of love but impatience. *Leave me alone, let me be,* he seemed to be saying. *I have dogs to hunt with, things to slay. I cannot be bothered with this naked, fleshy, needy woman.*

She walked on, studying one painting after another, trying to understand what made each one worthy of being hung in this great museum. By the end of the day she felt both exhausted by the intensity of the works and inspired by the potential of art to provoke thought and emotion. On her way out of the Louvre she stopped by another guard and asked, "Which way to the paintings of Monsieur Jean Millet?"

"Millet?" He scratched his head. "I've never heard of him. Is he dead?"

"Oh, no. He's still very much alive and painting."

"He has to be dead a long time before his paintings will be considered great enough to hang in the Louvre, mademoiselle."

"But people pay a lot for his paintings," she said.

"That may well be. But it is a pittance compared to what the works that hang here are valued at. By the time an artist arrives at the Louvre no one can afford to buy his paintings."

Berthe wondered if Armand was aware of the economics of art. Probably he hoped to achieve the same level of success as Millet, who could sell his paintings for enough to keep his large family happy, comfortable, well fed, and clothed. But even Millet was nowhere near achieving museum status, being a healthy man still in his forties.

She had a sudden insight. In art, fame meant money and

money meant one was free to follow one's passion and make even more money. But the point was, you had to have the passion in the first place. And then it hit her: She *did* have the passion. She knew it. Bolts and bolts of beautifully designed fabrics, dress after exquisite dress hung in the showroom of her mind. She realized she was back in a fantasy, but she didn't care. Because without a dream, she was without hope, and without hope she was dead. And death had no value except perhaps to the mausoleum builders, and museums. Success was possible only if fueled by passion. You just had to make sure you stayed alive to enjoy it.

Berthe burst into the ballroom. Catching her breath, she stood just inside the doorway and watched Armand paint. He lay on his back on the scaffolding, adding touches of purple to the dark sky. "I saw the *Venus de Milo* and *Venus and Adonis,* and wall after wall of beautiful paintings and statues. Why is Venus such a much-painted figure?" she asked breathlessly. Armand said nothing.

She could barely contain herself. She turned in circles, gesturing with her hands as she spoke.

"Why does one have to wait to die before you can become a famous artist? Why are there so many paintings of people fighting and horses being stabbed and women being dragged off to goodness knows where by their hair?" She was fairly bouncing up and down waiting for him to respond.

He sat up, gathered his brushes, and climbed down from the scaffolding. He studied the mural for a long time and then finally turned to look at her.

"So many questions. I gather you enjoyed the Louvre?"

"It was wonderful." She sighed happily. "I never imagined such beauty. Perhaps one day your art will hang there."

He frowned. "Not at the rate I'm going," he said, staring up at his unfinished work. "Besides, I am still just a student. I have much to learn. My dream is to go to Italy to study more."

Berthe's stomach twisted. "Why Italy? France is filled with artists."

"Italy understands and appreciates artists in a way France never has. Besides, the light is better in Italy. And who knows? Perhaps I could find my own Lorenzo de' Medici there."

He cleaned his brushes and rolled them up in a clean cloth, setting them inside an old leather case. Two minutes passed while both of them maintained their silence as they gazed at the mural. Finally, she couldn't stand it any longer and she said, "Do you think Monsieur Titian would be pleased with your work?"

"As long as Madame Rappelais is pleased that's all that matters, isn't it?" he said.

"You don't care one way or the other? You have no—what does Monsieur Millet call it—artistic integrity?"

"What do you, or Millet for that matter, know about artistic integrity?" he snorted, wiping his hands on a rag and throwing it on the floor.

"I suppose I know nothing since I am but an ignorant maid, but I thought you must have great respect for Monsieur Millet. Why else would you be an apprentice to him?" She felt her ears grow hot.

There was a long silence. And when he did finally speak she couldn't have been more surprised by his words.

"I'm sorry," he said in a quiet voice. "Please forgive me. I have spent so much of my life copying other people's art, especially Monsieur Millet's, that I suppose I have developed a resentment. Call it jealousy, if you will. I want so desperately to do my own work. I envy these great artists for being able to perfect their technique, to pursue their artistic visions. The luxury of being able to be original is one I fear I will never experience." He ran his hands through his hair and looked straight into Berthe's eyes.

"But they all had to start somewhere. The great masters must have been poor artists at the beginning."

"Poor artists with rich patrons or wealthy wives to support them. No, the painter's life is not for the lowly born." He walked over to one of the tall windows and looked out.

"Then what made you pick this profession?" She stared at his back.

He turned and laughed. She thought she had never seen anything quite so beautiful as the sight of his smile. It was like the sun coming out after many days of bad weather.

"I didn't pick it," he said ruefully. "It picked me. Once I started drawing as a young boy I was powerless to stop. I had my first paying customers when I was only eight years old. So, you see, it was my profession before I was old enough to realize what I was getting into."

"You started selling your art at such a young age?" she said, not quite believing him.

"I had a very particular subject matter, and what one might refer to as a built-in clientele." He smiled, and she felt brave enough to walk over and join him by the window. Standing next to him she noticed for the first time how much taller than her he was. Her head came only to his shoulder.

"My mother was a young and beautiful girl," he continued. "Too young and too beautiful and too ignorant in the ways of city men, having been brought up in the country. She came to Paris to work in the shops, was discovered by the wealthy son of a wine merchant, got pregnant, had me, and went into 'the profession' as the only way of supporting us." He recited this as if it had all happened to a character in a novel and not his own mother.

"The profession?" repeated Berthe.

"She was lucky enough to find a place in one of the city's better houses of prostitution. Only the most elite clientele frequented Madame Tourneau's establishment—men of great standing and considerable wealth. So I grew up surrounded by beautiful, half-clothed women. And they were my first subject matter." He turned and looked at her. Berthe had never seen such sadness in anyone's eyes.

"Many of the gentlemen who saw my drawings encouraged me and went so far as to commission certain poses for their own private collections. Even with Madame Tourneau taking her rather substantial cut I was able to earn enough to pay my way through art school. Madame bought several of my drawings herself and had them framed; as far as I know, they still hang on the walls of her brothel. They are considered, by those in the know, to be very fine pornography. You see, I benefited from an early and unusually intensive training in life drawing."

"Oh" was all Berthe could think to say. She turned her face from the window.

"Are you blushing, mademoiselle?" he asked, peering closely at her.

"I wasn't," she said, "but if you keep looking at me like that I am afraid I will start."

After seeking his attention for so long, she now found herself uncomfortable beneath his gaze. His blue, thick-lashed eyes held hers as though he was trying to read something in them that was somehow obscured.

"I've never told anyone this story before," he said.

"And your mother, is she still alive?" Berthe asked, studying her shoes.

"I had many mothers, but the one who gave birth to me died when I was ten."

"I'm sorry," she said, touching his arm.

He shook his head. "Don't be. She had a hard life and a quick death."

The death of Berthe's mother came back to her in a flash. She remembered the prolonged agony of the arsenic tearing away at her mother's innards, and she felt her eyes filling up.

"Please don't waste your tears on my mother. She chose her life," he said, reaching out to put a hand on hers.

"I wasn't thinking of her. I was thinking of my own mother and her death. She didn't have an easy one. But that was her choice, too," said Berthe, blinking hard, embarrassed by her sudden show of emotion. And in a rush of words she told him the story of her mother's sad life.

"It seems that our pasts are not so very different," he said, leaning closer.

"My mother was not a whore," she said, wiping her eyes. She looked up at him. "Oh, no, I'm sorry... I didn't mean..."

"It's all right. I meant we both had difficult childhoods, as it were," he said, smiling.

"Yes, I suppose you are right." She nodded. "But we did survive."

"And of that, I am very glad." Armand picked up her hand and slowly turned it over as if it were a small, fragile animal that he didn't want to alarm. He bent his dark head and softly kissed the inside of her wrist. She stopped breathing. From that one soft kiss, a current passed between them that erased every cross word, every misunderstanding they had had. Without letting go of her hand, Armand lifted his head and whispered, "Do you know that you are very, very beautiful, Mademoiselle Bovary?"

She closed her eyes, luxuriating in the sensation. She was so caught up in the tenderness of Armand's touch that she didn't hear any sound until it was too late.

"And is this what I am paying for?" Madame Rappelais stood in the doorway wearing her cape and bonnet. Her mouth was pressed into a thin, angry line; her eyes blazed. "Mademoiselle Bovary, I'm quite sure there is something else that needs your attention other than holding the hand of my very costly artist-in-residence," she said coldly.

"We were just talking, madame," Berthe said, turning quickly and tightening the strings on her pinafore.

"Leave us," ordered Madame Rappelais, turning to glare at Armand.

With one last glance at Armand, Berthe hurried from the room.

That night as Berthe was turning down Madame's duvet and spraying the sheets with lavender scent, her mistress called to her from the dressing room.

"Berthe, come and help me with this wretched corset."

She smiled over her shoulder as if she had forgotten her anger that afternoon. With shaking hands, Berthe untied the lacing in the back of the corset that held Madame's slender waist to an even smaller circumference. Her mistress's change of mood made her terribly uneasy.

"Ahhhh, that's ever so much better," breathed Madame Rappelais as the sateen corset fell away. She raised her arms so that Berthe could lift the thin cotton under-chemise over her head.

Then she turned to face Berthe, who lowered her eyes so she wouldn't have to stare at Madame's naked form or see her inevitable wrath.

"You are young and inexperienced and of course I forgive you for that," said Madame Rappelais. "But it is important for you to be aware that there is a certain type of man who is not to be trusted, whose main objective in life is to take advantage of young, innocent girls. I am speaking specifically of Monsieur de Pouvier."

"He didn't take advantage of me," protested Berthe.

"That's because he didn't have the time, my dear. And now I have seen to it that he won't have the chance."

"What do you mean?" Berthe dropped the under-chemise to the floor.

"I dismissed him this afternoon." Suddenly Berthe felt all the air go out of her lungs.

"But he did nothing wrong, madame. And his work, your mural, it isn't finished." She feared she would begin crying at any moment. She forced herself to try and stay calm.

"I will get someone else to finish it. Any half-decent artist can do it. It is, after all, only a copy." She looked at Berthe closely. "What is the matter with you? You look as if you are about to burst into tears."

"Nothing is the matter, madame." Her face reddened in an effort to stifle her emotions.

"Why don't you come and lie down for a bit? I can make you feel ever so much better." She reached for Berthe's hand.

Berthe pulled back as if the touch had burned and began busily folding her mistress's clothing.

"As soon as I've finished here, I'll bid you good night," said Berthe. Her voice was shaking. Did Madame Rappelais even recognize the irony of having dismissed Armand for his advances when she herself was the one who had made a habit of seducing her young, innocent maids?

"Suit yourself. You know I will never force you to do anything you don't want to do," Madame said, smiling as she slipped into her bed. Her smile sent a chill through Berthe's entire body.

CHAPTER 26

Dreams and Reality

NOT ONLY HAD ARMAND BEEN DISMISSED, BUT THAT SAME WEEK Berthe experienced another great loss.

She was walking outside during a rare break, trying to take her thoughts off what had happened with Armand, when a few blocks from the Rappelais house she passed a street with a number of small shops: a dress shop, a charcuterie, a pâtisserie, and a pawnshop. Something in the window of the pawnshop caught her eye. It was a Frenais Winged Sphinx butter dish, identical to the one that she had discovered underneath Hélène's bed only weeks before. It couldn't be the same one, could it? How could Hélène be so brazen, or so stupid, as to take it out of the house and sell it to the nearest neighborhood pawnshop? She hurried home, anxious to confront her friend before the theft was detected.

She heard loud voices coming from the kitchen. She was just in time to witness Madame DuPoix screaming at Hélène.

"Did you think no one would notice as one piece of silver after another disappeared from this household? Do you think I am blind?"

On the kitchen table were six silver napkin rings. Hélène stood in the corner of the kitchen, her arms folded, her attitude one of complete indifference. Madame DuPoix's usual cool demeanor had been replaced by hot rage. Her small white hands were clenched into fists. Berthe thought she might strike Hélène at any moment.

"What do you have to say for yourself, you ungrateful thief? Where is the butter dish and all the other things you've taken?"

Hélène merely shrugged her shoulders as if she were in the classroom and had been asked a question about a text that she had not yet read.

"I know where the butter dish is," Berthe said, hoping against hope to defuse the woman's anger and possibly avoid a disastrous outcome. Madame DuPoix whirled around and glared at her. "I just saw it in the window of the pawnshop on the corner."

"Ah, I should have known." Madame DuPoix's eyes narrowed and she leaned in so close to Hélène that their noses almost touched. "Your friend is in on this as well. No wonder you came with her high recommendation. You are both members of the same thieving gang. Madame will be so pleased to hear her precious maid is nothing but a common criminal."

"She had nothing to do with it. She don't have the nerve or the skill it takes to be a thief," Hélène said, laughing. "Just look at her face. She thinks the whole idea disgusting. Don't you, Miss Too-Good-to-Be-True?" Sarcasm dripped from her voice.

"Is that true, Berthe?"

Berthe shook her head then nodded, at a loss as to how to answer. Suddenly Madame DuPoix reached for a large butcher knife that had been lying on the wooden cutting board and pointed it at Hélène. Berthe screamed, fearing she was going to stab Hélène in the heart.

"Madame, please, put down the knife!"

"Let's just see where your loyalty lies. Go and fetch a *gendarme*," Madame DuPoix told Berthe. "I'll keep her here until you return." She held the knife at arm's length with the point only inches away from Hélène's apron-covered chest.

"If you stab me you'll get blood all over your perfect kitchen floor," said Hélène, wide-eyed, as she slowly backed toward the door.

"Stop! Stay where you are," said Madame DuPoix, following her with the pointed knife. Then Hélène did the worst thing possible: She began to laugh again. "Why you brazen little slut!" Madame DuPoix shouted, and she lunged with the knife just as Hélène jumped out of the way. Madame DuPoix lost her balance and fell to the floor, her black skirts ballooning around her. With one last guffaw, Hélène was gone, hurrying out the kitchen door.

Trembling, Berthe bent down to help the housekeeper to her feet.

"Leave me alone," she said, pulling away from Berthe. "It's all your fault. Bringing that garbage into this house. I will inform Monsieur and Madame. Now go and fetch a *gendarme* so I can report her."

There was always a *gendarme* standing on the corner of rue Payenne and rue Rivière. Berthe took her time as she made her way there.

"Your money or your life." She turned. Hélène was standing in an alleyway not far from the house, a grin spread across her freckled face.

"I would think you would want to put more distance between you and the scene of your crime," said Berthe, scowling.

"I still have some things under my bed. Will you get them for me?"

Berthe shook her head. "I've been ordered to fetch a *gendarme,* and that's what I'm trying to do. I'm going to walk very slowly, so if I were you I'd use the opportunity to vanish from this *arrondissement.*"

"Ah, you're angry at me. I'm the one who should be fumin', by all rights. Who asked you to be so bloody helpful? Oh, you'll find your precious butter dish at the pawnshop on the corner," she said in a poor imitation of Berthe's voice.

"I asked you not to steal from the Rappelaises. Now I'm sure I'll get into trouble for bringing you into the house."

"And they will forgive you. Their perfectly lovely lady's maid. Well, it's your life and you're welcome to it. It ain't for the likes of me."

"What are you going to do? How will you live?" Berthe forgot her anger, suddenly concerned for her friend.

"I'll do what I always done. I'll steal. And how will I live? In this city full of wonderful treasures, I'll live very, very well. You'll see."

"I fear you'll come to a bad end," said Berthe, touching her friend's arm.

"No need to worry 'bout me. But you take care. You're the one living in the den of sin, ain't you? I heard about that witch sackin' your lover, the mural man."

"He's not my lover," Berthe shot back.

"Not yet." Hélène laughed. "But I can tell you're hopelessly in love with him." Berthe started to protest but Hélène dismissed her with a wave of her hand. "I'll write and tell you where I'm livin' so when Madame Rappelais finally kicks you out you can come join me in my life of crime and luxury." And with a toss of her red hair, she was gone.

Instead of looking for a *gendarme,* Berthe made her way slowly back to the house. Madame DuPoix was standing at the front door, her arms folded tightly across her chest.

"Well, where is he?" she asked.

"Who, madame?" Berthe asked innocently.

"The *gendarme,* you little idiot!"

"Oh, I couldn't find one," said Berthe. "The man was off duty."

"A likely story. Protecting your thieving friend, as usual. Well, go on upstairs. Madame wants to see you immediately."

Berthe had no doubt that her time *chez* Rappelais was over. She didn't bother to remove her cape. She wished that she had just left with Hélène—they could have found a new place to live together. Now she would have no idea where her friend had gone in this huge city. She ascended the stairway, her fingers running along the damask-covered walls as if savoring their touch for the last time. Madame Rappelais sat in front of her dressing table mirror trying on a new bonnet.

"Is it true what Madame DuPoix has told me? Your friend has been stealing silver from right under our very noses?"

"Yes, madame." Berthe bowed her head and focused her attention on the tips of her boots. Forget living together, next time she saw Hélène she would throttle her.

"And did you know she was a thief when you recommended her to us?" Madame tilted the hat from one side of her face to the other. The black ostrich plume dipped over her eyes, giving her a mysterious air.

"Well, yes. But I thought she had reformed. She promised me that she had given up her bad habits."

"Bad habits!" snorted Madame Rappelais. "Biting your fingernails is a bad habit. Stealing heirlooms is a crime."

"Yes, madame." Berthe shifted her weight.

"Which makes you an accomplice in the eyes of the law."

Berthe's face burned. "Oh, no, madame, I never..." She grasped her hands together in what even to her was an overdone gesture of entreaty.

"Calm down, calm down. I know you're not a thief. But believe me, it took all my powers of persuasion to convince Madame DuPoix not to sack you immediately. And for that you shall be greatly indebted to me."

"Yes, madame," said Berthe, inhaling deeply.

"And to begin repaying that debt you may kiss my feet," she said with a sly smile.

"What?" Berthe began to laugh nervously.

"I mean it," said Madame Rappelais, removing her satin slippers. "Kiss my feet, slowly and lovingly. And gratefully. And don't forget to suck each toe." She held up one pink foot. Berthe was filled with disgust, which she didn't bother concealing.

Kiss your feet? Why, I would rather bite off your big toe.

"I'm sorry, madame, you must excuse me. I'm feeling quite ill." And with that Berthe left her mistress shoeless, speechless, and more than a little surprised.

Much later Berthe contemplated what Hélène had said about being in love with Armand. What exactly did love feel like? A fluttery feeling in her stomach? Well, she certainly had that every time she saw him. A desire to be with him whether he seemed to want her around or not? She had that, too. An overwhelming curiosity about who he was, what he thought, how he felt? Yes, she had that as well. But even if it was love, there was nothing she could do about it. It was just another luxury she could not afford right now.

Still, she thought of very little else but Armand. And just as she had with Renard on her grand-mère's farm, she created elaborate romantic scenarios involving herself and the young artist. As soon as she erased one fantasy from her mind another would appear like pages from a picture book.

She and Armand would live in a charming artist's garret.

They would lie abed in the mornings with nothing to do but exchange short, sweet kisses. He would bring her hot *café au lait* in a bowl and fresh bread smeared with sweet butter and orange marmalade. They would breakfast in bed and then make love. And there would be no bread crumbs in her fantasy bed.

She had a somewhat limited view of what making love entailed. Oddly enough, her knowledge of sex was limited to seeing Renard and the neighbor girl and what she had experienced under the tutelage of Madame Rappelais. She was, in the strictest sense, still a virgin.

After making love, she would watch Armand from underneath a soft duvet as he painted one magnificent canvas after another. But nothing was as magnificent as the sight of his smooth, well-muscled back. In her fantasies, he always painted with his shirt off. And that was how they would spend their days: he painting his masterpieces, she sketching out designs for her extraordinary fabrics.

As a young girl she had once listened to her mother telling Félicité's fortune. Berthe sat by the hearth as Emma Bovary peered into the maid's palm and outlined a future filled with romance and peopled by dark handsome strangers. Félicité blushed and giggled as her mistress spun the story.

"And one very hot summer day you will be walking down the road to the river," Madame Bovary said, tracing a line in Félicité's palm with her forefinger. "You will be very thirsty and very hot. You will hear the sound of hoofbeats behind. You won't look up because you are afraid and alone on a country road. Someone will grab you by the arm and swing you up and over behind him on a great white horse, and he will gallop off. You will have to hold on tight to his hard ribs and lean against his strong back because you will be afraid of falling off. And he will take you down to the river and leap off his horse and then he will gently help you down. 'Who are you?' you will ask. And you will realize then that you have seen him before in town, at the market. He is the rich marquis who lives in the castle on the outskirts of the village."

"A marquis!" Berthe and Félicité said at once. "A real marquis?" Berthe's mother smiled and nodded.

"A real marquis who has watched you and loved you from afar, but who had no way of telling you because you are from two different worlds. He adores you and cannot live without you. He will take you in his arms, kiss you on the neck and the shoulders and on top of your bare bosom."

"Oh, madame, my bosom is bare?" exclaimed Félicité, turning even redder than ever.

"Of course it is, you ninny," said Berthe's mother.

Berthe remembered Monsieur Millet mentioning that Armand lived not far from Millet's studio on the rue Jacob. On her next day off, she would find him. Nothing and no one, not even Madame Rappelais, could stop her.

The following Sunday Berthe walked down the narrow rue Jacob, her mind focused so hard on Armand's physical presence that every other man began to look like him. She felt that at any moment he might appear. She would find his lodgings, and if he wasn't there she would leave him a note.

She spent the next hour walking up one side of the street and down the other. At around five o'clock, when her feet began to feel like lumps of lead, she spotted Madame Millet getting out of a carriage at the end of the street. Berthe ran to catch up with her.

"Ah, Madame Millet, how good to see you," she said breathlessly. "Could you please tell me where I might find the lodgings of Armand de Pouvier?"

Madame Millet had a slight smile on her face.

"Of course. His room is up there," she said, pointing to the sixth floor of the building she was about to enter. "But you won't find him there."

"Is he at Monsieur's studio?"

"No, my dear. He left this morning. Gave notice and left my poor husband one apprentice short. He is off to Italy to study art, he says. Although I can't imagine what those Italians can teach him that Maître Millet can't."

Berthe stood in shock as Madame Millet patted her hand, then continued into the building.

He had left the country without a word to her. Was there anything worse than to love and not be loved in return? If there was any lesson Berthe should have learned from her mother, it was that the more a woman loved, the more love failed her. Berthe wiped her hand across her eyes as if to clear her vision, then she turned and headed for the prison that was the Rappelais home.

CHAPTER 27

The Birthday Ball

THE MORNING OF THE BIRTHDAY BALL BEGAN INAUSPICIOUSLY. Berthe had been instructed to be present in the ballroom to offer Madame Rappelais her opinion of the finished mural. She kept her head down to hide her swollen eyes; she had spent half the night before crying over Armand. Now she kept herself busy straightening the silk slipper chairs that lined the wall of the huge room. The artist who had come to replace Armand was applying final touches to the ceiling when Madame appeared in the entranceway.

She immediately flew into a terrible temper. "I told you: no partridge in the window. And what have you done but paint a stupid bird exactly there!" she yelled.

"But, madame, you wanted an exact copy," explained the trembling artist.

"I said an exact copy but without the hideous poultry," Madame said, stamping her small foot.

"You must have told the previous artist. You never said anything to me."

"Paint it over quickly," she hissed. "I detest birds." The poor young man immediately began adding earth tones to the blue-gray shape of the partridge. The result was that the brown and white spaniel pictured at Venus's feet looked as if he was barking at an unseen object somewhere in the hazy outdoors.

All Berthe could think about was Armand and how far away he was now. Watching his replacement finish the mural made her miss him all the more. She felt abandoned and lost. And angry, suddenly very angry. Armand had been free to escape while she was still a prisoner in this wretched house, subject to her mistress's every bizarre whim.

She shoved a chair hard against the wall and was alarmed to see she had left a small chip in the gold-painted chair rail. Glancing at Madame Rappelais, who stood with her neck craned to scrutinize every brushstroke, Berthe shoved another chair against the wall. *Someday I'll throw my own bloody grand ball. And when you try to gain entrance, I'll slam the door in your face.*

Fifty invitations to Madame's birthday ball had been mailed out a month earlier. Madame Rappelais had explained the number to Berthe.

"Fifty is the minimum number of people that one can have and still refer to it as a ball. My pitiful ballroom could hold more but I want there to be plenty of room for dancing so that one can properly see the gowns." Berthe knew by this she meant *her* gown, which Monsieur Worth had, in his words, "been slavering over for weeks"—without an ounce of credit to Berthe for the idea.

The gown was magnificent. An evening dress of white tulle over pink satin, it was simple and elegant, as Berthe had suggested. The bodice was very tight and Madame Rappelais's breasts swelled high above it. In her hair she wore a contrasting wreath of red roses which shone beautifully against her pale blond hair. Early in the evening she stood in front of her full-length mirror turning this way and that, clearly delighted by how she looked.

"I've never worn so plain a gown. But it seems to complement my coloring well." Finally, she turned to Berthe and said, "And I have just the dress for you, Mademoiselle Bovary." She retreated to the dressing room and returned with a ball gown in pale blue. "Here, put this on."

"But, madame, I can't wear that."

"Shush. It's important to look your best even if all you're doing is hanging up cloaks. It's an old gown of mine that I no longer wear. Now, don't dawdle. Get dressed. The guests will be here soon."

Berthe did as she was told. It was a beautiful dress, with short puffed sleeves and a lace-trimmed bodice. Madame scrutinized the dress and then reached over and removed the extra lace, revealing a low décolletage.

"Madame..." said Berthe, covering her half-bare bosom with both hands.

"Don't be a twit. There's no reason to hide what you have. Now go downstairs and be ready to see to my guests."

It was Madame's fortieth birthday and no detail had been overlooked. The food for the midnight supper had been ordered and the cook and her extra help had been preparing it for days. Musicians had been hired, wine and champagne delivered; extra livery men in red satin uniforms trimmed with gold braid were in attendance, and additional chairs had been rented and set up along the walls of the ballroom.

As the time of the party neared, Berthe found refuge inside the cloakroom in an effort to escape Madame's endless demands for just a few minutes. As she leaned against the wall, her thoughts drifted to the ball her mother had attended as a new bride. "One day I received an invitation from the marquis d'Andervilliers to dance at his château at Vaubyessard" was how she always began the story.

"You and Papa," Berthe would invariably remind her.

"Yes, yes, Papa and I," she said impatiently.

She would recount each detail of the evening as one would unpack a trunk of cherished mementos. The dinner, the sparkling cut crystal and gleaming china, the elegant silver-covered dishes. The succulent lobster, juicy steaming quails, roasts so tender you could cut the meat with a fork. And the wine. So much wine. And ladies drinking right along with the men—an unheard of thing at public parties. It was at this dinner that Emma Bovary first tasted pineapple—"a fruit as sweet as the sweetest candy." Finally, a maraschino ice in a silver gilt cup. Berthe watched her mother close her eyes as if retasting the cold dessert.

And then after dinner she had changed into her gown. This was Berthe's favorite part of the story: listening to her mother describe how she looked. There was no question in the child's mind that her mother was the most beautiful woman at the ball.

"I wore my hair in a simple chignon with waves on both sides. And a single rose on a stalk with artificial dewdrops on the tip of each leaf, which shook gently when I moved my head. My gown was of pale saffron..."

"What color is saffron?" Berthe invariably asked.

"A beautiful golden yellow," her mother always explained with irritation. "How many times have I told you?" She hated being interrupted at this point. "The gown was trimmed with three different bouquets of roses surrounded with green leaves. The skirt was huge and when I danced..."

"You danced?"

"It was a ball, silly."

"With Papa?"

"Of course not. I danced with gentlemen. So many handsome gentlemen. My skirt swirled around with the music, and I waltzed for the first time even though I had never before waltzed; it was as if my feet already knew how to move. The women who weren't dancing stood against the wall and watched as I twirled and spun around the entire floor, never getting dizzy, never getting tired, never wanting to stop."

Each time she told the story she would add new details: the candles, the perfume, the gilt-framed portraits of important people on the wall, the kindness of the marquis and marquise, the music, the château, and each time she would end the story with: "It was the most wonderful night of my life."

Now her mother lay rotting in her moldy mausoleum and it was to be Madame Rappelais's "most wonderful" night of her life. If only Berthe could stuff Madame into her mother's mausoleum and put her mother twirling about in the middle of the Rappelaises' ballroom floor. Wouldn't she love to give her mother another ball to remember and Madame Rappelais her just due?

Monsieur Millet and his wife were among the first to arrive. They greeted Berthe with great warmth even as they handed her their cloaks.

"How beautiful you look, mademoiselle," said Madame Millet. "Look, Jean, look at our own Mademoiselle Bovary. She is all grown up."

"Yes, I must get you to pose for me again one of these days, but this time without the cow, eh?" He laughed, and the couple continued inside. Berthe felt a deep blush move from her face down her neck to her bare shoulders.

Monsieur and Madame Worth made their entrance shortly after. Worth studied Berthe's dress. "I did this three seasons ago, I believe." He fingered one of the puffed sleeves. "But if I recall correctly it had lace over the bodice."

"Madame Rappelais removed it. I can reattach it if you wish," she said.

"Don't be silly. It's an excellent improvement—for both you and the neckline." He looked at her with such admiration, she suddenly did feel very beautiful. This was reinforced by the long looks she received from the men who passed by her as they escorted their wives into the ballroom. She ignored the men's glances and focused on their wives. Could she ever be one of these women? They had husbands and families and a secure sense of their place in society. She studied the pleased expression on each woman's artfully painted face. Was this happiness? It certainly looked like it.

The last guest had arrived. Berthe had promised herself a peek at the ball, so she peered through the narrow opening between the closed double doors. She watched as the dancers swirled around the floor, the ladies' skirts lifting and falling like enormous flower petals. The air was filled with the scent of perfume and pomade. The men were masterful in their straight-backed postures. They moved the ladies around the floor as if they were exquisitely dressed dolls.

She felt a sudden pang of jealousy. The beautiful story her mother had planted in her mind so many years before was being reenacted before her very eyes. But it all belonged to Madame Rappelais. Now she wished, just for a moment, that this could be her birthday, her home, her ball. She wished Armand were there with her, twirling her around in her beautiful gown as the guests stood by watching with admiration.

Suddenly she felt a hand on her shoulder, heavy and strangely familiar. She pulled away from the touch and turned. Her eyes widened as she recognized the man who towered over her. With the exception of a few more lines around his eyes, Monsieur Boulanger, her mother's old lover, looked exactly the same.

"Mademoiselle Bovary, how delightful to see you. And how you've grown! It's been... almost three years since last we met? What a surprise to find you here, a beautiful young woman in this most beautiful of all cities. I had no idea." He picked up her hand and started to kiss it, but she yanked it away before his lips touched her skin.

"Still the skittish one, I see." He laughed, apparently unbothered by her show of revulsion.

"Ah, Rodolphe, how naughty of you to be so late!" The doors to the ballroom had opened and Madame Rappelais stood fanning herself with her ostrich fan. "You've missed the first dance. And I see you've wasted no time in making the acquaintance of my pretty maid, you rascal."

"Oh, but Mademoiselle and I are very old friends. Very *good* old friends. Aren't we, mademoiselle? We come from the very same province. Her dear, departed mother was a particular favorite of mine." *A particular favorite of his? As if her poor mother were a prize horse or a vintage wine. How dare he?* Biting her lip to keep from expressing her disgust, Berthe glared at him.

"How very nice." Madame Rappelais smiled, a gleam in her eye. "But come, Rodolphe, the evening's half over. You must dance this next dance with me. That is, if I can tear you away from our Mademoiselle Bovary. Berthe, why don't you take Monsieur Boulanger's cloak and hat to the cloakroom?"

Berthe's hands were shaking as she hung Boulanger's things on one of the last remaining hooks. She longed to toss them into the nearest fireplace. The very sight of the man gave her a feeling of enormous dread. He couldn't possibly harm her here, she told herself. Not in the midst of this lavish ball, in the home of her well-respected employers, under the nose of her very possessive mistress. She tried to calm herself, but his proximity filled her with fear.

Instead of watching the dancers as had been her plan, she stole out into the garden, took a seat on the marble bench underneath a pear tree, and leaned her head against the trunk. It was a brisk December night and the cold air felt good against her skin. The evening was clear and the moon shone on the frost-covered garden, giving the dead grass and barren branches of the trees and bushes an almost magical glow. She took deep, slow breaths in and out. In a few moments, she began to feel steady again.

Berthe clearly remembered the look on her mother's face the day the apricots were delivered with Boulanger's last note. She remembered how her mother hadn't been surprised by the gift or the note that lay alongside them. It was as if she had known that this was the end of the love affair. Berthe wondered if she had always known. Even as she ordered her traveling outfit and trunk, as she planned her farewell note to her husband and daughter, had she somehow known that her life with Boulanger was never to be? Had she known when she had gone to Boulanger to beg him for enough money to save her family from bankruptcy that he would refuse? Surrounded by his furniture and art, his dogs and horses, he had turned her away without a franc. She had given him her love and he had robbed her of her hopes, her heart, and, finally and most painfully, her pride.

"Well, mademoiselle, it seems we are destined to keep meeting." Berthe sat up with a start. Monsieur Boulanger leaned against the stone balustrade, his arms folded and one elegant leg crossed over the other. "Which leads me to believe that perhaps destiny has something more in mind." He slowly uncrossed his arms and came toward her as if preparing to ask her to dance. "Yes, it seems to me that we are somehow meant to be together." She stood quickly and backed away as he came closer. "I remember you as a child looking up at me with those big eyes as I rode out of the courtyard in Yonville. You were a beautiful little girl. More beautiful even than your mother." Her back scraped against the high wall that separated the Rappelais garden from that of their neighbors. "Come, don't be afraid of me. I only want to help you." He extended his hand to touch her arm.

"And how do you think you can help me, monsieur?" She tried to keep her voice from wavering.

"I can take care of you. I told you that on the road outside of Millet's house. I've thought of you often since then," he said, peering down at her. She felt sick to her stomach.

"Why would you think of me? I am nothing to you," she said, lifting her chin and fixing him with her steeliest gaze.

"Perhaps because you, *chère* mademoiselle, had the temerity to refuse me. I don't think anyone has ever done that before. I must say that intrigued me. *You* intrigue me." He moved even closer and before she could move away he grabbed her arm, his fingers pressing into her flesh.

"Let me go," she hissed, trying to free herself. "Let me go or I'll scream." The threat sounded ridiculous even to her own ears.

"You have your mother's lovely white skin," he said, stroking her neck with his thumb. She felt her throat close. She wanted to scream but she could barely catch her breath. Fear had driven the very air from her lungs. His large form bent over her, blocking out the full moon. She was aware of his strong cologne, as well as the unmistakable scent of cognac. His mouth moved to her ear and he breathed into it. "The insides of your thighs, I wager they are like your mother's, too. Like white satin." He reached under her skirt. Now she did scream.

"Get away! Leave me alone!"

But he didn't stop. Using his whole body he pressed her against the wall and began to lift her skirt higher.

"Oh, ho, Rodolphe, up to your old tricks—deflowering young maidens. I thought you gave that up when you took up billiards. Aren't you getting a bit old for this?" Madame Rappelais stood a few steps away, watching them with amusement.

Berthe was never so glad to see anyone. Boulanger slowly lifted his head to look at Madame Rappelais. She was smiling at him fondly as if he were a mischievous child—as if there was nothing untoward about his behavior. "Of course, I can't say that I blame you, my dear," Madame Rappelais continued. "She is quite a beauty."

"And how very generous of you to be giving gifts on your birthday." His hand tightened its grip on Berthe's arm.

"A token from one fellow connoisseur to another. Forgive me, I must get back to my guests. I don't want to miss the supper." Madame Rappelais swirled around and without a backward glance floated up the garden steps.

Berthe then realized that her mistress, an advocate of sex in all its forms whether it was between consenting or nonconsenting adults, had planned this meeting from the beginning. She kicked out at Boulanger but he held her tightly by both arms. He marched her toward the back staircase of the house. She knew it was useless to scream. Nothing could be heard above the music from the orchestra. She could barely put one foot in front of the other. Sweat dripped down from her forehead, blurring her vision. She could not breathe. Never in her life had she experienced such all-consuming fear.

One hot summer afternoon when Berthe was quite young, Félicité had taken her to a nearby pond for a picnic. While the maid was unpacking the lunch, Berthe wandered into the water and fell in over her head. She could see the light of the sun and sky above, but no matter how hard she struggled she couldn't get out. One minute she was alive and breathing and the next drowning and dying. It was a feeling of total panic, but nothing compared to what she was experiencing now.

Inside Madame's bedroom, Boulanger pushed Berthe roughly onto the bed. He stood over her as he began to unfasten his velvet breeches.

She began striking Boulanger hard in the face with her fists. She was filled with rage.

"Ah, there's nothing I like better than a good fight," he said, easily catching her wrists and pinning her down with his entire body. "I see you are not going to go quietly. All the better."

"I'll kill you," Berthe hissed through clenched teeth. Boulanger threw back his head and laughed.

"Yes, of course, you'll kill me. But first you'll love me." He crushed his lips against hers. She bit his lower lip until she drew blood. "You little fox. So much for foreplay," he said, sucking his lip. While he held her down with one arm jammed across her neck he pulled up her skirt and ripped off her pantaloons. Totally immobilized by his considerable weight and height, she was powerless to move. He wrenched her legs apart and the next thing she knew there was a hard thrusting against her sex. She screamed. Her body resisted him. *He can't get in. I won't let him in.* But the pain was unbearable. He rammed against her over and over until she felt a sharp tearing inside, followed by a warm wetness. He continued thrusting for several seconds until he finally groaned, shuddered, and lay still. "Now, that wasn't so terrible, was it?" He pulled himself up and straightened his clothes.

Berthe couldn't look at him. Choking on her tears, she sat up and slipped quickly off the bed. There, in the center of Madame's satin duvet, was a red splash of blood. Her blood there for the whole world to see. She felt somehow separated from her body. It had become a dirty, disgusting thing. It wasn't so much that it now belonged to Boulanger, but that it had been so debased it couldn't belong to anyone. But the pain between her legs reminded her that she could not cut herself off from her physical self no matter how much she wanted to.

The sound of a throat clearing loudly caused Boulanger to spin around.

"What have we here? Your own little party, monsieur?" To Berthe's immense relief and shame Monsieur Rappelais stood in the doorway.

"I fear your supper is getting cold," Monsieur Rappelais said quietly. "And you, Mademoiselle Bovary, you look tired. You may go to bed. I'll arrange for one of the footmen to give the guests their cloaks."

She was shivering. Her legs felt as if they would give way any moment. She grabbed on to the bedpost to steady herself. Monsieur Rappelais took hold of her elbow and escorted her up the back stairs to the next floor and to her room.

"Go to bed. Try to forget about all this unpleasantness," he said kindly.

"Unpleasantness!" Her throat was as dry as paper. As if she had been screaming for hours. She wanted to scream now. She wanted to slap the old gentleman in his kind, concerned face. Instead she said, "Has your wife known Monsieur Boulanger for a long time?" She could barely get the words out.

"Oh, yes, they are old lovers. In fact, it was Boulanger who introduced her to Monsieur Millet. It is a very small place, this world of ours."

"And you don't care about 'this world of yours'? About what Madame Rappelais does?"

"I am too old to care." He sighed heavily. "My wife... She is a slave to her passions, the way we all are. She perhaps has more intense desires than most, but she means no harm."

"No harm? Letting that man have his way with me is what you call no harm? Oh, Monsieur Rappelais, how can you say that? How can you believe it? How can you let yourself be deluded like that?"

The old man shrugged his shoulders helplessly. "I am sorry if you were hurt, my dear. I'm afraid I am powerless over what goes on in this house." He patted her on the shoulder.

After Monsieur Rappelais left, she tore off the dress Madame had given her to wear, stuffing it into the closet where she wouldn't have to look at it. Then she washed herself between the legs. She stood in front of the small mirror and stared at her reflection. Suddenly she burst into deep, wrenching sobs. She wept for her father and for Monsieur Rappelais, men helplessly bewitched by women who took advantage of them, yet were guilty of perpetuating the world's evils through their passivity. She wept for her mother, who hadn't known how to love the decent man she had married. She wept for Armand, who might never learn how much Berthe cared for him. Finally, she wept long and hard for herself. And not one of the tears she shed that night offered her any relief whatsoever.

Berthe lay in bed the next morning staring at the ceiling. Except for a throbbing behind her eyes, she was numb all over. She could not convince her arms and legs to move. Eventually, the door flew open and Madame DuPoix stood in the room, her hands on her hips.

"What do you think this is, a national holiday for maids? You're lucky that Madame is good-hearted enough not to complain when you never appeared this morning. Now get up at once." Berthe dragged herself out of bed and walked slowly to the window. It was a bright blue day; she felt that even the weather was conspiring against her.

She did her chores listlessly, thankful that her mistress had gone out for the day. She was turning down the bed that evening when Madame Rappelais called to her from her bath.

"Come and scrub my back, dear girl." Berthe wanted to pretend she hadn't heard her. She wanted to flee from the room. The satin bloodstained duvet had been replaced with a new one. Was it that easy to erase all signs of a rape?

Berthe went into the bathroom, picked up the brush, and began to scrub Madame's pink back. She imagined how satisfying it would be to drown this woman in her own lavender-scented water. To hold her down until bubbles no longer escaped from her nose and mouth, until her eyes grew wide and blank. Berthe's brushstrokes became rougher and rougher until the bristles left red marks on Madame's skin.

"Ouch!" Madame shrieked. "*Mon Dieu!* Not so hard. You're hurting me." Madame tried to grab her by the arm, but Berthe slipped out of her soapy grasp. "What's the matter, *ma chérie*? Why are you angry? Come, let me kiss that frown away."

"No, madame."

"What do you mean, no?"

"No, you will not touch me. Not now, not ever." Berthe struggled to keep her voice steady and low.

"Do not worry, mademoiselle," her mistress said coldly. "I don't make a habit of raping young girls."

"No, you get an old friend to do that for you."

Madame acted as if she hadn't heard. "Hand me my towel and then you may go."

Berthe took the towel that was draped over the chaise, dropped it on the floor, turned on her heel, and left the room.

"Get me my robe! Do you want me to catch pneumonia?" Madame Rappelais shrieked.

Berthe picked up the robe from Madame's bed and returned to the bathroom. She looked down at Madame Rappelais, who was beginning to lift herself out of the tub, soapy water slipping down her wet body.

"Your robe, madame," she said, dropping it into the water. Berthe was pleased to see that her mistress was left speechless.

Four days later, a young girl appeared at the front door of rue Payenne. She was about thirteen years old and quite beautiful, with thick chestnut hair, brown eyes, and a fresh peach complexion.

"I have an appointment," the girl said shyly.

"Who shall I say is calling?" asked Berthe.

"Michelle Gossien. I have come from Monsieur Rappelais's mill in Lille. I was told there was a position available."

"Position?"

"Of lady's maid." The girl kept her eyes downcast as she played with the ribbons of her faded bonnet. "Monsieur Rappelais himself sent me money for my train fare."

Berthe considered warning the poor girl away, but her only option would be to return to the cotton mill, and Berthe shuddered at the thought of sending her back to that hideous place. Besides, Madame would only make her husband find another victim to fill her place.

"I am making a few staff changes," Madame Rappelais said when Berthe announced the visitor. She sat at her secretary, writing thank-you notes. "Mademoiselle Gossien will take on the position of lady's maid. After you train her you will be promoted to a position downstairs."

"Downstairs?"

"You will serve as downstairs housemaid."

We are like pieces on a game board, Berthe thought. *Everyone moves one space down to make room for the next poor fool.* She was to be moved to Hélène's old place and perhaps one day, if she worked hard enough and if Madame forgave her, she could take Madame DuPoix's place as housekeeper. She clenched her hands into tight fists, turned, and left the room. She felt like slamming the door, but she wouldn't give Madame the satisfaction.

She packed her few things, leaving the maid's uniform carefully folded on the bed. She was back in her homespun skirt once again. Then she went to say good-bye to Monsieur Rappelais, whom she found on the landing near the front door.

"In her way, my wife loves you, you know," he said, twirling his mustache nervously.

"She has an odd way of showing it."

"She has an odd way of showing everything." He smiled ruefully.

Berthe thanked him for the knowledge about fabrics he had imparted and for his kindness toward her. Then she quietly walked out and strode quickly down the street. As she turned the corner and glanced back one last time at the handsome house at 11, rue Payenne, she reflected that she might never again live at such an exclusive address. But instead of feeling sad, she felt a great sense of freedom. Now she must face the unknown. And what a boundless unknown it was.

PART 4

Work and Love

CHAPTER 28

Reunion

PARIS, 1858

IN THE ENTIRE CITY OF PARIS, BERTHE HAD ONLY ONE FRIEND she could turn to. Hélène had written her to tell her of her new address, a boardinghouse on the Left Bank near Saint Germain-des-Prés.

Berthe was surprised to see that the house was well maintained, with brass door fittings that had recently been polished and windows hung with clean lace curtains.

The landlady was a pretty, middle-aged woman with thick dark hair parted in the middle and worn in two large buns covering each of her ears. She was dressed in a blue silk dress with a clean white collar and cuffs.

"Ah, you are a friend of Mademoiselle Du Croix? I am so happy to meet you. She is out but will be back momentarily. Make yourself comfortable in our parlor." Berthe was surprised at the landlady's warm reception. Hélène must be doing well for herself. At least she must be paying her rent on time, Berthe thought.

The parlor was furnished with velvet couches, needlepoint

side chairs, fringed table lamps, gilded mirrors, and a fine, slightly faded Persian carpet on the floor. Twenty minutes later, Berthe heard a rustle at the door.

"Bonjour, Madame Laporte, comment ça va?" Berthe immediately recognized Hélène's husky voice.

"You have a visitor in the parlor," said the landlady.

Hélène swept into the room bringing with her a waft of gardenia. Berthe could hardly believe her eyes. If it hadn't been for the red hair she would have had a difficult time recognizing her old friend. She was dressed in a blue-gray striped jacket with turned-back pagoda sleeves trimmed in black braid and a matching blue-gray skirt. Underneath the jacket she wore a sparkling white blouse with long sleeves that hung down over her lower arms. She looked every bit the elegant young lady out for a day of shopping.

"Aha! So you finally got sacked as well!" said Hélène. She flung herself down on the velvet love seat. Her skirt rose up, revealing soft kid boots with gold buttons.

"Actually, I quit," said Berthe.

"Oh, and that makes you better than me, I s'pose?" said Hélène, removing her kid gloves one finger at a time.

"I didn't say that." Berthe shook her head.

"And what are you gonna do now?"

"I'm not completely sure." She twisted the ribbons of the bonnet on her lap. "That's why I'm here."

"Don't fret, my friend. I just might have an opening for you in my business," Hélène said, giving Berthe's hand a little pat.

Hélène's business hadn't changed. She was still stealing, but now she was focusing only on the big Parisian department stores. She had become very clever at how and what she stole. She disguised herself in wigs and different costumes and concentrated on the smallest, most expensive, most easily fenced items: jewelry, silk scarves, gold-framed eyeglasses, pearl collar studs.

"No more haulin' away iron birdbaths in the middle of the night," Hélène said with a laugh.

In addition, she occasionally employed the services of twelve-year-old Yvette, the daughter of the landlady. Hélène predicted that Yvette would one day enjoy a career on the stage. "Wait till you see her," she said. "She has a true talent, she does." According to Hélène, Yvette was well practiced in the art of temper tantrums, epileptic fits, and other small dramatic pieces designed to draw attention away from Hélène's shoplifting. "But the biggest boon to my business is those crazy kleptomaniacs," she said. "You can always spot 'em. They have a glazed look in their eye. And the clerks and guards in the store know 'em by sight. Poor things. So I puts myself next to one and wait for her to make her clumsy move. They have no skill at all. And, o' course the clerks have to bend over backward so as not to offend 'em, while at the same time they got to guard the merchandise. The kleptos are all from good families who can well afford to buy their luxuries. Oh, it all makes me laugh."

"Aren't you afraid of getting arrested, of having to spend the rest of your life in jail?" said Berthe. The very word conjured up visions of steel bars, stone floors, rats and rat droppings.

"Of course not. I'm too fast for the likes of them." Berthe had no desire to join Hélène's gang of two. It might be Hélène's idea of making a living but it certainly wasn't hers. She was determined to find a position where she could use her mind and her eye for design and fashion. Hadn't Messieurs Worth and Rappelais said that she had a real talent? And she did. She knew she did. The problem was, she didn't know where to begin.

"Well, I'm going to get a real job," Berthe said.

"What real job? You gonna be some other fancy lady's personal slave?"

"I'll never be a lady's maid again."

"How do you plan to pay your rent, then? And don't be lookin' to me; I got me own expenses."

"I'll have a job within the week," Berthe said with more confidence than she felt.

"Oh, then maybe you can hire me to be your lady's maid." Hélène laughed.

Berthe joined in the laughter. After everything that had happened in the last two years, it felt wonderful to be free again. She had forgotten how much she liked being with Hélène. Her energy and humor were contagious. Berthe began to feel alive and untarnished once more.

The only thing that was missing was Armand. Strange how she had known him for just a short time and yet his absence left a huge hole. Where in Italy was he? What was he doing? Was he thinking of her? She was certain he must have forgotten all about her, yet she ached to see him again. She wanted to find out if there was truly something between them or if it was all just a fantasy. But at this point in her life, a fantasy was better than nothing.

"Where are your clothes and such?" Hélène asked, jolting her back to reality. Berthe pointed to the small satchel at her feet. "Still the pretty little pauper, I see. Well, you can share my room until you get your job. And I'll lend you a proper dress. But I have to warn you, Madame Laporte will make you pay even though you're just sharin' the same room. Do you have any money at all?"

How could she have forgotten? Everything she had managed to save from her salary was in a little box underneath her bed in that horrible house. She couldn't go back. Besides, she felt even the money earned from the Rappelaises was dirty.

"Don't worry. I'm sure I'll have a position quite soon," Berthe said confidently.

"There she goes again with the 'position.' Just get yourself a bloody job, dear girl, and make it soon."

That very afternoon she went to Maison Gagelin on the rue Richelieu. All her hopes for a paid position rested on her connection with Monsieur Worth. She knew he had opened up his own establishment, but she wasn't sure where it was.

"Can you tell me where I can find Monsieur Worth?" she asked a short, balding man dressed in a brocade smoking jacket and velvet pants whom she took to be Monsieur Gagelin himself.

"Why do you ask?" he said, eyeing her up and down.

"I want to ask him about a job."

"Well, you are not in luck, mademoiselle. I understand that Monsieur Can't-Speak-a-Word-of-French has gone off to England with his *chèr ami* and benefactor, Monsieur Bobergh. I hope I've seen the last of him, the big arrogant Englishman. Good riddance to bad taste."

Berthe's heart sank. Worth had been her one chance. "Could you, perhaps, give me the address of Monsieur Worth's home?"

"It won't do you much good, but here it is," Monsieur Gagelin said.

When she inquired at Monsieur Worth's home she discovered that, indeed, he was in England with his wife and business associate and would not be back for at least a month. She couldn't possibly wait that long. She needed money and a job immediately. She wrote a note to Monsieur Rappelais asking him for help in obtaining a position in one of the many dress shops he did business with. The reply came back within the hour.

"My chère *mademoiselle, Unfortunately, due to my home situation, I am unable to assist you at this time."* Berthe tore the paper into shreds. How gutless could a man be? She knew Rappelais liked her and admired her talent with fabrics, and yet his fear of his wife was so great that he didn't have what little courage it would take to even write her a short reference.

She spent the next several days walking up and down the dingy streets of the Sentier in the 2nd *arrondissement* where many of the dress manufacturers were located. She applied for seamstress jobs, modeling jobs, clerking jobs, anything that was available. But without references and with no evidence of experience, she was turned away again and again.

Finally, she swallowed her pride and went in search of a position as a lady's maid. Applying at Première Placement Domestique, the largest establishment in Paris, she was told that a career as a lady's maid was closed off to her forever.

"Mademoiselle, I acknowledge the fact that you have the experience, but you also have the *mauvaise réputation.*"

"What?"

"Madame Rappelais, although kind enough not to report you to the police, has notified us in no uncertain terms that you are a thief and not to be trusted in a home which contains things of value. That, of course, would include every single one of our clients."

Berthe was furious.

"I am not a thief," she said, feeling the heat rise up her neck. "Madame has no right to say that."

"Are you calling your former employer a liar?"

"Oh, I could call her many, many more things," Berthe said, "but I don't have all day." She turned and marched out the door, holding her head as high as she could manage without falling backward.

Because she didn't have the rent for Madame Laporte, Berthe had avoided mealtimes at the boardinghouse. She hadn't eaten a decent meal since leaving the Rappelaises. She was starving and she was growing more fearful every day. How was she going to live? She had no other choice but to join Hélène in her shoplifting enterprise.

"Good," said a delighted Hélène. "I'll take you to my favorite store tomorrow."

CHAPTER 29

A-Shopping They Will Go

BERTHE ALLOWED HÉLÈNE TO SELECT HER COSTUME FOR THE morning foray to Le Bon Marché, the largest department store in Paris. The store was located at 24, rue de Sèvres on the Left Bank. In all her time in Paris, Berthe had never had a chance to visit the famous store.

"Ferme la bouche," said Hélène as they climbed down from the carriage and walked toward the entrance. "You're gawking." It was true. She stared at the stone with her mouth ajar. The outside of the huge building was encased in a beautiful metal framework, as if it had been gift-wrapped in wrought iron.

"This is the first time a metallic framework has been used in a building of this size," said Hélène, sounding every bit like a tour guide. "See, it's much lighter and stronger than stonework. It was designed by Monsieur Gustave Eiffel, an engineer who is a bit of a fanatic when it comes to metal structures."

"Where did you get all this information?" asked Berthe.

"I ain't a complete dolt, you know," said Hélène, reverting to her normal speech mode. "I make it me business to learn such stuff."

She pushed Berthe through the door. Sweeping staircases led up to the mezzanine that bordered the main floor. A ceiling bejeweled with fifty glittering chandeliers gave everything a festive and fanciful glow. The store was crowded with well-dressed women in huge bell-shaped skirts, who glided from one display to another almost as if they were on skates. The array of goods took Berthe's breath away. As she looked around from one counter to the next, she felt almost dizzy. The joy of seeing all this beauty and luxury momentarily lifted the weight off her mind. She drank in the sights and the fragrant scent of expensive perfumes. She had the strangest feeling that she was looking at this extravagant scene through her mother's eyes. The customers moved from one display to another, chattering excitedly to each other. Who were these women and what were their worries? Certainly not where they would get their next meal nor where they would find enough money to rent a roof over their heads. No, *their* minds were on the newest lace from Belgium, the softest Italian kid gloves, the latest look in bonnets.

Berthe had tried to make an honest living, and where had that gotten her? She promised herself that she would find a legitimate way to support herself. But first she had to survive. And if surviving required stealing, then so be it.

Hélène seemed very much at home in the opulent store. She gave a small wave of her hand to a distinguished middle-aged gentleman who stood in the corner. He was dressed in a beautifully tailored velvet jacket and well-cut wool slacks. He returned her greeting with a smile and quick nod of his head.

"Monsieur Proiret, the store manager," Hélène explained.

"He's the one who helps defray my expenses. Come on, I want you to meet him."

Berthe squeezed her hands together to calm her nerves, and followed Hélène down the aisle.

"Monsieur Proiret is not only the manager of this grand establishment, he is also my very dear and special friend," said Hélène with her newly acquired gentility. "Monsieur Proiret, this here is my dear friend, Mademoiselle Bovary."

"*Enchanté.*" Picking up Berthe's hand as if it were a delicate flower, Proiret bowed low and placed a kiss on her fingers. He was a short pinkish man in his forties with a pleasing well-fed look about him. He sported a tidy mustache and well-trimmed beard. His black hair glistened with pomade and he wore a pince-nez on the end of his upturned nose. Berthe noticed that he smelled strongly of bay leaves.

"Have you been to Le Bon Marché before, mademoiselle?"

"No, I haven't," said Berthe.

"Where in heaven's name do you do your shopping?" he asked, lifting one eyebrow.

"I'm afraid I'm not much of a shopper, monsieur." She smiled.

"That's probably just as well," said Monsieur Proiret, "since your friend Hélène more than makes up for you."

Hélène gave him a playful tap on the shoulder with her lace fan.

"But since this is your first time here, it is incumbent on me as the manager of Le Bon Marché to impart a few important facts to you."

Hélène placed her gloved hand over his mouth and proceeded to recite the following facts:

"Monsieur Boucicaut, the owner of Le Bon Marché, is the most brilliant of men. Among the many innovations he started are: the first store to offer free delivery; the first store to have prices clearly marked on every piece of merchandise; the first store to offer a catalog from which customers can order; and the first-ever white sale. Every January sheets and linens are reduced in price."

Monsieur Proiret removed Hélène's hand from his mouth and added, "He got the idea for the white sale from looking out one morning in January and seeing the rue de Sèvres covered in snow. He said, 'Each January we should have a special sale on sheets. And call it a white sale.' Brilliant, *n'est-ce pas?*"

"*Ma chère,* the day is slipping away from us. We got much shopping to do," said Hélène, pulling Berthe along.

"I don't understand. Doesn't he suspect what you are up to?" Berthe asked as they made their way to one of the crowded jewelry counters.

"He knows all about it," said Hélène with a smile.

"But . . ." Berthe frowned.

"Oh, look, there's a kleptomaniac now. Watch," said Hélène, pulling at Berthe's sleeve.

An elderly woman dressed in widow's weeds was trying on gold necklaces. While the clerk fastened one necklace on her neck she picked up another and placed it in her reticule. The clerk saw the whole thing and signaled to a man standing nearby.

"She comes here every day. Never pays for nothing," said Hélène. "They always stop her, just as she is leaving, and gently remove the items. The place is crawlin' with women like her. As Monsieur Proiret says, 'It is a veritable epidemic.' And they are all amateurs. In fact, I think they want to be caught."

"I feel sorry for the poor woman."

"Don't waste your tears. She'll never see the inside of a jail. It looks like the jewelry counter will be a good place for you to start. Me, I got a craving for expensive fountain pens today. I'll meet you back at the main entrance in thirty minutes."

"I don't have a watch."

"Well, steal one, silly girl."

Berthe tried on pair after pair of earrings—dangling crystal, gold filigree, pearl studs. She held up a mirror to examine each one. Then she selected various necklaces and bracelets to go with the earrings. Finally, as if nothing had quite met her satisfaction, she wandered away. Hélène was waiting for her at the front entrance.

"Well?" said Hélène. "How did you do?"

"I didn't. I couldn't. I don't want to do this," Berthe said.

"Oh, you want to starve in the streets instead?"

"No, of course not. I just didn't plan on spending my life as a thief."

"You're forgettin' you're the one who first talked me into stealing from department stores."

"That was when we were desperate."

"And you ain't desperate enough now? Come with me," Hélène said, dragging Berthe back to the jewelry counter. "Now get on with it. Either you pay your way or you can look for another place to live."

Under Hélène's watchful eye, Berthe managed to slip several pairs of earrings, a crystal necklace, and a mother-of-pearl pince-nez into a pocket hidden within the deep folds of the huge skirt Hélène had lent her.

"That's more like it," said Hélène as they were leaving the store. "You got the gift, you might as well use it." Berthe thought about her "gift" for fashion. She could say good-bye to that forever. She was back where she had started, scraping by, stealing, not knowing how she would survive from one day to the next. Tears of disappointment welled up and she turned her head away so that Hélène wouldn't see them.

Hélène treated them to a carriage ride home. She reached

MADAME BOVARY'S DAUGHTER 371

into her long sleeve and pulled out half a dozen gold and enamel fountain pens, a solid gold letter knife, and a mother-of-pearl card case.

"I don't understand. If Monsieur knows you are a professional shoplifter, how can he let you into his store? Why does he turn a blind eye to your stealing?" asked Berthe.

"He don't let me get by with anything. I'm well punished, I am. He likes to see me take things 'cause he knows there'll be a spanking later."

"He spanks you?"

"Oh my, yes. He loves spankin' me, don't he? That's the whole point. You should see how excited he gets."

"I don't think I care to," said Berthe, closing her eyes.

"And o' course I steal from other stores, ones that he has nothing to do with. I do know how to take care of me own self."

Hélène's relationship with Monsieur Proiret certainly gave her a leg up in her shoplifting venture. Maybe jail wasn't in their future, after all. Berthe tried to relax a little, but her stomach was still tied in knots.

Unlike Hélène, who seemed to think therein lay her fortune, Berthe knew that ultimately she would come to a bad end if she continued along this path. And being gifted with a vivid imagination, she could easily visualize just what that end might be: a dark cell with only the smallest barred window, the floor covered in grime; the bed, a wooden plank; and a blanket chewed by a large gray rat. And speaking of rats, she could see their eyes glowing from the dark corners of the cell. She pictured herself shivering and coughing beneath the thin blanket, wishing she had never embarked on a life of crime. Which was when one of the rats ventured forth to nibble her cold, bare foot.

She shuddered as she tried to shake the image from her mind.

CHAPTER 30

The Young Man from Germany

AFTER HÉLÈNE COUNTED THEIR BOOTY, SHE DRAGGED BERTHE to dinner with the other guests in the boardinghouse. In addition to Hélène, Yvette, and Madame Laporte, there were five men who took their seats around the long table. Berthe was now eighteen years old, in the full bloom of her beauty and used to stares from strange men. But she wasn't comfortable with how they made her feel. The men ogled Berthe as if she were that evening's dessert.

Madame Laporte introduced them. To Berthe's surprise, they were all in the *affaires de mode,* or fashion business. According to Hélène, Madame Laporte's boardinghouse was a popular stopping place because of its proximity to Paris's fashion district. Hélène had chosen the establishment for just that reason. "This is how I keeps up with what's the best stuff to steal from the stores. These men know what sells," said Hélène. Berthe looked at the guests with new interest. Perhaps one of them might even have a job for her.

"And finally, our newest guest, Monsieur Strauss, who is

stopping here on his way back to Germany," said Madame Laporte. Monsieur Strauss was a pale young man in his early twenties, with dark hair and a beard so dense it looked as if it was part of a disguise. He had a large head that dominated his very narrow shoulders, a high forehead, and soft, wide-set eyes. His mouth, too, was soft and sensual. When he stood up to shake hands Berthe noticed he was a good three inches shorter than she.

She smiled at the young man and he immediately lowered his head as if he was too shy to meet her gaze.

"Actually, I am on my way to California, in America," he said to his potage.

"Ah, California!" Madame Laporte clapped her hands.

"The Wild West and Indians!" said Madame Laporte's daughter, Yvette, leaning forward across the table.

"I understand that it ain't safe to walk down the streets alone. That men on horseback come galloping by and swoop you up and carry you off and do heaven knows what with you," said Hélène excitedly.

"And do the men shoot each other on the street? And are the ladies' dresses really lined with gold?" asked Yvette.

"It's not the dresses, dear. It's the streets. They are paved with gold," corrected her mother.

"Once they is done with you they hand you over to the Indians, who strip you of all your clothes and cut your hair, turn you into a slave, and make you have their babies," said Hélène. Berthe felt torn between Yvette's streets paved with gold and Hélène's dire accounts of rape, bondage, and babies. The former sounded too good to be true and the latter too likely a possibility, as she knew all too well.

"And every third man is a millionaire," added Madame Laporte. "I read it in the newspaper."

This could be Berthe's chance at a fortune. She imagined a country filled with millionaires, with every third man dressed in a top hat and tails. At the same time, she saw herself tied up to a tree in front of a band of Indians ready to ravish her.

"Don't believe everything you read, madame," said one man. The rest of the men went back to their food, too busy eating to take part in the conversation.. The women were all focused on Monsieur Strauss, much to his embarrassment.

"Have you ever seen an Indian?" asked Yvette, her eyes bright with excitement.

"What do they eat, these Indians?" asked her mother.

"I bet they dine on fat millionaires," said Hélène.

The women never gave him a chance to answer. The barrage of questions and observations went on through the soup and the main course. The other guests continued to concentrate on their food, ignoring the conversation as if it were taking place in another room. One by one, they excused themselves and left the table. Strauss was still eating. He piled food into his mouth as if he hadn't eaten in days. Finally, Berthe decided to engage him in a serious conversation.

"Monsieur, what exactly takes you to California?" she asked. He looked up and met her inquiring smile. He put down his fork.

"That's a very good question," he said. But apparently not as good as the answer. Once he started talking there was no stopping him. "I left Germany when I was fourteen. I joined my two brothers, Jonas and Louis, who had a successful textile and tailoring business in New York. After a short stay there I went on to Louisville, Kentucky, where my uncle Goldman had a ranch. That was where I learned English. My uncle wanted me to take over the ranch but I'm afraid that the open road called to me.

Once a peddler, always a peddler," he said, laughing and helping himself to a second portion of the casserole.

"More *haricots verts*?" asked Madame Laporte. He nodded and took another helping of the green beans without losing the thread of his story. "When the gold rush started, I had to join the throngs. Not for the gold, but for the glory," he said, laughing again. "I made my way to San Francisco to sell my notions, my scissors and bolts of fabric. My brother and I opened a dry goods business and were doing very well. In talking to the miners I heard many complaints of their torn breeches, and one day I had a brilliant idea." He paused and leaned back in his chair, waiting for the women to respond. Hélène, Madame Laporte, and Yvette were busy eating. They seemed to have lost interest just around the time Monsieur Strauss had begun telling his story.

Finally, Berthe, taking the hint, said, "What was your brilliant idea, Monsieur Strauss?" He beamed at her.

"Well, I had a huge supply of canvas cloth for making tents and covers for the wagons. And it occurred to me that this fabric would be ideal for making overalls. I went back to Germany to raise money from family and friends for my new enterprise, which I truly believe will not only be a benefit to the men who toil in the mines but enrich my family as well."

"But what brings you to Paris?" Berthe said.

"Ah, I have always wanted to see Paris. I decided to treat myself to a few days before sailing back to America." How easy it was for these men, Berthe thought. Monsieur Strauss was free to travel and do business wherever he chose, just as Armand could pack up his paintbrushes and go anywhere in the world.

Strauss turned to Madame Laporte, catching her in the middle of a yawn. "Delicious dinner, madame. Particularly the casserole. May I ask what was in it?"

Madame Laporte suddenly came to life.

"*Tripes à la mode de Caen,* a great specialty of mine," she said.

"And what is it composed of?" he asked politely, wiping his mouth with a napkin.

As the subject of California had freed Monsieur Strauss's tongue, so his question to Madame warmed her to the topic of her cuisine.

"You take cloves and garlic, a leek and onions, some flour and apple brandy and a carrot, and you place them at the bottom of a large pot," she said as if conducting a cooking class. "Add to that four pounds of tripe and a trotter's foot. Then you cook it all slowly for about fifteen hours until the tripe is tender."

"Trotter's foot?" said Monsieur Strauss.

"The foot of a pig," said Madame Laporte.

"Did you say pig?" Strauss clutched his throat.

"Yes. The recipe calls for the hoof of the ox, but I prefer that of the pig. It has more flavor."

"*Oy Gott!*" He turned the color of a raw turnip. "Excuse me, please," he said, rushing from the room with his napkin held to his mouth.

The sound of Monsieur Strauss retching in the *salle de bain* kept Berthe up for hours. Finally, around two in the morning, Hélène sat up in bed.

"Tell your friend to get out of the bloody bathroom," she said. "I have to use it."

"He's not my friend and use your chamber pot," said Berthe. Finally, taking pity on the sick man, Berthe knocked on the bathroom door.

"Are you all right, Monsieur Strauss?"

"I am dying. I am dying a goy's death," he moaned.

She opened the door and found him clutching the porcelain toilet bowl. He was pale and sweating.

"You must have *la grippe*," she said, handing him a towel.

"No, it is the *traif* I stupidly ate." And with that he vomited once again. His vomiting was making her sick. When it seemed that he was finally done she helped him to his feet and supported him as he wobbled to his bedroom. He fell into bed and she placed a cold wet cloth over his head.

"*Oy vey iz mir,*" he moaned. "I should be buried in the dirt along with the other filthy dishes," he said in a loud voice.

"Hush," she said. "You'll wake the whole house."

"Such terrible *traif.*"

She had no idea what he was talking about. She thought he was delirious.

"Sleep now," she said. "You'll feel better in the morning."

"The foot of a pig. *Mein Gott.*"

She pulled the blanket over him and started to leave, but he grabbed her hand.

"Don't go. Please. I don't want to die alone."

"You're not dying, Monsieur Strauss." But despite herself her heart went out to him. There was something about his solitariness that touched a place deep inside her. He was in a strange city far away from family and friends. Whom did he have to love? Who loved him?

His hand in hers was cold and small. He looked like a little boy wearing a grown man's beard. Still holding his hand, she sat on the floor and leaned her head against the bed. Soon both of them were asleep.

The next morning he was still weak but clearly happy and grateful to be alive.

"You are an angel, Mademoiselle Bovary. You saved my life. How can I ever thank you?"

"Nonsense. I did nothing," she said, getting up from the floor. Every bone in her body ached. She saw a pair of light colored overalls folded on top of the bureau.

"And are these your famous overalls, Monsieur Strauss?"

"Yes," he said, lifting his head from the pillow. "As you can see they are quite durable."

"The fabric is so stiff," she said, feeling the rough material. "They must chafe terribly."

"Oh, some have complained. But these are meant to be work clothes, not evening wear."

"This is good for a tent perhaps, but not for human skin."

She remembered the conversation she had had with Monsieur Rappelais and Monsieur Worth about a fabric that French peasants wore that was both durable and soft. *"Serge de Nîmes,"* she said suddenly.

"What?"

"I know just the thing. I'll see if I can get a sample to show you."

Berthe put on her cloak and bonnet and was about to go out when Hélène stopped her at the door.

"Where are you going? We have shopping to do. There's a new store that's just opened on the avenue de l'Opéra."

"Not today."

"What do you mean?" Hélène demanded, hands on hips. "Do you expect me to do this all by myself?"

"Get Yvette to go with you."

"Yvette's little dramatic scenes is getting out o' hand. She's actually learned to foam at the mouth. It's disgusting," Hélène said with a toss of her head. "She cares more about the audience and the attention than doin' the job right. Come, change your clothes, time's a-wasting."

"I have other plans. Ones that don't involve stealing."

"Oh, really. Did someone just die and make you Empress of France?"

"Don't worry. I can take care of myself." But could she? she wondered. If she didn't steal, she had no idea how she was going to support herself. She owed Madame Laporte for her room and board. Occasional stealing had been necessary to survive, but making it a profession was wrong, not to mention it was tempting fate. Besides, she wanted more. She had promised herself a life of integrity, whatever that was.

And she had a plan. One that might put her on the road out of her desperate life.

CHAPTER 31

A New Opportunity

BERTHE HAD READ IN THE NEWSPAPER THAT MONSIEUR WORTH was back from England and doing business at his own shop on the rue de la Paix. She was nervous that he would refuse her the way Monsieur Rappelais had. After all, Madame was one of his most important clients. But now Berthe had an excuse to approach him on a different matter, the fabric for Monsieur Strauss. And while she was there she would ask him for a job; the worst that could happen was that he would say no. As she hurried along the busy Paris streets she thought about the American streets, supposedly paved with gold. Maybe, if Worth refused her, she could persuade Monsieur Strauss to take her with him to America.

With each step she grew more and more confident. She would not be a thief, a maid, or, worse, a mill worker. She would not rely on the support of a man either, the way her mother had. She would earn a fortune for herself. And she would use some of it to help the children forced to work in cotton mills, so that not another child would have to die like poor Antoine, and not another girl would find herself lured into serving Madame Rappelais.

She arrived breathless at the rue de la Paix. It was an elegant street and the House of Worth seemed to be the most elegant shop on it. She was standing outside, admiring the imposing exterior of the building and gathering her courage to enter, when she felt someone touch her on the shoulder.

"Ha, I see you are in exuberance over my new shop," Monsieur Worth said in his usual bad French. "Well, don't just stand there with your head open, come in. Come in."

He was happy to see her and more than delighted to show off his new establishment. The shop was beautiful. The French windows were draped in wine-colored velvet, and brocaded slipper chairs were set around low, graceful tables. On every table were long-stemmed red roses arranged in sparkling crystal vases. Even though Charles Worth was now the owner of a sophisticated fashion house on the most elegant street in Paris, he hadn't changed his style of dress. He still affected *la mode bohème,* wearing his usual black skullcap, loose bow tie, and oversized brocaded smock. He gestured to an elderly man who stood in the corner, dressed far more conservatively in a morning coat and dazzling white shirt.

"And here is my great benefactor, my dear Otto. Monsieur Bobergh, may I present Mademoiselle Bovary. Bobergh, show my friend your money."

Bobergh chuckled, clearly used to Worth's sense of humor.

"Show her my money? All she has to do is look around her. What you see is the last of my meager fortune, mademoiselle. All wasted by this mad Englishman."

"Mademoiselle Bovary has a real flair for fabrics," Worth said to Bobergh. "Although I fear that has not extended to her own taste in dress." He covered one eye with his hand as if what she was wearing pained him. "And to what do I owe this pheasant surprise, mademoiselle? Are you here to purchase a gown, I hope?"

"I'm afraid not, Monsieur Worth." She laughed. His warm greeting had reassured her that she was not unwelcome, but still she hesitated, worried that his reaction would change once she raised the possibility of a job. "I wanted to ask you where I might find the fabric called *serge de Nîmes* that you once spoke of."

"Of course, I can give you a name. But what do you want that ugly fabric for? It's not fit for anything but the wiping of one's boots."

"It's not for me. It's for a friend who is going into the manufacturing business."

He narrowed his eyes. "I understand you are no longer a member of the House of Rappelais."

She nodded.

"You're well out of there. It was not a good place for a young woman. Especially a young woman with a brain on her shoulders."

Monsieur Bobergh interrupted. "The applicant for the assistant's position has arrived, Charles."

"Ah, yes. Excuse me, Mademoiselle Bovary," he said, "I am currently searching for an assistant. My dear Bobergh thinks I need another pair of feet. I'll be just a moment."

Berthe's heart sank as Monsieur Bobergh escorted a tall, poised young woman into the room. She was dressed in the very latest fashion and carried herself like a ballet dancer. She extended her hand toward Worth, ignoring Berthe.

"Monsieur Worth, I am Mademoiselle Therault. I was recommended by Madame Carton of the Beaux Modes School. I have studied design with her. Here are my references." She handed Worth a packet of letters. He looked them over.

"Very good. Now, did Madame Carton explain the position to you?" asked Monsieur Worth.

"Yes, she said it involved dress design."

"You are feasting your eyeballs on the premier dress designer in the world. And here is my plan: I will employ the most beautiful models to wear all my latest creations and invite the creamery of Paris to view them. Women will be seduced into ordering my dresses. That is where you would come in, mademoiselle. Madame Carton mentioned in her recommendation that you have knowledge of silk and luxury fabrics and trims. You will help my clients make their selection. Women tend to become confused and dazzled by the beauty of my creations. It is important that they understand they have a choice in fabrics. But most important, I don't want my designs ruined by their bad taste. Which is why you must manhandle their selections. What do you think? Does the job interest you?"

"I was hoping to have the opportunity to do my own designs," said Mademoiselle Therault.

"A woman designer! Don't be rarified!" exclaimed Worth.

Mademoiselle Therault sniffed and then looked about her at the elegant surroundings.

"How much does the position pay?" she finally asked.

"Forty francs a week." Worth looked at Monsieur Bobergh, who nodded, a pained expression on his face.

"I shall have to consult my father about it," she said. "I am afraid he is very much against me working in the trades."

"The trades!" shouted Worth. "This is not the trades! This is the House of Worth! And speaking of trades, where did you get that horrified hat?"

The young woman turned bright red. She touched the brim of her feathered bonnet as if she was reassuring a frightened child.

"By all means, think it over, mademoiselle," said Monsieur Bobergh, quickly escorting the young woman out. He returned within seconds. "That is the fourth applicant that you've managed to insult this week," he said. "You had better settle on someone soon or you will run out of prospects."

"Oh, monsieur, I could do that job. I would be very good at it," Berthe said, surprising even herself at her audacity.

Worth looked at her and smiled indulgently.

"You are too young, too inexperienced, and too undressed."

"But I could learn. You yourself said I had a flair for fabrics. Please, monsieur, if you would just give me a chance."

"Why not, Charles?" put in Bobergh, clearly relieved that here was someone willing to work with Worth.

"I don't mean to assault you, mademoiselle, but it is a question of class. My patrons are wealthy, demanding women. One has to be able to withstand their artichoke."

"After Madame Rappelais, I can withstand anyone's 'artichoke,'" she said. "Please, if you aren't happy with my work, you can fire me."

"Why not fire you now and save myself the aggravation?" joked Worth.

"Monsieur, please. You won't be sorry, I promise you."

He removed his skullcap and rubbed his head.

"All right, we'll give you a trial. You will start next week."

Berthe was ecstatic. To work in Monsieur Worth's beautiful atelier, helping women select fabrics and trims for his wonderful gowns, to actually be paid for something she loved doing was a dream come true.

"How much will my pay be?" she asked, holding her breath.

"Shall we say twenty francs a week?" said Worth, looking at Bobergh, who nodded his head happily in agreement.

Berthe thought for a moment.

"But you offered the other girl forty francs a week," she finally said. She could feel the perspiration collecting underneath her bonnet.

Monsieur Worth looked at her.

"Oh, so she has a head for numbers, as well as an eyeball for fashion," he said to Bobergh. "I better watch out. Pretty soon she will be taking over my business." He turned to Berthe. "All right, mademoiselle, forty francs it is."

"Oh, sir, thank you, thank you," said Berthe, clasping his hands and shaking them vigorously. She wanted to cry or laugh, she didn't know which.

"Be careful of The Instruments," he said, pulling his hands away and holding them up as if they were those of a concert pianist. "And perhaps later, if you work out, we will add a small commission. Is that agreeable with you, Monsieur Moneybags?" he said, turning to Bobergh.

"As you wish, Monsieur Masterpiece." Both men laughed uproariously.

Berthe had started daydreaming about the first gown she would create. She thought of the illustration she had carried around with her for so many years. She could modernize that once adored dress, keeping the basic structure but removing the roses, leaves, and crystals and replacing them with simple lilies of the valley. Intead of spotted tulle trimmed in velvet she would use a double layer of plain silk tulle. But for now she would keep her designs in her head. Clearly Worth was not looking for someone to challenge his control over what was produced in his studio.

"You wanted the name of a supplier of *serge de Nîmes*?" Worth reminded her.

"Oh, yes, please," Berthe said, coming back to reality. "My friend will be grateful. I think it is just the fabric he needs for what he has in mind." She completely put aside her alternative plan to go to America. *I am much better off here in Paris without the Indians to worry about.*

Worth wrote down the address of a wholesale dry goods company that would give her a sample and, ultimately, a fair price on a large order of *serge de Nîmes*.

Berthe took a sample of the fabric back to the boardinghouse to show Monsieur Strauss. He was in his room about to partake of a meal of bread and cheese on top of his bed.

"I see your appetite is back, Monsieur Strauss. You must be feeling better."

"I can't take any chances with Madame's cuisine. I will be taking all my meals in my room until I leave." He held out a piece of bread. "May I offer you something, Mademoiselle Bovary?"

"Thank you, no. But I have something for you." She unwrapped the package and held out the fabric to him.

"And what is this?" He fingered the material, then held it up to his nose to smell.

"It's *serge de Nîmes*, a fabric that is made in the town of the same name. As you can see it's quite soft but very durable. Our farmers wear it for its sturdiness. This is what you should be making your overalls from."

He took the small piece of cloth over to the window and held it up to the light, pulling it this way and that. It seemed like so many years ago that Monsieur Millet had done the same thing with the homespun cloth as he demonstrated the importance of texture. She felt as if she had grown threefold since that girl in the pasture.

Monsieur Strauss pulled at the fabric with all his strength.

"This is marvelous. You have performed a great service to my family and me, mademoiselle. A very great service indeed." Berthe gave him the name of the dry goods store where she had obtained the sample.

Two days later there was a knock on her door. Monsieur Strauss stood in the hallway, twirling the brim of his hat round and round.

"Mademoiselle Bovary, I am planning to travel to Nîmes to negotiate the best price for this new fabric," he said. "But before I go, I have a proposition for you. Come to America with me. I will give you an important position in my company. You have already made an enormous contribution. I want you to continue to prosper with us." He looked up at her with his sad brown eyes.

For a moment she felt a giddy surge of pride. In a short time, she had received two excellent job offers. Other people were willing to pay her for her knowledge, for what Monsieur Worth had called her "flair for fabrics." It had nothing to do with her youth, or her beauty, or her body. Monsieur Strauss wasn't interested in those things. And Worth was too involved with himself and his creations. It was the first time Berthe truly believed that she could not only take care of herself, she could succeed. But now she had to choose. Should she go to California with Monsieur Strauss? She could leave the legacy of her mother, the tragedy of the Bovary name far behind. Or should she stay in Paris and work for Monsieur Worth?

Out of nowhere, an image of Armand's long arms reaching up to paint the mural on Madame Rappelais's ceiling came back to her. *Oh, those arms, those deep-set blue eyes.* She shook the vision from her head. She couldn't afford to dwell on what she didn't have.

"Are you completely sure?" asked Monsieur Strauss when she told him her decision. "I cannot say anything that will change your mind?"

"No, monsieur, my future is here. But thank you, truly, for your kind offer."

"It is not kind, mademoiselle. I am a businessman. I don't make business decisions from the heart." He took her hand. "And I repay my debts."

"You don't owe me anything, monsieur."

"I don't. But Levi Strauss and Company surely does. May I write to you?"

"Oh, please do! I will be happy to hear news of your venture."

Monsieur Strauss returned to America loaded down with several thousand yards of *serge de Nîmes* while Berthe began work at the House of Worth.

CHAPTER 32

A New Chapter

WITH HER NEW SALARY, BERTHE WAS ABLE TO AFFORD HER OWN room at Madame Laporte's. She didn't want to stay a minute longer in Hélène's room; she was afraid that at any time a *gendarme* could come knocking at the door looking for stolen goods. And she knew that half the merchandise from Paris's department stores lay hidden underneath her friend's bed. As a gesture of grudging goodwill, Hélène gave Berthe a lovely frock to wear to her new job.

"And don't be forgettin' where that come from," said Hélène.

"From you, my dear friend."

"No, from Le Bon Marché."

As she settled into her new employment, Berthe found herself in a constant state of excitement and awe watching Monsieur Worth create his art. He never seemed to stop thinking of new ideas. The atmosphere at the atelier was alive with his creative energy.

Often, the models just stood around in their cage crinolines, bell-shaped frameworks formed from a series of horizontal hoops and suspended with tapes from the waist, that made it difficult to sit. Worth, meanwhile, dashed from one model to the next, draping and undraping fabric, attaching trim, standing back, squinting his eyes, removing his skullcap, and scratching his head. Nothing seemed to please him.

On one such day, finally, one of the models said, "My feet are killing me." Sitting down suddenly on one of the small side chairs, her crinoline rose up, exposing her bloomers. Everyone laughed except for Worth.

"Genius is having a brainstorm!" he said, clapping his hands. "We are going to do away with the underskirt. The time has come for me to use my brilliant idea. Yes, this is the moment." He instructed one of the girls to put on a dress without the crinoline cage. Then he draped and pinned the fabric in the back, thereby creating a whole new silhouette.

"The lady's bottom is now the new royalty," he proclaimed. "And here is where we put the crown." He added a large bow to the bunched up fabric. "I christen you the Bustle. Write this down," he said to Berthe. "From here on out, all great dress designs will focus on two places: the *bustier* and the *derrière*."

One morning Berthe arrived to see Worth rushing around gathering swatches. He was in an even higher state of agitation than usual.

"The Empress is coming! The Empress is coming!" he announced. "Find me some silk. In blue. No, burgundy. No, saffron."

"The Empress is really coming?" asked Berthe.

"Did I not say so? Now hurry. Gather up the most gargantuan of our fabrics."

An hour later, the Empress Eugénie herself arrived. She was

one of the most beautiful women Berthe had ever seen. She had wide-spaced violet blue eyes, a small straight nose, and the smallest rosebud mouth. Her hair was worn in a simple chignon at the back of her long white neck. Her arms were graceful and beautifully plump and her hands were so tiny they looked as if they belonged to a child. She was cold and aloof, as befitted an empress. Berthe wondered why she had come to the shop. She could have easily had Worth call upon her at the palace.

She soon explained. "I wanted to see what all the fuss was about, and to view *all* of your dresses, Monsieur Worth."

"All of them?" he said, bouncing on the balls of his feet.

She didn't even bother to nod her head. He clapped his hands loudly and called out: "Girls, girls, quickly. Gown yourselves." What followed was to be known thereafter as the world's first fashion show. After much commotion, Worth's models came out one by one, dressed in his most recent creations. One after another bowed and then turned slowly, according to Worth's direction, in order to show off every angle. The Empress sat unsmiling. Worth fluttered about, describing each gown in his flawed French, pointing out and praising various details.

"As you can see, Your Exaltedness, I have created a new sleeve in this visiting dress. I call it the Polonaise."

The Empress had no comment.

"And you will notice my new silhouette. I have christened her the Bustle."

Again not a word from the Empress.

"The fabric you are fingering is called... I forget the French term. What is it called, Mademoiselle Bovary?"

"*Velours de peluche,*" Berthe said, flattered to be called upon in the presence of the Empress Eugénie.

"I know what plush velvet is, monsieur," said the Empress, lifting her chin to an even more regal angle.

When every last dress had been paraded, Monsieur Worth rubbed his hands, waiting for some reaction from the Empress. Berthe stood in the corner, a notebook readied to write down her special instructions.

"Tell me, Monsieur Worth, your honest opinion of what I am wearing." Empress Eugénie stood up and turned around. She was wearing a walking dress of mustard-colored brocaded silk. The sleeves hung down to her wrists, from which cuffs of muslin peered out. Over the dress she wore a double cape of red velvet with a lace flounce trimmed in a line of velvet ribbon. Covering her dark hair was a bonnet of matching mustard-colored velvet with a white plume. Berthe thought that both the color and the style were terribly unflattering.

Worth stood back, his chin in his hand, studying the whole effect.

"Well, Your Majestiness, I can honestly say that this is the ugliest ensemble I have ever opened my eyelids to."

Berthe gasped. The Empress lifted the edge of her cape and studied it. Finally, she looked at Worth and said, "Exactly my feelings, monsieur. Let us begin. We obviously have much work to do."

As Worth led the Empress toward his inner sanctum, Berthe followed, almost breathless with excitement. *Perhaps I could help them with the color choices.* She knew what color she would choose first: a pale peach to complement the Empress's lovely complexion.

At that moment, there was a loud ringing of the doorbell. Monsieur Worth turned to Berthe.

"Whoever it is, tell them to come back tomorrow. I have all I can chew on now," he whispered. He escorted the Empress into the fitting room. With a sigh, Berthe made her way to the entrance of the atelier. She could hear someone shouting from the street.

"Wake up! Wake up! Where is everyone? La Pearl has arrived."

Berthe opened the door a few inches. There, standing on the steps, was the most notorious woman in Paris, the courtesan and actress Cora Pearl. Berthe had read about her in the papers, as had everyone else in the country.

"I have an appointment with Monsieur Worth. Where is he?" she said, pushing past Berthe.

"I'm so sorry, madame, but he is occupied at the moment."

"Occupied? But I am supposed to choose the fabric for my opening night gown today. I am in rehearsals every day. I have no other time." She spoke French fluently but with an English cockney accent.

Her high cheeks were flushed with frustration. She was a pretty woman—not beautiful, but she exuded a sweet sexuality, an irresistible combination of innocence and intrigue. Her thick auburn hair was worn in a casual upsweep. Her soft full mouth was pushed out in a rosy pout.

"Perhaps I can help you, madame."

"And who are you, may I ask?" the actress said, one eyebrow arched.

"I am Monsieur's assistant. I can show you some fabrics until he is free."

"Well, I suppose there is nothing else to be done." The actress followed Berthe into the room where long tables were stacked with bolt after bolt of fabric. Immediately she saw something she liked. "What about this?" Madame Pearl said, running her fingers along a heavy brocade. "I love this. Wouldn't it make a stunning gown?"

The fabric she'd chosen, of brocaded lampas and silk, was a copy of a tapestry woven for Catherine the Great. The medallions enclosed alternating pairs of peacocks and swans. It was better suited to an upholstery fabric, Berthe thought. But how could she redirect the woman away from the horrid material? Should she flatter Madame Pearl's taste or tell her the truth? She remembered Worth and the Empress and how he had spoken his mind without fear of disapproval from the most powerful woman in France. She took a deep breath.

"I'm afraid a dress made out of that would make you look like a chaise longue." She had followed Worth's example, but he was Charles Frederick Worth and she was nobody. Had she gone too far?

There was a long silence as Cora Pearl studied Berthe closely. To Berthe's great relief, Madame Pearl finally threw back her head and laughed boisterously.

"A chaise longue? Something to lie upon? That's not such a bad idea." She patted Berthe on the cheek. "I like you. You tell the truth. How very refreshing. Well, mademoiselle, since you are so wise, you tell me which fabric I should select. And make sure it's not one of Monsieur Worth's most expensive or I will begin to suspect you of collusion."

Berthe selected two fabrics: an embroidered silk brocade of gold and white, and a silver lamé with embossed *fleurs-de-lis*. "I can't decide. What do you think?" Madame Pearl asked, holding up each to her chin.

"Why not use both in one dress," suggested Berthe. "You could have a bodice of the gold and white, and carry it over with insets in the silver skirt."

"Won't that cost me twice as much?"

"I will have to speak to Monsieur Worth."

"Has anyone combined these two fabrics in one dress before?"

"No, not that I know of, madame."

"Well, let's do it, then. Hang the price," said the actress, clapping her hands.

To Berthe's amazement, she became a great favorite of Cora Pearl's—so much so that whenever the woman came to order new dresses she asked to see Berthe first.

"The little one understands the need not just to look beautiful but to make a statement as well," she said to Monsieur Worth. Berthe was counting on the fact that Worth would appreciate her efforts and ultimately reward her with a raise in salary. But as time went on and it became apparent that he was not going to offer an increase, she decided to ask him herself. What would happen if he was so angry at her for asking that he fired her instead? She was very nervous. But she knew she had proven herself. She had to take the chance.

"Monsieur, are you satisfied with my work?" she asked one day.

"I am as happy as an oyster," he said, ripping a flounce off the bottom of a new black silk gown. "Why do you ask?"

"I would like an increase in my pay." He looked at her as though she had just asked him if he minded if she poked him in the eye with a pair of pinking shears. She immediately began to lose her nerve. *You had to open your mouth. Now see what you've done. You'll be out on the street again.* There was a long silence. She had never experienced a silent Worth before. She longed for his fractured French chatter. She wanted to take back her request, but instead she pressed her lips together and clasped her hands behind her so that he wouldn't see them shake.

"A raise? A raise? I pay you forty francs a week. That is a very generous salad for a girl your age," he finally said. It was just as she feared. He was very, very angry. But at that moment, she had the strangest sensation: She opened her mouth and someone else's words came out. A braver, bolder, more businesslike someone else.

"Not as generous as eighty francs," she said.

"Eighty francs? A week? Are you trying to bankrupt me? Do you think I am made of molasses?" he cried.

And now what are you going to do, you greedy girl? Return to the cotton mill? Beg Madame Rappelais to take you back in any position she chooses? There were the two voices: the one inside her head, growing more hysterical and fearful by the minute, and the other that was busy negotiating better terms with her employer.

"Not molasses, monsieur, but certainly money. Yes, I think you are made of money and have a good and generous nature."

Despite himself, he was pleased by this latter. "Yes, I am a generous man. And you are a bad girl to take advantage of me like this." He shook his ringed finger at her.

"And, monsieur, one more thing, " she said.

"What now?"

"A commission on dresses I help you design." *You idiot. Now you've really gone too far.*

"A what? A commission! My ears cannot believe what they are seeing! Is she serious? Now she is a designer who deserves a commission? From me, God's gift to French fashion? Me, who taught her everything she knows? Oh, I think I am going to have a cat!" With great dramatic flair, Worth pulled a lace handkerchief from the sleeve of his smoking jacket, drew it across his brow, and stumbled back into a chair, whereupon he immediately collapsed, closing his eyes as if in pain.

Despite her fear, she stood firm, and in the end, fuming and muttering, repeatedly asking for "smelling sugar," he agreed to raise her salary to eighty francs a week plus a commission. "If she happens to be lucky enough to sell any of her so-called designs."

Berthe's innovative choice and use of fabrics for Cora Pearl created a stir in the French press, which was exactly what both the actress and Berthe wanted.

"Madame Cora Pearl made a great splash at the Café Vendôme wearing a tea dress of striped silk in vertical red and blue stripes, embroidered with silken tassels at the sleeves and a bodice of black lace tapestry. Her *chapeau* was composed of the same stripes but set in a horizontal design." This did not go unnoticed by Parisian society. As Worth's business grew, so did the demand for Berthe's expertise. Her commissions grew accordingly.

"I am raising you to one hundred and fifty francs a week, but don't let it go to your foot," said Worth, patting her on the shoulder.

"Thank you, monsieur."

"And since you are earning such a nice large sum I would like to do away with the commission. According to Bobergh, there is too much beekeeping involved."

"No, monsieur, given the choice, I would rather do away with the salary and keep the commission."

"As you wish."

"But given your generous nature, I think you would like me to have both."

"Ach, there it is again, my fatal 'generous nature.'"

They both laughed. Berthe was able to send substantial checks to her great-aunt Charlotte and to her grand-mère's old friend Madame Leaumont.

She was earning more money than she had ever dreamed possible. And she was fulfilling her fantasy of creating beautiful things. Wasn't that all she had ever wanted? Yes, but still she was alone and lonely. There was no one to love and no one to love her. Perhaps this was the trade-off, she thought. Lucky in work, unlucky in love. She felt the sadness of not having anyone to share her good fortune with.

She sat at the small writing table in her bedroom at Madame Laporte's house and gazed out the window. If only her mother could see her now. Wouldn't she be surprised? Wouldn't she be proud? Berthe imagined showing her around Monsieur Worth's atelier. Then she would take her into the fabrics room and let her pick out her favorite material. Monsieur Worth would make up a special ball gown. It would be simple and very elegant, showing off her mother's ivory skin and dark satiny hair. Berthe knew just the fabric her mother would have picked. Monsieur Rappelais had brought it in the day before: a midnight-blue silk embroidered throughout with wine-red roses.

Berthe shook her head. What was she doing? Designing a dress for a woman who had been dead these many years?

She cried then for a mother who was gone, whom she had never really had in the first place. She cried because she had no one to be proud of her, to say, "That young woman is my daughter; see how well she has turned out?" *Stop it,* she told herself, angrily brushing away tears. *I'm* proud of you and that is quite enough.

Cora Pearl continued to monopolize her time and applaud her talents. Berthe knew that her future earnings were sewn directly to Madame Pearl's satisfaction with her.

"I want a dress just like the one Worth designed for the Empress," Cora Pearl said one day in late November. The dress she spoke of was one the Empress planned to wear to the December

Ball. It was a magnificent pink tarlatan gown with a huge double skirt. The upper skirt was looped with large bows of black velvet ribbon. The tarlatan sleeve plaited into the armhole was topped with a black velvet epaulette. "I want this very same dress, only disguised as something slightly different."

"Is that wise?" asked Berthe, worried that copying Empress Eugénie's dress could be foolhardy to say the least.

"Silly girl. You know I don't wear 'wise.' Besides, no one will notice. Their eyes will be on the Empress. Who would look at me?" said the woman whom all of Paris followed with obsessive curiosity.

Berthe reasoned that this was a golden opportunity for her. The Empress's ball was the ideal venue to show off her talents. To prove that she was capable of making a gown every bit as beautiful as Monsieur Worth's. Once that was proven she could ask for yet another raise. How could he refuse her?

Berthe found a crimson damask, which she trimmed with heavy drapery cords and tassels instead of the black velvet. The result was a dress of a similar design but, she thought, a totally different effect.

The day arrived and Berthe was a bundle of nerves. Her fingers shook as she made the final adjustments to Madame Pearl's gown moments before the ball was to begin.

"Please, madame, don't flaunt yourself or your gown in front of the Empress, I beg of you," said Berthe, worried that perhaps she had gone too far in copying Monsieur Worth's original.

Madame Pearl looked down at Berthe, who was tacking up a bit of the hem which had come undone.

"Of course not. Do I look like a fool?"

"No, actually, you look quite beautiful," said Berthe, standing up and admiring her handiwork. In her opinion, Madame Pearl had never looked lovelier.

The ball was held at the Élysée Palace. Berthe was too anxious to stay home. She knew that there was an anteroom where ladies' maids and manservants could get a view of the festivities, so she put on her best dress and watched the attendees gather for the reception line and the arrival of the Empress Eugénie and Napoléon III. There were rows and rows of women in the most exquisite and elaborate gowns. She spotted Cora Pearl making her way to the front of the line.

No, no. What are you doing? Not the front row! Berthe anxiously bit her nails, something she hadn't done since she was five years old.

Suddenly there was a hush as the lovely Empress Eugénie made her entrance, followed by her less-than-lovely husband.

Berthe heard the excited titters from the ladies' maids around her.

"Do you see? Madame Cora Pearl is wearing the same dress as the Empress!"

"No. It can't be!"

"But she is! The nerve!"

"The gall!"

The Empress stopped, looked Cora Pearl up and down, and, frowning ever so slightly, floated on.

Berthe went home in despair. She didn't sleep a wink the entire night.

"Are you crazy?" Charles Worth screamed the next day. "Are you trying to ruin me? It is my name over the door, not yours. All of Paris thinks I have tried to make a fool of our beloved Empress. That's it! You are *flambéed*!" His face was purple with anger. He pointed to the door. "Never darken my window again."

And just like that she was fired from her beloved dream job.

For the first time in what seemed like ages she had no work to go to in the morning. She felt empty, as if she didn't quite exist. She lay in bed listening to the rain on the slate roof. How had everything gone so wrong so suddenly? The truth stabbed at her: She had wanted too much too quickly. She had wanted to enhance her reputation, to increase her income, to have more things. She had recently started thinking she might even begin saving for a house. A house! Was she really any different from her mother? It seemed the Bovary women knew only how to destroy the things in life that mattered most.

Berthe desperately needed cheering up, so she forced herself out of bed and went to see Hélène, who was now living with Monsieur Proiret in a sunny apartment on the rue Malebranche. Hélène had left the boardinghouse and married her benefactor some months before.

"You can go back to lifting," said her friend, holding a fine china demitasse, her little finger pointing skyward. "You always had a talent for that, even if you didn't want to admit it."

"Thank you, no. I have learned a legitimate trade and I want to earn my living doing what I know I'm good at."

"Earn your living? You call workin' fourteen hours a day living? What you need is a man to marry you. Someone like my dear Proiret." She lifted the china pot and offered Berthe more coffee, seeming every inch the perfect lady.

"So have you finished with stealing?" Berthe asked, slumping down in the velvet-covered couch.

"Let us say, I is semi-retired," said Hélène, tucking a stray curl into her coiffure.

"Does he still spank you?"

"Oh, yes." She laughed. "But he does it so sweetly, don't he? It's a small price to pay. You could do worse yourself, my dear." She pulled Berthe off the couch and walked her over to the gilt-framed mirror on the wall. "Look at yourself. You're young and beautiful. Don't let it go to waste by *workin'*." She said the word with such distaste that Berthe had to laugh. "I'm serious."

"I'm not going to marry someone just so I can be taken care of," Berthe said, turning away from the mirror.

"Oh, what? You're going to wait for love to come and sweep you away? Don't tell me you're still pinin' for that starving artist."

"And what if I were?"

"And I always thought you was the one with the brain in her head. If I recall, his pockets was as empty as yours. Only thing he owned was his good looks." Berthe didn't answer. "And where is the lucky fellow now?"

"I believe he's in Italy," Berthe said, sighing.

"Well, that don't do much for you in your time of need, do it?"

She spent the week trying to find work in other dress shops and fabric houses. At Madame Touquet's Dresses for the Discerning Woman on rue Tabac there was actually a sign in the window:

Help Wanted. Inquire Within.

She was able to catch the proprietress herself just as she was opening the shop.

"I would like to apply for the position," Berthe said.

Madame Touquet studied her approvingly. Berthe was well dressed in a gray silk and cashmere day dress that had been returned by one of Worth's clients for lack of payment.

"And do you have experience working in a dress shop?"

"Why, yes, madame. I have, until recently, been employed by Monsieur Charles Frederick Worth."

Madame Touquet raised a rose-colored kid glove to her lips.

"Oh, no! You're the one who caused the ruckus at the Empress's ball. For shame, embarrassing the great master like that!" She gave a little smile. "Not that he doesn't deserve a comeuppance, the arrogant little Englishman. Well, my dear, I certainly wouldn't hire you. Nor, I imagine, would anyone else in Paris. Oh, no, I have enough business problems of my own without adding one to our employ."

At Chavet's House of Silk and Fine Fabrics she met with the same amused rejection.

"Why, it's little Miss Fashion Forgery."

She noticed the salesgirls separating huge bolts of silk at long tables. They looked at her and then proceeded to giggle and whisper among themselves. She thought about going to Monsieur Rappelais and begging him for a job in one of his mills. But she knew it was no use. He was too tied in with Worth's business to risk helping her, and besides, Madame Rappelais would never allow it. No one would hire her after her fiasco at the Empress's ball. She began to worry in earnest. How long would her savings last? Would she have to go back to stealing to survive? And she knew where that would eventually lead: to prison, rats, disease, and death.

Early one morning less than a week later there was a loud banging on her door.

It was Charles Worth. His face was crimson and wet with perspiration. His skullcap had slipped off to the side of his head. He almost fell into the room when she opened the door.

"Come back at once! The orders are snowing in. They are lined up down the street. They want copies. They want originals. They want anything with my name on it. I need you. I forgive you. I cannot revive without you." Surprised, Berthe was at first overcome with relief. But the relief was quickly replaced by something strange and new: a wonderful feeling of confidence.

"I'll need a raise in my commission, monsieur."

"A raise? How can you talk about money at a time like this?"

Berthe simply stared at him, careful to reveal nothing in her face.

"Besides, if my memory serves me correctly, I've already given you a raise or two. Or three. Not to mention a generous commission. Why are you being so fattening?"

Berthe turned around and, keeping her back to him, fluffed the feather pillows and straightened the coverlet on her bed as if she were alone in the room.

"This is ridiculous. A woman earning this much money." Berthe did not respond.

"All right. All right. I'll increase your commission to ten percent."

"Twenty percent."

"Fifteen percent," countered Worth.

Berthe put on her bonnet and cape and opened the door to leave.

"Wait. Wait. All right. Twenty percent commission. Not a centime more."

Berthe was dizzy with joy. She had gone from the depths of despair to a commission of twenty percent on every dress she helped design and sell. Anything was possible. She could see that Monsieur Worth, despite his protests, was as happy as she was. Flushed with victory, she pushed her advantage.

"And I want an official position in the business."

"Position? What position?"

"I want to be an assistant designer."

"You can be whatever you want, dear girl. You can be queen of the commode." He sighed. "Just come back. We have too much business and it's giving me sunburn."

Berthe's popularity continued to grow. Charles Worth had more clients than he could handle, and he welcomed her success as long as it didn't take away from his name. She created many in-novations for which he took credit.

For the wedding dress of the daughter of the comtesse d'Arbe she selected a fine white muslin trimmed with Valenciennes lace edging. No one had ever used something as simple as muslin for a society wedding.

For Madame Estienne, a cousin of the Empress, Berthe chose a steel-colored silk, a color never seen in an evening dress before. It served as the perfect background for the heavy point lace edg-ing.

Madame Fouret, a wealthy widow of advanced years, was dis-pleased with her new opera dress. "Too boring. I am not dead yet," she said. Berthe repeated her trick of draping a light silk tulle over the solid color satin, giving the gown a gauzy, cloudlike effect.

But her greatest contributions were to the ever-expanding ego of the master himself.

"They come, they demand, I create, they go away happy, and I am left with what? Nothing, nothing. They just use me up like an empty sock!" he cried.

"But you are the most famous, most revered couturier in all of Paris," said Berthe.

"What is that, a couturier? I am nothing more than a tailor to rich women."

"You are an artist," said Berthe. "What you create are not just gowns; they are works of art. You should sign them, like artists sign their paintings."

"My little genius!" He pinched her on the cheek. He imme-diately designed a label with his name which was to be sewn into every dress that left his shop. And not stopping there, he created his own coat of arms, featuring a stylized cornflower with a snail, which was mounted over the entrance to the rue de la Paix store as well as inserted into the wrought-iron gates of his country home in Suresnes. "Let your Monsieur Millet sign all the canvases he wants. I'll wager I now have my name on more pieces of art than he does," he said. And finally, he even created a fragrance in his name. *Parfum de Worth* sold at his salon for the exorbitant price of one hundred francs per ounce.

One day Berthe received a letter from America. It was a short note from Monsieur Strauss.

> *Chère Mademoiselle Bovary, I just wanted you to know that the streets in my new country are certainly paved in gold. And my overalls are now riveted in copper. My partner Mister Davis and I have patented our design. U.S. Patent 139,121. My everlasting gratitude goes to you for your help.*

Enclosed was a picture of a newspaper advertisement showing two horses chained to a pair of overalls in an attempt to rip them apart—proving how sturdy the *serge de Nîmes* fabric was. Berthe felt nothing but happiness for the little German. It seemed to her that success came to everyone if they worked hard and long enough.

Madame Pearl continued to be a devoted client of Berthe's, but as much attention as her wardrobe attracted in the press, her lack of wardrobe created even more of a sensation.

"Did you see the morning papers?" asked Monsieur Worth, chuckling.

"No," said Berthe. She was examining bolts of new fabric that had been delivered the day before.

"I am afraid if this trend catches on, your dear Madame Pearl will put us out of business." He proceeded to read from the society column:

> *"At a private dinner party at her home, Madame Cora Pearl entertained and astonished her guests when she was carried to the dining table on a large silver platter. The lovely demoiselle was lying on a bed of freshly picked violets with garnishes of parsley appropriately placed around her naked body. One can only imagine the look on her guests' faces. The question of white meat or dark was deemed irrelevant."*

The celebrated actress herself appeared later in the day carrying a copy of the newspaper.

"Where is my precious *styliste*?" she called out. "Where is my *belle* Bovary?"

"I'm here, madame," Berthe called from the fabric room.

"Did you see the papers?" Madame Pearl asked, waving her copy.

"I don't understand, madame. If it was a private party, how did it get into the papers?"

"I have no idea," said the actress, winking. "But wait till you read about what I'm wearing, or not wearing, in the opening act of my next show. Come, *chérie,* after all this *nudité* Madame Pearl feels the need for a new frock."

Cora Pearl was Paris's ultimate trendsetter. One day she appeared with her hair dyed mahogany red to match the upholstery of her carriage. Soon women all over Paris followed suit. She brought more and more business to Worth's salon. And she continued to rely on Berthe for her fashion sense.

"Monsieur Worth dresses women for his own glory. You,

dear girl, understand my essential spirit. You know that under-neath all my flamboyance is a delicate flower that just wants to be protected and nourished."

"You are a rare orchid, madame."

"Exactement."

It occurred to Berthe that she possessed a valuable talent she had instinctively learned at her mother's knee: how to cater to a larger-than-life ego. Madame Pearl was not unlike Madame Rappelais in her need to be the most important, most beautiful, most talked-about person in the room, in any room. Instead of feeling overwhelmed by Madame Pearl or Monsieur Worth, Berthe began to rely on her own strength and skill in dealing with their importunate personalities.

But as successful as she was, she was lonely. And that was one quandary she felt completely incapable of solving.

CHAPTER 33

Sunday Afternoon

BERTHE HATED SUNDAY. IT WAS HER ONE DAY OFF. THERE WAS no work, nothing to occupy her time, and although she never stopped creating gowns in her head, the day always spread out before her like an onerous chore. For her it was the loneliest day of the week.

To console herself, she strolled along the Seine, browsing among the bookstalls. She kept her eyes averted from the many lovers who strolled hand in hand as though they were reenacting a romantic painting. She was aware that men—men on the street, fellow lodgers in the boardinghouse, even the husbands of women who frequented Worth's atelier—found her attractive, but for whatever reason—natural shyness, a fear of being hurt as her mother had been—she never encouraged them.

It was a warm afternoon and, looking up from a book she had been perusing, she suddenly saw, or thought she saw, Armand! He was sitting by the side of the river with a drawing pad. She closed her book, stood, and slowly walked closer. He wore a long linen shirt, black breeches, and boots. His dark hair was even longer than before and his skin had been tanned to a golden brown.

Over the last two years she had imagined him so many times in so many places that she could not believe her eyes. Had her mind simply conjured him up? Her stomach fluttered uncontrollably. She couldn't take a deep breath. It was as if a band of steel had tightened around her chest. She was surprised at the strength of her reaction.

She stood behind him for a long time watching as he captured the movements of the Sunday strollers in quick, thick strokes of his charcoal. Instead of focusing on the river as his subject, he was sketching women as they walked by.

She could see that his were not the kind of sketches designed to attract an audience or, ultimately, a paying customer. Some artists painted pleasant landscapes of the river and its surroundings. Others had set up outdoor studios, complete with easel and stool, where they would create overly flattering pastel portraits of passersby for a franc or two. Clearly, this was not what Armand was interested in. He worked intently, glancing up only long enough to study the movements of the people who passed.

He was even more handsome than Berthe remembered. He had filled out. His hands seemed larger, his shoulders broader, his bones denser. It was a warm day and his shirt was open at the neck, and the sleeves were rolled up to his elbows revealing his strong forearms.

"I'll give you a franc for that," she said.

"My sketches are not for sale," he said, not looking up.

"Your work reminds me very much of the great Armand de Pouvier," she said. "Do you know him, perhaps?"

He turned then, his smile brilliant. "Why, it's little Mademoiselle Bovary, all grown up."

"I've always been grown up, Monsieur de Pouvier. When did you return from Italy?"

"How did you know I went to Italy?"

"Oh, it was the talk of the Parisian art world. Nothing of any note has been painted since you've been gone."

He studied her for a long time, still smiling. "You're angry with me. Why? Because I didn't say good-bye?"

"I'm not angry with you, Monsieur de Pouvier," she said, hating him a little for guessing the truth.

He stood up. It seemed he had grown even taller.

"Well, if you're not angry then you'll have tea with me and we can catch up on old times."

"I'm afraid we have no old times to catch up on." Armand seemed charmed by her bad humor. He packed up his sketch-book and charcoal, and then took her firmly by the elbow and led her toward a café. She hoped he wouldn't notice that she was trembling all over.

She was so happy to see him again. Why couldn't she just tell him that? But something prevented her. They had a way of talking to each other that seemed to always result in some kind of disagreeable exchange.

Suddenly he stopped and turned to her.

"I have an idea. Would you like to see my work?" Her stomach and her heart seemed to collide with each other.

"Yes, yes, I would," she said finally.

Armand had a room on the fifth floor of a badly maintained apartment house in an industrial section of the 8th *arrondissement*. As they walked up the five flights, the smell of garbage permeated the air. His garret was totally unlike the one Berthe had fantasized about years before. In her vision she had pictured a huge room with windows and skylights, a large four-poster bed in the corner, a couch covered with a beautiful piece of drapery, and a small table and chairs set up for romantic dinners by the French windows.

Instead, an easel and a stool took up the majority of the space and a small table covered with paints filled the remainder. Stacks of canvases stood against the wall. A lumpy cot was wedged under the eaves. There was but one soot-covered window.

Pulling over a stool for her to sit on, Armand began to show her his work, reverently holding up one canvas after another as if waiting for a response from her. The paintings were of ordinary people doing ordinary things: a little girl playing with a cat; a couple walking hand in hand through a garden; a woman peeling an apple. Berthe was surprised how different his work was from the copy of the Titian that he had done for Madame Rappelais. He painted in loose brushstrokes, not paying attention so much to details as to the feeling and movement of the figures. The colors seemed to be soaked in sunlight.

"I know nothing about art . . ." she began.

"Then don't say anything stupid." He grinned.

"I was going to say they are beautiful paintings, but if you think that's stupid then I happily retract it," she said. Her face grew hot. She stood up to leave.

"Wait, I'm sorry. I'm the stupid one. Forgive me. I'm not in the habit of showing my work to anyone."

"You're not in the habit of showing your good manners, either."

"There's one more I want you to see." He reached over and turned the last canvas around. The painting was of a young woman lying on a chaise longue. She was totally naked with the exception of a gardenia in her hair, a thin gold necklace, and a pair of satin mules. These few items seemed to emphasize her nakedness all the more. Her hand rested on her upper thigh, not so much hiding as drawing attention to the thick bush of her pubic area. Behind her stood a man fully dressed in formal wear. His hand rested on her shoulder a tantalizing few inches from her breast. He gazed down at her as if mesmerized by the sight of her bare skin. The expression on the woman's face could only be described as triumphant. It seemed to say, *I have my lover and I have you the viewer as well and I defy anyone to look away.*

Berthe thought there was something familiar about the woman. And then it hit her: It was her own face.

"This is supposed to be me?" she said. He nodded. "Without my clothes?"

"As I imagined you without your clothes. Unfortunately, I only had my imagination to inspire me."

"You had no right to paint me without my permission!" Berthe's voice broke.

"If I had asked you to pose for me like this, would you have?"

"No, of course not."

"And yet you posed for the illustrious Monsieur Millet. Is it because I am a nobody?" Armand moved to stand in front of her, his hands on his hips. His eyes flashed with anger.

"How did you know I posed for him?"

"My dear Mademoiselle Bovary, his painting of you sitting by the stream hung in his studio waiting for the highest bidder, which turned out to be your own Madame Rappelais."

"I was just a child. I didn't know what I was doing."

"You certainly knew how to take off your clothes." She raised her hand to strike him. He caught her wrist, pulled her arm behind her, and kissed her long and hard. Finally, he released her. "You're free to slap me now," he said, smiling.

"I don't want to touch you," Berthe said, wiping her mouth with the back of her hand.

Armand grabbed her by the waist and pulled her to him.

This time, even though he held her firmly, he placed the gentlest of kisses on her lips. His mouth was slow and sweet, his tongue tentative, giving Berthe control over whether to respond or to stop him. Soon she softened into his arms. He kissed her ear, the side of her neck, the hollow of her collarbone. He kissed her forehead, underneath her chin, and then her mouth again, and then again.

It seemed as if someone else was breathing for her. Berthe moved in his arms, pressing herself into him. She reached for his hand and placed it against her breast.

"Tell me what you want," Armand whispered in her ear. She felt him harden against her. With one hand he managed to unbutton each of the many buttons that ran up the back of her dress. He pulled down one shoulder and slipped his hand inside her chemise, cupping her breast. With his forefinger he gently tickled her nipple back and forth. "Tell me."

He lowered his head to her breast and ran his lips lightly over the skin. She lifted her chest up, offering her nipple, but he ignored it. He ran his fingers and then his tongue around and around her breast, covering every inch except for the obvious and aching nipple.

"More." Berthe moaned with pleasure. "Please, more."

He took her nipple in his mouth, the tip of his tongue continuously caressing it. A current of warmth ran through her body. She felt a tightness in her throat. Suddenly, she couldn't breathe; she couldn't swallow; she couldn't see. She felt paralyzed, and then just as suddenly her body exploded into a million spasms. Surge after surge, beginning below and moving from her toes through her legs and up her back. She emitted a strange groan that she didn't recognize as coming from her.

"Oh, my!" Armand laughed. "And we haven't even begun."

He led her over to the cot and gently helped her out of her clothes. She tried to get under the blanket to hide her nakedness but he made her stand so he could gaze at her while he stripped. He had a beautiful body, lean and muscular—covered all over with fine dark hair. His thick penis stood out from his body like an unexpected guest. He took her in his arms and she felt the thrill of him and his bare skin next to hers.

He began kissing her all over. And again Berthe felt a calling—no, *a screaming* out for him. She needed him inside her as she had never needed anything in her life. She fell back on the bed and he moved on top of her. She opened her legs, feeling the wetness there, and he thrust himself tenderly into her. Instead of the terrible, sharp, tearing pain she had felt when Boulanger raped her, she felt the wonderfulness and rightness of Armand's strong sex inside her. Pushing, pushing, slowly, ever so slowly at first, and then faster and faster until she was carried along with his motion. Her hands held his smooth hard back. Her legs wrapped around his waist and all she was aware of was his breath on her neck, his lips at her ear, moaning, "*Chère* Berthe, *douce* Berthe, *belle* Berthe." And then he uttered a long guttural sound and collapsed on top of her.

She began crying. She had wanted Armand to be the first. Oh, how she had longed for that. Now she felt used, sullied, unworthy.

"What's the matter? Did I hurt you? I'm so sorry."

She couldn't answer. He hadn't hurt her. That was the trouble. Boulanger had already done the damage. He had stolen her virginity before she or anyone else had a chance to value it. What should have been a wonderful moment was full of misery.

"Please, tell me what's wrong." Armand's breath was warm against her neck.

Finally she told him.

"You were not my first," she sobbed. He was quiet for a long time.

"Don't tell me. I don't want to know," he said in a low tone.

"But I want to tell you. He...I..."

Armand put his hand over her mouth. "Whatever happened before has nothing to do with us."

Berthe wanted to tell him about Boulanger and the night at the Rappelais house. She had a tremendous need to rid herself of the awful memory. But somehow she knew that putting it into words wouldn't help. It would just make it all come back to her.

"What's done is done," Armand said. "All that matters is now. And right now, dear girl, I have to sleep." And with that he promptly fell asleep.

Berthe eased herself out from under him and got up. She found an old robe of his and put it on. And then she sat in the only chair in the room, waiting for him to wake. But he slept on. It was beginning to grow dark, so she dressed and went down to the street to buy some bread and cheese. As she looked for the nearest *boulangerie* she was struck with a great feeling of loneliness. How had she gone from feeling as close to anyone as she ever had in her life to this? She had given herself to Armand and now she felt exposed and defenseless. How could he be sleeping when she needed him so much? If this was love she wasn't sure she wanted any part of it. She thought of her mother and understood a little of her sadness and her pain.

When Berthe returned, Armand was sitting on the edge of the bed. He looked up at her and smiled, then pulled her down next to him and kissed her.

"My dear Mademoiselle Bovary, where have you been? I thought I had been abandoned."

"You forget it is you who abandoned me," she said. "And furthermore, you snore." They both laughed, and her sadness vanished.

"Ah, you've brought food for the great starving artist," he said, grabbing the bread from her.

"What's so wonderful about starving?" she said. "Do you think you are better than me because your ribs show?"

"Actually, I do. Look, don't I have beautiful ribs?" he said, pulling down the sheet and exposing his chest.

"They're good and bony," she said, poking him hard with her finger. He grabbed her hand and pulled her on top of him.

"Take off your clothes and I'll show you something good and bony."

"You're an impossibly disgusting man," she said, smiling. She felt quite the sophisticated woman, and supremely happy.

"I captured your face in my painting but not your body," Armand said later, after they had made love again.

"You made my breasts far too large."

"You're still young. They could grow."

"They're not going to grow," she said obstinately.

"I added just a little, to satisfy my painterly instincts. Here and here." He traced one nipple and then the other with the tip of his finger. "And this needs to darken and get much fuller." He ran his fingers lightly over her pubic hair. "Wait. I have an idea for another picture. Here's an area I've entirely missed in my other painting." He spread her legs apart, leaned back on his heels, and narrowed his eyes as though working out the perspective.

"Armand!" she gasped.

"Hold this pose while I get my charcoal."

"No, no." She was breathless with laughter. She covered herself with the sheet.

"You are my model, my muse. You must do as I say," he growled. He tried to pull the sheet off her but she prevailed.

Berthe had never felt like this before. She was flying. But with that delicious sensation came this awareness: the possibility of crashing to earth. She shuddered briefly and then pushed the thought out of her mind.

CHAPTER 34

Busy Days, Beautiful Nights

THE TIME BERTHE SPENT WITH ARMAND WAS FILLED WITH LOVE and laughter. They rarely fought, and if they did, their disagreements dissolved into more love and laughter. But she bemoaned the fact that they had so little time together. She worked long hours, and he painted from sunup to sunset and even late into the night by oil lamp. She longed to see more of him, which is how she came up with the idea of speaking to Monsieur Worth.

"Monsieur, I know just what your salon needs," Berthe announced to her patron a few weeks later.

"Another pair of hands, another set of eyes, another brilliant mind like mine." He was working on a new gown for the Empress, using one of his models for a fitting. "But alas, there is no one like me in all the world." He sighed. "So many bosoms and bottoms, so little time."

"You need to elevate your salon to the level of your genius."

She had his attention. "Go on," he said. "I don't have all day to stand and chew."

"I propose you have a mural painted. A work of art that cel-

ebrates *your* art. On that wall over there." She pointed to an area
just inside the entrance to the atelier. "So that when your customers walk in they are immediately made aware of the fact that
they are entering not just a dress salon, but a museum of art.
Your museum."

He needed no further convincing. She recommended
Armand, and Monsieur Worth readily agreed. He remembered the
Rappelais mural and had been impressed with the painter's skill.

Berthe was thrilled. If she could find Armand permanent
work, then perhaps they could eventually afford a house, get
married, raise a family. *To think, only six years ago I was struggling
to learn how to milk a cow.* Looking back, she began to see a
theme not just of survival but of great progress. It was only two
years since she walked out of the Rappelais home with no job, no
home, and no idea of how she would earn her living. And now
she was gainfully employed, even highly respected by Monsieur
Worth. She was earning an excellent salary with the confidence
of more to come. She was eighteen years old, and for the first
time in her life she envisioned a future filled with promise and
great success.

Her stomach did a nervous dance. Why did that worry her?
Why did she continue to have the feeling of a hovering shoe
about to drop?

"I don't need you to peddle my wares," Armand said angrily that
evening. Berthe was taken aback.

"Oh, no. Of course not," she said sarcastically. "You're doing
so well on your own. Look at this wonderful gallery you use to
show your work. People are lined up on the dingy stairway just
for a viewing." She opened the door and shouted down the stairway, "Messieurs and mesdames, the De Pouvier studio will be
open shortly. Please be patient and have your money ready."

She wasn't sure who was more surprised by her outburst, Armand or she. But he was the first to laugh.

"All right, all right, I'll talk to the great Monsieur Worth. But no copies of a Titian."

"No, no," she assured him. "Monsieur Worth will want something totally original, completely your own creation."

"This is what I have in mind," said Monsieur Worth, stroking his beard. "I want Titian's Venus here." Worth waved his hand as if he were conducting an orchestra. "Only instead of her lying naked, I want her to be dressed in one of my newest gowns. I will show you which one." Berthe put her hand on Armand's arm, but it was too late.

"Clothing the naked Venus! Are you out of your mind?" Armand practically spit.

Worth seemed to ponder this as if it were a question that required an answer.

"I think you misunderstood, Monsieur Worth," said Berthe evenly. "Monsieur de Pouvier doesn't just paint Venuses by Titian. His real strength is in his own original work."

"I don't know," said Worth, taking off his skullcap and rubbing his head. "All I have seen of his work was what he did for Madame Rappelais."

"I would think you, of all people, would want something unique, something that was an emblem of your genius," Berthe gently reminded him.

"*Emblem* sounds more expensive to my trained earlobe," said Worth, frowning.

"It will be a fair price, I assure you," said Armand.

"In that case, the two of you decide what to paint. I have too much originality on my brain as it is." He returned to his work, leaving Armand and Berthe grinning at each other.

Berthe took Armand to the nearest café, an elegant establishment on the corner of the rue de la Paix, where the price of a *café au lait* was what she had not very long ago spent on room and board for a week. "My treat, to celebrate," she told him. It was late afternoon and the café was almost empty. They sat at a linen-covered table by the window.

Berthe came up with a plan that she thought would satisfy both men.

"You know those sketches you did of women walking along the Seine? Why not turn them into a painting, but have them wearing dresses that have been designed by Worth?"

"But that's absurd. He designs nothing but ball gowns. What would women be doing walking along the Seine in ball gowns?" Armand downed his coffee in one gulp and set the cup down in the saucer with a clink.

"No, you're wrong. He creates visiting dresses and walking dresses. He designs scarves and hats. He has even created a fragrance."

"I can't paint a fragrance," said Armand, throwing up his hands in frustration.

"Of course not. But don't you think it's a good idea? Your wonderful women strolling along in his beautiful designs."

"I think it's crass and commercial, and I would not call it art. It's nothing more than an advertisement for Charles Worth."

"Not to mention an advertisement for yourself."

Despite himself, Armand finally smiled. He reached across the table and ran his finger along her cheek.

Monsieur Worth approved the sketch for the mural immediately. And he had another idea.

"At the end of the year, you can paint new dresses on the ladies. So that the mural keeps up with the fashion. What say you?" Armand considered this. "Of course I will be happy to put you on a handsome retainer. But you must not do this for any other dressmaker. It will be exclusive to my salon. Do you agree?" Armand continued to ponder the proposition, as if he were deciding what to have for lunch. Berthe gave him a push.

"I'm sure he agrees, don't you, Armand?"

Armand nodded his head.

"I like you," said Monsieur, slapping Armand on the shoulder. "You are as imperious as I am. We arrogant artists must fasten together."

It took Armand three months to complete Worth's mural, and it was a huge success. Portrait commissions from Worth's customers began pouring in. Armand was able to move to a bigger, brighter studio on the rue Bonaparte. One morning Berthe woke up before dawn and decided to surprise Armand with breakfast in bed. She stopped at the bakery on the corner of rue Bonaparte, where they were just taking the bread out of the oven. She bought a baguette and hurried up the stairs of his apartment house. She wanted to make him coffee before he woke.

As she entered the apartment she looked at him from across the room. His mouth was open, his head thrown back. His long narrow foot stuck out from under the covers. She felt tears well up. She never knew she could be so happy or feel so full of love. And then as she watched him it suddenly hit her: He wasn't breathing. *He's dead!*

He had died during the night. All the hard work and late hours had taken their toll. His poor heart had given out; he was gone, leaving her forever alone.

She fell to her knees at the side of his bed and pressed her ear against his chest. She heard the clear strong beat of his heart. *You silly fool,* she said to herself. *He's not dead. He's only sleeping.* He opened his eyes and smiled at her. It was then that she knew for certain. She wanted to spend her life with this man. "Are you my dream or am I awake?" He pulled her into bed with him and began kissing her.

"It's a dream." She laughed. "You must wake up now and go to work. Fame and fortune await you."

"Let them wait," he said. "First I have to ravish someone in my dream." And he proceeded to make slow, sleepy love to her. Afterward, he fell promptly asleep again. She lay there filled with happiness, and sheer joy. Armand had come back into her life because she had wished for it and dreamed of it. And now he loved her. It was what she had wanted from the very beginning. They belonged together.

But the minute she felt the sureness of this, she experienced the loss of it. It was like opening the door of a warm room onto a winter day. She forgot the warmth and only experienced the cold. Because if she could create this very real love, wasn't she also capable of creating the opposite? She tried to shake the blackness from her mind. *Just enjoy your happiness and good fortune. Nothing untoward is going to happen.* But she didn't believe it. Everything in her life had somehow proven otherwise. Not only did she not trust her fortuity, but she knew in her heart of hearts that she would have to pay dearly for it. And probably far sooner than she was ready to.

Carriages lined the street outside the shop on rue de la Paix from early morning until late at night. Every day Worth attracted more and more clients. They were women of the very highest status. All of society it seemed was attracted to the salon. Women would wait for hours in the second salon for a chance to confer with the master on either a new dress or his predictions for the forthcoming fashion season. They hung on Worth's every word and seemed to welcome his rather sharp criticism. Gossip abounded as the ladies gathered each afternoon, and that was how Berthe came to hear about Le Petit Manoir on the avenue Bois de Boulogne.

"It is such a pity about the Gautiers. They've lost everything. His ship not only didn't come in, it sank in the Bay of Biscay," said Madame DuPlesse, carefully choosing a chocolate from a box on her lap.

"They owe millions to their creditors. They've fled the country," said the wasp-waisted Madame Filet, who held out her hand for the box of chocolates. Madame DuPlesse appeared not to notice, so intent was she on making the right choice.

"Their home is in foreclosure. The bank has taken it over," added Madame DuPlesse. Madame Filet turned her attention to her nails, admiring each one as if she had just grown them that day. When Madame DuPlesse finally offered the box of chocolates to her, she pretended she was no longer interested.

"What a shame!" said Madame Filet. "A lovely home. Not a *grand château* but it has its charms."

"An excellent location," agreed Madame DuPlesse. "I talked to Georges about buying it for our youngest. It is a veritable steal. But he thinks the garden too small." Berthe was no longer listening. Early the next morning on her way to work she made a detour and stopped by the small house on the avenue Bois de Boulogne near the park. There was a sign posted on the front door:

FORCLUSION. Par Banque de Paris.

She felt a great wave of pity for the people who once lived in this house. She remembered the day the bank had foreclosed on her parents' house, taking away every piece of furniture. To lose a house was to Berthe second only to the loss of a parent. It was like forfeiting your place in the world.

Le Petit Manoir, by far the smallest house on the street, was situated on a lovely square. It was three stories high, built of granite. The French windows were graced by intricate wrought-iron railings and the mansard roof was trimmed with copper. She walked around to the back of the house. A gardener was cutting back some of the ivy that threatened to close in on the windows.

"Do you know how much they are asking for this house?"

The man put down his shears, wiped his brow, and looked Berthe up and down.

"All I knows is there ain't no takers. No one in this neighborhood is interested. It's too small for them that could afford it and too big for the likes of you, mademoiselle."

She looked around at the garden of roses and wildflowers, planted between rows of Belgium block. The garden was not at all too small for her. And it was right here in the heart of Paris. With a house like this, she would be safe from the wolf she always imagined about to knock at her door. She had lost her home so many times in her young life; a house like this would provide her and Armand with a safe haven. Owning her own house would finally give her the security she longed for.

She began to decorate it in her mind as though she already lived there. She started with apple green and white striped curtains for the parlor. *No, first things first.* She placed a huge wing chair in front of the fireplace in the parlor, and in it she put Armand with his feet up on a hassock and a sketchbook on his lap. *No, no, he would work on the top floor where the light was so much better.* She moved him up there and placed him next to his large easel and table full of paints. *There, that's perfect.*

She had to have this house. She had a job; she had considerable savings from the many commissions she had earned. She took one last look at Le Petit Manoir. She feared it wouldn't stay ownerless for long, so she headed straight for the bank.

"How much is the small house on avenue Bois de Boulogne?" she asked the banker, who glanced up briefly before returning to his ledger.

"I am afraid it would be beyond your means, dear young lady," he said.

"I am an employee of Monsieur Charles Frederick Worth and he has bade me inquire the price. However, if you are not interested in selling it . . ."

The man looked up with sudden interest. "Oh, well, in that case." He shuffled through a pile of papers. "Number eighteen, avenue Bois de Boulogne . . . oh, this is truly a *bon marché*. Be so kind as to tell Monsieur Worth it could be his for just fifty thousand francs."

Berthe swallowed hard. Though far beyond her savings as the figure was, there was great relief in knowing the actual number. It was real and it wasn't in the millions. Still, it was more than twice what she had.

"Thank you, monsieur." She started to leave and then turned back. "And does one have to pay the entire amount at once?"

"Oh, no, a down payment of twenty percent is all that is required. We will gladly arrange a mortgage with the proper person." A mortgage. That wasn't something she had considered. It was a huge financial burden. She thought of her mother's disastrous indebtedness and how it had cost her family everything. A mortgage meant that she wouldn't fully own the house. If she lost her job again before she'd paid it off, the house might be repossessed. No, if she was going to buy a house, she wanted to own the house.

For the next several days, she thought of nothing but the

pretty little place on avenue Bois de Boulogne. The house represented the life she wanted for herself and Armand. Wasn't that worth the risk? At the same time, she felt it was crucial that the house be her responsibility, that she not ask Armand to help pay for it. He was only finally starting to earn a real income from his art. In fact, she wouldn't tell him about the house at all—it would be a surprise. Gradually, she came up with a plan to put all her savings toward the house. But she vowed that if she wasn't able to come up with the rest of the money, she would walk away. Was this the kind of insane thinking her mother had indulged in? No, this was very different, she reasoned. For one, she wasn't relying on a man to take care of her. She was taking responsibility for her own dreams.

"I thought it was Monsieur Charles Frederick Worth who was interested in the house," said the banker when she presented her proposition.

"No, in fact it's me, monsieur."

"And what does your husband do, may I ask?"

"I'm not married." Berthe took a deep breath. "But I hope to be soon."

"Correct me if I'm wrong. You are an unmarried woman and you are putting your life's savings toward a partial, albeit considerable, payment on a house that you may never be able to afford. Forgive me for saying this, mademoiselle, but you could lose everything. I strongly suggest you instead make a minimal down payment and take out a mortgage for the rest, thereby protecting your assets."

"Rest assured, monsieur, I will have the balance of the money, I promise you."

"Well, it's your neck, mademoiselle."

"No, monsieur, it's my life and I plan to live it in Le Petit Manoir."

He sighed. "The payment you are proposing will suffice to hold the house for a period of twelve months."

"Then the house is mine?" Berthe could barely catch her breath.

"For twelve months. Then if you haven't secured the rest of the money for the full payment, it will revert back to the bank." He raised his eyebrows and looked at her grimly over his spectacles. "You will forfeit everything."

Despite the banker's warnings, Berthe floated on an air of joy and anticipation for several days; she was confident that soon the house would be hers. But eventually the old familiar cloud of impending doom returned. She began to worry in earnest about losing the house, losing her money, and losing Armand's love. She felt anxious, tense, and afraid.

So when Rodolphe Boulanger appeared in the foyer of Worth's salon one evening Berthe thought, *This must be the terrible thing that I've been dreading.* The other employees, including Monsieur Worth, had left an hour before. It was almost dark outside. Her heart began to pound and she had difficulty breathing. She started to run to the back room and then she stopped. He wouldn't dare try anything here, would he? They were in plain sight of the passersby strolling up and down the rue de la Paix. If he tried to attack her someone would see or hear. Taking a deep breath and hiding her trembling hands behind her back, she turned and approached him.

"Monsieur Boulanger, what brings you to the House of Worth?"

"Ah, my *chère* Mademoiselle Bovary." He looked her up and down with a leer that made her shiver. "What else, but you? My good friend Madame Rappelais told me I might find you here. And here you are, even lovelier than ever."

"I'm afraid I cannot show you any of our gowns as the models are not here, but you may want to look at Monsieur Worth's collection of fashion accessories. However, I must warn you, it is almost closing time." She kept her voice firm and steady. She prayed that Boulanger wouldn't realize she was alone in the shop.

Boulanger began to remove his gloves. "I want to tell you, mademoiselle, that I am a man with few hobbies and even fewer interests. I have grown tired of the opera. I no longer play chess. I have collected all the art I care to. In the summer I hunt. In the winter I travel to the south. But you, Mademoiselle Bovary, continue to hold my interest. I believe I have turned you into an obsession. As I told you once before, a woman who says no is a woman I can never forget. Your mother and I were very much alike in this way."

Eyes suddenly blazing, Berthe hissed, "Don't you dare speak of my mother!"

Boulanger ignored her. "Furthermore, I am determined to get my way no matter what it takes. By flattery or, if necessary, by more force. Which shall it be?" he asked pleasantly, as if he had just offered her a choice of after-dinner liqueurs. He smiled his awful smile and waited for her response. It took everything in her not to scream. She found his perfect calm and composure absolutely terrifying. She walked over to a table at the end of the room, opened a drawer, removed a pair of twelve-inch seamstress scissors, and pointed them at Boulanger.

"Which shall it be? These scissors buried in your neck, your eye, or your precious manhood?"

"*Quel courage!*" He laughed. Then he lunged forward and grabbed her wrist, twisting her arm behind her back until she had no choice but to drop the scissors. She tried to knee him in the groin but her full skirts made the attempt useless. He bent her backward over the table and pressed his body hard against hers. His mouth forced her lips open and it felt as if his tongue was thrust halfway down her throat. She gagged. Her heart was pounding so frantically she thought for a moment she might actually faint from fright. She struggled to keep calm, to think, to find a way to escape what seemed inescapable. She fought him with all her strength but it was no use. And then, in the middle of her panic, she thought of her mother's feelings for Boulanger, and the way he had rejected her, and an idea came to her.

She suddenly stopped struggling and forced her body to relax. Wasn't this the way she dealt with difficult customers—to give them what they thought they wanted? She wrapped her arms around his neck. As he ground himself against her, she moaned and returned his kiss. His tongue retreated in surprise.

She spoke the words she remembered hearing her mother say, that day in the woods. "Oh, Rodolphe," she breathed. "Kiss me, love me. I am yours."

He pulled back and looked at her, chuckling nervously.

"Well, well, you do surprise me, mademoiselle," he said.

She traced her fingers lightly along his cheek.

"I can no longer lie to you or myself. I want you. Desperately," she said, sighing. "Please, Monsieur Boulanger, if you only knew how I've dreamed of this moment." She wondered if she was overdoing it. Would he realize this was just an act?

"Stop it, mademoiselle. You forget yourself," he said, pulling out of her grasp. She saw the hesitation creep into his eyes.

"But I've never forgotten you. Ever since I was a little girl, when I watched you take my mother riding, I wanted you for myself. I'll live with you and you'll take care of me. We'll be married!" She threw herself against him and began covering his face and neck with kisses.

"Enough." He shoved her away and retreated several steps. "Wh-what in heaven's name has gotten into you?" he stammered.

"My dear monsieur, don't you understand? You have inflamed me, just as you inflamed my mother. Can't you see? I am not unlike her. I want what she wanted," she said, reaching for him. With a horrified look on his face, he backed away from her. Quickly wrapping his cloak around him, he turned and fled before she had a chance to utter another word. As Boulanger rushed through the door he bumped into Armand, who stood there, fury and outrage darkening his handsome face.

CHAPTER 35

Old Friends, New Money

BERTHE RAN TO ARMAND BUT HE PUSHED HER AWAY.

"You little whore!"

"Wait!" Berthe said. She grabbed his arm but he yanked himself out of her grasp. "Let me explain."

"Explain what, that you were making love with a man twice your age? There's nothing to explain. I have eyes, you know." He paced back and forth, his hands running through his hair as if he were trying to pull it off his head.

She burst into tears. "He was my mother's lover . . . he found me when I was working for the Rappelaises." She forced herself to say what she had dreaded telling him all this time. "The night of Madame's birthday ball—he raped me," she said, rushing to get the words out. "He came here tonight and tried to seduce me again. The only way I could think to escape was to turn the tables on him."

"And you expect me to believe that?" He refused to look at her.

"Of course I expect you to believe it."

"Why?"

"Because I've never lied to you. Because . . . I love you," she said, reaching out to touch his arm.

He moved out of her reach. She could see there was a part of him that wanted to believe her, and a part of him that would find it hard to trust her again. *He is the son of a prostitute. Of course he believes the worst of women.* She knew there was nothing more she could say. She had told him everything. He stared at her for a long moment, his jaw clenching and unclenching. And then, without another word, he turned on his heel and left. She ran to the door, opened it, and called down the street. "Wait. Armand. Please!" But he had already turned the corner.

As the months passed, they formed an uneasy alliance. Although no longer angry, Armand remained distant; his lovemaking became less passionate. At the same time, his reputation as an artist continued to grow. Most of his day was taken up with painting portraits of wealthy women, with the occasional dog or child as a prop. He wasn't happy in his work, but he was well pleased with his improved fortune.

Berthe threw herself into her work. It seemed more important than ever to earn enough money to buy her home. She would surprise Armand with it. It would be proof of her love, of her commitment to him. With a home, marriage, and hopefully, in time, a family, their rift would be nothing more than a bad memory.

Meanwhile, Berthe was growing more and more indispensable at the House of Worth. She not only helped select fabrics but she was now designing them as well. There was a continued demand for one-of-a-kind fabrics to be used in Monsieur Worth's gowns.

"How many unique fabrics can I come up with?" complained Monsieur Rappelais. "There is an end to originality. A *fleur-de-lis* is after all still a *fleur-de-lis*."

"Don't worry, Monsieur Rappelais, I will have some new fabric designs for you," said Berthe.

"I fear I am far too old for this business," Rappelais said.

"Of course you are," said Monsieur Worth. "But that's what we have Mademoiselle Bovary for. We will feed upon her brain."

"There is a woman here who says she is a good friend of yours," said Monsieur Worth one afternoon when Berthe had returned from lunch. "She is looking at accessories in the blue room." Berthe hurried out to find Hélène trying on shawls while her husband, Monsieur Proiret, stood watching her, a smile on his face.

"*Bonjour,* my dear Berthe. You remember my darling husband, Monsieur Proiret, don't you?" Hélène kissed Berthe on both cheeks.

"Of course. Hello, monsieur," said Berthe, extending her hand.

"Well, we are here to say hello and, of course, to shop." Hélène smiled in the direction of Worth, who had followed Berthe into the room.

"I don't know if you'll find anything you'll like here," said Berthe, desperate to get her thieving friend out of her place of employment. "Perhaps you'll find something in one of the shops down the street."

"What? Your friend's money is too good for the likes of me?" said Monsieur Worth. "Try this one, madame, it suits your clavicle." He draped a rust-red and gold paisley shawl around her shoulders.

"And how goes the dress business?" asked Monsieur Proiret, pulling Worth aside.

Berthe didn't want to lose sight of Hélène, who she knew could not be trusted around the expensive accessories. But then, she was a married woman now, so perhaps she had turned a new leaf. How lucky Hélène was to be enjoying the security of marriage to this dull but dependable man.

Berthe watched her old friend as she moved casually among the displayed goods. Surely Hélène couldn't be up to her old tricks, could she? Before Berthe could react, Hélène lifted a silk scarf, studied it in the light, and then quickly stuffed it down her bodice.

"Hélène!"

"What?" said Hélène, looking for all the world like an innocent. She turned her back and quickly picked up a pair of gloves. Worth was busy expounding on the importance of using machine-made lace when Berthe pulled Proiret over to the window.

"Monsieur, you must take her away from here," she whispered. "This is my place of employment. I can't have her stealing Monsieur Worth's merchandise. He will take it out of my pay."

"Not to worry, Mademoiselle Bovary. I am opening an account here and you will be so kind as to put her 'purchases' on it." Then he turned to Hélène and said, "Come, *chérie*, I see what you are doing. You are a bad, bad girl. I am taking you home immediately."

"Yes, Papa. Please don't be angry," she said, smiling. Worth turned just in time to see Hélène stuffing one last item down her already lumpy bodice as she and her husband hurried out the door.

"What is going on here?" Worth said to Berthe. "This woman is supposed to be a friend of yours and you are allowing her to steal me naked?"

It was a measure of Worth's trust in her that he was able to accept her explanation of Hélène and her strange relationship with Monsieur Proiret.

"Well, charge them an additional ten percent. Call it handling charges," he said finally.

Berthe made yet another payment toward the house on avenue Bois de Boulogne, but the deadline for the remainder of the principal was fast approaching. She thought about asking Monsieur Worth for an advance on her salary, but she knew what he would say: "A woman owning a house in her own name? What an extraordinarily odd concept!"

It was on this same morning that Cora Pearl approached Berthe just as the salon was opening at eleven.

"What am I doing up at this ungodly hour?" she said, readjusting her hat in the mirror. "I never dreamed there were actually people in the streets at this time of day."

"Are you here for your fitting? Your gown isn't ready," said Berthe.

"No, I am here for my portrait."

"Your portrait?"

"Your precious artist has refused me. He claims he is too busy to do my portrait now. I must wait in line like everyone else? *Impossible*. This is to be a birthday gift for the duc de Graisville. He is turning seventy in a few months. He won't live out the year. The poor dear has done so much for *la Perle*. I have promised him. You must speak to De Pouvier. I beg you, and you know I never beg anyone for anything. This is a sincere plea from my heart."

That night in bed Berthe tried to convince Armand to paint Cora Pearl's portrait.

"Just because she's your friend doesn't mean I should drop everything to paint her."

"Why not?"

"It's interesting. When I first met you, you were a sweet and obliging maiden. And now you have become as demanding as any of your rich and spoiled clientele," he snapped. She turned her back to him, pulling most of the quilt with her.

"Oh, now I have offended *la demoiselle*."

She said nothing.

"Do you love me?" he asked, twirling a piece of her hair around his finger. She had told him that so many times since the Boulanger incident. But no amount of reassurance seemed to convince him.

"Do you? Do you love me?" he repeated.

"No," she said finally, exhausted by his constant interrogation and knowing that nothing she said would be enough.

"You're lying. You're a liar. Dear God, I'm in love with a liar," he joked.

She jumped out of bed.

"Well, that's your problem, isn't it? Next time you'll have to choose better." Her cheeks were flushed with anger. How could he so strongly affect her feelings with just a few words? She had given him this power, and now she wanted to take it back.

"Unfortunately, there won't be a next time," he said, smiling sadly up at her.

"Why unfortunately?"

"Because I'm afraid that you, my temperamental wench, are it." He stretched his arms above his head and sighed. "I should have fallen in love with a rich woman. Someone who could be my patron so I would never have to take on another commissioned portrait again."

"Well, why don't you?" she said through clenched teeth.

"Now she's calling my bluff. How does one deal with a

woman like this?" He tilted his head, addressing his question to some unseen authority figure.

Berthe stood with her hands on her hips, glaring at him. "You're still passably handsome. And there are hundreds of women to choose from. I see many of them in the shop. There are even some women who don't care about character or intelligence. I could introduce you."

Suddenly, his jesting tone was gone.

"Could you?" he said, his voice now tightly controlled and as cold as she had ever heard it. "That would be very kind." She saw the fury on his face and she realized that she had gone too far.

"Of course. And at the same time I can tell them that you snore like an asthmatic goat," she added. His face began to soften. The glimmer of a smile began to form. He tried to fight it. Finally he laughed, despite himself.

"No, I don't. Take it back." He pulled her down onto the bed and began making snoring sounds in her ear. "Take it back or suffer the consequences." He bit her softly on the side of her neck.

"I won't," she said, her anger melting away and a warm wave of desire taking its place. He unloosed her hair and ran his fingers slowly through it, as though caressing the finest silk. Holding her gaze in his, he slowly lifted her arms, raising them high above her head and removing her nightgown.

"Don't move," he said. He began kissing the inside of her thighs. He worked his way around and around her inner thighs and stomach until the throbbing desire was more than she could bear. Finally, when she thought she would scream in frustration, he put his mouth between her legs and slipped his tongue into her most private parts. And then she did scream, only this time in pure ecstasy.

"Shall I stop?" he said.

"No, don't stop," she moaned.

His tongue worked away at her until spasms ran up and down her body and she cried out. He looked down at her and smiled.

"Can I move now?" she whispered.

"I will move you." He raised her legs up and onto his shoulders. "I'm the artist, remember? And this is my art." And with that, he plunged his smooth hardness into her again and again until she thought she would die from too much pleasure.

She lay in his arms exhausted, and relieved that their anger had been transformed into passion. But she knew this wouldn't be the last storm on their horizon. At least she was reassured that the intensity of their fighting was well matched by their lovemaking.

And Armand had agreed to start Cora Pearl's portrait the next day.

CHAPTER 36

A New Gown

THE FOLLOWING WEEK, BERTHE RECEIVED A COMMISSION CHECK
from Monsieur Worth for the dresses she had sold in the previous six months. She gasped. It totaled over ten thousand francs.

"Don't spend it all in one place," cautioned Worth.

"That's exactly what I plan to do," she said when she finally
caught her breath. She put it in her reticule. With this check, she
had enough to purchase the house on avenue Bois de Boulogne,
the home where she and Armand could live and start a family.
Armand would no longer have to work for the patrons he disliked and could do what he loved: paint for the joy of painting.

She knew she was treading on dangerous ground. Women
were not supposed to have their own money and certainly not
their own ideas about what to do with it.

She would not let finances poison her relationship with
Armand. He would never feel the burden of responsibility
toward her. She would never have to beg him for anything. If he
needed her to support him while he pursued his art and his fortune, then she would do it gladly. Theirs would be a love unfet-

tered by obligation. And she would have her home—a home that no one could take from her, ever. She would finally be able to have a family, the family she had lost so long ago. Then, perhaps, she would find the security and abiding happiness that had always evaded her.

Berthe spent a sleepless night planning exactly how to share the news with Armand. She decided to tell him everything the next day.

She rushed over to his studio that evening after work. She would show him the latest check, watch his face light up with surprise and joy, and then tell him about the house.

"I don't understand. What is he paying you for?" he asked, his eyes narrowing as he studied the check.

Berthe explained about her commissions.

"This is a huge sum of money." He shook his head.

"I know," said Berthe, delighted.

"A man doesn't pay a woman this much money to work for him," he said, flinging an empty canvas against the wall.

She was stunned by his reaction. And then she was angry. "Well, this man does," she said, folding her arms over her chest.

"There's more to it than that. You were his lover. You *are* his lover." He grabbed her arm and yanked her to him.

"Don't be ridiculous!"

"Why are you so afraid to admit it? Just as you were afraid to admit that Boulanger was your lover. Tell me the truth."

She pulled away.

"And why are you so afraid to accept the fact that I have contributed greatly to Worth's business? Do you think I'm only good for what I can do in bed?"

"No, but..."

"You don't believe that a man can respect and value me for

my skill and knowledge?" He seemed somewhat mollified by her anger.

"It's a lot of money," he said again.

"Yes, he gave me this check and many others because of the mad passionate love we make on the cutting table while the clients are changing into their gowns."

Armand began cleaning his brushes so violently it was as if he were trying to pull the bristles from the wooden handles. Seeing his frustration, her anger evaporated. She felt a sudden tenderness toward him, knowing he was hurting and wishing she could fix the damage between them. Wanting to ease his pain, she put her arms around him. She was desperate for him to see things her way.

"Oh, Armand, think of what we can do with this money." She was about to tell him about the house.

"It's your money. You earned it. Do with it what you will. I want no part of it." He turned away from her.

That night they didn't make love. She lay awake all night wondering how such good fortune could turn so quickly into such devastation. She worried about the wisdom of sinking all the money into a house. And then she began to be concerned about how Armand would react to the whole idea of a house in the first place. Not just the house, but their home, their family, her plan for their happy future. She tried to reassure herself. Money was only a means to an end. It couldn't change one's heart, could it?

She arrived early at the *atelier* and busied herself straightening the ribbon sample books. She tried to shake her feelings of dread. She and Armand had argued before and they had gotten through it. He would soon realize his jealousy was ill-founded. He would begin to see how much the money would mean to them and their future. Just give him time, she thought. But the fear in her stomach felt all too real.

Monsieur Worth bounded into the office.

"Good morning, my little cauliflower," he said cheerily. He unwound the long scarf from his neck and peered down at her. "Why, mademoiselle, you have suitcases under your eyes. You look as if you haven't slept in a week. Am I overworking you?"

"No, monsieur." She forced a smile, determined to act as though her life were not crumbling around her.

"Then I must try harder," he said, chuckling to himself. "I see Monsieur Rappelais has not arrived for our appointment. That man is always late. Well, the early bird gets the serpent."

Worth's huge success had reversed the roles of the two old friends. Rappelais now brought his swatches and samples to Monsieur Worth's salon for him to choose. They still enjoyed a warm, albeit one-sided, relationship. Rappelais was happy for his friend's enormous popularity and stature in the world of fashion. Worth, on the other hand, seemed to forget what part the Rappelais fabrics had played in the success of his clothes. He tended to give much more credit to Berthe and her new designs than he did to his friend. Monsieur Rappelais bore it all in good humor—until Worth went too far.

"My dear friend, what has happened to your taste?" Worth said, pushing aside the books of new swatches Rappelais had brought in. "These fabrics aren't fit for a pedestrian."

"You mean a prostitute?" said Monsieur Rappelais, his eyes narrowing.

"Stop inserting words into my mouth. But yes, I mean a prostitute. Mademoiselle Bovary, tell me honestly, what do you think of these hideous brocades?"

"I think they're quite lovely. If used with some of the new

trims they would make beautiful gowns. For instance this trimmed with this," she said, holding a piece of black lace trim against a yellow and white brocade, "could be stunning."

"Perhaps, perhaps." Monsieur Worth studied the example she had laid before him. "But still, Rappelais, I think you are losing your touch. My customers don't want these big shouting designs anymore. They want new ideas. You must open your eyes, keep up with the times. Mademoiselle Berthe, show this man some of your work."

She showed Rappelais a series of sketches she had been working on that utilized elements of the simple country life she had experienced at her grand-mère's farm, but in very elegant and sophisticated patterns: morning glories twined around slender ribbons, Queen Anne's lace dotted with golden bumblebees. One of her more striking designs featured geese afloat on a background of vivid blue.

"What is this, fabric goes to the farm?" asked Monsieur Rappelais.

"I think the fusion of commonplace elements with your most sumptuous fabrics will catch on," she said.

"Very nice. I always welcome Mademoiselle Bovary's ideas, but I remind you, dear Charles, that my *hideous* fabrics are what have sold your ridiculously expensive dresses." Berthe had never seen the elderly gentleman so angry. His face had turned the color of his red cravat.

"You would do well to remember, dear friend: Pride goeth before a fumble," misquoted Worth.

"Oh, for heaven's sake, Worth. You've been in this country for fifteen years. Isn't it time you learned the language?"

"Isn't it time you learned not to bite the hand that feeds you?"

"Finally, he gets the words right but the man all wrong. I'm finished with you, you arrogant tailor. You can find your fabrics elsewhere."

"Gentlemen, gentlemen," Berthe said. She hated to see the two old friends fight.

"He's no gentleman," said Worth. "He's a...a..." He struggled to find the right word.

"You see. You can't even call me names. You have the vocabulary of an idiot," sneered Rappelais.

"Tell me when he's gone," Worth said to Berthe. "I will be in my studio sketching." He turned his back and marched out of the room.

Monsieur Rappelais sat down in one of the dainty slipper chairs and buried his head in his hands.

"Now I've gone and done it. What an idiot I am. I had to pick a fight with him, today of all days when I desperately needed to ask a favor."

"What favor, monsieur?"

"A new gown for my wife."

"Oh, Monsieur Rappelais, you know how busy he is—"

"But she must have something soon. It will be her last gown."

"What are you saying?"

"I'm afraid Madame is quite ill. She wants Worth to create the dress she is to be buried in. She has selected the fabric. She has talked of nothing else for the past month."

"Oh, I'm so sorry. I had no idea."

The two men made up that very hour. When Monsieur Worth heard of Madame Rappelais's illness he put aside his other work and set out immediately to design a new gown for her.

————

Two weeks later, when the gown was finished, Berthe decided to deliver it herself. Enough time had passed since she last laid eyes on her former mistress that she no longer felt the anger toward her that she once had. Madame Rappelais had, after all, taken Berthe under her wing, and that had set her on the path to working with Charles Worth. The fact that she had taken her in far less desirable ways Berthe was now willing to forgive.

There was another part of her that wanted to show Madame Rappelais how well she was doing, how far she had come from being a mere lady's maid. She hoped to have a chance to tell her that she had even found Armand again.

Madame DuPoix answered the door. She looked as if she had aged twenty years. Her glossy chignon was faded with gray. Berthe looked down. There on her hands and knees, scrubbing the marble floor, was Michelle Gossien, the young girl from Lille who had taken Berthe's place as Madame Rappelais's maid. She, too, seemed to have aged. Gone was the peach complexion. Her hair underneath the blue kerchief was dry and dull.

"Mademoiselle Gossien, is it?" said Berthe. The girl looked up. Her eyes were filled with sadness. Berthe's heart went out to her. "You are no longer Madame's maid?" The girl shook her head. "Well, I suppose this is better than the cotton mill."

"Oh, I could never go back there," said the girl. "I lost my brother to the mill, and my four younger sisters suffer there still."

"What was your brother's name?" Berthe asked.

"Antoine. He was just a baby. But he was so proud to have a job."

"I believe I knew him," Berthe said, remembering the horrible accident. "I was there when he was killed."

"Enough, Gossien. Back to work, if you please," snapped Madame DuPoix.

Berthe heard a terrible scream coming from the upstairs bedroom and she flinched. *Who was it? What was it?* Perhaps she had best just leave the dress and go. But before she could get out the door, Madame DuPoix spoke.

"She is waiting for you. Go on up, but please don't tire her. Although that seems impossible. She goes on and on. The madness seems to fuel her."

Berthe trudged slowly upstairs. When she caught sight of her former mistress, she froze in the doorway. Gone was any evidence of Madame's beauty. Her golden hair was now a sad, colorless beige. It lay spread out on the pillow like old harvested hay. Her skin was almost the same color as her hair: sallow, yellow, interrupted by blotches of red at her neck and under her eyes. Saliva was leaking from both corners of her mouth. It seemed as if she was almost choking on it. To Berthe's horror, Madame Rappelais leaned over and let the saliva run into a basin that had been placed at her side. She had great difficulty speaking. Her swollen tongue made it hard for Berthe to understand her.

"Ah, Berthe, my beautiful Berthe, come closer. Here, sit on the bed. You see this," she said, indicating the half-filled basin. "I am making a perfume of my own. You must tell Monsieur Worth about it. I will call it *L'eau de l'esprit*. He can sell it in his salon. We will make millions."

Berthe could see that her arms and her chest were covered with red sores. With great difficulty, she turned toward Berthe, lifting herself up on one elbow.

"This damned mercury treatment is worse than the disease. But it's working wonders." She spewed out more saliva. "Yes, it is working. I will be up and about in no time. All those gossips who have gotten so much pleasure talking about how Madame Rappelais contracted the great scourge will be mightily surprised." She extended a dry hand toward Berthe. "Here, help me up so that I may try on the . . . what is the word for it? I cannot for the life of me remember."

"The gown," said Berthe, thinking how terribly sad this was, and yet how just.

"Ah, yes, the gown. My beautiful gown." Berthe helped her stand. "Ooooooh," she screamed. "It hurts so to move."

"Perhaps you should try it on when you are feeling better, madame," Berthe said, trying to hold her old mistress upright.

"No, now. I must get ready for the ball. The Empress is coming. She is jealous of me. Always has been. When she sees me in my beautiful dress, she will certainly kill me." She sat down on the edge of the bed as if waiting to gather her strength before attempting to rise again. Suddenly she raised a finger to her lips.

"Shhh. Open the wardrobe. Quickly, quickly. Someone is hiding there. Open it." Berthe did as she was told. The wardrobe was stuffed with gowns of every color, overflow from Madame Rappelais's dressing room.

"There is nothing here." She pushed aside the dresses to demonstrate. "Nothing but your gowns, madame."

"Who are you?" Madame Rappelais said. Her eyes were wide with fear.

"It's Berthe, madame." She felt another wave of pity for the woman.

"Oh, Berthe, come sit with me. I have the most terrible taste in my mouth. Did you bring me any chocolate?" Berthe shook her head. "Well, no matter. Let me put on the gown."

The dress that Worth had created for her was one of his new bustle designs in a rich cranberry-red silk. It was meant to be worn without a crinoline. Row upon row of pleats, ruching, and frills created the fullness in the back. Berthe helped Madame remove her robe, and saw with horror that her entire body was covered in the red sores. Madame Rappelais supported herself by holding on to one of the bedposts while Berthe stood behind her buttoning the many buttons that ran up the back of the dress. It hung loosely on her bone-thin body.

"It fits perfectly," said Madame Rappelais. "He is still a genius, I grant him that." She turned to gaze at herself in the mirror. The red of the dress just made her pallor all the more ghastly. "Am I not a vision?" she said, and then she slowly crumpled to the floor.

Appalled and terrified, Berthe bent down to help her up.

"Get away from me," Madame Rappelais screamed. "Help, help, I am being raped. The devils are after me. Someone help me." The cords on her neck stood out like ropes. Berthe struggled to get her on the bed, but the woman's arms flailed about and her elbow struck Berthe's head so hard that she saw stars.

Madame DuPoix was suddenly at her side. She held Madame Rappelais firmly in her arms.

"Hush, madame, it is only Mademoiselle Bovary with your ball gown. No one will hurt you."

"They are crawling inside me. I can feel it. Please, please, make them stop." She twisted and cried in Madame DuPoix's embrace. "I'll be good, I promise. No more. No more." Suddenly she raised her head and screamed at Berthe. "How dare you! I am not a whore! I am not your whore!"

Madame DuPoix turned to Berthe.

"It is better if you go now. Leave her to me; I know how to calm her," she said.

Berthe couldn't move. She stood staring at Madame Rappelais.

"It's so sad," she said. Madame DuPoix looked up at her.

"Why do you care? She never did anything for you."

"I don't know," said Berthe. But she did know. It was her

mother all over again. All the horror of that time came back to her. All the feelings of fear, loathing, and even love. Madame Rappelais had once been the center of her life, just as her mother had been. She had wielded enormous power over Berthe and inflicted terrible pain. But there was no power here. Only illness. There was no beauty. Only the ugliness of a wasted life. She felt a great pity for this woman, as she did for her mother. She leaned over Madame Rappelais and gently kissed the top of her head.

Berthe walked slowly to the door. She felt as if there was something she had to say but could not find the words. She glanced back in time to see Madame DuPoix gently stroking Madame Rappelais's forehead.

"Shhh, *ma petite,* it's all right. I'm here. No one will hurt you."

"How do I look, DuPoix?" said Madame Rappelais.

"Beautiful as always, my darling girl."

As Berthe slowly descended the stairs of the Rappelais house, a scene from her childhood came back to her—something she hadn't thought about in years. Her mother, as usual, had been busy trying to cover her shopping debts before her husband discovered them. She had taken to selling her old clothes, hats, gloves, even the silver dessert spoons her father had given the Bovarys for a wedding present. On this particular afternoon Berthe found her mother on her knees before an old trunk in the attic. She was sorting through pieces of lace and lengths of ribbon, holding each item up to the light to see if it was in good enough condition to merit selling. There were dust motes swirling around her head. Her usually smooth coiffure had come loose and a sheen of perspiration covered her worried face.

Berthe was old enough to understand what was going on. She sometimes accompanied her mother and had heard her trying to convince various merchants of the value of what she was trying to sell. She had seen the looks of scorn on their faces as her mother extolled the qualities of this moth-eaten cape or that misshapen bonnet. She remembered the anger she felt toward her mother at the time. Anger and shame.

Now, remembering all this, a swell of emotion suddenly hit her. It was so strong she had to stop and grab hold of the banister. The feeling started in her stomach and moved to her chest and up to her throat. She felt her jaw slacken and her face collapse. And then the tears began, pouring down in unchecked streams. At that moment she felt a tremendous longing for her mother. Is this where her heart had been hiding all along? Had she stuffed the feelings down so far that she couldn't even recognize them for what they were? Had she been that afraid of loving her mother? She wiped her face with her hands and gulped for air.

It was then that she finally let go of all the anger and began to understand. Her mother had only been trying to get through life, to give herself what she thought she needed to be happy. Berthe knew how lucky she was to have found a trade, to be good at what she did. Her talents and skill were real. The money she earned was real. The ability to take care of herself—it was all real. No one and nothing could take that away from her. And as for her love for Armand? She thought of her old friends, the Homaises. Their love, their home, their family, for all its clutter and chaos, was as solid as a city sidewalk. That was what she wanted with Armand and that was what she would work for.

Berthe wasn't surprised when word came to her two weeks later that Madame Rappelais had died. She made one last visit to the house at 11, rue Payenne, whereupon she met with Madame DuPoix.

"I am taking Mademoiselle Gossien away."

"Oh, and pray tell what do you plan to do with her?" Madame DuPoix's eyes were red and swollen as if she had been weeping for days.

"I am offering her a position as my housekeeper," Berthe said, neglecting to mention that she had yet to own a house that required keeping.

"The girl is not capable of that." Madame DuPoix laughed. "Why, she can barely make a bed, let alone run a household."

"I will train her," said Berthe.

She took the girl by the hand, and when they arrived at the boardinghouse she put her to work performing small duties for Madame Laporte. When she cashed her commission check, she gave Mademoiselle Gossien the ten thousand francs.

"Oh, no, mademoiselle, I couldn't . . ."

"Send this home so that your sisters no longer have to work in the mill," Berthe insisted. Only for a moment did she worry that this was the money for her house. Then she remembered that, business being what it was, there would be plenty more where that came from.

CHAPTER 37

Love and Work

MONSIEUR RAPPELAIS, EVER THE LOYAL HUSBAND, FOLLOWED his wife to her grave within weeks. Their home was boarded up, awaiting the return of the Rappelais *fils* when they came of age; the boys had been shipped off to a distant cousin in England.

Meanwhile, Berthe continued putting all her energy into her work. Her subsequent commission checks sat locked in a box in her desk. Armand's contempt for her income had kept her from completing the remaining payment with the bank. She wanted to move carefully, to make sure he knew that her efforts were for both of them. But first she had to give him time to get over his irrational anger. No amount of explaining was going to work when he was in this kind of state. She had learned from experience to let his storm blow over.

The more she thought about the house, the more she imagined how she and Armand would fill it with a family. She began to think seriously about children, many children—four, six, eight—enough to ensure that even with the occasional inevitable infant death she would never be alone or feel like an orphan again. She had a vision of herself surrounded by all these beautiful, happy children whom she and Armand would dote on.

How many bedrooms did the house on avenue Bois de Boulogne have? Not enough for her brood. She could put several small children into one nursery, but ultimately they would have to move to larger quarters. Suddenly, she had to laugh at herself; Armand was barely speaking to her and she already had him installed in a new house surrounded by their offspring.

"Why must you toil so?" Armand asked her one night. "You act as if you are in danger of starving to death. I have enough money for both of us."

"You forget, I love my work," she said.

"Yes, it's quite clear. You love your work more than you love anything, including me."

"Who said I loved you at all?" she said in an attempt to be playful. He gave her a long look. Was he hurt? Was he angry? Had she gone too far? Then he lunged for her.

"You love me. Admit it." He pulled her over his knee and began spanking her.

"I'll admit nothing," she said, laughing.

"It's not natural." He pulled her up. "You work like a man."

"Do I feel like a man?" she said, taking his hand and slipping it down the front of her dress.

"Let me see." He ran his fingers lightly over her nipple until it became hard and erect.

Soon, they began to make love. "Isn't this better than all the money in the world?" he whispered when they were through. She took his face in her hands and held it a few inches from hers.

"The money I work so hard for is for us, for our house, our home. Our family."

"What? What house? What family?" He pulled back, alarmed.

"Of course there's no family. Not yet. But there is a house," she said, excited to finally be sharing this with him, "I have been wanting to tell you that I do have my eye on a place. After we are married—"

"Married? Who ever said anything about marriage? And a house? Why, you are full of little surprises. And big ideas." He clucked his tongue at what he obviously thought to be a ridiculous notion. "So, my darling Berthe longs to be a homeowner." He laughed.

"It's not a joke," she said.

Suddenly he grew serious.

"You have great ambitions for one so young and so female. Be careful that they don't get the best of you." He slipped his hand between her legs.

"What do you mean by that?" She pulled his hand away.

Armand gently pushed her hair back off her face.

"Just don't let your dreams take the place of reality. A house is a nice dream," he said, placing her hand on his erect penis. "But this is reality."

"It may be your reality, but I prefer mine to be a bit larger and better built." Armand tried to turn Berthe over his knee again but she stood and faced him, her eyes flashing. "And what about marriage? Is that just a nice dream as well?"

"Suddenly everything has gotten so very serious. Aren't we happy just as we are? Aren't we having a wonderful life? What more can you want?"

She looked at him for a long moment. How could she tell him she had almost completely paid for their dream home when he wasn't even considering the idea of a house, or marriage, or a family?

"I'm late for work," she finally said, feeling completely defeated. On her way to Worth's that morning the house loomed large in her head. In her mind's eye moving men carrying various pieces of furniture were stopped in their tracks. They looked at her, awaiting further instructions. Move in? Move out? Just tell us where to put all these things. She sighed. How could her good news have turned so bad?

That evening Berthe left Worth's and bought a roasted duck, a loaf of fresh bread, a wedge of Camembert, and an expensive bottle of Beaujolais. Then she hurried to Armand's studio. She would surprise him with a picnic on the floor in front of the fireplace. They would make love and he would come to realize how much he adored her and how he wanted to spend the rest of his life and have a family with her. And once he came to this realization she would tell him that she had nearly finished paying for the house. She would be patient and give him time to come to the obvious conclusion—that it was where they were meant to be.

Carrying her packages and hurrying up the stairs to his studio, she knocked on the door with her foot. There was no answer. Perhaps he was sleeping. She put down her purchases and tried the door. It was unlocked. She turned the knob and entered the large, dark room.

"Armand?" He wasn't there. Where could he be at this time of evening? she wondered. She busied herself putting the food on the table and starting a fire. Then she lay down on his bed and before she knew it she was asleep.

She woke to the sound of someone bumping into a piece of furniture. She turned up the lamp at the side of the bed. It was three in the morning. Armand was leaning against the table, devouring a drumstick. Duck fat covered his hands and chin. He had a silly grin on his face and she could see that he was drunk.

"Where have you been?"

"Painting. Where else would I be?"

"Painting at this time of night?" She felt her face grow hot. "Who were you painting?"

"The Mona Lisa." He stumbled across the room, fell on the bed, and immediately began to snore.

Berthe spent the rest of the night lying awake, trying to quell her anger. By the time the sun came up she had decided that her best course of action was to act as if nothing had happened. For nothing had, had it? She sat in a chair waiting for him to awaken. She studied him as he slept. She loved the way his thick lashes shuttered his eyes. His strong chin was thrust up in the air, his mouth was ajar, and his hair, which seemed to grow in so many different directions, was a black tangle against the white pillowcase. His face had all the innocence of a child. She could imagine him as he must have been as a little boy, a bundle of energy, his body a series of sharp angles always in motion. His mouth moved in his sleep as though he were finishing the last of a delicious meal. She felt she could live her entire life exploring that mouth. She loved how quickly his whole face could change from dark and brooding to bright with humor and mischief. She admired his intensity, his energy, and his ambition—and how they drove him.

"Do you love me?" she whispered. "You know I cannot live without you. I would die without your love. You are my heart, my soul. I love you, Armand. Don't ever leave me."

"What?" He yawned, his long lashes flickering open. He stretched his arms above his head. He seemed to have difficulty focusing. "What did you say?"

"Nothing."

And then he smiled and said, "I'll never leave you."

She realized with a pang that she had spoken aloud her love and her need for him, and he had heard her. And now he knew how she felt. Worse, *she* knew how she felt.

How many times had her mother's heart been broken by a need so great that no man could fill it? Berthe had vowed never to fall into the same trap. But that was before this man. This tall, lean, beautiful man with his mirrored eyes, his long lashes, his beautiful mouth and tongue.

For the first time, she understood the powerful pull a man could have on a woman. She began to see how her mother could forget everything while under Boulanger's spell. Berthe could begin to understand Emma's obsession, but still she couldn't forgive it. For it was during the time of Boulanger that her mother was the most dismissive of her daughter.

She got up and began to tend the fire. She would pretend she hadn't said anything. That was the best way, the safest way. She knew those words and feelings could ruin her. It was poison, this terrible passion. She was determined to be light and carefree. And yet despite her resolve the next thing out of her mouth was the last thing she should have said.

"And so," she said, stirring the embers in the fire, "who were you painting last night?"

"Your friend Cora Pearl." He swung his legs out of bed.

"I thought you had finished her portrait weeks ago." She unwrapped the cheese she had bought the night before and put it on a plate.

"This is a new one. A nude portrait," he said, splashing water on his face. Berthe suddenly felt nauseated. Was it the smell of the Camembert so early in the morning?

"Oh?" She tried to match his casual tone but she felt her whole body stiffen with tension. "And how goes it?"

"It's boring work."

"Painting Madame Cora Pearl in the nude? That doesn't seem boring to me." She laughed but it sounded brittle even to her own ears.

"She talks and talks—never runs out of words. She goes on all night. It's exhausting."

"Do you think she has as beautiful a body as everyone says?"

He shrugged. "It's a body. It's no different from any other woman's body."

"That's not true. Her breasts are enormous. I know. We have a terrible time fitting her bodices."

"Why are you asking me all these questions? If you want to see what she looks like, ask her yourself. She has no difficulty taking off her clothes. She does so without a moment's hesitation. In fact, you don't even have to ask." He wiped his face with a towel and threw it on the floor.

"I want to know what you think of her, that's all."

Stop it, Berthe, she scolded herself. *You're making a fool of yourself.* But she couldn't stop. "Do you find her beautiful?"

Armand shut his eyes as if trying to remember Madame Pearl's face.

"Of course I find her beautiful. She *is* beautiful. She's famous for her beauty."

"Do you think about making love to her?" Her mouth felt dry.

"That's all I think about. When I'm painting her, I think to myself if only I could get my brush on her bare flesh instead of this dry canvas. If only I could..." His eyes flashed and his mouth tightened into a thin line. He sat down on the bed and pulled on his boots.

"Armand..."

"Wait," he said with a sharp laugh. "I know your next question before you even ask it. Do I find her more beautiful than you? More desirable? More the woman I want to be with?" He threw up his arms in a gesture of exasperation. "Why, of course I do. I am just biding my time until she forsakes everything for me."

She knew he was toying with her, but still anger boiled inside her. With shaking hands she put the cheese and bread on the small table. She filled the kettle with water from the jug and put it on the fire. Every move was an effort designed to steady herself before asking the only question that really mattered to her.

Finally, she turned and asked in a voice tense with emotion, "Did you sleep with her?"

His eyes sparkled with thinly disguised amusement and his lips twisted into the mischievous grin she loved.

"*Bien sûr,* I slept with her. Everyone sleeps with her. That's what she's for. In fact, *ma chère,* I have smuggled her into my room. She is under the bed right now, waiting for me to make love to her again as soon as you leave." He invited her to have a look for herself.

As if by magic, her anger dissolved into relieved laughter and she fell upon him, pummeling him with her fists.

"Stop it. You're teasing me. You're being cruel."

"Yes, my little fool, I'm teasing you. I can't help it. I get too much pleasure out of it."

Somehow his teasing told her she had nothing to worry about. And that he did love her. And that perhaps, just perhaps, it was safe to love him back.

The next night Armand dropped in unexpectedly at Worth's workroom, which was located on the top floor of the salon.

"Come, I will take you out to supper," he told Berthe.

"She is not going anywhere," said Monsieur Worth. "Not until she finishes helping me select the fabrics for my spring collection."

"Oh, Armand, can you wait, please? Just a little while."

"I'll be in the showroom, flirting with the models," he said.

Berthe was under a great deal of pressure. As Worth grew

more and more popular, the demands on her grew greater. On this particular night she was experiencing something few Victorian women ever had to face: the struggle between her job and her family. For that was how she thought of Armand. He was the beginning of her long-awaited family. And Monsieur Worth was the means by which she would be able to provide her family with a home. So while she worked to finish the fabric selections with Worth, her mind was in the room below with Armand.

Two and a half hours later, she put on her cloak and bonnet and hurried down to the salon.

Armand was gone.

She rushed to his studio to find him working on a new painting. He was working in a style she had never seen before, using colors that were totally different from his usual palette. Purples, reds, and oranges gave the painting a garish, almost ghoulish effect.

Berthe was stunned by the violence of the picture. A spasm of fear gripped her stomach. A woman was lying on a bed, while a man stood over her with a knife. The woman's mouth was wide open as if in mid-scream. The man had a sweet, almost loving smile on his face and he held the raised knife above the woman's naked form. There were already several red stab wounds in the woman's white breast.

"What do you think? It is part of my new dramatic series," Armand said. He took a long drink from the bottle of wine at his side.

"I hope you don't plan on trying to sell it. It's grotesque."

"You don't know anything about it," he said angrily. "You think those pretty pictures I paint of rich women are art? *This* is art. This is *me*. I believe this is my best work yet." He finished off the last of the wine.

"Yes, well, I'm just not sure anyone would want to hang it in their parlor," she said, trying to keep the conversation light. He threw the empty bottle across the room. "Armand!" she screamed, frightened by his sudden burst of temper.

"That's all you think about: selling things, making money. You have no real sense of what is beautiful or meaningful in life."

Now she was angry and she turned on him, her eyes flashing.

"You call that beautiful and meaningful?" she said, pointing to the painting. "A woman getting stabbed to death? And who is that poor woman supposed to be?"

"It's a painting of my mother."

His mother? She felt as though she'd been punched in the stomach.

"How lovely. You're murdering your mother. Is this one of a series? Will you be murdering me in another painting?" Why was she so angry?

"Actually, I am planning a painting of *your* mother. She was just as much a whore as mine was."

She slapped him hard across the face and left.

Armand appeared outside of Worth's the next day with an armful of flowers.

"Oh, Berthe, Berthe, my beautiful Berthe," he sang loudly to the tune of a popular love song.

She came rushing out of the store.

"Stop it. You're making a scene."

"I know. That's what mad artists do. We make scenes."

"Go away. I have customers."

"Not until you forgive me." He began to sing again. "Berthe, Berthe, my beautiful Berthe." He had a terrible voice. And he still had the odor of alcohol about him. He looked as if he hadn't slept at all.

"Please, can't we talk about it later? People are staring." Fashionable passersby were, in fact, staring at them.

"Accept my apology. My mother was a whore. Yours was not."

"And you are an idiot," she said, frowning.

"And I am an idiot," he said, holding out the flowers to her and bowing low.

CHAPTER 38

The Other Shoe

BERTHE HAD ONLY ONE WEEK TO PAY THE REMAINDER OF WHAT she owed at the bank. She wanted this house for herself—with or without Armand's help. She loved him, but she didn't trust her love. She had seen for herself that the harder she worked at her profession, the more she learned and the greater were the rewards. But the same principle didn't seem to apply to love. She understood now that having a house didn't guarantee a haven, love, or a family.

Berthe paid a visit to the bank shortly before the last payment was due. She knew that completing the purchase and moving into Le Petit Manoir without resolving things with Armand could tear them apart forever. She just needed a few more days to convince him.

"I am earning an excellent living. I have the money. But there is a personal issue . . . I just need more time."

"A contract is a contract, mademoiselle. May I suggest that perhaps, as a single woman, you have gotten in over your head."

"What then? I am to lose my money *and* the house?" she asked, her eyes filling with tears.

The banker shook his head.

"You have until the end of the week. But that is as much as I can do, mademoiselle. If you don't have the rest of the money by that time, the property will be put on the market. And I must warn you, I have a couple who is already very interested."

As she walked back to the boardinghouse, Berthe was suddenly overcome by nausea. She vomited into the gutter, wondering what was wrong with her. She hadn't felt right for the past few days. Any strong smell bothered her. She hadn't been sleeping, which she'd chalked up to stress. As she hugged herself, she realized that her breasts felt unusually tender as well.

The knowledge moved through her like a wave of awe: She must be pregnant. Suddenly she was swept up in so many different emotions she didn't know what to think or how to feel. She was stunned, humbled, amazed, and terrified. But most of all, she was happy. She felt a strange and sudden satisfaction—a feeling of rightness unlike anything she had ever experienced in her life. *This is our baby, our love. A sign that we belong together, forever.*

Armand was in his studio working on a portrait of Madame Darelle, the wife of a wealthy French banker. It was an unusual portrait. The young woman was sitting in a chair reading a novel. Armand had captured a look of total absorption on her face. She was dressed in the most beautiful lace *peignoir.* Light from an unseen window accented each delicate ruffle of the skirt. The softness and femininity of the costume was shown in sharp relief against the dense dark background.

Armand stood on a short stepladder adding finishing touches to the woman's auburn hair. Just the smallest stroke of ochre added to the twist of her chignon made it feel as if the day was drawing to an end and she was drinking up the words on the page before the last light drained from the room.

Berthe smiled with delight when she saw it.

"I feel as though she must be reading the most wonderful novel. It is so engrossing a story that she never managed to get dressed for the day. It is a love story. The young lovers are just about to consummate their love and she doesn't want to miss a word."

"You have a wonderful imagination," he said.

"And you, dear Armand, have a wonderful gift for pulling the viewer into your paintings. She reminds me of my mother, a little—she was always lost in a book."

He turned and smiled at her. There was paint smeared on his forehead where he had pushed back his hair to keep it from falling into his eyes. He stepped down from his ladder, kissed her quickly, and then returned to his painting.

She watched him for a long while. Then: "I have an exciting new commission for you. A portrait of an infant."

"Impossible. One can't paint babies. They squirm too much," he said, adding a shadow to Madame Darelle's face.

"Oh, that's too bad. I was so hoping you could do a portrait of ours."

He paused, paintbrush raised as though not quite understanding what she'd said. He slowly turned and looked at her. She couldn't read the expression on his face.

"You're with child?"

"It appears so." She picked up a clean rag, poured a little turpentine on it, and proceeded to wipe the paint from his forehead. She had decided not to bring up the subject of marriage. One thing at a time, she told herself. She was so absorbed in what she was doing that she failed to notice that a storm was brewing in his dark eyes.

He threw down his brushes and walked to the window. He looked out for a long time before turning and facing her.

"You must get rid of it. It will ruin everything." His voice cut through her quiet reverie like a crash of thunder.

All the air was sucked out of her. Her legs felt as if they were made of ribbon. She sat down quickly on a small stool.

"What? What are you saying? This is our child. Our baby." Her voice quavered.

He strode back and forth across the room, his arms gesturing wildly.

"You know I adore you, Berthe. But we are artists, you and I. Our work is what is most important." He indicated the painting he had been working on.

"But I can still work. You can certainly work. You can paint to your heart's content. A baby is not going to stop you."

"It will take away what little time we have together. I won't have it."

"*You* won't have it! *You!* Who do you think you are?" She jumped up from the stool, reached for a glass jar that was filled with clean brushes, and flung it across the room. It fell against the far wall and broke, strewing brushes and shards of glass all over the floor. She stood, her hands clenched, all the color drained from her face.

"Why would you want to bring another child into this world? Life is hard enough as it is," he said, shaking his head from side to side.

"Whose life are you talking about? Yours or your child's?"

"Working and raising a child do not go hand in hand. I well remember my mother working. She had no time for me. The busier her particular business got, and it flourished for many years, the more in the way I was," he said bitterly.

"This is different, Armand. I'm not a prostitute. Don't you

think we are capable both of working and of loving and caring for a child?"

His silence was her answer. She felt a pressure building behind her eyes until she thought her head would explode with the effort of holding back her tears. She had been so happy about the baby, so sure that he would be happy as well. She grabbed her shawl and moved quickly to the door.

"Wait. Where are you going?"

"Home, to kill myself." She wanted to shock him, to hurt him as he had hurt her. But he let her leave without saying another thing.

Berthe stared at the bleak rain outside the House of Worth. Monsieur Worth was in the fitting room dealing with the comtesse Grenoble, one of his most demanding clients. The comtesse was a woman of enormous proportions, weighing nearly three hundred pounds. She didn't consider herself the least bit fat and consequently refused to pay for the extra fabric required to make her dresses. Worth literally had his hands full.

She went into his office, found *Le Figaro,* and quickly turned the pages looking for Madame Claudine's advertisement. She knew that abortion was permitted in France, but only in order to save the life of the mother. Nonetheless, many were performed to rid poor mothers of another mouth to feed or wealthy women of the inconvenience of an unwanted pregnancy. The notorious Madame Claudine actually advertised surgical abortion and abortifacient drugs.

Finally, she found it:

A Simple Remedy
Parents must ask themselves the difficult question. Is
it advisable to increase their families regardless of

consequences to themselves, or the well-being of their offspring, when a simple, easy, healthy, and certain surgical remedy is within our control? Inquire also about our Female Monthly Regulating Pills which will cure all cases of suppression, irregularity, or stoppage of the menses.
Madame Claudine, 28, rue du Bac, Paris VI.

Berthe threw the paper down. It would be easy to get rid of the baby and go on with Armand just as they were before. Did she have to choose between their child and him?

She walked over to the full-length mirror and turned sideways. Placing both her hands on her middle, she felt the beginning swell of her belly underneath the folds of her full skirt. *Forget about fantasies. This baby is real and must be dealt with.* She strode over to the desk and sat down abruptly. *Damn him to hell.* How horrible to realize that she was as much a fool as her mother had been.

At that moment Monsieur Worth, his face covered with perspiration, his tie untied and his skullcap askew, stormed into the office.

"Save me from the fat of the land," he groaned. "Comtesse Grenoble will be the finish of me." Suddenly he noticed her sitting in the chair.

"My dear Mademoiselle Bovary, you have been liquidating. What is the matter?"

"Nothing, monsieur. It is the dust. I fear I am allergic," she said, turning away and wiping her eyes.

"Well, then call the wretched maid and have her clean in here. Dust! We cannot have dust in the House of Worth."

Worth insisted she take the rest of the day off, to go home

and "blow off your nose." She left, grateful to have some time to herself.

Once home she tried to think of what to say to Armand. She knew what she wanted from him but had no idea how to get it. As a young girl, she had seen her mother go after something she desperately wanted and fail. Perhaps that was the answer. Not to be desperate. She would compose herself, appeal to him on a strictly rational basis, calmly making him see the advantages of marriage, of a family, of a stable home. As long as she kept her wits she would have no trouble persuading him what a blessing this was for his career, and for the happiness and well-being of them both.

She knew words alone wouldn't convince him. She had to remind him of his love for her. She looked in the mirror. Her eyes were red and swollen, and her nose looked as if rouge had been applied to it. Her hair had all but come undone. She looked like a wild and desperate woman. This wouldn't do.

She tore off her dress and threw open her armoire. What should she wear? Something serious, sedate, and mature. What the mistress of a happy household would wear. She pulled out a navy blue finishing dress with red piping and tiny red bows down the back and put it on. She turned to the mirror and burst into fresh tears. She looked as if she was wearing a mother's dress. Not her mother, but someone's mother. It wouldn't do to dress the part until he had accepted the role.

She pulled off the dress and went back to the armoire. Something soft and appealing, feminine and vulnerable. Something that would persuade Armand that parenthood wouldn't change the relationship they had. She pulled one dress after another out of the armoire and flung them on the bed. She had nothing to wear! Finally, she settled on a rich russet silk that was edged in black grosgrain ribbon. It had a plunging neckline that showed off the tops of her creamy breasts to their full advantage. The russet brought out the delicate color in her cheeks and complemented her copper hair.

She applied an ivory powder under her eyes, hoping it would conceal the evidence of her crying. And then she tackled her hair. Her hands were shaking so much that it took her several tries to get it into the simple upsweep that Armand always preferred.

She took one last look at herself in the mirror. *Do I look like a woman a man would want to spend the rest of his life with?* She turned and walked back to the bed. Falling to her knees, she clenched her hands in prayer—and then realized this was something she had never done before and didn't know how to begin.

Finally, she just whispered, "Please, God, make Armand see our future as a family."

It was nearly ten o'clock that evening when Berthe arrived at Armand's studio. She could see from the street that his lights were on. Of course, he would be working on yet another painting.

The scene that greeted her was one that at first did not surprise her: Armand's smooth muscled back, his firm round buttocks moving up and down, thrusting forward and back. It was a picture she carried around in her head of the two of them making love. In the middle of a busy day she would conjure up this same scene. It would excite her and make her count the hours until she could be with him again. But the legs that were now wrapped around Armand's neck were not her legs. In the very next moment it struck her like an explosion that the body he was pushing himself into was not hers. She cried out in horror.

Quickly he twisted his head around and stared at her.

"Ah, chérie, quelle surprise!" said Cora Pearl, lifting her elaborately curled but very disheveled head off the pillow.

Berthe stood paralyzed. She tried to speak, but no sound

came out. She shut her eyes, hoping to erase the scene before her, and then she felt pain in both of her hands and looked down. Her nails had cut into the palms and they had begun to bleed. She spun around and managed to get out the door before the tears began spilling down her cheeks.

Stupid. Blind. Idiot. Fool. She sank down on her bed. She had known that Armand's art was his first love, but she'd truly believed that she was his second. She thought back to his teasing about Cora Pearl and realized he had been telling her the truth. He had slept with her when he'd painted her portrait.

What were they doing making love in his studio? They could have had their rendezvous in Cora's home. That was when Berthe realized that he had done it on purpose. He wanted to be caught. Was he that desperate to end it all? She didn't bother to answer her own question.

A loud knocking sounded at her door.

"Berthe, please, let me in," called Armand.

"Go away," she said in a cold voice. Her heart was pounding in her ears and she realized that she had stopped breathing.

"Just let me see you for a moment," he pleaded. She was silent.

"I won't leave until you hear me out."

Finally, she opened the door. Armand had a wild, disheveled appearance. His shirt was buttoned wrong and only half tucked into his breeches. Dark circles lined his eyes and he had neither shaved nor combed his hair. She turned and walked back to the window, where she stood gazing out. She could smell the faint sweet scent of gardenia, Cora Pearl's favorite perfume. It was all she could do not to pick up the nearest candlestick and throw it at him.

"She means nothing to me," he said quietly.

"Well, then, I suppose I should be gratified that Madame Pearl and I share the same place in your affections." She remembered then the enormous betrayal she had felt when she walked in on the farm boy Renard making love to the neighbor girl in his barn. She suddenly felt cold and hard and strong. How could she have forgotten a lesson she had learned so well?

"Don't you understand? None of them meant anything."

"None of them? There were others?" Her fists clenched in an effort to control herself.

"How do you think I got all my commissions?" he said sadly.

"Silly me. I assumed it was because of your talent." She felt a sharp pain behind her eyes.

"Talent is useless without connections. You must have learned that by now," he said with a touch of bitterness. "I fear that my greatest talent is between the sheets." He reached out a hand to touch her shoulder and she whirled around. He pulled back as if he had been burned. "I believe I have ruined everything," he said in a soft voice.

Her eyes flashed with fury. "So when you accused me of having an affair with Boulanger it was only because that's what you've been doing all along. How stupid I am."

"There is nothing I can say?" He looked up. Tears filled his eyes, which just enraged her all the more. *How dare he do the damage and shed the tears as well.*

"You have always been better with actions than words. And your actions have spoken volumes." She walked across the room and opened the door. Armand gave her one last look and left. She slammed the door after him. And then she opened it and slammed it a second time, even harder.

How Berthe had worked to avoid her mother's fate. And she had been so sure she had succeeded. Emma Bovary had spent her whole life looking out the window waiting to be rescued by some man. Berthe had been determined not to ever repeat her mother's mistakes, and yet here she was in exactly the same place. Except now she was pregnant, without even the presence of a tolerant husband to give her baby a name. Emma had been wise enough to marry, if not well, at least securely.

Berthe remembered all the times she had condemned her mother for being deluded by visions of wealth and power and, finally, for being unlucky, so very unlucky, in love. Now she had to face the most painful fact of all: She was, and perhaps always had been, her mother's daughter. *Oh, Mother, I am so very, very sorry. Forgive me.*

How had she ever thought she could outsmart her own destiny?

The house was to go on the market the next day. Berthe found herself wandering down to the bookstall where she had first spotted Armand after his return from Italy. Everything had seemed possible then. As she browsed through the books, she picked up a copy of *Pride and Prejudice,* and the moment she did, a kind of peace came over her. As she thumbed through the well-worn pages, she marveled at how everything turned out in the end. Couples were reunited, marriages were arranged and paid for, old feuds were forgotten, and everyone lived quite happily ever after. How had Mademoiselle Austen figured it out? So that each disparate piece, each wildly different personality managed to achieve a kind of harmony in the end?

If I think of all this as just a story, then perhaps I can change it. She finally understood that there was a narrative that she had unconsciously been following. She now knew she was free to rewrite her life in her own words with her own feelings and desires.

She was alone. And for now that was fine. She patted her belly and thought of the life growing inside her. She would be responsible for her own happiness. She was strong. She would prevail. And as she understood this, she burst into a fresh flood of tears.

The next morning she woke with a plan. She looked in her mirror and saw, not surprisingly, that her eyes were almost swollen shut from all her tears of the night before. She applied cold compresses. Then she chose one of her best dresses, a dove-gray striped jacket with turned-back pagoda sleeves trimmed in black velvet piping and a matching skirt. She had purchased it from Worth at a fraction of the price because the woman who had ordered it had died unexpectedly. She chose a black velvet bonnet with a black ostrich feather and pearl earrings and necklace to complete the outfit. She checked her image in the mirror one last time before leaving. *Good,* she thought. *Very good.*

Cora Pearl lived in a seven-room apartment on the rue Boulard. Her maid answered the door.

"Madame is still asleep," she informed Berthe. It was now almost noon.

"No matter, I won't be long," said Berthe, sweeping past the maid and down the hall to Madame Pearl's bedroom. She knew where it was, having been there before to check the alterations on one of Monsieur Worth's gowns.

Cora Pearl was completely buried underneath a pile of satin duvets. Berthe pulled back a corner and uncovered the actress's still-coiffed head. She was wearing a lace-trimmed sleeping mask. Sitting down on the side of the bed, Berthe gave the sleeping woman a light tap on her cheek.

"Mimi, please, let me sleep."

"I'm sorry, Madame Pearl, but we have a little business to take care of."

Cora Pearl pulled off the mask and sat up.

"Why, it's the beautiful Mademoiselle Bovary. What brings you here in the middle of the night, my dear? You haven't come to kill me, have you?"

"Hardly," said Berthe, handing the actress her robe. "I have come to make a proposition that I think will benefit you as well as my employer."

An hour later Berthe left with a check from Cora Pearl as a deposit on ten gowns to be created by Worth at a considerable savings to the actress.

"I never thought of taking money for gowns I have yet to make," said Monsieur Worth. "Now I can order fabrics ahead of time and negotiate a discount for myself." He handed Berthe a check. "Here is your most recent commission, my dear girl. But I see I shall have to write you a second check for this coup with Madame Pearl. Business is even better than even I imagined. We are to be constipated, the two of us."

Berthe smiled. What a fool she had been to worry about her money affecting Armand's pride. Where had his pride, or lack of it, gotten them? She was thrilled with the money. It was hers and no one could take it away. She knew exactly what she would do with this windfall.

Berthe asked Monsieur Worth for permission to run a quick errand. Then she hurried over to the bank, where she surprised the banker by signing over both checks. Together with her earlier commission, they were more than enough not only to buy the house on avenue Bois de Boulogne outright—but have money left over for furniture.

Once the banker recovered from his shock, he cleared his

throat. "We will have the ownership papers drawn up for you within the week. Uh . . . will you need to give notice at your current residence? When do you plan to move in?"

Berthe looked down and placed her hands carefully across her belly. "Immediately." She smiled. "You see, I'm having a baby, and I want her to be born there."

She gave birth on a Saturday morning.

"It's a girl," said Hélène, handing Berthe the baby. For the first time she could remember, Berthe thought she saw tears in her friend's eyes.

"A perfect baby," said Mademoiselle Gossien, now happily employed in Berthe's household. She held out a soft baby blanket she had just finished embroidering that morning.

"I'll call her Emma." Berthe gazed down at her daughter and then glanced out the window at the garden below. The pink peonies were in bloom. The air was sweet with their scent. The lawn was freshly mown and at the peak of its late spring greenness. It was her garden, her lawn, her flowers. This was her bedroom with its green and white silk curtains and cream-colored damask walls. She looked down. And this soft being, this precious bundle, was her most beautiful daughter.

Tiny pink fingers curled against her mother's breast. More than the house with its large light-filled rooms and the garden with its sweet blossoms, this small silent creature was the dearest prize of Berthe's life.

Who knew that true happiness would come to her as simply and naturally as the blessed creature she held in her arms? Berthe's heart filled and overflowed with love. She felt a part of her had been healed. Of all the lessons she had learned from her mother, this had been the most important of all: She must first love herself and then, and only then, could she give her heart to another.

Epilogue

EMMA'S SECOND BIRTHDAY WAS TO BE CELEBRATED WITH A GARden party.

It was a bright blue spring day and the garden at the house on avenue Bois de Boulogne was in full bloom. The guests, dressed in varying shades of white, lazed about as they observed the two children at play. Céline Proiret was six months younger than Emma Bovary. Hélène and Monsieur Proiret watched as their redheaded daughter crawled over to little Emma and grabbed a blue-and-white-striped pinwheel out of her hands. Emma's little mouth opened in surprise and dismay.

"Céline. No! That ain't yours. It belongs to Emma. Give it back." Hélène turned to Berthe. "I don't want her following in her mother's footsteps." But Emma had already pulled the pinwheel back out of Céline's hands.

Monsieur Millet and his wife sat under a large umbrella. He was busy sketching the two little girls. He had turned them into bedraggled peasant children picking potatoes in a field.

Mademoiselle Gossien sat under the oak tree with her two

younger sisters, whom Berthe had brought to her home from the mill in Lille. Their sister was helping them learn some intricate stitches on samples of silk that were to be presented to Monsieur Worth for his approval.

"Ah, the goslings are learning well," Worth observed.

"Michelle is an excellent teacher and her sisters seem to have a real talent for fine needlework. I think you'll be able to feature their work in your next collection. Which brings me to a point of business," said Berthe.

"No, no, not now," pleaded Worth. "Can't you see I am half asleep?"

"What better time?"

"Go on, speak your brain, you will anyway," he sighed.

"We have ten more girls coming from the mill to learn embroidery and fine detail. I don't have enough room to put them up here. We are already bursting at the seams, so to speak."

"And you want me to find them a nice house to live in."

"Monsieur Worth, you are always one step ahead of me. Yes, we need to give them a house and money enough to live on while Michelle and I teach them."

"Why do I feel like I am being masticated?"

"It's all to better serve you, monsieur. You have the need for fine needlework, do you not?"

"Yes, but do we have to rescue the entire population of mill workers?"

Berthe smiled and patted his hand. Worth looked past her at a figure that was just entering the garden. His heavy eyebrows lifted in surprise.

"Ah, look what the canary dragged in," he said.

Berthe looked up and saw Armand for the first time since that awful day. He had been in Italy for the past two years and had never laid eyes on his daughter. Berthe, thinking it was time they finally met, had sent word for him to come to the party.

She rose to greet him.

"According to Monsieur Millet you have gained quite a reputation in Italy. Your paintings have enjoyed great success."

"I've come to understand that success can be measured in other ways than what one does for a living. You may find this hard to believe, but I've learned a great deal since we last met."

"Oh?" She smiled.

"I've changed," he said, taking her hand and looking down at her.

"Into what?" she asked, cocking her head. His face took on a pained expression. She was sorry the moment she said it. She took a deep breath. "Armand, *chèr* Armand. I harbor no ill feelings toward you. None at all." And as soon as she said it she knew it was true. All her anger, her resentment toward him, had vanished. And in its place she was infused with the most extraordinary feeling of lightness and peace. What was it? It came to her. It was forgiveness. For him, for her mother, her father, her grand-mère, even Madame Rappelais—anyone who had inflicted pain on her in the past. Who would have thought that the simple, or not-so-simple, act of forgiveness could feel so full of grace?

Armand stood behind Berthe's chair in the garden as they watched Emma toddle after the two geese who had been sunning themselves by the small fishpond. Céline, who could still only crawl, watched Emma with admiration and envy. A large shaggy dog of indeterminate breed lay dozing in the shaded corner of the house, happy to escape the children's attention for a change.

"She looks like me," said Armand, unable to stop smiling.

"Some might say so."

"I will do a beautiful portrait of you. Mother and daughter."

"If you can get her to sit still long enough." Berthe laughed, picking up her sketch pad and adding some final touches to a new fabric design she had been working on.

Emma took a tumble and Armand moved to pick her up. Berthe put her hand on his arm to stop him.

"No, wait. Watch." The child shook her head, her dark curls glistening in the sunlight. Then, laughing, she pushed herself back up on her pudgy legs and continued her pursuit of the geese.

"She looks like me, but I see she has your determination. Her mother's daughter. I think she'll get everything she wants in life," said Armand.

"Well, she certainly won't lack for love if I have anything to say about it," said Berthe.

Armand gently touched her shoulder. "And, thankfully, you do."

Author's Note

One of the joys of writing *Madame Bovary's Daughter* was having the opportunity to read up on the fascinating cultural, artistic, and scientific advancements happening in France around the time that Gustave Flaubert lived, and to imagine what his character Berthe Bovary might have encountered had she been able to leap off the pages of *Madame Bovary* and wander around. Because I wanted to share the rich intellectual life of France with my readers, and because *Madame Bovary's Daughter* is a novel, not a history lesson, I took liberties in the story with a few dates:

Jean-François Millet's *The Gleaners* was completed in 1857. Berthe sees an unfinished version of the painting on an easel in Millet's studio in 1852. This is plausible, as earlier versions of *The Gleaners* are known to exist, and Millet completed *The Sower,* the first in the trio of paintings that included *The Gleaners* and *The Angelus,* in 1850. It would have been a shame not to call readers' attention to this influential painting that speaks volumes about life in the French countryside.

Louis Pasteur began working on a solution to the epidemic that was killing silkworms in Alais, in the south of France, in 1865. Georges Audemars began developing the first artificial silk around 1855; commercial production began in 1891 but faced various issues, and ultimately it was improvements made in 1904 that finally made artificial silk comparable to the real thing. The term "rayon" wasn't adopted until 1924. What I wished to show in the scene in which Charles Frederick Worth, Monsieur Rappelais, and Berthe discuss Pasteur and artificial silk were the technological advancements that influenced the fashion industry in ways we take for granted today—and which most readers wouldn't otherwise have been aware of.

Le Bon Marché, which Hélène and Berthe visit in 1858, began as a small shop in 1838 and grew into a successful department store by 1850. A new building was constructed in 1867, and it wasn't until the 1870s that the store brought in Gustave Eiffel to construct its metal framework. But what a wonderful opportunity to give readers a glimpse of the man whose Eiffel Tower, built years later in 1889, would instantly become France's most iconic symbol.

Levi Strauss was in San Francisco for the Gold Rush in 1853, which historically was a few years earlier than when Berthe meets him in the boardinghouse, but I wanted to give readers a taste of what was happening in America around the same time. The bigger license I took was in imagining that *serge de Nîmes* might have been the material he first used to make his miner's dungarees. Denim was in American usage since the late eighteenth century. The word "jean" was used to describe a lighter cotton material and comes from the French word for Genoa, Italy (*Gênes*), where the first denim pants were made. The fact is, my heroine Berthe had absolutely nothing to do with the creation of jeans, Levi's or otherwise.

Acknowledgments

At first I thought this was going to be the hardest page of all to write.

How to mention all the dear friends and family who have so lovingly cheered me on?

How to acknowledge who was truly responsible for this book?

Then it became glaringly simple.

Thank you to Caitlin Alexander, my wonderful, awesome editor.

And to Natasha Kern, my very dedicated agent.

Finally, to Gustave Flaubert, wherever you are.

MADAME BOVARY'S

Daughter

Linda Urbach

A Reader's Guide

A Conversation with Linda Urbach

Random House Reader's Circle: Where did the idea for *Madame Bovary's Daughter* originate?

Linda Urbach: Directly from the great master himself, Gustave Flaubert.

To make a short question long: After graduating from college I knew I wanted to be a writer. I thought the best place to do this was Paris, and the best way to do it was to find a garret and live the life of a starving *artiste*. I found a garret, or rather a furnished room without a bathroom, on the Left Bank, and proceeded to starve, which seemed to take up all my writing time. What little time I had left I spent trying to earn a few francs. I got a job teaching English—I could barely speak French, by the way—for five francs an hour. I lived this way for a year.

Even though on the surface it seemed like a wonderful adventure for a twenty-two-year-old, it was pretty depressing. No one would talk to me (my bad French), so I did what I've always loved to do: I read books. This was when I encountered *Madame Bovary* for the first time. I remember thinking *How sad, how tragic.* Poor Emma Bovary. Her husband was a bore, she was desperately in love with another man (make that two men), and she craved another life, one that she could never afford (I perhaps saw a parallel to my own life here). Finally, tragically, she committed suicide. It took her almost a week of agony to die from the arsenic she'd ingested.

But twenty-five years later and as the mother of a very cherished daughter, I reread *Madame Bovary.* And now I had a different take altogether: What was this woman thinking? What kind of wife would repeatedly cheat on her hardworking husband and spend all her family's money on a lavish wardrobe for herself and gifts for her man of the moment; most important of all, what kind of mother was she?

When Berthe was born, Emma Bovary did the opposite of rejoice. The epigraph to my novel describes how she greeted her daughter's arrival in *Madame Bovary:* She fainted in distress! How, I wondered, did the ignored, unloved Berthe overcome such a childhood? Her father was too busy trying to make a living and her mother barely acknowledged her existence. I wondered how it felt to grow up as the child of one of literature's worst mothers. When I wrote this book, I wanted to make sure Emma's child not only survived but triumphed in the end. I guess you could say I adopted Berthe as a sort of second daughter.

RHRC: *Madame Bovary* was recently called "the most scandalous novel of all time" by *Playboy.* Do you agree with that assessment? How did you approach writing a continuation of Flaubert's story 150 years later, when society has different standards (or do we?) for what is scandalous?

LU: I laughed when a friend pointed out the *Playboy* cover. In all the many editions of *Madame Bovary* that have been published over the last century I don't know of one with a centerfold. And, no, I don't agree with *Playboy*'s assessment of *Madame Bovary* as the most scandalous novel of all time. For heaven's sake, they're totally forgetting about the Marquis de Sade's various novels, just to mention one example. Now you're talking scandalous.

I really would never claim that Berthe's story was a continuation of *Madame Bovary*. Flaubert's exquisite novel is an impossible act to follow. But I can say that it was ever so much easier for me to write a novel that's a bit risqué than it would have been in Flaubert's time.

RHRC: What interested you about exploring the roles of women in Victorian times?

LU: I've always been drawn to the Victorian period, perhaps in part because of my love of Victorian furniture (I still own some very uncomfortable, very impractical pieces that belonged to my great-grandmother!). Thanks to some wonderful websites, I was able to plunge headlong into the period when it came time to do research for my novel. I found myself in an era when most women did not work outside the home—I'm speaking only of the upper class here. And in that home they were responsible for putting multicourse meals on the table, children in their beds, occasional musical entertainment, and always exquisite needlework.

And as far as women owning property, the following is from the French Civil Code:

A wife, even when there is no community, or when she is separated as to property, cannot give, convey, mortgage, or acquire property, with or without consideration, without the husband joining in the instrument or giving his written consent.

In other words, a woman could only inherit from her family or her husband. If she were separated from her husband, he got the children and, of course, the house. I decided to write a story about flouting all these conventions and codes, thereby allowing Berthe, a single woman (gasp!), to acquire her beloved house.

In *Madame Bovary's Daughter* I have Berthe working her way toward a career in fashion. A career per se was a rare thing for a woman of the times. Unless of course the business was operating a house of ill repute. Being born a girl in Victorian times was certainly no piece of cake. In reading Dickens's *Dombey and Son* I ran across this passage:

But what was a girl to Dombey and Son! In the capital of the House's name and dignity, such a child was merely a piece of base coin that couldn't be invested—a bad Boy—nothing more.

RHRC: I happen to know that mother-daughter relationships are a particular passion of yours. Tell us a little bit about the ways in which you've explored that topic outside of *Madame Bovary's Daughter.*

LU: Well, it all started with the adoption of our two-and-a-half-day-old Charlotte, who is, in my opinion (as well as hers), the perfect daughter. Becoming a mother was the single best thing that ever happened to me. I really believe that mother-daughter relationships, although sometimes difficult, are to be cherished.

I began writing about Charlotte when she casually announced that she had 209 days left before she got her driver's license. How could that be? She had just recently learned to walk!

Where had the time gone? Writing was a way of capturing my daughter and my feelings about her before she literally drove out of my life. I kept a daily journal for the next six months. It allowed me to indelibly engrave Charlotte in my mind—it was like bronzing the memories instead of the baby shoes. This was when I came up with the idea of the MoMoir.

I published a couple of magazine articles about MoMoirs and began a writing workshop at the Theater Artists Workshop in Norwalk, Connecticut. This turned into a theater piece called *MoMoirs: The Umbilical Cord Stops Here!* which has been performed in New York City and throughout Fairfield, Connecticut.

I now lead other MoMoirs workshops. I've seen how women (even those who've never written before) can write easily and beautifully about a subject that is near and dear to them.

I am presently working on another historical novel, about yet another orphan girl who longs for a mother-daughter relationship of her own. It's currently called *Sarah's Hair* and is the story of Sarah Bernhardt's hairdresser. But these days I also find myself writing about my mother, who's been deceased for many years, and remembering how very patient and loving she was with me. Writing about her now almost makes up for my years as a sulky, smart-mouthed teenage ingrate.

RHRC: The fabrics and fashion in this novel are so vividly described that I never had trouble picturing what the characters were wearing or talking about—and I wanted every single one of those gowns that Worth and Berthe create! Tell us about your personal favorite Victorian dress.

LU: That's hard. I have a big fat file of Victorian dresses I downloaded from two wonderful websites about *Godey's Lady's Book*.

The periodical came out every month for years and years. The illustrations and descriptions are absolutely delicious. What the women didn't possess in personal freedom they made up for in ribbons and ruffles. Here's one of my favorite descriptions:

Evening dress of straw-colored silk, the skirt trimmed with four flounces of Brussels lace, and caught up with small bouquets. The bouquet for the waist is of the same flowers as the wreath, as is usual in full evening costume. [What's a wreath? We must use our imagination here.] *Wreaths of purple heath, or mingled blossoms of aquatic plants, are the most fashionable this season. The heath is worn with ringlets, and made to droop at the side, while the others form small bouquets. Flowers are the most simple and natural ornaments a young lady can wear.* [Yes!]

I love the fashion, the furniture, the hairstyles of those times. Women knew how to dress. Even the most humble of frocks had a style. In my opinion, no other era in fashion was quite as becoming to the female form.

RHRC: Did you know you were going to write about Charles Frederick Worth when you started this book?

LU: Not really. Actually, I didn't meet Monsieur Worth until more than halfway through my first draft of the book. I knew that Berthe was headed for the world of fashion, but little did I imagine that she would one day end up employed by the world's first great couturier. I should have realized he would play a big part in the book, of course. Who else had more influence on the world of fashion than he did? The man was a genius. When I discovered that he hadn't gone to France until he was nineteen years old, I thought back to what a hard time I had with the language when I lived in Paris at around the same age. Needless to say, Worth ends up speaking French in the novel almost as poorly as I did.

RHRC: I'm curious about Millet, as well. How did he end up in the novel?

LU: Although Millet painted his famous *The Gleaners* five years after I placed him in Berthe's life, I couldn't resist manipulating the dates so that they could meet. Who better to encounter on a summer day in the beautiful French countryside than this brilliant, iconic artist of that era and place? Millet was truly a man of the country. He honored the homespun that Berthe's grandmother forces her to wear and featured it in the dresses of the gleaners. He never forgot his family, who gave up their life savings to support his studies in art. What a striking counterpoint to Berthe's own struggles to rise above her circumstances! It's interesting to note, too, that Millet was an important source of inspiration for Van Gogh as well as Monet, as you can see in Monet's paintings of the Normandy coast. There was so much going on in France artistically during that period that has continued to influence our culture today.

RHRC: Now here's something many readers might be curious about: Armand. Are you with him or against him?

LU: By the end of the book I still hadn't decided whether Berthe should end up with Armand or not. As with any relationship there are pros and cons. On the plus side, he is handsome, talented, on his way to having a very successful career as an artist, and, oh yes, the father of her child. On the minus side, he is self-centered, temperamental, and unfaithful—the kind of classic "bad boy" that women through the ages have fallen for. By the time Armand comes back onto the scene, Berthe is enjoying a full and happy life. Is there room in that life for him? I just could never decide, so I left it up to the reader to imagine what happens to them after the last page of the book is turned.

RHRC: How do you think Flaubert would feel about your sequel? If you could sit down for a drink with him, what would you want to know?

LU: Honestly, I think he would hate it. He was a craftsman. Every word was edged in gold. It took him more than four and a half years to write his masterpiece, *Madame Bovary*. Not that I didn't sweat over *Madame Bovary's Daughter,* but, hey, Flaubert's novel is often considered one of the two greatest novels ever written, second only to Leo Tolstoy's *Anna Karenina*.

As a writer I am humbled by Flaubert's genius. I would be terrified to sit across the table from him. According to author Lydia Davis in the introduction to her highly acclaimed new translation of *Madame Bovary,* he was known to "bellow... while having dinner with friends." Flaubert was a notorious perfectionist in his writing, always searching for *le mot juste* (the right word). I think if I were to sit down for a drink with him, I would be rendered *sans voix* (speechless).

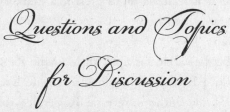

Questions and Topics for Discussion

1. Berthe spends part of her life in the countryside, part in small cities, and part in Paris. In what ways does each setting affect her personally? How does each come to influence her work and her choices?

2. Discuss Jean-François Millet's role in Berthe's life. What did you learn from Millet's paintings about the class issues of the period? Are those issues still relevant today? In what ways does Millet inspire Berthe, and how, if at all, does he hold her back?

3. Discuss Berthe's relationship with Hélène throughout the book. How are the two girls alike? How are they different? How is Hélène important to the story?

4. Do you think Berthe was justified in stealing when she worked at the mill? What would you have done if you were in her position?

5. Emma Bovary was a notorious romance reader, and those stories are frequently blamed for her downfall. Do you agree or disagree? If you've read *Madame Bovary,* compare and contrast Flaubert's depiction of Emma Bovary with Linda Urbach's portrayal. Why was literature so important to Madame Bovary?

What does Berthe take from her mother's love of romance novels? How are books and reading significant to her own life? Discuss your own approach to literature: Do you expect a novel to reflect life as it really is or to present a fantasy of how life might be?

6. Discuss Berthe's relationship with Madame Rappelais. Why does she seduce Berthe? Why does Berthe feel so conflicted about it? Did the author's reversal of gender roles vis-à-vis Madame and Monsieur Rappelais surprise you? What was the author able to explore in their relationships with Berthe that wouldn't have been possible otherwise?

7. During the dinner party scene, Millet and Charles Frederick Worth disagree vehemently about what qualifies as art. Whose position do you support, and why? Do you think that art still contributes as vitally to shifts in society's thinking today as it did in the nineteenth century?

8. *Madame Bovary's Daughter* can be regarded as metafiction in the way it continues Flaubert's story as well as prompts readers to consider the themes of the original novel in a new context. Linda Urbach has created a rich intersection between literature, art, and fashion; by setting a story about another author's fictional character amid real historical figures, in what ways has she encouraged readers to examine the cultural and societal contexts in which novels are written?

9. Why does it take Berthe so long to quit her job in the Rappelais household? What keeps her there? In what ways did the lives of Victorian women, as portrayed in the novel, differ from those of women today?

10. Berthe is one of the first women to work in the Paris fashion world. How is her background a challenge as she rises professionally? How does it help her?

11. Why does Worth take Berthe back after the public snafu with Cora Pearl? What does Berthe learn from the incident?

12. Compare Armand and Boulanger. In what ways are they similar? In what ways are they different? How was Berthe's relationship with Armand shaped by her mother's relationship with Boulanger?

13. Do you think Berthe has a moral compass? If so, where did she get it? Discuss some of the influences in her life and what she has learned about morals from each of them.

14. Why is owning a home so important to Berthe? What does it signify to her?

15. Ultimately, how was Berthe like her mother? How was she different? If you have read *Madame Bovary,* is this what you would have expected for Berthe's life?

16. What kind of mother will Berthe be? What does the future hold for Berthe and Armand? For Berthe's daughter?

About the Author

LINDA URBACH is the founder of MoMoirs Writing Workshops For & About Moms. She lives in Black Rock, Connecticut.